GRAND CENTRAL
PUBLISHING

LARGE
PRINT

NOVELS BY NELSON DeMILLE
Available from Grand Central Publishing

By the Rivers of Babylon
Cathedral
The Talbot Odyssey
Word of Honor
The Charm School
The Gold Coast
The General's Daughter
Spencerville
Plum Island
The Lion's Game
Up Country
Night Fall
Wild Fire
The Gate House

WITH THOMAS BLOCK

Mayday

Nelson DeMille

A NOVEL

The Lion

GC

GRAND CENTRAL
PUBLISHING

LARGE PRINT

Copyright © 2010 by Nelson DeMille

Grand Central Publishing
Hachette Book Group
237 Park Avenue
New York, NY 10017

www.HachetteBookGroup.com

Printed in the United States of America

First Large Print Edition: June 2010
10   9   8   7   6   5   4   3   2   1

Grand Central Publishing is a division of Hachette Book Group, Inc. The Grand Central Publishing name and logo is a trademark of Hachette Book Group, Inc.

Library of Congress Cataloging-in-Publication Data

DeMille, Nelson.
    The lion / Nelson DeMille.—1st ed.
        p.   cm.
      ISBN 978-0-446-58083-0 (regular ed.)—
      ISBN 978-0-446-56693-3 (large print)
        1. Corey, John (Fictitious character)—Fiction.   2. Ex-police officers—Fiction.   3. Terrorism—Prevention—Fiction.
4. New York (N.Y.)—Fiction.   5. Large type books.   I. Title.
PS3554.E472L555   2010
813'.54—dc22
                                                    2010007804

To my family—
Sandy, Lauren, Alex, and James,
with love

AUTHOR'S NOTE

The Anti-Terrorist Task Force (ATTF) represented in this novel is based on the actual Joint Terrorism Task Force, though I have taken some literary license where necessary.

The Joint Terrorism Task Force is an organization of dedicated, professional, and hardworking men and women who are in the front line in the war on terrorism in America.

The workings and procedures of the Task Force, as well as the New York Police Department and other law enforcement and intelligence agencies represented in this novel, are factual or based on fact, though I have taken some dramatic liberties. I have also altered some facts and procedures that were told to me in confidence.

PART I

New York and New Jersey

CHAPTER ONE

So I'm sitting in a Chevy SUV on Third Avenue, waiting for my target, a guy named Komeni Weenie or something, an Iranian gent who is Third Deputy something or other with the Iranian Mission to the United Nations. Actually, I have all this written down for my report, but this is off the top of my head.

Also off the top of my head, I'm John Corey and I'm an agent with the Federal Anti-Terrorist Task Force. I used to be a homicide detective with the NYPD, but I'm retired on disability—gunshot wounds, though my wife says I'm also morally disabled—and I've taken this job as a contract agent with the Feds, who have more anti-terrorist money than they know how to spend intelligently.

The ATTF is mostly an FBI outfit, and I work out of 26 Federal Plaza, downtown, with my FBI colleagues, which includes my wife. It's not a bad gig, and the work can be interesting, though working for the Federal government—the FBI in particular—is a challenge.

Speaking of FBI and challenges, my driver today is FBI Special Agent Lisa Sims, right out of Quantico by way of East Wheatfield, Iowa, or someplace, and the tallest building she's previously seen is a grain silo. Also, she does not drive well in Manhattan, but she wants to learn. Which is why she's sitting where I should be sitting.

Ms. Sims asked me, "How long do we wait for this guy?"

"Until he comes out of the building."

"What's he going to do?"

"We're actually here to find out."

"I mean, what do we have on him? Why are we watching him?"

"Racial profiling."

No response.

I added, to be collegial, "He is an Iranian military intelligence officer with diplomatic cover. As you know, we have information that he has asked for his car and driver to be available from one P.M. on. That is all we know."

"Right."

Lisa Sims seemed bright enough, and she knew when to stop asking questions. Like now. She's also an attractive young woman in a clean-cut sort of way, and she was dressed casually for this assignment in jeans, running shoes, and a lime green T-shirt that barely concealed her .40 caliber Glock and pancake holster. I, too, wore running shoes—you never know when you might be sprinting—jeans, black T-shirt, and a blue sports jacket that concealed my 9mm Glock, my radio, my pocket comb, and breath mints. Beats carrying a purse like Ms. Sims did.

Anyway, it was a nice day in May, and the big ornamental clock across the street said 3:17. We'd been waiting for this character for over two hours.

The Iranian Mission to the U.N. is located on the upper floors of a 39-story office building off Third Avenue, between East 40th Street and 41st. Because of the U.N., Manhattan is home to over a hundred foreign missions and consulates, plus residences, and not all of these countries are our buds. So you get a lot of bad actors posing as diplomats who need to be watched, and it's a pain in the ass. They should move the U.N. to Iowa. But maybe I shouldn't complain—watching bad guys pays the rent.

I was the team leader today, which is a guarantee of success, and on this surveillance with me were four agents on foot, and three other vehicles—another Chevy SUV and two Dodge minivans. The other three vehicles also have one NYPD and one FBI agent, which means at least one person in the vehicle knows what he or she is doing. Sorry. That wasn't nice. Also, FYI, each vehicle is equipped with the whole police package—flashing lights in the grille, siren, tinted windows, and so forth. Inside the vehicle we have 35mm digital Nikon cameras with zoom lenses, Sony 8mm video cameras, handheld portable radios, a portable printer, and so on. We all carry a change of clothes, a Kevlar vest, MetroCards, Nextel cell phones with a walkie-talkie feature, sometimes a rifle and scope, and other equipment, depending on the assignment. Like, for instance, a little gadget that detects radioactive substances, which I don't even want to think about.

In any case, we are prepared for anything, and have been since 9/11. But, you know, shit happens even when you have a shit shield with you.

High-tech toys aside, at the end of the day, what you need with you is an alert brain and a gun.

When I was a cop I did a lot of surveillance, so I'm used to this, but Special Agent Sims was getting antsy. She said, "Maybe we missed him."

"Not likely."

"Maybe he changed his plans."

"They do that."

"I'll bet they do it on purpose."

"They do that, too."

Another fifteen minutes passed, and Special Agent Sims used the time to study a street and subway map of Manhattan. She asked me, "Where do you live?"

I looked at the map, pointed, and said, "Here. On East Seventy-second Street."

She glanced out the windshield and said, "You're not far from here."

"Right. You have a map of Iowa? You can show me where you live."

She laughed.

A few minutes later, she asked me, "What is that place behind us? Au Bon Pain."

"It's like a coffee shop. A chain."

"Do you think I can run out and get a muffin?"

Well, she had running shoes, but the answer was

no, though maybe if Ms. Sims got out of the SUV, and if Komeni Weenie came out of the building and got into a car, then I could drive off and lose Ms. Sims.

"John?"

"Well . . ."

My radio crackled and a voice—one of the guys on foot—said, "Target exiting subject building from courtyard, out and moving."

I said to Sims, "Sure, go ahead."

"Didn't he just say—?"

"Hold on." I looked into the courtyard that separated the subject building from the adjacent building where two of my foot guys were helping to keep New York clean by collecting litter.

The radio crackled again, and Sweeper One said, "Target heading east to Third."

I saw our target walking through the courtyard, then passing under the ornamental arch and clock. He was a tall guy, very thin, wearing a well-cut pinstripe suit. We give nicknames or code names to the targets, and this guy had a big beak and moved his head like a bird, so I said into my radio, "Target is henceforth Big Bird."

Big Bird was on the sidewalk now, and all of a sudden another guy—who I profiled as being of Mideastern extraction—came up to Big Bird. I couldn't make this new guy, but Big Bird seemed to know him, and they seemed happy and surprised to see each other, which is pure bullshit. They shook hands, and I thought something was being passed. Or they were just shaking hands. You never know. But they know or suspect that they're being watched, and sometimes they screw with you.

Anyway, Big Bird has dip immunity, and we're certainly not going to bust him for shaking hands with another Mideastern gentleman. In fact, now we have two people to watch.

Big Bird and the unknown separated, and the unknown began walking north on Third, while Big Bird stayed put. This was all captured in photos and video, of course, and maybe someone at 26 Fed knew this other guy.

I said into the radio, "Units Three and Four, stay with the unknown and try to ID him."

They acknowledged, and Ms. Sims said to me, "I don't think that was a chance meeting."

I did not respond with sarcasm and I didn't even roll my eyes. I said, "I think you're right." This was going to be a long day.

A minute later, a big gray Mercedes pulled up near Big Bird, and I could see the dip plates—blue-and-white, with four numbers followed by DM, which for some unknown reason is the State Department's designation for Iran, then another D, which is Diplomat, which I get.

The driver, another Iranian gent, jumped out and ran around to the other side of the car like he was being chased by Israeli commandos. He bowed low—I should get my driver to do that—then opened the door, and Big Bird folded himself into the rear seat.

I said into the radio, "Big Bird is mobile." I gave the make and color of the car and the plate number, and

Unit Two acknowledged. Unit Two, by the way, is the second Dodge minivan, driven by a guy I know, Mel Jacobs, NYPD Intelligence Unit detective. Detective Jacobs is Jewish, and he speaks a little Hebrew, which he uses when interrogating Arabic-speaking suspects. That, and the Star of David that he wears, sends these guys into orbit, which is kind of funny to watch.

Anyway, the other guy with Mel today is George Foster, an FBI Special Agent who I've worked with and who I like because he knows from experience how brilliant I am.

The Mercedes headed north on Third Avenue, and Special Agent Sims asked me, "Should I follow him?"

"That might be a good idea."

She threw the SUV into gear and off we went, threading our way through heavy traffic. New York drivers are divided between the good and the dead. It's Darwinian. Ms. Sims would evolve or become extinct. And I'm sitting in the passenger seat to witness one or the other.

The Iranian chauffeur, who I think I've followed before, was an erratic driver, and I couldn't tell if he was driving like that to lose a tail or if he was just a really bad driver. Like the last thing he drove was a camel.

Meanwhile, Special Agent Sims had her chin over the steering wheel between white knuckles, and her right foot was moving from the brakes to the accelerator like she had restless leg syndrome.

The Mercedes made a sudden left on 51st Street and Ms. Sims followed.

Unit Two continued on Third where he'd hang a left on 53rd and run parallel to us until I could tell them what the Mercedes was doing. You don't want a parade following the subject vehicle; you want to mix it up a bit.

We were heading west now, and we passed beside St. Patrick's Cathedral, then crossed Fifth Avenue. The subject vehicle continued on, which I reported to Unit Two.

I had no idea where Big Bird was going, but he was heading toward the Theater District and Times Square, where these guys sometimes went to experience American culture, like strip joints and titty bars. I mean, you don't get much of that back in Sandland. Right?

The Mercedes made the light on Seventh Avenue, but we didn't and we got stuck behind three vehicles. I couldn't see the Mercedes now, but I had seen him continue on 51st. I hit the lights and siren, and the vehicles in front of us squeezed over, and Ms. Sims squeezed past and barreled through the red light, cutting across the southbound traffic on Seventh Avenue.

We got across the avenue, and I killed the lights and siren, and we continued west on 51st.

Ms. Sims glanced at me as though she wanted a compliment or something, so I mumbled, "Good driving."

I radioed Unit Two with our position and said, "I have subject vehicle in sight."

We drove through the area called Hell's Kitchen, formerly a nice slum, which has gone downhill with an influx of yuppies. I had no idea where Big Bird was going, but if he continued west, maybe he was headed for a Hudson River crossing. I said to Ms. Sims, "He may be going to Jersey."

She nodded.

In truth, ninety percent of our surveillances go nowhere. Abdul is just out and about, or he's trying to draw us off from something else that's happening. Or they're just practicing their countersurveillance techniques.

Now and then, though, you get the real thing—like one of these dips meeting a known bad guy. We do more watching than arresting or interrogating, because these characters can tell us more by keeping them under the eye than they'd tell us in an interrogation room. With the dips, you can't question them anyway, and getting them booted out is left to people with a higher pay grade than mine.

Now and then we do make an arrest, and I'm on the interrogation team, which is a lot more fun than following these clowns. I mean, *I'm* having fun; they're not.

The goal, of course, is to prevent another 9/11 or something worse. So far, so good. But it's been too quiet for too long. Like over a year and a half since that day. So, are we lucky, or are we good? For sure, the bad guys haven't given up, so we'll see.

The Mercedes continued on toward Twelfth Avenue, which runs along the Hudson River and is the place where civilization ends. No offense to New Jersey, but I haven't gotten my malaria shots this year.

I radioed Unit Two that we were traveling south on Twelfth.

There isn't as much traffic in this area of warehouses and piers, so the Mercedes picked up speed, and Ms. Sims kept up without being obvious.

The Mercedes passed the turns that would have led to the entrance of the Lincoln Tunnel and continued south toward Lower Manhattan.

Ms. Sims asked again, "Where do you think he's going?"

"Maybe one of the piers. Maybe he's got a rendezvous with a Saudi yacht that's carrying a nuclear device."

"Jeepers."

"Please don't swear."

"Shit."

"That's better."

We were making pretty good time down Twelfth Avenue, and I could see Unit Two in my sideview mirror, and we acknowledged visual contact. By now, the Iranian driver should know he was being followed, but these guys are so dumb they can't even find *themselves* in a mirror, let alone a tail.

Maybe I spoke too soon, because the guy suddenly slowed up, and Ms. Sims misjudged our relative speeds, and we were now too close to the Mercedes with no one between us and him. I could see Big Bird's head in the back right seat, and he was talking on his cell phone. Then the driver must have said something to him, and Big Bird twisted around in his seat, looked at us, then smiled and gave us the finger. I returned the salute. Prick.

Ms. Sims said, "Sorry," and dropped back.

I advised her, "You have to watch their brake lights."

"Right."

Well, it's not the end of the world when the subject is on to you. It happens about half the time when you're mobile, though less on foot.

There is a Plan B, however, and I called Unit Two and explained that we'd been burnt. I told Ms. Sims to drop farther back, and Unit Two passed us and picked up the visual tail.

We all continued on, and I kept Unit Two in sight.

I could have called for another surveillance vehicle, but the Iranians weren't doing any escape and evasion, so I just let it play out. They damned sure weren't going to lose us, and if I screwed up their plans today, that was a good day's work.

We got down below the West Village, and Unit Two radioed that the subject was turning on West Houston. Jacobs also said, "I think this guy made us."

"Then pull up alongside and give him the finger."

"Say again?"

"He flipped me the bird."

I heard laughter on the radio, then Unit Two said, "Subject is turning into the entrance ramp for the Holland."

"Copy."

In a few minutes, we were on the entrance ramp to the tunnel.

There are no toll booths in this direction so traffic was moving quickly into the tunnel entrance. I passed on a tidbit to Ms. Sims: "Almost none of these dip cars

has E-ZPass—they don't want their movements recorded—so when there's a toll booth, they're in the
cash lane, which is very slow, and if you go through
the E-ZPass lane, you'll be ahead of them, which you
don't want."

She nodded.

Unit Two was in the tunnel and we followed.

Inside the long tunnel, Ms. Sims asked again,
"Where do you think he's going?"

This time I knew. "New Jersey." I explained,
"That's where the tunnel goes."

She didn't respond to that bit of Zen, but she informed me, "Iranian diplomats may not travel more
than a twenty-five-mile radius from Manhattan."

"Right." I think I knew that.

She had no further information for me, so we continued on in golden silence. The tunnels under the
rivers around Manhattan Island are, of course, A-list
targets for our Mideast friends, but I didn't think Big
Bird was going to blow himself up in the tunnel. I
mean, why put on such a nice suit for that? Plus, you
need a big truck bomb to actually open the tunnel up
to the river. Right?

We exited the tunnel, and it took me awhile to ad-
just my eyes to the sunlight. I couldn't see the Mercedes, but I did spot Unit Two, and I pointed them
out to Ms. Sims, who followed. Unit Two reported the
subject in sight.

We were in Jersey City now, and we got on to the
Pulaski Skyway, from which we had a scenic view of
belching smokestacks.

I asked Ms. Sims, "Where do you think he's going?"

She recognized the question, smiled, and replied, "How do I know?"

We approached the interchange for Interstate 95, and I said, "Ten bucks says he goes south." I added, "Newark Airport."

She asked, "What's to the north?"

"The North Pole. Come on. You betting?"

She thought a moment, then said, "Well, he's been traveling south, but he has no luggage for the airport—unless it's in the trunk."

"So, you pick north?"

"No. I say he's going south, but not to the airport. To Atlantic City."

I wasn't following the train of thought that led Ms. Sims to Atlantic City, but I said, "Okay. Ten bucks."

"Fifty."

"You're on."

Unit Two radioed, "Subject has taken the southbound entrance to Ninety-five."

"Copy." So it was either Newark Airport or maybe Atlantic City. I mean, these guys did go down to AC to gamble, drink, and get laid. Not that I would know about any of that firsthand. But I have followed Abdul down there on a number of occasions.

I could still see Unit Two, and they could see the subject vehicle, and Jacobs radioed, "Subject passed the exit for Newark Airport."

Ms. Sims said to me, "You can pay me now."

I said, "He could be going to Fort Dix. You know,

spying on a military installation." I reminded her, "He's a military intel guy."

"And the chauffeur and Mercedes are cover for what?"

I didn't reply.

We continued on, hitting speeds of eighty miles an hour on Route 95, known here as the New Jersey Turnpike.

Ms. Sims announced, "He's past the twenty-five-mile limit."

"Good. Do you want to keep following him, or kill him?"

"I'm just making an observation."

"Noted."

We continued on, and I said to Ms. Sims, "You know, maybe I should call for air."

She didn't reply, so I further explained, "We have an air spotter we can use. Makes our job easier." I started to switch the frequency on the radio, but Ms. Sims said, "He's booked at the Taj Mahal."

I took my hand off the dial and inquired, "How do you know?"

"We got a tip."

I inquired, "And when were you going to share this with me?"

"After I had my muffin."

I was a little pissed off. Maybe a lot.

A few minutes later, she asked me, "Are you, like, not speaking to me?"

In fact, I wasn't, so I didn't reply.

She said, "But we've got to follow him down there to see that he actually goes to the Taj and checks in." She informed me, "We have a team down there already, so after they pick him up we can turn around and head back to the city."

I had no reply.

She assured me, "You don't owe me the fifty dollars. In fact, I'll buy you a drink."

No use staying mad, so I said, "Thank you." I mean, typical FBI. They wouldn't tell you if your ass was on fire. And the Special Agents, like Ms. Sims and my wife, are all lawyers. Need I say more?

I radioed Unit Two with my new info, though I advised Mel and George to stay with us in case our info was wrong and Big Bird was heading elsewhere.

Mel asked, "How did you find this out?"

"I'll tell you later."

We continued on, and Ms. Sims said, "We have about two hours. Tell me all you know about surveillance. I'd like to know what you've learned in the last forty years."

It hasn't been quite that long, and Ms. Sims I'm sure knew that; she was just making an ageist joke. She actually had a sense of humor, a rarity among her colleagues, so to show I was a good sport, and to demonstrate to her the spirit of joint FBI/NYPD cooperation, I said, "All right. I talk, you listen. Hold your questions."

"Will there be a test?"

"Every day."

She nodded.

I settled back and imparted my extensive knowledge of surveillance techniques, interspersed with anecdotal and personal stories of surveillances, even the ones that went bad.

The criminals I've followed over the years were all pretty dumb, but when I got to the Task Force, I realized that the guys we were following—diplomats and terrorist suspects—were not quite as dumb. I mean, they're certainly not smart, but they *are* paranoid, partly because most of them come from police states, and that makes them at least savvy that they're under the eye.

Ms. Sims, true to her word, did not interrupt as I held her spellbound with my stories. I really don't like to brag, but this was a teaching moment, so how could I avoid it? And, as I say, I was honest about the screw-ups.

On that subject, and on the subject of smart bad guys, I've run into only two evil geniuses in my three years with the Task Force. One was an American, and the other was a Libyan guy with a very big grudge against the USA, and not only was he evil and smart, he was also a perfect killing machine. My experience with the Libyan had less to do with surveillance than it did with hunter and hunted, and there were times when I wasn't sure if I was the hunter or the hunted.

This episode did not have a happy ending, and even if there were any lessons to be learned or taught, the whole case was classified as Top Secret and need-to-know, meaning I couldn't share it with Ms. Sims, or with anyone, ever. Which was fine with me.

But someday, I was sure, there would be a rematch. He promised me that.

CHAPTER TWO

About three hours after Ms. Sims did not get her muffin in Manhattan, we pulled into the long, fountain-lined drive of the Trump Taj Mahal. The Taj is topped with bulbous domes and minarets, so perhaps Big Bird thought this was a mosque.

Ms. Sims had the contact info for our team here, and she'd called ahead to let them know the subject was on the way so they could get to reception. She also described what he was wearing and let them know, "Subject is code-named Big Bird."

I radioed Unit Two, who were parked a distance from the entrance, and told them, "You can take off."

Mel Jacobs and George Foster volunteered to stay— above and beyond the call of duty—and I replied, "Do whatever you want. You're on your own time."

The nature of this job and of this Task Force is such that we all trust one another to do the right thing. There are rules, of course, but we're informal and free of a lot of the bureaucratic crap that keeps the job from getting done. And the thing that really makes the Task

Force work, in my opinion, is that about half the agents are retired NYPD, like me, which means we're not worried about our careers; these are second acts, maybe last acts, and we can improvise a lot and not worry about crossing the line. Plus, we bring NYPD street smarts to the table. Results may vary, of course, but we mostly get the job done.

The driver pulled away in the Mercedes without Big Bird, who went inside carrying an overnight bag. We couldn't give the fully equipped SUV to the parking attendant, so we just parked near the entrance and locked it. I flashed my creds and said, "Official business. Watch the car." I gave the parking guy a twenty and he said, "No problem."

We entered the big ornate marble lobby, and I spotted Big Bird at the VIP check-in, and I also spotted two guys who I recognized from the Special Operations detail. We made eye contact and they signaled they were on the case.

Great news. Time for a drink.

I didn't think Big Bird could recognize us from our brief, long-distance exchange of salutes, so I escorted Ms. Sims past where he was checking in. I mean, he knew he'd been followed here, but he wasn't looking over his shoulder. He wasn't supposed to be this far from Third Avenue, but we don't make an issue of it unless someone in Washington wants us to make an issue of it. The dips from most countries can travel freely around the U.S., but some, like the Cubans, are confined to New York City, or a set radius, like the Iranians. If I had it my way, they'd all be living and working in Iowa. Bottom line here, we have had no diplomatic relations with Iran since they took over our embassy and held the staff hostage, but they were U.N. members, so they were here. Also, since we had no diplomats in Iran, we could mess with these guys without worrying about them retaliating back in Sandland. In fact . . . stay tuned.

Anyway, we each made a pit stop, then went into the casino area, and I asked Ms. Sims, "Would you like a muffin?"

"I owe you a drink."

I headed directly for the Ego Lounge, which late at night becomes the Libido Lounge. We sat at the bar, and Ms. Sims inquired, "Have you been here before?"

"I think I may have been here on business."

The bartender—actually a tendress with big . . . eyes—asked what we were drinking, and Ms. Sims ordered a white wine while I got my usual Dewar's and soda.

We clinked glasses, and she said, "Cheers," then she asked me, "Why are we here?"

I replied, "Just to be sure Big Bird is playing and not meeting someone."

She reminded me, "We have a team here. Also, B.B. can have a meet in his room and we wouldn't know."

I replied, "The SO guys would know." I advised her, "You want to be around if something goes down. Being in the right place at the right time is not an accident." I asked her, "Were you listening to my stories?"

"Every word."

"You got someplace else to go?"

"Nope."

"Good. We'll give it an hour."

Actually, there was no reason to stay, except I needed a drink. Plus, I was pissed off at Big Bird for giving me the finger. That wasn't very diplomatic of him. I mean, it's my country. Right? He's a guest. And I'm not his host.

"John? I said, sorry I couldn't tell you about this." She explained, "They wanted to run it as a standard surveillance so that the subject couldn't guess by our actions that we knew where he was going." She added, "Only I knew in case we actually lost him."

"Right. Whatever." I had no idea whose brilliant idea that was, but I could guess that it was the idea of Tom Walsh, the FBI Special Agent in Charge of the Anti-Terrorist Task Force in New York. Walsh is somewhere between a genius and an idiot, and there's not much space separating the two. Also, he loves the cloak-and-dagger stuff and doesn't quite get standard police work. I mean, this secrecy crap would never have happened when I was a cop. But it's a new world and a new job and I don't take it personally.

To change the subject, I said, "Call the SO team and get a fix on Big Bird."

We all have these Nextel phones that, as I said, have a bling feature—a walkie-talkie capability—and Ms. Sims blinged one of the SO people and reported our location and asked that we be called if Big Bird left his room and came down to the casino or wherever.

So we chatted, mostly about her living and working in New York, which she didn't like personally, but did

like professionally. Lisa Sims reminded me in some
ways of my wife, Kate Mayfield, who I met on the job
three years ago on the previously mentioned case of the
Libyan asshole. Kate, too, is from the hinterland, and
she wasn't initially thrilled with the New York assignment, but after meeting me she wouldn't live anywhere
else. And then there was 9/11. After that, she wanted
us to transfer out of New York, but after the trauma
wore off—we were both there when it happened—she
rethought it and realized she couldn't leave. Which
was good, since I wasn't leaving.

I had a second drink, but Ms. Sims—now Lisa—
switched to club soda because I told her she was driving back.

Her cell phone blinged, and she took it and listened, then said to the caller, "Okay, we'll probably
head out." She signed off and said to me, "Big Bird is
alone at a roulette table."

"How's he doing?"

"I didn't ask." She called for the check, paid, and
we left the Ego Lounge.

She turned toward the lobby, but I said, "I just want
to get a close look at this guy."

She hesitated, then deferred to my professional
judgment and nodded.

We made our way into the cavernous casino, and
Lisa blinged her contact on the SO team and got a fix
on Big Bird. Within a few minutes, we spotted him
sitting at a roulette wheel with a drink in his hand.

The Iranian's sinful behavior was not my problem—in fact, we record all this on film and it can be

useful—but I think there's something deep down schizo with these people, a total disconnect that is not good for the head.

Lisa said, "Okay? There he is. Let's go."

I observed, "Satan has entered his soul."

"Right. I see that."

"I need to help him."

"John—"

"Let's get some tokens and hit the slots."

"John—"

"Come on." I took her arm and we went to the cashier, where I got a hundred one-dollar tokens on my government credit card—the accounting office will get a good laugh out of that—and we headed for the dollar slots, from which we could see Big Bird's back.

Lisa and I sat side by side at two poker machines, and I asked her, "You ever play the slots?"

"No."

"You play poker?"

"I do."

So I divided up the silver coins and briefly explained the machine to Lisa, and we played slot machine poker. They should have a slot game called Sucker. You get a row of five suckers and the machine kicks you in the nuts and swallows all the coins in your tray.

We each got a drink from a passing waitress, and I inhaled the secondhand smoke of a catatonic fat lady sitting next to me.

Anyway, we were up and down, and Lisa was getting into it, hoping to retire early on the Zillion Dollar Jackpot. Meanwhile, Big Bird is sinking deeper into the fires of hell with each spin of the wheel. I had to save him.

After about half an hour, Big Bird cashed out and got up. He drifted over to the blackjack tables, then hesitated and decided to go somewhere else.

Lisa got four kings and the machine chimed and disgorged a stream of coins into her tray.

I said to her, "Big Bird is moving. Stay here and play my machine. Call the Special Ops team and tell them I've got him."

She glanced around, noticing her surroundings, then said, "Okay . . ."

I headed across the casino floor, hoping that Big Bird would head to the elevators, or the men's room, or the boardwalk—any place where we could be alone for a chat.

He walked like he needed to take a leak, and sure enough he headed out toward the restrooms. I followed him into a corridor and saw him go through the men's room door. I followed.

These guys don't piss at the urinal—they like privacy when they pull out their pee-pees—and Big Bird was in one of the stalls.

There were two guys at the urinals and one at the sink. Very quietly and diplomatically, I showed my creds and asked them to move out quickly, and I asked one of them to stand outside and keep people out.

They all exited, and I stood at the sink, looking in the mirror. The stall door opened—without a flush. In fact, Big Bird didn't even go to the sinks.

I turned and he gave me a glance and I could tell he

didn't recognize me. But then he made his move. He suddenly rushed me and somehow managed to smash his balls into my fist. Well, that took me by surprise, and I stepped back as he made his next aggressive move, which was to sink to his knees and make threatening groans at me. His eyes were rolling like the wheels on a slot machine, and then he slumped forward and lay on the floor, breathing hard, ready to attack again. I didn't want to cause an international incident, so I excused myself by saying, "Fuck you," and left.

Out in the corridor, I released my deputy and went back into the casino, where I ran into Lisa, who was carrying a plastic container filled with tokens. She asked me, "Where were you?"

"Men's room."

"Where's Big—"

"Time to go."

We headed toward the lobby, and she asked me, "What do I do with these tokens?"

"Give them to accounting."

We got outside and headed toward the SUV.

Lisa asked, "What happened? Where's Big Bird?"

The less she knew, the better for her, of course, so I said, "Men's room."

She asked, "Who's covering him? Is he moving?"

"Uh . . . not too much."

"John—"

"Call the SO team and report his last location."

We got to the SUV and I said I'd drive. She gave me the keys, we got in, and I pulled away.

Lisa called the surveillance team and told them I'd

left Big Bird in the men's room, which they already knew. She listened, then signed off and said to me, "Big Bird . . . had a fall or something."

"Slippery when wet."

I headed out of town toward the Jersey Turnpike.

After a few minutes, she asked me, "Did you . . . have an encounter with him?"

"Hey, how'd we do? What do you have there?"

She glanced at the container on the floor and said, "I think we won ten bucks."

"Not bad for an hour's work."

She stayed silent, then said, "Well . . . I suppose he's not in a good position to make a complaint."

I didn't reply.

We got onto the Turnpike northbound toward the city, which was about 130 miles away, less than two hours if I pushed it. The sun was below the horizon and the western sky was rapidly fading into darkness.

Lisa asked, "Are we, like, on the lam?"

"No. We are the law."

"Right." She added, "They told me I'd learn a lot from you."

"Am I a legend?"

"In your own mind." She then observed, "You seem like a nice guy and you're smart. But you have another side to you."

I didn't reply.

She further observed, "You're into payback."

"Well, if I am, I'm in the right business."

She had no response to that, and we continued on in silence.

Awhile later, she said to me, "If something comes up about tonight, you were never out of my sight."

I assured her, "Nothing will come up. But thanks."

"And maybe you'll do the same for me someday."

"No maybes about it."

She glanced at me, then stared out the windshield at the dark road ahead. She said, as if to herself, "This is a tough business."

And what was your first clue? I replied, "And getting tougher."

She nodded, then said, "Good."

I stopped at a turnpike rest area, and Lisa Sims got her muffin, I got gas, and we both got coffees to go.

Back on the road, we talked mostly about living in New York, and a little about me being at the Towers when they were hit. It changes you. Seeing thousands of people die changes you.

We took the Holland Tunnel into Manhattan, and I dropped her off at 26 Fed, where she had some work to do. I reminded her, "Give the tokens to accounting."

I continued on to my apartment on East 72nd and got in the door a little after 10 P.M.

Kate was home, watching the ten o'clock news, and she asked me, "How did it go?"

"Okay. The target went down to AC and we followed."

"Drink?"

"Sure." I asked, "How did your day go?"

"Office all day."

We made drinks, clinked, smooched, and sat down and watched the news together.

I was waiting for a story about an Iranian U.N. diplomat who was found in the men's room of the Taj Mahal Casino with his nuts stuck in his throat, but apparently this was not going to be a news item.

We shut off the TV, and Kate and I chatted about our day of fighting the war on terrorism. After exhausting that subject, she reminded me that we were going upstate for the weekend—skydiving.

This was not my favorite subject, though she was excited about it.

Aside from the fact that I don't like trees and woods and bears and whatever else is north of the Bronx, I damned sure don't like jumping out of planes. I have no particular fear of heights or even death, but I see no reason to put myself in danger for fun. I mean, I get enough danger on my job. And all the fun I want. Like tonight.

But I'm a good guy and a good husband, so I've taken up skydiving. And in the spirit of quid pro quo—as the diplomats say—Kate has taken up drinking and oral sex. It works.

I went out to my 34th-floor balcony and looked south down the length of Manhattan Island. What a view. Gone from view, however, were the Twin Towers, and I held up two fingers in a V where they used to be. Victory and peace.

Not in my lifetime, but maybe someday.

Meanwhile, the name of the game, as Lisa Sims figured out, was payback.

—PART II—

California

CHAPTER THREE

Asad Khalil, Libyan terrorist, traveling on a forged Egyptian passport, walked quickly down the Jetway that connected his Air France jetliner to Terminal Two of Los Angeles International Airport.

The flight from Cairo to Paris had been uneventful as had the flight from Paris to Los Angeles. The initial boarding at Cairo Airport had been even more uneventful thanks to well-placed friends who had expedited his passage through Egyptian passport control. In Paris, he had a two-hour layover in the transit lounge and did not have to go through a second security check, which could have been a problem. And now he was in America. Or nearly so.

Khalil walked with his fellow Air France passengers toward the passport control booths. Most of the people on board the flight were French nationals, though that included many fellow Muslims with French citizenship. Perhaps a fourth of the passengers were Egyptians who had boarded the flight in Cairo and like him had waited in the De Gaulle Airport

transit lounge to board the Boeing 777 non-stop to
Los Angeles. In any case, Khalil thought, he did not
stand out among his fellow travelers and he had been
assured by his Al Qaeda friends that this particular
route would get him at least this far without a problem. All that remained was for him to get through
American passport control with his forged Egyptian
documents. Customs would be no problem; he had
nothing to declare and he carried nothing with him
except his hate for America, which he could easily
conceal.

There were ten passport control booths operating,
and he stood in the line with other arriving passengers. He glanced at his watch, which he had set to the
local time: 5:40 P.M.; a busy hour, which was part of
the plan.

Asad Khalil wore a bespoke blue sports blazer, tan
slacks, expensive loafers, and a button-down oxford
shirt—an outfit that he knew gave off the image of a
man of the upper middle class who may have attended
the right schools and was no threat to anyone except
perhaps his drinking companions or his financial advisor. He was a westernized Egyptian tourist by the
name of Mustafa Hasheem, carrying a confirmed reservation at the Beverly Hills Hotel, and in his overnight bag he had a Los Angeles *Fodor's* guide in
English, which he spoke almost fluently.

He scanned the passport control officers hoping
there was not an Arab-American among them. Those
men or women could be a problem. Especially if they
engaged him in a seemingly friendly conversation.

"And in what quarter of Cairo do you live, Mr. Hasheem?" And if the friendly conversation was in Arabic, there could be a problem with his Libyan accent.

Asad Khalil walked quickly, as most passengers did, to the next available booth. The passport control officer was a middle-aged man who looked bored and tired, but who could also become alert in an instant. The man took Khalil's passport, visa, and customs declaration form and stared at them, then flipped through the passport pages, then returned to the photo page and divided his attention between the photograph and the man standing before him. Khalil smiled, as did most people at this juncture.

The man, who Khalil thought could possibly be Hispanic, said to him, "What is the purpose of your visit?"

To kill, Khalil thought to himself, but replied, "Tourism."

The man glanced at Khalil's customs form and said, "You're staying at the Beverly Hilton?"

"The Beverly Hills Hotel."

"You're here for two weeks?"

"That is correct."

"What is your next destination?"

Home or Paradise. Khalil replied, "Home."

"You have a confirmed return flight?"

In fact he did, though he wouldn't be on that flight, but he replied, "Yes."

"You have a reservation at the Beverly Hills Hotel?"

He did, though he knew not to offer to show it unless asked. He replied, "Yes."

The man looked into Khalil's deep, dark eyes, and Khalil could tell that this passport officer, who had seen and heard much over the years, had a small doubt in his mind that could grow into a larger doubt in the next few seconds of eye contact. Khalil remained impassive, showing no signs of anxiety and no feigned impatience.

The man turned his attention to his computer and began typing as he glanced at Khalil's passport.

Khalil waited. The passport itself, he knew, looked genuine, with just the right amount of wear and a few entry and exit stamps, all from European countries, with corresponding entries to Cairo. But the information in the passport was not genuine. His Al Qaeda friends, who knew much about American airport security, did not, unfortunately, know much about what the computer databank was capable of knowing or detecting—or suspecting. As always, it came down to the man.

The passport officer turned away from his computer screen, looked again at the Egyptian tourist, then hesitated a second before opening the passport and stamping it. He said, "Welcome to the United States, Mr. Hasheem. Have a pleasant visit."

"Thank you."

The man made a mark on the customs form, and Khalil collected his documents and moved toward the baggage carousels.

He was now one step closer to the security doors that he could see beyond the customs inspection area.

He stood at the luggage carousel and waited for it

to begin moving, aware that he and his fellow Air France passengers were being watched on video monitors. It was here that people sometimes revealed themselves, unaware or forgetting that they were being watched. Khalil assumed the pose and the blank gaze of the other tired passengers who stared at the carousel opening.

In truth, his heart had sped up just a bit at the passport control booth, which surprised and annoyed him. He had long ago trained himself—or his mind—to remain calm under any circumstances, and his body obeyed; his skin remained dry, his mouth remained moist, and his face and muscles did not tense or betray fear. But he had not yet learned to control his heart, which if it could be seen and heard would reveal all that his mind worked to overcome. This was interesting, he thought, and perhaps not a bad thing; if he had to fight, to kill, it was good that his heart was ready, like a cocked gun.

A harsh buzzer sounded, a red light flashed, and the carousel began to move. Within five minutes he had retrieved his one medium-size bag and wheeled it toward the customs counters.

He was able to choose his counter and his inspector, which he thought was poor security. He chose a counter with a young man—never choose a woman, especially an attractive one—and handed the man his customs form. The man looked at it and asked him, "Anything to declare?"

"No."

The man glanced at the black suitcase that was

behind Khalil and said, "If I looked in there, would I find anything you're not supposed to have?"

Asad Khalil answered truthfully, "No."

The young man joked, "No hashish?"

Khalil returned the smile and replied, "No."

"Thank you."

Khalil continued on. The security doors were ten meters away and it was here, he knew, that he would be stopped if they intended to stop him. He had no weapon, of course, but he felt confident that there were not many men whom he could not disable or disarm, and he was close enough to the doors to escape into the crowded terminal. He might not make good on his escape, but if he had one of their weapons he could kill a number of them and shoot a few passengers while he was at it. Death did not frighten him; capture frightened him. A failed mission frightened his soul.

A few meters from the doors, Khalil stopped, let go of his luggage handle, and made a pretense of checking his pockets for his papers and his wallet, the way many passengers did before exiting the security area. Anyone who was watching could plainly see that he was not overly anxious to get out of the area. And he could see if anyone seemed too interested in him. The Americans, he knew, especially the FBI, did not often make preemptive or premature arrests; they followed you. And kept following you. And they saw who you met and where you went, and what you did. And a week or a month later they would make the arrests and then thank you for your help.

Asad Khalil walked through the security doors into the crowded terminal.

A small group of people waited near the doors for their arriving friends or family members. Another group, livery drivers, stood in a line holding up signs with the names of their expected passengers.

Khalil moved past them and followed signs that directed him to the taxi stand. He exited Terminal Two and stood in a short line of people as taxis moved up the line and took on passengers. Within a few minutes, he and his suitcase were in a taxi and he said to the driver, "The Beverly Hills Hotel."

As the taxi moved toward the airport exit, Khalil noted absently that it was a very fine day. He had been to Los Angeles once before, and also to the area north of the city, and every day seemed to be a fine day. Why else would anyone live in this place?

The driver asked him, "First time in LA?"

"No."

"You like it here?"

"I keep returning."

"Business or pleasure?"

Killing Mr. Chip Wiggins would be both a business and a pleasure, so Khalil replied, "Both."

"I hope you have fun and make lots of money."

"Thank you."

Khalil took his guidebook from his overnight bag and pretended to read it, and the driver settled into a silence.

Khalil slipped a pocket mirror from his bag and placed it into the book that he held in front of his face.

He scanned the traffic to his rear but couldn't see any vehicles that appeared to be following them as they entered the freeway and continued north toward Beverly Hills.

Within half an hour, they pulled into the long, palm-lined drive that led to the pink stucco hotel on the hill.

The vegetation was very lush, Khalil noticed, and on this fine day in May thousands of flowers were in bloom. It was, he imagined, what the Garden of Eden must have looked like. Except here, there were many serpents, and here, bare flesh would never be an embarrassment.

Khalil paid the driver, allowed a porter to take his suitcase, but not his overnight bag, and entered the hotel lobby and checked in under his assumed name. The receptionist, a young lady, assured him that all charges, including incidentals, were prepaid by his company in Cairo, and that no credit card was necessary. He let the receptionist know that he might not be returning to the hotel this evening and that he did not require turndown service, a wake-up call, or a newspaper in the morning. In fact, he required nothing but privacy.

He was shown to his room in the main building, a spacious and sunny suite on the second floor overlooking the pool.

Asad Khalil stood on the small balcony and looked out at the swimming pool where men and women paraded and lounged, and he wondered at men who would allow their wives to be seen half naked by other men. He did not wonder at the women who had no shame; women were shameless if it was allowed.

He found himself aroused at the sight of these women, and when his doorbell rang he had to remove his jacket and hold it in front of him as he answered. Yes, that was another thing his mind had trouble controlling.

The bellman entered with his suitcase and asked if the accommodations were satisfactory and if he required anything further.

Khalil assured him everything was satisfactory, and when the bellman left, Khalil put the DO NOT DISTURB sign on his door, then unpacked his suitcase. He sat at the desk with a bottled water and waited for his call.

The phone rang, and he answered, "Hasheem."

The voice at the other end said in English, "This is Gabbar. Are you well, sir?"

"I am. And how is your father?"

"Quite well, thank you."

The sign and countersign having been given, Khalil said to Gabbar, "Five minutes. I have a flower for your wife."

"Yes, sir."

Khalil hung up and went again to the balcony. Many of the men, he now noticed, were fat, and many of them had young women with them. Waiters carried trays of beverages to the lounge chairs and tables. It was the cocktail hour; the time to cloud one's mind with alcohol. Asad Khalil recalled the Roman ruins in his native Libya, and he imagined fat Romans in the public baths drinking wine poured by slave girls. "Pigs," he said aloud. "Fat pigs to the slaughter."

CHAPTER FOUR

Asad Khalil, carrying a flower from his room, walked through the lobby of the Beverly Hills Hotel, noticing a few men whom he recognized as fellow Arabs—men who aped the dress and the manners of the Americans and Europeans. These men, he knew, were more dangerous to Islam than the infidels. They would be dealt with next, and without mercy.

Khalil walked out of the lobby and a doorman asked if he needed a taxi. Khalil had noticed on his last visit here, three years before, that no one walked anywhere in this city. Even a trip of a block or two necessitated an automobile. In fact, he was surprised that the hotel did not provide sedan chairs for guests going to the pool. Roman pigs.

He replied to the doorman, "I am waiting for a car."

"Yes, sir."

A blue Ford Taurus that had been sitting nearby moved forward and stopped at the doors. The driver did not exit, but signaled to Khalil, who got quickly into the passenger seat, and the car moved off.

The driver, whom he knew as Gabbar, said in Arabic, "Good evening, sir."

Khalil did not respond.

The driver headed down the long driveway and said, "I have taken a room under my own name at the Best Western hotel in Santa Barbara."

Khalil nodded and asked, "And what is your name?"

The driver replied, "It is Farid Mansur, sir," but he did not ask his passenger what his real name was.

Khalil inquired, "And what do you do here, Mr. Mansur?"

"I deliver parcels, sir."

"Good. And do you have my parcels?"

"I do, sir. They are in my hotel room, as instructed." He added, "Two locked luggage pieces for which I have no keys." He inquired, "Is that correct, sir?"

Khalil nodded and asked, "Do you have the other two items I requested?"

"Yes, sir. They are in the trunk."

"And the card?"

Mansur handed Khalil a plastic card without comment.

Khalil examined the card, which had little information printed on it for security reasons—not even the name of the airport where it could be used, nor the specific security gate that it would open. In fact, it had only numbers printed on it.

Khalil asked, "How did you get this card?"

Mansur replied, "In truth, sir, I did not get it. It was given to me by our mutual friend here." He added,

"I was told to tell you that it is on loan from another friend, a man of our faith who will not be needing it for two days. But I must return the card to our mutual friend so that it can be returned to its owner." Mansur further added, to reinforce his ignorance of this matter, "I do not know the airport in question or the area it will allow you to access, but I trust, sir, that you do."

Khalil asked, "Why do you say airport?"

Farid Mansur realized his mistake and tried to cover it up by saying, "Our mutual friend . . . he may have used that word . . . but I may have misunderstood, or—"

"No matter."

"Yes, sir."

Khalil put the card in his pocket.

They came to the end of the driveway, and Farid Mansur asked, "Do you wish to go now to Santa Barbara?"

"I do."

Mansur began to turn right on Sunset Boulevard, but Khalil said, "Go straight."

Mansur crossed Sunset Boulevard and continued on Canon Drive, which was lined with large private homes.

Khalil glanced in the sideview mirror, but saw no vehicles that seemed to be following. He said to Mansur, "This is a rental car, correct?"

"Yes, sir." He added, "I have taken it for three days, as instructed."

"Good." So the vehicle would not be missed until Monday.

Khalil stared out the side window, and Mansur commented, "The wealthy live here. Movie stars and those in the film industry."

Khalil observed, "Sin pays well here."

Mansur replied, as was expected of him, "Here, yes. But there is a higher price to pay in Hell."

Khalil did not respond to that and asked, "Where in Libya are you from?"

"Benghazi, sir."

"Why are you here?"

Mansur hesitated, then replied, "To make money for my parents, sir, and the parents of my wife who are in Benghazi." He was quick to add, "My dream is to return to our country."

"You will."

"Yes, sir."

"And your wife? Is she here with you, Mr. Mansur?"

"Yes, sir. And our four children."

"Good. And are they instructed in our faith?"

"Of course, sir. They study the Koran in a school at our mosque."

"Good." Khalil asked, "And your wife knows you will not be returning home for two or three days?"

"Yes, sir."

The two men fell into a silence, and Farid Mansur realized that this man made him nervous. He had seen men like this in Libya, and sometimes here, at the mosque. They shared with him the same faith, but in a different way. And this man . . . his voice, his manner, his eyes . . . this man was different even from the others who were different; this man frightened him.

Farid Mansur, unsure of where to go but suspecting that his passenger was concerned about someone following them, made a few random turns and continued on.

They entered a street lined with expensive-looking shops, and Mansur commented, "This is Rodeo Drive, sir. Only the very rich can shop here."

Khalil stayed silent.

At the end of the shop-lined street, Khalil said, "Santa Barbara."

Mansur turned right onto Wilshire Boulevard and headed west into the sinking sun.

They continued on along the wide boulevard lined with shops and tall buildings that held apartments and offices. Traffic was heavy and moved slowly.

Mansur observed, "Many vehicles here."

Khalil responded, "They suck the oil from the earth."

Mansur allowed himself a small laugh and said, "And pay well for it."

"Yes." Khalil asked, "How long have you been here?"

Mansur hesitated, then he replied, "Eight years, sir." He added, "Too long."

"Yes, too long." Khalil said, "So you were in Benghazi when the Americans bombed the city."

"Yes. I remember that night. April 15, 1986. I was a young boy."

"Were you frightened?"

"Of course."

"Did you wet your pants, Mr. Mansur?"

"Sir?"

"I did."

Farid Mansur did not know how to respond to that, so he stayed silent.

Khalil continued, "I, too, was a young boy living in the Al Azziziyah compound in Tripoli. One of their aircraft flew directly over the rooftop where I was standing and released a bomb. I was unhurt. But I wet my pants."

Farid Mansur managed to say, "Allah was merciful, sir."

"Yes. But my mother, two brothers, and two sisters ascended to Paradise that night."

Mansur took a deep breath, then said softly, "May they dwell with the angels for eternity."

"Yes. They will."

They drove on in silence, then Khalil asked, "Why are you doing this?"

Farid Mansur considered his reply. To say that he was doing this for his country or his faith was to admit that he knew there was more to this than assisting a countryman on his visit. Farid Mansur had done nothing illegal—except perhaps for the plastic card—and if the man sitting beside him was going to do something illegal, he did not want to know about it.

"Mr. Mansur? I asked you a question."

"Yes, sir . . . I . . . I have been asked to do a favor for a countryman, and—"

"Have you ever come to the attention of the authorities?"

"No, sir. I live quietly with my family."

"And your wife. What does she do?"

"What a good woman does. She tends to her house and family."

"Good. So, a little extra money would be of help."

"Yes, sir."

"The price of oil has gone higher again."

Mansur allowed himself a small smile and replied, "Yes, sir."

"Our mutual friend here has paid you, I believe, a thousand dollars."

"Yes, sir."

"I will give you another thousand."

"Thank you, sir."

"And this flower for your wife." Khalil threw the bird of paradise on top of the dashboard.

"Thank you, sir."

Mansur took the Pacific Coast Highway north toward Santa Barbara. He informed his passenger, "It should be less than two hours to the hotel."

Khalil glanced at the dashboard clock. It was just 7:30 and the sun was sinking into the ocean. In the hills to his right, large houses faced out to the sea.

Farid Mansur said, "This is the more scenic route to Santa Barbara, sir. On Sunday, we can take the freeway back, if you wish."

Khalil did not care about the scenery, and neither he nor Farid Mansur would be returning to Beverly Hills on Sunday. But to put the man's mind at ease, he replied, "Whatever you wish." He added, "I am in your hands."

"Yes, sir."

"And we are both in God's hands."

"Yes, sir."

In fact, Khalil thought, Mr. Mansur would be in God's hands within two hours, and then he would go home, finally.

And as for Mr. Chip Wiggins, who was one of the pilots who had bombed Tripoli seventeen years ago and had perhaps been the one to murder Khalil's family, he would be in Hell before the sun rose again.

And then to New York to settle other unfinished business.

CHAPTER FIVE

A few miles north of Santa Barbara, Farid Mansur pulled into the entrance of the Best Western hotel. He drove around to the back of the hotel and parked in a space facing the building.

Khalil exited the car and said to Mansur, "Open the trunk."

Mansur opened the trunk and Khalil peered inside. Sitting on the trunk floor was a long canvas carrying case, which Khalil opened. In the case was a heavy crowbar, and also a butcher's saw. Khalil touched the sharp, jagged teeth of the saw and smiled.

He slammed the trunk closed and said to Mansur, "Lock the car."

Mansur locked the car with the remote and Khalil took the car keys from him and motioned toward the hotel.

Khalil followed Mansur into a rear entrance that Mansur opened with his passcard. They turned down a corridor, and Mansur stopped at Room 140, which had a DO NOT DISTURB sign on the doorknob. Mansur opened the door with the card, and he stepped aside to let his guest enter first, but Khalil waved him in, then followed and bolted the door behind him. He took the passcard from Mansur and put it in his pocket.

It was a pleasant room with two large beds, and on one of the beds sat two pieces of luggage—a black suitcase and a black duffel bag.

Khalil asked Mansur, "When did you check into this room?"

"At three, sir. For two nights. The checkout time is at one P.M., the day after tomorrow."

"And you carried these bags yourself?"

"Yes, sir. From where we have just parked."

Khalil walked to the bags on the bed, and from his wallet he retrieved two small keys that had been given to him in Cairo.

He unlocked and unzipped the duffel bag and saw that it had a few changes of clothing for him, but mostly it was filled with some other items that he had requested for his mission.

Farid Mansur had moved to the window and was staring out at the parking lot.

Khalil zipped and locked the duffel bag, then opened the suitcase. Inside were the other things he needed to complete his mission—cash, credit cards, forged passports and documents, plus a few maps, binoculars, and a cell phone and charger. Also in the suitcase was a copy of the Koran.

Within the suitcase was also an overnight bag, which he opened. In the bag he found the instruments of death that he had requested—a .45 caliber automatic pistol with extra magazines, a very large butcher's knife with a well-honed blade, and a few smaller knives. There was also a pair of leather gloves and a garrote. And finally, there was the ice pick that he'd asked for.

Satisfied that all was in order, he glanced at Mansur's back, then slipped on the leather gloves and removed the piano wire garrote from the bag.

Khalil said to Mansur, "Close the drapes."

Mansur pulled the drapes shut, but remained facing the window.

Khalil came up behind him, and Mansur said, "Please, sir."

Khalil quickly slipped the wire noose over Mansur's head and twisted the wooden grip. The wire tightened, and Mansur tried to pull it from his throat as a high-pitched squeaking sound came out of his mouth. Khalil tightened it further, and Mansur lurched about, finally falling facedown on the floor with Khalil on his back, keeping the wire taut. A line of blood oozed around the man's throat and neck where the wire bit into his flesh.

Mansur kicked his legs and his body began to heave. Then he lay still.

Khalil remained on top of him and waited a full minute before he loosened the wire. He said to Mansur, "The angels shall bear thee aloft."

Khalil knelt beside the dead man and removed his wallet from his pocket, then rolled him over on his back. Farid Mansur's eyes stared up at Asad Khalil and his mouth was open in a silent scream.

As Khalil went through the man's pockets, he noticed that Mansur had wet his pants. His sphincter, too, had opened, and there was a faint odor in the room that Khalil found annoying.

He retrieved his garrote, then rolled and pushed the dead man under one of the double beds.

From the suitcase, he took a wind-up alarm clock and set it for 2:30 A.M. That would give him about four hours' rest, which was enough.

Khalil removed the Colt .45 automatic from the overnight bag. He checked the magazine, chambered a round, and stuck the pistol in his belt.

He also took the Koran from the suitcase, then he turned off all the lights except for the reading lamp and lay down fully dressed on the bed. Khalil opened the Koran and read a verse for the man lying under his bed. "Wherever ye be, God will bring you all back at the resurrection."

Then he read a few more favorite verses, shut off the light, and closed his eyes.

He thought he heard a sound from under the bed, but perhaps it was just gases escaping from the corpse.

He reflected briefly on his past visit here, and on how he had been cheated of his final revenge on the last living pilot of the air raid on Tripoli. Mr. Wiggins would not escape his fate this time, nor would the man who had cheated him of his revenge—John Corey.

And others.

Asad Khalil did not sleep. Like the lion, after whom he was named, he rested his body and kept his senses awake. He recalled an old Arab proverb: "On the day of victory, no one is tired."

CHAPTER SIX

The alarm clock did not waken him—he was awake—but it told him it was 2:30 A.M.

Asad Khalil swung out of bed, used the bathroom, drank some water, then left the room, ensuring that the DO NOT DISTURB sign was still in place. By the time Mansur's body was found— by a cleaning person or the next guest—Khalil would be far from California.

He went out into the cool, dark morning, got into the car, and drove out of the parking lot. On the way, he removed the cash from Mansur's wallet and threw the wallet into a drainage ditch along with the flower from the dashboard.

There was no traffic on the roads, and within ten minutes he was approaching the northeast corner of Santa Barbara Airport. This part of the airport was away from the main terminal, and it was reserved for private aircraft, charter companies, and air freight.

He had been told to be alert for the airport patrol car that made periodic sweeps of the area, but he saw no moving vehicles beyond the chain-link fence. He drove through the open gate into a long, narrow parking lot where several low buildings backed onto the aircraft parking ramps. Most of the buildings were dark, but one of them had a lighted sign that said STERLING AIR CHARTERS, which would be his second destination.

He continued past a few more buildings, noting that there were a total of three vehicles parked in the lot, and he saw not a single person or moving vehicle at this hour. So far, his information had been correct. Al Qaeda in America had not made his mission possible—as they believed—but, he admitted, they had made it easier. Asad Khalil, The Lion, had killed the enemies of Islam all over Europe and America without help from anyone, but Al Qaeda had made him an offer of assistance with his American mission in exchange for his carrying out a mission for them in New York. And so he would do that, but not until he completed his personal mission of revenge.

About two hundred meters from the Sterling Air Charters building was a lighted sign that read ALPHA AIR FREIGHT—Mr. Chip Wiggins's place of employment. In fact, Khalil saw a dark Ford Explorer parked near the freight office that matched the photograph he had been shown in Tripoli. Mr. Wiggins—formerly United States Air Force Lieutenant Wiggins—was apparently working this evening, as scheduled. Today was Friday, and Mr. Wiggins was not scheduled to work again until Sunday night, but in fact this would be Mr. Wiggins's last day of work.

Khalil parked the Ford Taurus in a space opposite

Alpha Air Freight, next to Wiggins's vehicle. He shut off the lights and the engine, then got out and checked the license plate number of the Explorer, confirming it was Wiggins's vehicle. He opened his trunk and removed the canvas carrying case that contained the crowbar and the butcher's saw and slung the case over his shoulder.

Khalil walked quickly across the parking lot toward the open space between the freight building and the building beside it. There was a high security fence and gate between the two buildings that led to the airport ramps. Khalil used the access card that he'd gotten from Farid Mansur—may he be rewarded in Paradise for his sacrifice—opened the gate, and slipped into the secured area.

The space between the buildings was not well lighted, and he walked in the shadow close to the Alpha building, then knelt beside a trash container at the corner of the building and scanned the area around him.

Here behind the row of buildings were the parking ramps for the aircraft, and there were a number of small and medium-size aircraft up and down the line. Close to the rear of the Alpha building were two small twin-engine aircraft with the Alpha markings on their tails. These aircraft, as he'd been told, were two of the three aircraft that were operated by Alpha, and they normally returned to the ramp between midnight and 1 A.M.—and they had apparently done so this morning. The third aircraft in the Alpha fleet—which was not parked on the ramp—was a white twin-engine Cessna piloted by Mr. Wiggins, whose pickup and drop-off route would not usually get him back here until three or four in the morning. Khalil looked at the luminous dial of his watch and saw it was now 2:58 A.M. He hoped that Mr. Wiggins had made good time on his route and that he would be arriving shortly.

Khalil remained crouched in the shadow of the trash container and stared out at the airport. In the far distance he could see the lights of the main terminal and also the lights of the runways. There were not many aircraft landing or departing at this hour, but he did see the lights of a small aircraft as it came in low over the closest runway.

The aircraft touched down, and a few minutes later Khalil saw the beams of two white landing lights cutting through the darkness and illuminating the taxiway that led to the ramps.

He remained still, listening for any sound that someone might be close by. If he encountered anyone, he had two options: the crowbar or the gun. Fleeing was not an option. He had waited a long time for this moment, and he was now very close to Mr. Wiggins, the last of the eight pilots who had dropped their bombs on the Al Azziziyah compound in Tripoli where he had lived, and where his family had died.

The twin-engine aircraft continued taxiing toward him, and he prayed that this was the aircraft he had been waiting for. As it drew closer, he saw it was white and he thought he saw the Alpha marking on its tail. He opened the canvas carrying case and took out the heavy crowbar.

The aircraft entered the ramp and came to a stop not more than ten meters from him. Within moments the aircraft lights had been extinguished, both engines shut down, and the night was again dark and quiet.

Khalil watched and waited. He heard a few creaking sounds from the aircraft, then he saw the airstair door on the left side of the fuselage swing down, and a moment later a man stepped out and descended the stairs.

There was little illumination in the ramp area, and Khalil could not be certain that this pilot was Wiggins, but this was the aircraft he flew, and it was his vehicle in the parking lot, and his arrival time was correct. Khalil would not have been troubled if he killed the wrong man, except that would alert Wiggins—and the authorities—that he, Asad Khalil, was back.

The pilot was carrying something—wheel chocks on ropes—and he turned and bent down to place the first chock into position behind the aircraft's left tire.

Khalil grabbed the canvas carrying case and sprang forward, covering the ten meters between him and the aircraft in a few seconds.

The pilot was now placing a second chock in front of the left tire, but he heard a sound, turned, and stood.

Khalil was right on top of him, and in an instant he recognized the face from photographs as that of Chip Wiggins.

Wiggins stared at the man and said, "Who—?"

Khalil had dropped the canvas bag and was now holding the crowbar in both hands, and he swung the heavy steel bar around in an arc and smashed it down on top of Wiggins's left shoulder, shattering his clavicle.

Wiggins let out a bellowing cry of pain, staggered backward, then fell to the ground.

Khalil swung again and shattered Wiggins's right kneecap, then again, smashing his left shin bone, then a final swing that broke his right shoulder.

Wiggins's cries of pain were barely audible now, and Khalil could see that the man was passing into unconsciousness.

Khalil looked around quickly, then threw the crowbar and the carrying case with the saw up into the plane's cabin. He knelt beside Wiggins and pulled him up by the front of his shirt into a sitting position. Khalil hefted the semi-conscious man over his shoulder, stood, then made his way quickly up the stairs, which he closed behind him.

The freight cabin was dark and the ceiling was low, so Khalil moved in a crouch toward the rear bulkhead, where he dropped Wiggins into a sitting position with the man's back against the wall.

Khalil retrieved his butcher's saw, then knelt astride Wiggins's legs. He took an ammonia ampoule from his pocket and broke it under Wiggins's nose. The man's head jerked back, and Khalil slapped him across both cheeks.

Wiggins moaned and his eyes opened.

Khalil put his face close to Wiggins and said, "It is me, Mr. Wiggins. It is Asad Khalil who you have been expecting for three years."

Wiggins's eyes opened wider, and he stared at Khalil but said nothing.

Khalil put his mouth to Wiggins's ear and whispered, "You, or perhaps one of your deceased squadron mates, killed my mother, my brothers, and my sisters. So you know why I am here."

Khalil drew back and looked at his victim. Wiggins was staring straight ahead, and tears were running down his cheeks.

Khalil said to him, "Ah, I see you are sorry for what you did. Or perhaps you are just in physical pain. Surely you have never experienced the mental pain I have carried with me since I was a boy. And, of course, you never experienced the physical pain of a house collapsing on you and pressing the life out of your body."

Wiggins's lips moved, but all that came out was a soft moan that trailed off into a whimper.

Khalil could tell that the man was about to pass out again, so he slapped him hard and said loudly, "Listen to me! You escaped me once, but now I have a very unpleasant death planned for you, and you must be awake for it."

Wiggins closed his eyes and his lips trembled.

Khalil reached back and drew the butcher's saw from the carrying case. He held it in front of Wiggins's face and again slapped him.

Wiggins opened his eyes and stared at the saw with incomprehension, and then he understood. His eyes widened, his jaw dropped, and he managed to wail, "No . . . !"

Khalil shoved a handkerchief deep into the man's open mouth and said, "Yes, a butcher's saw. You are an animal, and I am your butcher."

Wiggins tried to defend himself, but both arms and legs were useless. He began shaking his head from side to side, but Khalil grabbed him by his hair, then put the teeth of the saw against the left side of his neck.

Wiggins let out a muffled scream through the handkerchief as Khalil drew the saw across his neck. He continued his screams as Khalil slowly and patiently sawed into his flesh and muscle.

An increasing amount of blood began to pour from the open neck wound, and it ran over Wiggins's white shirt and began puddling on the floor of the cabin. Wiggins's movements and sounds grew weaker, though Khalil knew he was still experiencing the pure pain and terror of having his head cut off.

Khalil kept the saw blade toward the rear of the man's neck to avoid severing the carotid artery or the jugular vein, which would kill Wiggins too quickly. Khalil now felt the teeth of the saw scrape the man's vertebrae. There were unfortunately no more cuts to be made that would cause pain without causing death.

Khalil had done this once before, in Afghanistan, where a Taliban fighter had instructed him on the finer points of beheading. The victim was a Western aid worker, and the instrument used was a large Afghani knife that Khalil admitted he had difficulty with, especially in severing the neck bones. This was much easier, and therefore more enjoyable for him—though not for Mr. Wiggins.

Khalil pulled Wiggins's head back by his hair and looked at him. His face was chalky white, and his eyes, though open, seemed dull and lifeless.

There was no more pleasure to be drawn from this, so Khalil sawed quickly, first severing Wiggins's left carotid and jugular vein, which gushed blood over Khalil's hands and arms. Then he sawed through Wiggins's windpipe, then his right carotid and jugular, until only the man's vertebrae connected his head to his body. Amazingly, Wiggins's heart still pumped blood, but soon it stopped.

Khalil pulled straight up on Wiggins's hair and sawed through his vertebrae, lifting his head from his body. He held the head by its hair and stared at Wiggins's face as the head swung slightly from side to side. He said, "You are in Hell now, Mr. Wiggins, and my family rejoices in Paradise."

Khalil threw the saw aside, then stood and carefully placed Wiggins's head in the man's lap. He then took the crowbar and shoved it down into Wiggins's open neck until it was half into his body.

Khalil left the aircraft and closed the airstairs behind him. He took the time to complete Wiggins's job of putting the two remaining chocks under the other wheel so the aircraft would attract no attention.

If his information had been correct, this aircraft would sit here until Sunday evening when Mr. Chip Wiggins, who was unmarried and lived alone, was to report back for his scheduled flights. Mr. Wiggins would be late—or one could say early since he had never left the aircraft—and by the time Wiggins was discovered, he, Asad Khalil, would have crossed the continent and crossed more names off his list before anyone even knew he had returned to America.

Khalil walked quickly across the ramp, passed through the security gate, and within a few minutes he was in his car, driving out of the airport.

He returned to the Best Western hotel and disposed of his bloody clothing under the bed, where Farid Mansur lay.

Khalil showered and changed into another sports jacket, trousers, and shirt, then spent a few hours reading the Koran. At 6 A.M., he prostrated himself on the floor, faced east toward Mecca, and recited the Fajr, the predawn prayer in remembrance of God.

He then collected his luggage, left the room, and exited the hotel through the rear. He put his suitcase and duffel bag in the trunk and his overnight bag on the passenger seat and made the ten-minute drive back to the airport.

There was more activity at this hour, and Khalil parked in a space near Sterling Air Charters. He gathered his luggage, locked the car, and walked into the Sterling office.

A young man looked up from his desk and inquired, "Can I help you, sir?"

Khalil replied, "I am Mr. Demetrios, and I have reserved a charter flight to New York."

The young man stood and replied, "Yes, sir. Your billing information is here and ready, the pilots are here and ready, and the aircraft is ready. We can take off anytime you're ready."

Khalil replied, "I am ready."

PART III

Upstate New York

CHAPTER SEVEN

Skydiving.

I've done a lot of stupid things in my life, and it would be hard for me to list them in order of stupidity. Except for Number One. Skydiving. What was I thinking? And I couldn't even blame this one on my dick.

But I *could* blame my wonderful wife, Kate. When I married her three years ago, I didn't know she had once been a skydiver. And when she confessed this to me about six months ago, I thought she said "streetwalker," which I could forgive. What I can't forgive is her getting me to agree to take up this so-called sport.

So, here we were—Mr. and Mrs. John Corey—at Sullivan County Airport, which is basically in the middle of nowhere in upstate New York, a long way from my Manhattan turf. If you're into nature and stuff, the Catskill Mountains look nice, and it was a beautiful Sunday in May with clear skies and temperatures in the mid-sixties. Most important for what lay ahead, it was a nearly windless day; a perfect day to jump out of an airplane. Does it get better than this?

Kate, looking good in a silver jumpsuit, said to me, "I'm excited."

"Good. Let's go back to the motel."

"This is my first time jumping from a Douglas DC-7B," she said.

"Me too," I confessed.

"This is a fabulous addition to our jumper's logbook."

"Fabulous."

"This is the last flying DC-7B in the world."

"I'm not surprised." I looked at the huge, old four-engine propeller aircraft taking up most of the blacktop ramp. It had apparently never been painted, except for an orange lightning bolt running along the fuselage, nose to tail. The bare aluminum had taken on a blue-gray hue, sort of like an old coffee pot. To add to the coffee pot image, all the windows of this former luxury airliner had been covered with aluminum—except, of course, the cockpit windshield, which I guess could be thought of as the little glass percolator thing . . . well, anyway, the plane looked like a piece of crap. I asked my wife, "How old is that thing?"

"I think it's older than you." She added, "It's a piece of history. Like you."

Kate is fifteen years younger than me, and when you marry a woman that much younger, the age difference comes up now and then, like now when she continued, "I'm sure you remember these planes."

In fact, I had a vague memory of seeing this kind of aircraft when I went to Idlewild—now JFK—with my parents to see people off. They used to have these observation decks, pre-terrorism, and you'd stand there and wave. Huge thrill. I reminisced aloud and said, "Eisenhower was president."

"Who?"

When I met Kate three and a half years ago, she showed no tendency toward sarcasm, and she had once indicated to me that this was one of several bad habits that she'd picked up from me. Right, go ahead and blame the husband. Also, when I met her, she didn't swear or drink much, but all that has changed for the better under my tutelage. Actually, she'd made me promise to cut down on the drinking and swearing, which I have. Unfortunately, this has left me dim-witted and nearly speechless.

Kate was born Katherine Mayfield in some frozen flyover state in the Midwest, and her father was an FBI agent. Mrs. Corey still uses her maiden name for business, or when she wants to pretend she doesn't know me. Kate's business, as I said, is the same as mine—Anti-Terrorist Task Force—and we are actually partners on the job as we are in life. One of our professional differences is that she's an FBI agent, like her father, and a lawyer, like her mother, and I'm a cop. Or as I said, a former cop, out of the job on three-quarter disability, which is not actually disabling, but good enough for a steady check every month. This disability, for the record, is a result of me taking three badly aimed bullets up on West 102nd Street almost four years ago. Actually, I *feel* fine, except when I drink too much and Scotch spurts out of my holes.

Kate interrupted my thoughts and said, "The ATTF should give us jump pay, like the military does."

"Write a memo."

"This is an important skill."

"For what?"

She ignored my question and turned her attention to the sixty or so skydivers who were milling around aimlessly in silly colored jumpsuits, giving each other dopey high fives or checking one another's pack and harness. No one, and I mean *no one*, touches my rig, not even my wife. I have literally trusted her with my life, and she's trusted me with hers, but you never know when the ladies are having a bad day.

Kate belatedly replied, "My theory is that mastering difficult skills like skydiving or mountain climbing gives you confidence on the job even if the skill is not directly related to your work."

My theory was that the FBI should first master some basic police skills, such as how to use the subway system or how to follow a suspect without getting hit by a taxi. But I didn't verbalize that.

The concept of this joint task force is to create synergy by joining Federal agents—who all seem to be from Iowa, like Lisa Sims, and who think mass transit means driving to church—and NYPD, who know the city intimately and do a lot of the street work. The concept, in practice, actually works in some weird way. There is, however, some tension and a few small misunderstandings among the men and women of these two very different cultures, and that, I suppose, is reflected in my marriage. And maybe in my attitude.

Anyway, while Kate was checking out our fellow skydivers, I looked at the pilot standing under the wing of the DC-7B. He was peering up at one of the engines. I don't like it when they do that. I observed, "The pilot looks older than the plane. And what the hell is he looking at?"

She glanced toward the aircraft, then asked me, "John, are you getting a little . . . ?"

"Please don't question my manhood." In fact, that's how she got me to agree to skydiving lessons. I said to her, "Be right back."

I walked over to the pilot, who had a close-cropped beard the color of his aluminum plane. He looked even older up close. He was wearing a Yankees baseball cap that probably covered a bald head, and he had on jeans and a T-shirt that said "Beam Me Up, Scotty." Funny.

He turned his attention away from the possibly problematic right outboard engine and asked, "Help ya?"

"Yeah. How's your heart?"

"Say what?"

"Do you need a part?"

"Huh? Oh . . . no, just checking something." He introduced himself as Ralph and asked me, "You jumpin' today?"

What was your first clue, Ralph? The black-and-blue jumpsuit? Maybe the parachute rig on my back, or possibly the helmet in my hand? I replied, "You tell me."

He got my drift and smiled. "Hey, don't let the looks of this old bird fool you."

I wasn't sure if he was referring to the aircraft or himself. I pointed out, "There's oil dripping out of the engines." I drew his attention to the puddles of oil on the tarmac.

Ralph agreed, "Yep. Oil." He informed me, "These old prop planes just swim in oil." He assured me, "When it's time to add more, we just pump it up from fifty-five-gallon drums. Problem is when you *don't* see oil."

"Are you making that up?"

"Hey, you people have parachutes. I don't. All you got to worry about is getting up there. I got to land this damn thing."

"Good point."

"This was once an American Airlines luxury liner," Ralph confided.

"Hard to believe."

"I bought it for peanuts and converted it to haul cargo."

"Smart move."

"This is my first time hauling skydivers."

"Well, good luck."

"You weigh less, but cargo don't ask questions."

"And cargo doesn't unload itself at fourteen thousand feet."

He laughed.

An even older guy ambled over, and Ralph and he spoke for a minute about things I couldn't understand, but which didn't sound good. The older gent shuffled off, and Ralph said to me, "That's Cliff. He's my flight engineer."

I thought he was Ralph's grandfather.

Ralph further informed me, "No computers on this aircraft, so it takes three cockpit crew to fly this old bird." He joked, "One to fly and two to flap the wings."

I smiled politely.

He continued, "Cliff works the engine throttles, the mixture controls, and all that stuff. He's a dying breed."

I hoped he didn't die after takeoff.

Before I could ask him if he and Cliff had new batteries in their pacemakers, a girl wearing jeans and a sweatshirt, who looked about twelve years old, came up to us and said to the pilot, "Ralph, Cliff and I did the walk-around. Looks okay."

Ralph replied, "Good. I'm gonna let you do the takeoff."

What?

Ralph remembered his manners and said to me, "This is Cindy. She's my copilot today."

I must have heard him wrong, so I ignored that and walked back to Kate, who was in a conversation with one of the guys in our so-called club, a putz named Craig who desperately wanted to fuck my wife.

His stupid smile faded as he saw me approach, and Kate said to me, "Craig and I were discussing the scheduling for our jumps in the next few weeks."

"Is that what was making Craig smile?"

After a moment of silence, Craig said to me, "Kate

was just telling me that you had some concerns about the plane."

"I do, but I could reduce the takeoff weight by sending you to the hospital."

Craig thought about that, then turned and walked away.

Mrs. Corey said to me, "That was totally uncalled for."

"Why did you tell him I was concerned about the plane?"

"I . . . he asked why you were talking to the pilot, and I . . ." She shrugged, then said, "I'm sorry."

I was really pissed off, and I said, "We'll discuss this after the jump."

She didn't respond to that and said, "We're starting to assemble for boarding."

I saw that our group was drifting toward the big aircraft. They seemed like a happy, excited bunch of idiots, in stark contrast to paratroopers, who look appropriately somber and purposeful as they form up to board. Paratroopers have a mission; skydivers are having fun. I'm not having fun. So I must be on a mission.

Actually, I was carrying my Glock 9mm in a zippered pocket and Kate was carrying her .40 caliber Glock. Someday, someone will explain to me why the cops and the FBI agents carry the same make of gun, but in different calibers. What if I ran out of ammunition during a shoot-out? "Kate, can I borrow some bullets?" "Sorry, John, my bullets are bigger than yours. Would you like some gum?"

Anyway, we didn't need our guns for skydiving, but, as per regs, we couldn't leave our weapons in the motel, or even in the trunk of our car. If you lose a weapon or it's stolen, your career is in serious trouble. So we were packing heat. Hey, there could be bears in the drop zone.

We continued toward the aircraft, and Kate took my hand and said to me, "Let's just make this one jump and pass on the next two."

"We paid for three, we'll make three."

"Let's decide when we get on the ground." She suggested, "I think I'd rather go antiquing."

"I'd rather jump out of an airplane than go antiquing."

She smiled, and squeezed my hand. She knew I was still pissed. Sometimes you milk these things for all they're worth and hold out for a blow job. Other times, like now, you just let it go. So I said, "We'll play it by ear."

A guy from the skydiving club was standing on the tarmac marshaling people into their jump groups. As I understood this, there would be two large groups exiting en masse to attempt a prearranged join-up formation. They were trying for some sort of record. Like Biggest Circle of Flying Assholes.

Kate had enough experience to join either of the groups, but I did not, so Kate and I would be jumping together along with some single jumpers and a few groups of two or three. Although I technically didn't require a jumpmaster any longer for my solo jumps, Kate would be my jumpmaster so we could practice some relative work during the free falls. Someday, I would be qualified to be part of a big hook-up formation that looked like a flying eggbeater.

I actually enjoyed the free fall without the work and concentration of trying to maneuver to hold hands with strangers. The air resistance as I fell at over a hundred miles an hour allowed me to position my body and arms to slow myself, or speed up, even do loops and rolls, and it felt more like flying than falling. In truth, it made me feel more like Superman than I already did.

The guy from the skydiving club was now standing at the rolling stairs that led to the big cargo opening in the rear of the fuselage. He was holding a clipboard, checking off names as the jumpers assembled.

As we walked toward the clipboard guy, I asked Kate, "Are we in first class?"

"We are, until we step out of the plane."

We approached the clipboard guy and I announced, "Corey. Mr. and Mrs."

He consulted his chart and said, "Okay . . . here you are. A third-stage two-jump. You can board now. Go all the way forward. Row Two."

"Is this a lunch flight?"

Clipboard guy looked at me, but did not respond to my question. He said to me, "Have a good and safe jump, Mr. Corey."

How about a safe landing?

Kate led the way up the portable metal stairs, and I followed her into the dark cavernous cabin.

When I'm flying in a commercial airliner, I always

like to see nuns and clergy on board. But parachutes are good, too. Nevertheless, I suddenly had a bad feeling about something. I've been in law enforcement for over twenty years, and it sounds clichéd, but I've developed a sixth sense for trouble and danger. And that's what I felt now.

CHAPTER EIGHT

Kate led the way toward the front of the aircraft.

The windows, as I said, had been covered with aluminum skin, so it was darker in the cabin than I expected. A few dim light fixtures were mounted along the sidewalls, which revealed that the interior had been stripped bare to convert this airliner into a cargo plane. Apparently we would be sitting on the floor, like cargo.

The only other light in the cabin was sunlight coming in from the cargo opening and from the cockpit windshield up ahead. I noticed that there was no door leading to the cockpit; just an open passageway through the interior bulkhead. The required anti-hijacking door was not there—and why should it be? If we got hijacked, we could all jump out of the plane.

On the floor I saw cargo rings, which I guess were used to secure pallets but that now secured nylon straps for us to hang on to.

The cabin was only about ten feet wide, which was considered a wide-body aircraft in nineteen-fifty-something. The first four skydivers had already boarded and were sitting abreast on the floor facing us, packed together across the full width of the airliner's cabin.

There were row numbers taped to the walls and we easily found Row 2, which was logically just aft of Row 1.

Kate asked me, "Port or starboard?"

"I'll have a port." I added, "You take the window seat."

She sat near the wall on the left side, and I sat beside her, with my hand on the cargo strap, and said, "Fasten your seat belt."

"Are you done with the stupid remarks?"

"Seat in the full upright position for takeoff."

The two people who had boarded after us—a guy and a girl—sat in their places on the right side of Row 2, and the rows farther aft in the cabin started filling up.

I looked around the cabin. The cargo opening, as I'd noticed when we entered, was very wide, but now I also noticed that there was no door—just that large opening. I brought this to Kate's attention, and she explained that they had to remove the big cargo door for this jump because it couldn't be operated in flight—it was a clamshell that opened outward—and the smaller hinged entry door next to it was only one person wide. She further explained, "The group jumpers need all the space they can get to exit en masse."

I thought about that and said, "It's going to be cold and noisy in here without a door."

"Very noisy." She added cheerily, "I won't be able to hear you."

"Sit closer." I asked, "Hey, what's the name of that Italian guy?"

"*What* Italian guy?"

"The one whose name we're supposed to yell when we jump."

"John, what—?"

"You know . . . Ah! Geronimo!"

A few heads turned toward us, and Kate slid closer to the wall and stared at where the window used to be.

The jumpers continued to board. My thirty-five-pound parachute rig was making my back ache in this position, and my butt, which is all muscle and no fat, was starting to feel the hard floor. This totally sucks.

It's like skiing—you know? A long trip to the middle of nowhere, lots of expensive equipment, surrounded by fanatical half-wits who think they're having a great time waiting around forever; then a few minutes of adrenaline rush—or pure terror—and then it's over. Sort of like sex.

My first wife, Robin, who was also a lawyer (I like screwing lawyers for a change), was a skier, but it was a starter marriage of short duration, so I never got beyond the beginner slopes before she skied happily out of my life. Now I'm a friggin' skydiver. I mean, I've spent most of my professional life in dangerous situations—is this any way to relax?

"John?"

"Yes, darling?"

"One jump, then we're going home."

"Sweetheart, I want to log *three* jumps from a DC-7B today."

"I am spraining my ankle when I land, and you and a paramedic will help me into the car."

I was feeling a wee bit guilty now, so I said, "No, no. I really enjoy this. I'll behave. Let's make this fun."

"You embarrassed me in front of Craig."

"Who's Craig?" Oh, the guy who wants to fuck you. "I'll apologize to Craig when we all go out for drinks tonight." I'll corner him in the men's room. That's my specialty. "Okay? Hey, I'm looking forward to the après-jump party. Great group of skydivers."

She looked at me closely for signs of insincerity.

I saw Craig coming toward us, walking between the skydivers. He was some sort of officer in the club, and thus he had official responsibilities that included checking to see that everyone was happy, seated properly, and hadn't forgotten their parachute.

I wanted to make amends to Craig—and to Kate—for my uncalled-for remark, so I shouted out to him, "Hey, Craig! Let's get this bird airborne. We're gonna have a helluva jump today, bro!"

Craig gave me a weak smile and continued on into the cockpit.

I looked at Kate, who had her eyes closed. I made a mental note in my logbook: *Have Craig followed. Possible terrorist.*

The guy with the clipboard came into the cabin to check names and groupings. I mean, what happened to personal responsibility? If you don't know where the hell you belong or who you're supposed to be with, maybe you shouldn't be doing this.

Anyway, the clipboard guy got to the front rows and double-checked our names and positioning.

Craig came out of the cockpit and asked clipboard guy, "How's it look, Joe?"

Joe replied, "We have two dropouts and one last-minute sign-on for a total of sixty-three jumpers."

"Okay," said Craig, "we'll probably lose a few for the second jump."

What?

Craig continued, "The pilot is ready when we are."

Joe, I noticed, wasn't wearing a jumpsuit or a parachute, so I deduced that he was staying on the ground with the manifest, just in case something not good happened. I pictured him crossing off sixty-three names as the aircraft plummeted to the ground. Bad luck for that last-minute sign-on. Meanwhile, one of the no-shows shows up out of breath and says, "I got stuck in traffic. Am I too late?" *Fate.*

Joe was off the plane now, and Craig started for his place among the group jumpers, but then turned to me and said, "I assume you will be making all three jumps today, John."

I replied enthusiastically, "Hey, Craig, I'm here to *jump!*" I informed him, "I'm buying you a beer tonight."

Craig glanced at Kate, then turned and found his place on the floor near the cargo opening. He wasn't wearing his helmet, and I noticed he had a big bald spot on the back of his head.

In fact, most people weren't wearing their helmets at this point, though a few people had put them on. One guy had boarded with his helmet on, and instead of goggles, which most skydivers wear, he had a tinted helmet shield that was pulled down. As a cop, things like motorcycle helmets with tinted face shields or ski masks automatically grab my attention. But I wasn't in full cop mode and I made little note of it.

There was an undercurrent of babble in the cabin, punctuated by occasional laughter. I noticed that Craig was chatting up a very pretty lady sitting next to him. The pig probably made up the jump order so he could hold her hand on the way down.

I had been a bachelor most of my adult life, and I really didn't miss it—well . . . sometimes maybe just a little—but I certainly didn't envy Craig, who I'm sure was lonely, and who probably couldn't get laid in a cathouse with a fistful of fifties. Kate has really made my life . . . more . . . very . . . incredibly . . . totally . . .

"John."

"Yes, sweetheart?"

"I love you."

"And I love you." I squeezed her hand.

Kate had never been married, so she had no way of knowing if I was a normal husband. This has been good for our marriage.

I heard one of the engines firing up, then another, then the last two. I pictured Cindy in the cockpit saying to Ralph, "So, like, all those propeller things are spinning round and round."

And Ralph replies, "Very good, sweetie. Now we

have to taxi to the runway. Take your feet off the brakes, sweetheart."

And sure enough, we began moving. The noise of the engines was deafening, and the aircraft seemed to be squeaking and squealing as it turned toward the taxiway.

I was close enough to the cockpit to hear Cindy asking, "Ralph, can I take off from here?"

"No, darling, wait until we get to the runway."

Maybe I was imagining that.

We taxied for a minute or two, then turned and stopped at the end of the runway. Cindy ran up the engines (remembering to keep her feet on the brakes), and the old plane vibrated and strained forward like a sprinter, ready to make the dash down the long stretch of blacktop.

Was that a miss in one of the engines? Did I hear a backfire? Cliff, turn up your hearing aid.

I could hear some radio traffic coming from the cockpit, and Cindy replied, "Hi, Tower. Can I, like, use the whole runway?"

Okay, just kidding.

The aircraft began to roll, gathering momentum, and I could feel it lighten as it approached takeoff speed.

Before I knew it, the aircraft nosed up and we were airborne.

Cindy shouted, "Ralph! I did it! I did it! What do I do now?"

The aircraft nosed up and we held on to the strap. Then Kate put her arm around my shoulder, drew me close, and said in my ear, "I like sharing things with you."

Right. Next time we'll share one of my cigars.

The DC-7B banked to the right, gaining altitude as it began a wide corkscrew turn. The drop zone, which was a big, hopefully bear-free meadow, was not far from the west side of the airport, so most of this thirty-minute flight would be vertical until we reached 14,000 feet.

I noticed that the loadmaster was sitting near the open cargo door with some kind of intercom phone in his hand, which I assumed he used to communicate with the cockpit, so he could let them know when everyone had jumped.

I wondered if Cindy knew this was a skydive. I mean, I could imagine her coming into the cabin and being startled to see that everyone was gone, then running back into the cockpit shouting, "Ralph! Cliff! Everyone fell out of the plane!"

Kate put her lips to my ear and said, "It's nice to see you smiling." Then she gave me a wet willy.

I squeezed her hand and gave her a kiss on the cheek.

Now that I was up here, I was actually looking forward to the free fall and the nice easy parachute float to the ground. It really is spectacular, and statistically less dangerous than doing what I did for a living.

CHAPTER NINE

The cabin was very cold now, and everyone had put on their helmets and gloves.

I turned toward Kate and blew a cloud of breath toward her. She blew a cloud back and smiled.

The aircraft droned on, continuing its slow spiral climb.

"John?"

"Yes, darling?"

She put her mouth to my ear and said, "Review the maneuvering sequence we discussed. Ask me any questions you might have."

"What color is your parachute?"

"When you stabilize, you need to watch me."

"I love watching you."

"You weren't watching me last time."

"Have we done this before?"

"We don't want to collide in free fall."

"Bad."

"We'll do some relative work, as discussed, then I will initiate the separation."

Same as my last wife did. Divorced in six months.

"We'll both deploy our chutes at twenty-five hundred feet. Keep an eye on your altimeter." She reminded me, "And you need to keep at least a hundred feet between us. We don't want our chutes getting tangled."

I patted the emergency hook knife on my harness and said, "I can cut you loose."

She continued, patiently going over a few other small details having to do mostly with safety and not dying.

Kate, I understood, was very brave to jump with a novice. New guys caused accidents. Accidents caused certain death. I assured her, "I got it. I got it."

We both retreated into silence as the aircraft continued climbing.

I glanced at the digital altimeter on my left wrist. Ten thousand feet.

How the hell did I get here? Well, I went to skydiving school, which was my first mistake.

That was last November, after Kate and I had successfully resolved the curious case of Bain Madox—the previously mentioned evil genius—who wanted to start a nuclear war, but who was otherwise a pleasant man.

Our bosses at the ATTF had suggested we take a few weeks' leave time as a token of their appreciation for us saving the planet from nuclear annihilation. Also, this was a very sensitive case, so the bosses wanted us out of town and away from the press. Kate suggested Florida, and I started packing my Speedo.

Then the thing about skydiving came up, and without getting into that interesting discussion, I soon found myself in a Holiday Inn across the street from a sky-diving school in Deland, Florida.

Deland, like everything that has to do with this sport, is in the middle of nowhere, far from the beach and palm trees that I imagined.

Kate took a ten-day refresher course, and I discovered that she actually holds a United States Parachute Association "C" license, which qualifies her to be a jumpmaster. I wish I'd known this before I slept with her.

As for me, I took a two-week basic course that started, thankfully, in the classroom but progressed rapidly to 14,000 feet and something called the accelerated free fall, which is two big guys named Gordon and Al jumping out alongside me, and the three of us falling through the open sky together with them holding on to my grippers. I got sixty seconds of instruction before they pushed off, waved, and left me falling through space.

I've made maybe a dozen weekend jumps since that wonderful two weeks in Florida, and I've earned my USPA "A" license, which allows me to make solo sky-dives and begin some basic relative work with a jump-master, who today would be the lucky lady next to me.

The prop engines changed pitch, and I looked at my altimeter. Fourteen thousand feet.

I commented, "We're at cruising altitude. They'll begin the beverage service soon."

"We're actually leaving the aircraft soon."

In fact, the loadmaster shouted for those in the first group to get up and get ready.

There was a flurry of activity in the cabin as about twenty skydivers nearest the exit door stood up and adjusted their equipment, then began their rehearsed shuffle toward the open cargo door.

The aircraft seemed to slow, then with a loud verbal command from their group leader, the first group began to quickly exit the aircraft and disappear silently into the deathly void of space. Or, one could say, they jumped merrily into the clear blue sky. Whatever.

As the aircraft circled back to the drop zone, the second large batch of skydivers jumped to their feet, and the process was repeated until the entire rear two-thirds of the aircraft was empty, except for the load-master.

It was kind of weird. I mean, a few minutes ago the plane was full, and now I was looking at empty floor space. Where'd everybody go?

Kate informed me, "There is a cameraman on the ground, and one in each group." She said, "I can't wait to see those jumps on tape."

Neither could the personal injury lawyers.

We remained seated as the aircraft again began to circle back over the drop zone.

A few minutes later, the loadmaster gave us a two-minute warning, and the last group, who were all solo and small-group jumpers, got to their feet, including me and my jumpmaster.

The loadmaster looked at us and held up one finger, and I was glad it wasn't his middle finger.

There were about ten people in front of us lined up to make their two- or three-person jumps, and behind us were four people who were making solo jumps. We all put on our goggles or lowered our face shields and did a final equipment check.

By now, the two big groups of jumpers were on the ground, gathering their chutes, doing high fives and hugs, and climbing into the buses that would take them back to the airport for jump number two. I had a rare moment of empathy as I stood poised to follow my fellow club pals into the void, and I sincerely hoped that they'd set whatever hook-up record they were trying for, and that they had all landed safely. Even Craig. You hear that, God?

The loadmaster shouted, "Ready!" Then he shouted, "Go!"

The skydivers in front of me began to exit in their prearranged groups of two and three with a brief interlude between them.

The couple who'd sat abreast of us on the right side of Row 2 were ahead of Kate and me and were next to jump. I moved closer to the cargo opening, and I could feel the whirling wind and see the green-and-brown field three miles below. What if I got vertigo and fell out of the plane?

The couple ahead of us joined hands and took a step in unison, then literally dove together out of the aircraft—like lovers, I thought, jumping to their . . . well, jumping into a swimming pool.

I stepped up to the opening, and I could see a few people in free fall, which is a very strange sight. I also saw a few brightly colored chutes deploy, and suddenly I wanted to jump—to fly through the sky at the speed of a diving eagle and then to float gently down to earth.

I was ready to take the plunge, but I felt a hand on my shoulder, and I turned my head to see Kate smiling at me, and I smiled back.

I noticed now that the solo jumper directly behind Kate was crowding her more than he really should. He needed to let her clear the airplane before he jumped. Maybe he was nervous.

The loadmaster said something, and I realized I was holding up the show.

I turned back to the cargo door and without thinking too much about what I was about to do—and without yelling "Geronimo"—I dove face-first, leaving the solid floor of the aircraft behind me. And there I was, falling through the sky.

But my mind was back in the aircraft, and I had two split-second thoughts: one, Kate had yelled something just as my feet left the airplane; two, the guy behind her was the same guy I'd noticed earlier in the black jumpsuit and the full-tinted face shield. He had sat in front of us, so he should have jumped ahead of us. Why was he behind us?

CHAPTER TEN

Even with the helmet covering my ears, the roar from the wind stream sounded like a freight train going through my head.

I forced my body into a medium arch, then extended my arms and legs, and the airstream began to stabilize my fall. I was dropping now at about 110 miles per hour, which was terminal velocity for the position of my body.

I expected to see Kate appear on my right, as we'd planned, but when I didn't see her, I twisted my head to the right and upward but still didn't see her. This move altered the aerodynamics that were steering me, and I began to rotate away from the direction I'd turned. I quickly went back to my fully stabilized position with my body in a medium arch and my arms and legs extended and symmetrical. I began to stabilize again. *Where the hell was Kate?*

Just as I was about to attempt another look, I saw in my peripheral vision that Kate was catching up to me. This should have happened much sooner, and she should have been much closer to me to do our relative work. I had the feeling that she'd delayed her jump by a second or two. But why?

Kate was about fifty yards off my right shoulder now, and I saw the skydiver in black, who I'd thought was too close to her in the plane, and I realized he was actually hanging on to her. *What the hell . . . ?*

He had his right arm wrapped around her body, and he appeared to be holding on to the gripper on the left side of her jumpsuit with his left hand. I saw, too, that he had his legs wrapped around hers.

They were falling faster than I was because of their combined weight and because of how their bodies were positioned in the airstream. Within a few seconds, they were below me and falling farther away.

I couldn't believe what I was seeing, and my heart started to race. What was this? Maybe, I thought, one of them had a problem of some sort and grabbed on to the other. Maybe the guy panicked, or somehow he'd hooked up with the wrong skydiver for relative work, or—I couldn't understand this or make sense of it.

Kate and the guy were now a few hundred yards below me as they continued their joined-up free fall at an accelerating rate. It hit me that this guy might be trying to commit suicide and for some sick reason he was taking Kate with him.

Then I saw the small pilot chute stream out from Kate's pack, and it blossomed into an open position. The pilot chute lifted the main canopy out of its container, and her parachute began to fill with air.

Thank God.

Kate's white canopy with red markings was fully extended, and her rapid free fall ended in a jerk that reduced her drop speed to about a thousand feet per minute. As I continued my free fall, I could see that the hitchhiker was still attached to her, and they both swayed under her canopy.

I shot past them in a blur, then out of training and habit I glanced at the digital altimeter on my wrist: 8,400 feet. Why did she deploy her chute so soon? I grabbed my ripcord, arched my body, and looked around to be sure I was clear of any other chutes—then I pulled the ripcord.

I did the required count—*one thousand, two thousand*—waiting to see if I needed to go to my reserve chute. I looked over my right shoulder, as trained, and saw my pilot chute streaming upward. I turned back and felt a jerk as the pilot chute filled with air, then another jerk as the pilot chute dragged my main chute out of its container.

I looked up to visually confirm that the rapid deceleration I felt was, indeed, the result of my main chute being fully deployed, and that I had no need for the reserve chute.

I now had full control, and I scanned the space around me to see if Kate and her hook-up guy had caught up.

I spotted Kate and her passenger about two hundred feet above me, and about a hundred feet to my front. She was again descending at a slightly greater rate because of the weight of the guy holding on to her.

The noise of the airstream had been reduced considerably now, so I shouted to her, "Kate!"

She seemed to not hear or see me, but the guy with her looked toward me.

"Kate!"

I needed to get closer before Kate's faster rate of descent caused her and the guy to drop too far below me—but canopy relative work is inherently dangerous, and a wrong move would get the two chutes tangled, which results in everyone falling like a rock. They'd shown us a horrifying film of this very thing in Deland, and everyone in the class got the message.

Just as they came abreast of me, I pulled on my front risers, which caused me to match their rate of descent and allowed me to maneuver my chute closer to theirs. In less than a minute, only about fifty feet separated our parachutes, which was almost too close.

"Kate!"

She looked at me.

I shouted, "What's wrong?"

She shouted something, but I couldn't hear her.

I carefully maneuvered closer, and now I could see that there was a short cord between them, attached to Kate's gripper and to the guy's gripper, and that explained how he'd stayed with her from the time of the jump, through the free fall, and during the rapid deceleration of her chute deployment. But what was going on? Who was this idiot?

"Kate!"

She called out to me again, but all I could hear was "John," and then something that sounded like "Eel."

I shouted at the guy, slowly, distinctly, and loudly. "What—are—you—doing?"

He seemed to hear me and waved.

I shouted, "Who—are—you?"

He reached up and pulled Kate's left riser, which caused her chute and them to slip toward me on a collision course.

Good God . . . I let go of my risers and my rate of descent slowed as theirs continued faster, and Kate's chute passed under my feet with only about ten feet separating us. This guy was crazy. Suicidal. My heart thumped and my mouth went dry.

Using my risers again, I increased my rate of descent, and within a minute we were again within fifty feet of each other.

I let go of my risers, pulled off my right glove, and unzipped the pocket that held my Glock. I had no idea who this guy was or what he was up to, but he'd done a very dangerous thing, and he was strapped to my wife; if I could get a shot off safely, I was going to kill him.

Kate, too, had her Glock in her jumpsuit, though I didn't think she could get to it with that guy all over her.

I was now just about where I was before that turd brain made a kamikaze run at me. I shouted at him, "Get—away—from—her! Now! Unhook! *Unhook!*"

The guy turned toward me, then lifted his face

shield. He was grinning at me. He shouted, "Hello, Mr. Corey!"

I stared at him.

Asad Khalil.

My heart started to race again.

I heard Kate shout, "John! It's Khalil! Khalil! He's got a—"

Khalil punched her in the face and her head snapped back.

I drew my Glock and took aim, but I was swaying under the canopy, and Khalil had twisted himself and Kate so that she was between me and him. I could not fire safely, but I *could* fire, and I squeezed off two rounds, wide to the right.

That got Khalil's attention and he positioned himself closer to Kate.

I pocketed the Glock and worked the risers until I was again abreast of them with about fifty feet separating us.

Asad Khalil.

Libyan terrorist. Known in international anti-terrorist circles as The Lion. Known to me as pure evil.

It had been my misfortune to cross paths with him three years ago, when I was new with the Anti-Terrorist Task Force. I never actually *met* him, though Kate and I did have some interesting cell phone conversations with him while we spent a bad week following the trail of blood and death he was leaving from New York to California.

Khalil pulled on Kate's risers, and again they drifted

toward me. He called out, "I promised you I would return, Mr. Corey!"

I looked at Khalil and we stared at each other. Seeing him hanging there, floating in the clear blue sky, I recalled that Asad Khalil had demonstrated a high degree of showmanship and originality in committing his murders—in fact, he'd pushed it in our faces— and I was not surprised that he'd chosen this method of reappearing. Did I sense his presence today?

He shouted, "Your wife seems unhappy to see me!"

Come on, Kate. Get on this. But I could see she'd been stunned by the blow to her face.

Khalil shouted, "I want you to witness this!"

I now noticed a glint of reflected sunlight coming from Khalil's right hand. A gun.

I pulled my Glock again as they got closer.

I could see Khalil's face peeking over Kate's left shoulder, and that's all I could see of him. I had no shot, but he had an easy shot at me dangling from my parachute.

Our chutes were now less than ten feet apart and on a collision course again. I had to do something; I could have pulled the emergency release on my main chute, and gone into free fall, then deployed my reserve chute, and that would get me away from him and his gun. But that wouldn't do Kate any good, so I let Khalil drift closer, hoping I'd get a shot before he fired.

Our chutes were almost touching and we were staring at each other. I remembered those dark, deep-set eyes from a dozen photos I'd looked at for too long. I kept my gun trained on his face, wondering why he didn't fire at me.

Khalil flashed me another smile and answered my question. "Today she dies! And you live to see it! Tomorrow, *you* die!"

I steadied my aim at his face, but before I could squeeze off a round, he ducked his head behind hers. Then I saw his right hand go up, and I realized that the metallic object in his hand was not a gun. It was a knife. His hook knife or hers.

I saw the flash of the blade as Khalil brought it down in a slashing motion. Kate made a quick movement, and I could see her left hand go toward Khalil's face, then she screamed, and almost immediately I saw blood shooting into the airstream.

Oh, God . . . I had no shot, but I fired over their heads.

Khalil made a sudden movement, and I saw that he'd cut the cord that attached them, and in a second he'd released his hold on her and was in a head-down free fall.

I could have gotten off one shot, but there were people on the ground, and Khalil was not the problem now.

I looked quickly at Kate, who was dangling from her chute, her blood flying up into the airstream.

I shoved my gun into my pocket and pulled on my risers to get closer to her. Khalil's push-off had caused her to rotate so she was facing me now, and I could see the blood gushing from her throat. I shouted, "Kate! Pressure! Pressure!"

She seemed to hear me and her hands went to her throat, but her blood kept flying into the air. *My God . . .*

I glanced at my wrist altimeter: 6,500 feet. Seven more minutes until we reached the ground. She'd be dead by then.

I needed to do something, and there was only one thing that might save her.

I steered my parachute directly toward hers, then, just as the two chutes were about to touch, I swung my body in an arc, and as the chutes collided I reached for her gripper with my left hand and got hold of it. I caught a glimpse of her face, and saw that her nose and mouth were bleeding where he'd hit her, and I saw the blood gushing through her fingers from the right side of her throat where he'd sliced into her jugular vein or her carotid artery. *Bastard!*

"Kate!" She opened her eyes, then closed them again, and her hands dropped from her throat.

The tangled chutes were collapsing, and we were starting to fall rapidly, so I did the only thing I could do; I yanked the emergency release on her main chute and it immediately flew away, pulling me and my entangled chute with it, and putting Kate into a free fall. I yanked my own main chute release and both entangled chutes were gone. We were both now in a feet-first free fall.

I looked down and saw her dropping a few hundred feet below me, with her arms above her head. She was either unconscious or close to it, and she was unable to stem the bleeding or control her free fall. She was accelerating toward absolute top speed of close to 200 miles per hour. I did a forward roll so that my head was pointed straight down, and I tucked my arms and legs in so that I, too, could accelerate to maximum speed. We were both rocketing at terminal velocity toward the ground, which was rushing up at me at a rate I'd never experienced before at this low altitude. The features and details on the earth were doubling in size with each passing second, and there was nothing I could do now except wait.

The barometric devices on our chutes were supposed to pop the reserve chute if the skydiver fell through a thousand feet at a high rate of descent and didn't pull the ripcord because of panic, malfunction, or unconsciousness. Kate, I thought, was unconscious by now, and the damned barometric device should have deployed her reserve chute, and mine too, but so far nothing was happening except a fatal, high-speed fall to the ground.

I could have manually pulled my ripcord and deployed my reserve chute, but I wasn't going to do that until I saw Kate's chute open.

My altimeter read two thousand feet, and I knew that these chutes had to open *now*. I stared at Kate falling a few hundred feet below me, and just when I gave up all hope, I saw her reserve chute stream out of its pack and begin to fill with air. *Yes!*

I grabbed my ripcord, but before I could pull it my barometric device kicked in, and I felt my reserve chute pop. In a few seconds the small chute was fully deployed, and it jerked my body from terminal velocity to a fast but survivable rate of descent.

I kept watching Kate as she fell. Her arms were hanging at her sides now and her head was slumped against her chest. She was definitely unconscious . . . not dead . . . unconscious.

Her chute drifted toward a thick woods, and I steered toward her. She had about thirty seconds before touchdown, and I prayed that she'd land in the open field before she hit the trees. In either case, her touchdown would be uncontrolled and she might break some bones—or worse if she fell into the trees.

I took my eyes off her for a second and scanned the field below. Everyone had realized that something was very wrong, and the people on the ground were running toward Kate's drifting parachute. I saw, too, that the standby ambulance was racing across the field. Where was Khalil?

Kate hit the ground about twenty yards from the tree line, and before her chute collapsed around her, I could see that she'd hit hard, without any movement to make a controlled landing. *Damn it!*

I hit the ground hard, collapsed my legs, shoulder-rolled, then jumped to my feet and released my reserve chute as I sprinted toward Kate. I barreled through the crowd that was gathering around her, shouting, "Let me through! Get back!"

The crowd parted, and within a few seconds I was kneeling beside my wife.

She was on her back and her eyes were closed. Her

face was deathly white, except for the streaks of blood. She was bleeding from her lips and nose where he'd hit her, and her neck wound was still bleeding, which meant her heart was still pumping.

I pressed very hard against her carotid artery below the wound and the flow of blood stopped. I kept my fingers on her artery and felt for a pulse with my other hand. She had a rapid pulse as her heart raced to compensate for the diminished volume of blood and to keep her blood pressure from collapsing. Another minute or two and there would have been no blood to pump.

I lowered my face toward hers. "Kate!"

No response.

I put my hand on her chest and felt her heart racing, and also saw her chest rise and fall in shallow movements. Not good.

The crowd around me was very silent, but some guy behind me asked, "What the hell happened?"

I looked around and saw the ambulance pull up and stop ten feet away. Two guys jumped out with a stretcher and medical equipment and raced toward us. I shouted to the paramedics, "Severed artery!"

I turned back to Kate and said to her, "It's all right. It's okay, sweetheart. Just hang in there, Kate. Hang on."

The two paramedics were joined by a woman who was the ambulance driver, and they sized up the situation very quickly.

One of the paramedics said to me, "Keep the pressure on."

The other paramedic got a breathing tube in Kate's throat, while the first guy took her blood pressure and checked her breathing, then started a saline drip in one arm and another drip in her other arm. The second guy attached a bag to the tube and began squeezing it to force air into her lungs.

They briefly discussed immobilizing her neck with a collar, but decided it was too risky with a severed carotid. The paramedics log-rolled Kate to her side and the ambulance driver slid a backboard under her, then they rolled her back and immobilized her with straps. They quickly transferred her and the backboard to a rolling stretcher and again strapped her down while I kept the pressure on her artery. The driver raised the lower part of the stretcher to elevate Kate's feet above her head.

The paramedic team wasn't sure I should ride with their patient unless I, too, was in need of hospital care. I flashed my creds and said, "Federal law enforcement. Let's get moving."

Within a minute we were all in the ambulance and it was moving as quickly as possible across the rough field. The paramedics, whose names were Pete and Ron, looked very grim, which confirmed my own prognosis.

I stood over Kate, my fingers pressed on her throat as the two paramedics cut away her jumpsuit and quickly examined her for other injuries, but found nothing external, though they wondered aloud about broken bones or internal injuries.

I've seen all or some of this performed many times in my twenty years as a cop, and I'd always maintained a detachment toward these desperate life-saving procedures—even when it was me lying in the street with three bullet wounds. But now . . . well, now my mind was focused on every breath that Kate took.

When the paramedics seemed satisfied that she was stable, they put EKG leads on her chest and turned on the monitor. Pete said to his partner, "Normal sinus rhythm . . . but tachycardia with a rate in the one-forties."

I didn't ask what that meant, but I did ask, "How far is the hospital?"

Pete replied, "We should be there in ten minutes."

Ron asked me, "You okay?"

"I'm fine."

"You hit hard." He suggested, "Why don't you take a break? I'll keep the pressure on."

"This is my wife."

"Okay."

I said to the medics, "In my wife's jumpsuit you will find her FBI credentials case, her gun, and maybe her cell phone. I need those items."

Pete went through the remnants of Kate's jumpsuit and retrieved her creds case, which he gave to me, saying, "There's no gun and no cell phone."

I put the creds case in my pocket. Maybe she hadn't been carrying her cell phone. But she *was* carrying her gun.

We crossed the field and got onto a farm road. The driver hit the lights and siren and we accelerated quickly.

I bent down and put my lips against Kate's forehead. Her skin was cold and clammy.

The driver was on the radio, and I could hear her saying, "Requesting trauma room." She added, "Real critical."

The paramedics monitored Kate's heart, blood pressure, and breathing, felt her pulse, and checked her temperature. I asked them for a sterile wipe, and I cleaned the blood off her face.

I looked at Kate.

She'd made a defensive move just as Khalil was cutting her throat, and he'd missed her jugular vein and other veins and arteries. And that had probably saved her life, because Mr. Asad Khalil was a very accomplished killer, and he rarely, if ever, left an intended victim alive.

Regardless if Kate lived or died, Asad Khalil still had some unfinished business—with me. And that was good, because he'd stick around at least long enough for me to finish my business with him.

Finally, I asked, "Prognosis?"

Neither man answered for a second, then Ron replied, "Her condition is very serious."

Pete asked me, "What the hell happened?"

I replied, "This is a knife wound."

Neither man replied.

I asked them, "Did you see the guy in the black jumpsuit who was hooked up to her?"

Ron replied, "Yeah . . . he steered his chute over on

the other side of the woods." He added, "I couldn't figure that out . . . now I get it." He asked me, "Do you know who that was?"

Indeed, I did. This was our worst nightmare. The Lion has returned.

CHAPTER ELEVEN

As the ambulance raced to the hospital, I used my cell phone to call 911. I identified myself to the 911 dispatcher as a retired NYPD homicide detective and a Federal law officer. I quickly explained that I was reporting the attempted murder of an MOS—member of the service—and I asked to be transferred to the State Police.

A few seconds later, I was speaking to a desk officer at the State Police station in Liberty, New York.

I described the incident to him and added, "I am also the husband of the victim, who is an FBI agent. The assailant is still at large." I gave him the location of the incident and said, "You should get some troopers over there to see if you can locate the assailant."

"Will do."

But I knew that Asad Khalil was not wandering around in his jumpsuit or repacking his parachute. He had a vehicle parked on the far side of the woods and he was long gone.

The desk officer asked me, "And you're now on the way to the Catskill Regional Medical Center?"

"Correct, and I'm requesting a police presence at the hospital, and I would also like a senior homicide investigator to meet me there."

The desk officer replied, "Let me transfer you to the back room."

"Thank you." The back room is where I used to work.

About thirty seconds later, a man came on the line and said, "This is Investigator Harris. My desk man has explained the situation and passed on your request for a police presence at the hospital."

We spoke, cop to cop, for a minute, and Investigator Harris said, "We've dispatched troopers to the scene to look for the perpetrator, and I'll send some troopers to the hospital. I'll see if I can locate a senior homicide investigator to meet you there."

"Thank you."

"How is your wife?"

I glanced at Kate and replied, "Critical."

"Sorry . . ." He asked, "Can you describe the perpetrator?"

"Yeah. He's a Libyan national, age about . . . thirty, name of Asad Khalil, tall, dark, hooked nose, armed and dangerous." I suggested, "Call the FBI duty officer at 26 Federal Plaza in New York, and they'll give you the particulars on this guy and e-mail you a photo." I informed him, "This man is wanted by the Justice Department for multiple murders in the

U.S. He's an international terrorist, also wanted by INTERPOL and half the world."

There was a silence on the phone, then Investigator Harris said, "Okay . . . wow. Okay, I'll get hold of Senior Investigator Miller, who will meet you at the hospital."

"Thank you." I gave him my cell phone number, hung up, took a deep breath, and looked again at Kate. Her skin was chalky, and blood seeped around her breathing tube.

I looked at Ron and Pete and said to them, "You are not to repeat anything you just heard."

I kept my fingers pressed tight against Kate's artery, aware that by keeping her from bleeding to death, I was also reducing blood flow to her brain.

The paramedics had shone a penlight into her eyes a few times, and they seemed optimistic that there was still brain activity. I pushed back her eyelids and looked into Kate's blue eyes. I thought that the life in them was dimming.

We were still in a semi-rural area, and I was concerned that we were far from the hospital. But then I saw a white six-story building up ahead, and the red letters across the building said CATSKILL REGIONAL MEDICAL CENTER.

A trauma team was waiting for us at the emergency entrance, and they took Kate directly into the trauma room. I quickly filled out some paperwork, then a nurse led me into a small surgery waiting room and said to me, "The surgeon will be Dr. Andrew Goldberg. He's the best vascular surgeon on staff. He will see you when he comes out of surgery." She suggested, "You should call whoever you need to call."

There was no one in the waiting room, so maybe that was all the accidents in Sullivan County on this Sunday in May. At least for now.

On that subject, I unzipped the pocket that held my Glock. I didn't know if the State Troopers were here yet, and I would not put it past Asad Khalil to know that this was where Kate would be taken, dead or alive, and that this was where victim number two, John Corey, would be. If a trained killer tells you he will kill you tomorrow, don't take that timeline too literally; tomorrow could mean later today.

A nurse came into the waiting room, and I was sure she had bad news for me. But she handed me a plastic bag and said, "These are your wife's personal effects."

I hesitated, then took the bag. "Thank you." I waited for her to say something about Kate, but she said, "When you get a moment, please stop at the nurses' station and sign for those items."

"Okay . . ." I asked, "How is she?"

"Being prepped for surgery."

I nodded and the nurse left.

I looked at the items in the bag and saw Kate's wallet with some cash inside. Also in her wallet was a photo of me. I took a deep breath and looked at the other items—a comb, a pack of chewing gum, tissues, and a tube of lip gloss. In the bottom of the bag I found her wedding ring.

I put the bag in a zippered pocket of my jumpsuit. I had to assume that Khalil had her gun. But what about her cell phone? Had it fallen out of her pocket? Or had she left it in the motel room or the car? I wouldn't want to think that Asad Khalil had her cell phone, complete with her phone directory.

Regarding cell phones, I went into the corridor and pulled out my own phone. *You should call whoever you need to call.* Meaning next of kin. I started to dial Kate's parents, who lived in Minnesota—but what was I going to say? Her father, as I said, was an FBI agent, now retired, and I could speak to him, man to man, law officer to law officer . . . husband to father. But maybe I'd have more news—better news—later.

The call I needed to make was to my office.

I was supposed to call the FBI Ops Center, but on weekends that would get me an FBI duty officer who could be a clueless rookie. That was who Investigator Harris would be speaking to now. But since 9/11, NYPD detectives could dial a direct, private number and get the watch command, manned by an NYPD detective, which I preferred—protocol notwithstanding.

I dialed the private number, and after a few rings a female voice said, "Detective Lynch."

I knew her and replied, "Hi, Janet. It's Corey."

"Hi, John. What's up?"

I replied, "I'm reporting an attempted murder of a Federal agent by a known terrorist."

"Oh . . . God. Who? I mean, who is the victim?"

"Kate."

"Oh my God! How is she? Where are you?"

"She's . . . critical. We're at the Catskill Regional Medical Center."

"Oh, John, I'm—"

"Are we recording?"

"Yes. Recording."

"All right. The assailant was Asad Khalil."

"Asad . . . ? The Libyan?"

I made a full and hopefully intelligible report of all that had happened, up to and including me standing now in the hospital corridor, looking up and down the hallway to see if a nurse or surgeon was approaching to give me some good or very bad news.

Janet was upset and did not ask too many questions, except about Kate. She told me she would pray for Kate, and I thanked her. I said, "Call Walsh and Paresi and tell them The Lion is back."

"Okay . . ."

Janet was new to the Task Force, and she had little knowledge of Asad Khalil's visit to the U.S. three years ago, and what little she did know had mostly to do with the fact that Khalil had murdered three people from the Task Force—Nick Monti, NYPD, Nancy Tate, a civilian receptionist, and an FBI agent named Meg Collins. The details of Asad Khalil's last visit to the U.S. were classified and on a need-to-know basis, but the names of our people whom he had murdered were passed on to each new member of the Task Force.

Janet had also seen, hanging on the wall in the coffee room of the ATTF at 26 Federal Plaza, the wanted poster of Asad Khalil that over the past three years had been annotated by a number of agents with words

such as "scumbag" and "cop killer." I myself had written, "You're mine, asshole."

Well . . . now I'd get my chance.

I said to Janet, "I've asked the State Police here in
Liberty to call the FBI Ops Center and request e-mail
or fax photos of Asad Khalil, and also the rap sheet on
this bastard, and the wanted poster. Check with the
Ops Center and make sure this was done, and done
right."

"Will do."

"And we want a news blackout. This is classified."

"Right. John, I'm so sorry."

"Thanks."

I hung up and found a men's room, where I washed
Kate's blood off my hands. I watched her blood draining into the sink, and I flashed back four years to
102nd Street when my own blood was draining out of
me and into a storm sewer, and my partner, Dom
Fanelli, now dead, was standing over me saying, "Hang
in there, John. Hang on." *Hang on, Kate. Hang on.*

I splashed water on my face and drank from the
tap.

When I came out of the men's room, a nurse was
waiting for me, and my heart skipped a beat. She said,
"There's a State Trooper here to see you."

I followed her to the nurses' station where a man
with a sports jacket was speaking to one of the nurses
and making notes in a detective's notebook. He saw
me, glanced at my bloodstained jumpsuit, then walked
toward me, extending his hand.

We shook and he introduced himself as, "Senior

Investigator Matt Miller, Bureau of Criminal Investigation." He added, "Troop F, Liberty."

He already knew who I was and who Kate was, so I said, "Thank you for coming."

Investigator Miller had secured a small coffee room for us, and we sat on plastic chairs with a table between us. He wore jeans and a golf shirt under his sports jacket, and I had the impression—reinforced by the smell of charcoal smoke—that he'd hastily left a barbecue. He was an intelligent-looking man, as one would expect of a Senior Investigator with the state Bureau of Criminal Investigation, and I placed his age at about forty, which was young for this job, so he was either very smart or well connected. I hope smart.

He began by saying, "I'm sorry about your wife."

"Thank you."

Investigator Miller politely asked to see my identification and also asked me some preliminary questions.

The State Police are a good organization, highly trained and disciplined, and we actually had a few state troopers from the BCI assigned to the Anti-Terrorist Task Force. I was sure they were up to this task, though I was also sure that the FBI would descend on Sullivan County and take over. But for now, what I needed was for the State Police to flood the area with troopers and look for Asad Khalil before he got away. Or before he showed up here.

On that subject, Investigator Miller said to me, "I just got a call from the troopers who went out to the scene, and they found tire tracks at the edge of the woods. The tracks led to a road." He added, "We didn't

find a jumpsuit or a parachute. But we're still looking."
He filled me in on the manhunt, but concluded correctly, "If those tire tracks were from the perpetrator's
vehicle, then he had about a twenty-minute head start
on us, and we don't even know what kind of vehicle
we're looking for. But we are setting up roadblocks and
looking for a guy who fits the description. Or who
maybe has a jumpsuit or a parachute in his vehicle."

I said, "You're not going to find those with him." In
fact, unless Asad Khalil had gotten very stupid in the
last three years, he had planned his escape with at least
as much care as he planned his attack. Still, it wasn't so
easy getting out of a rural area when the State Police
were tightening the net. I said, "Tell your troopers this
guy is armed and very dangerous, and he wouldn't
hesitate to kill a cop."

He replied, "He's already tried to kill an FBI agent—
your wife. So we know that." He added, "I remember
the Khalil case. About three years ago. This is the guy
who arrived at JFK under armed escort and killed his
escorts and some people on the ground." He recalled,
"That was the same day as the arrival of that airliner
with the toxic fumes that killed everyone on board."

"Right." It was, in reality, the very same flight. Asad
Khalil had personally arranged for the "toxic fumes"
that killed everyone on board, except himself. But that
case had been so tightly wrapped in national security
and government disinformation that very few people
knew what really happened. I was one of the few who
did, but I didn't need to share much of that with Investigator Miller. I had to give him only enough informa-

tion to do his job, and I said to him, "The suspect was at that time thought to be working for Libyan Intelligence." I added, "He's a professional assassin."

Investigator Miller, like most cops, was not overly impressed. The word "assassin" didn't appear in his mental dictionary. The suspect was simply a killer. Works for him, and works for me.

Investigator Miller got down to specifics and informed me, "Investigator Harris tells me that you've spoken to him and that he's also spoken to your office, and he's given me some details about what happened." He assured me, "We've stationed uniformed and plainclothes troopers in the lobby and on this floor. One outside the OR. We've also received from your office two e-mailed photos of the alleged perpetrator, which we are electronically circulating to all state highway patrol vehicles and local police in this county and surrounding counties."

"Good."

"Your office also e-mailed a wanted poster, and I see there is a Justice Department reward for this individual of one million dollars."

"That's correct."

"He is a fugitive from Federal justice and wanted for the murder of Federal law enforcement agents." He said, "I assume that would be his armed escorts on that flight."

"That's right." Plus three more on the ground.

"But there were no specific details of his . . . escape and what he did subsequent to those murders." He looked at me for more information.

I replied, "Well, I hate to use the words 'national security,' but that's the bottom line on that." I further informed him, "With that in mind, I and my office would very much like your troopers here to keep the news media out of this hospital, and I'd like you to inform your headquarters and this hospital that there are to be no medical reports issued—no names, and no details of the attack. No *nothing*."

"Your office has made that clear." Investigator Miller was probably wondering how this had landed in his lap on a quiet Sunday afternoon up in God's country.

He didn't pursue the national security issue, and asked me, "Are you positive that this individual you saw during your skydive is the same individual on the wanted poster? Asad Khalil?"

"I am." He would have taken me at my word, but I added, "I—and my wife—worked the case that involved the murders referred to on the wanted poster."

He thought about that, then said, "So . . . this guy attacked your wife because . . . she worked that case?"

"Apparently."

He asked, "Did you or your wife ever have personal contact with him? Interrogate him? Piss him off?"

Well, Kate and I had a few cell phone conversations with him, and I'd definitely pissed him off. But if I'd had personal contact with him, there would have been no interrogation, and one of us would now be dead. I replied, "I can't give you any details, but I will tell you that this is his second attempt on our lives."

His eyebrows rose and he made a note of that, then asked, "And the first attempt was three years ago?"

"Correct."

"So you and your wife were working together on that case?"

Investigator Miller had to ask the standard questions, but they weren't relevant to this investigation, or to apprehending the assailant, and as I was trying to tell him, this was classified information. But I did respond and said, "Yes, we were working together." To change the subject and to interject a personal touch into our interview, I said, "She actually wasn't my wife then." I explained, "We met on that case."

And now, he was thinking, she may have been murdered on this case, by the same guy.

I said to him, and to myself, "She'll be okay."

He looked at me, wondering, I'm sure, why I thought that. This wasn't what the nurses had told him, and he'd already figured this was probably a homicide. I've been in his position too many times, not knowing if the victim is going to make it—so you don't know what verb tense to use.

Investigator Miller asked me, "Do you think this guy had any accomplices?"

"He's a loner." I added, "Last time he was in the U.S., he had a few unwitting and unwilling accomplices, but he killed them. So you may get a body or two turning up in the area."

He made a note of that, took a sip of coffee, then asked a few more standard questions, which I answered.

I wanted to be cooperative in helping the State Police apprehend Asad Khalil, but they weren't going to do that using standard detective work. If they did catch him, it would be the result of a lucky car stop by State Troopers, or because some local citizen had reported a strange-looking guy in the 7–Eleven asking for a camel burger.

Also, there was a possibility that Khalil was actually in this hospital right now.

I said to him, "We're dealing with a professional, highly trained killer who doesn't make the usual mistakes that we count on when we're looking for the stupid killers. Asad Khalil has no fear the way we understand fear, but neither is he suicidal. He is very goal-oriented, and his goal today was to kill my wife and let me live to see it. He failed in that goal . . . which he may or may not know. So I'm requesting that you maintain around-the-clock police protection in the hospital and outside her room until I can get my wife moved back to the city."

He nodded and said, "Done," then asked me, "Do you want protection as well?"

"I can protect myself."

I'm sure he thought, *Famous last words*, but again, he was polite and professionally courteous, and he said, "All right." He asked me, "You carrying?"

"I am."

"Good." He then asked, "Where is your wife's weapon?"

I replied, "It was not in her jumpsuit." I added, "The perpetrator may have it, or it may have fallen out over the drop zone. It's a .40 caliber Glock 22, FBI issue."

Investigator Miller made a note of that and said, "We'll get a citizens' search team out to the drop zone."

I suggested, "The paramedics can pinpoint the exact area where we landed." I added for his incident report, "The crime took place about eight thousand feet above there."

He nodded to himself and said, "Incredible."

"Indeed." I advised him, "This skydiving club had a video camera on the ground so maybe this incident was captured on film."

He noted that and inquired about the skydiving club.

I replied, "It's a loose organization, and I'm sure that Asad Khalil is not a regular dues-paying member." I suggested, "Get hold of a guy named Craig Hauser. He can fill you in." I wondered if the club made their next two jumps. I said to Investigator Miller, "They may still be at the airport." I also informed him, "The skydiving club are all staying at the High Top Motel in Monticello."

He asked me, "Where are your wife's creds?"

"I have them." I let him know, "Her Nextel phone seems to be missing."

He thought about that and said, "If the perpetrator has her phone, he has her entire phone directory. Unless you need a code to access it."

Incredibly, you didn't need an access code to see the phone directory. You could also access text messages without a code. Only voice mail was secured by a code, so if an agent's cell phone got into the wrong hands—as it possibly had—the unauthorized person, Asad Khalil in this case, had the agent's phone directory and could also access every text message received as well as send a few of his own. Also, the walkie-talkie directory was stored in the phone. I said to Investigator Miller, "There is no code for the phone directory, or the push-to-talk directory, or for text messages."

He raised his eyebrows, but said only, "We'll have the search team look for the cell phone, too."

"Good."

Assuming Khalil did have Kate's cell phone, and based on my last experience with him, I would not be at all surprised if Asad Khalil called me to offer his condolences on Kate's death.

I suggested, "You should also send a trooper to our motel to check out our room and see if my wife's phone is there. Also, see if anyone has inquired about us."

He didn't seem too annoyed that I was telling him how to do his job and replied, "Will do."

"And could you do me a favor? I don't think I'll be returning to the motel, so could you have someone check Mr. and Mrs. Corey out of the motel and retrieve our personal things?"

He nodded, and saved me from telling him the next part of his job by saying, "We'll place a surveillance team there to see if anyone comes looking for you."

"Good thinking." I said to him, "Another favor. My car is parked at the airport—"

"We'll get it for you."

"Thanks." I suggested, "Look in the car for her phone." I gave him my keys and registration and asked him to have the vehicle, a Jeep Cherokee, delivered to the hospital with my and Kate's luggage. There is, indeed, a strong bond between cops all over the world, and we will extend to each other every professional courtesy that is requested—even unreasonable requests—if possible. So I said to Investigator Miller, "If you do apprehend this individual, will you notify me immediately?"

"Of course."

"Will you give me ten minutes alone with him?"

He forced a smile, hesitated, then replied, "If you tell me it's in the interest of national security, I will."

"Thank you." I also suggested to him, "Check to see if my vehicle has a newly installed tracking device, and look through our personal things for anything that doesn't seem to belong there."

He did not make a note of that, and he asked me, "Do you think this individual has that level of . . . sophistication?"

"I do."

He didn't want to ask why I thought that and hear the words "national security" again, so he said, "All right. We'll do that."

Investigator Miller and I discussed a few more details of the incident and our immediate goals, which included protection, road stops, checkpoints, and circulating Khalil's photo. In truth, Asad Khalil was most probably long gone from Sullivan County and the surrounding counties—unless he was in the corridor now, wearing scrubs.

We briefly discussed the usual procedures of sending troopers or investigators with photos of the suspect to motels, car rental agencies, restaurants, rest stops, train and bus stations, toll booths, and so forth to see if anyone could ID this guy.

On the subject of fugitive travel, Khalil had also used private charter aircraft the last time he was here, so he may very well have flown into and out of Sullivan County Airport. I passed on this thought to Investigator Miller, and he said he'd send an investigator to the airport to see who had arrived and departed by chartered aircraft. The thing that had impressed me most about Khalil, aside from his intelligence and his resourcefulness, was the speed of his attacks and escape. Maybe more impressive was his sixth sense for danger.

I could not give Investigator Miller any details of Asad Khalil's previous murders, which were partly classified, but I did fill him in on the suspect's M.O., including Khalil's ability to assume many identities to get close to his victims. I said, "This morning, for instance, he was a skydiver. Now he may be a hospital orderly." I continued, "His compatriots call him The Lion because of his fearlessness. But it goes beyond that—he has the instincts of a cat. A big, nasty cat."

Senior Investigator Miller did not make a note of that either, and I didn't think he'd mention this at a briefing.

I could have added that Khalil liked the taste of human blood. Literally. And this made me wonder if he'd . . . I put that out of my mind and said to Investigator Miller, "Consider the mind of someone who would go through all that trouble to cut someone's throat."

Investigator Miller had apparently already considered that. "Yeah. It's like . . . these ritual killers."

"Correct. The killing is secondary. The ritual is primary."

He nodded and observed, "Which is why he didn't go for you this time." He had an interesting thought. "He'll come for you next—so you really don't have to look for him." He added, unnecessarily, "He'll find you."

I nodded.

"But you won't know where or when."

"Anytime and any place is okay with me."

He had no reply to that.

I felt that I'd given Investigator Miller my full cooperation and had passed on some good information and suggestions. I needed to speak to other people, and he needed to get a lot of things rolling, so I stood and said, "I'll be here in the hospital until further notice." I gave him my card with my cell phone number, and he gave me his.

He said to me, "I promise you we'll do everything we can to get this guy. Don't worry about anything except your wife." And not wanting any more victims on his turf, he added, "Watch yourself."

We shook hands and I left.

Well, I always knew this day would come, but I didn't think it would come at 14,000 feet above a cow pasture in upstate New York.

Khalil always picked *his* time, *his* place, and *his*

method of attack. But this time, I knew his mind a little better. Also, his element of surprise was gone, but for him that made the game just a bit more interesting.

I recalled the last words that Asad Khalil had said to me on Kate's cell phone three years ago. *I will kill you and kill that whore you are with if it takes me all of my life.*

If he hadn't hung up, I would have made a similar promise to him, but he knew that. Now, three years later, we both knew that one of us would be dead before too long.

CHAPTER TWELVE

I went to the nurses' station to sign for Kate's personal effects and to see if they had any information about her surgery, and also to check on the security arrangements.

The hospital staff knew by now that Kate was not an ordinary accident victim, and they knew who I was. The supervising nurse, Mrs. Carroll, assured me that there were uniformed troopers outside the operating room and at the elevators. Everyone on duty, including hospital security staff, had been briefed to be on the lookout for a man whose photograph they'd been given by the State Troopers.

As for Mrs. Corey's condition, the nurses had no new information, but Mrs. Carroll strongly suggested that I stay in the surgery waiting room because that was where Dr. Goldberg would look for me. I also had the impression that no one wanted me wandering around in my bloody skydiving outfit.

I promised to return to the waiting room, but I needed to be a cop while I waited, so I went instead to the elevators where two uniformed State Troopers stood, one at each elevator.

I showed them my creds and identified myself as the husband of the victim, which explained my blood-stained jumpsuit.

Both troopers had been briefed, and they appeared intelligent and alert. If they were a little incredulous regarding the possibility of the perpetrator showing up at the hospital to check on his victim, they hid it well. I asked to see the photo they had of the suspect, and the older of the two, Trooper Vandervort, gave me the photo in his hand.

I looked at the color photograph that had been taken in the American Embassy in Paris three years ago when Asad Khalil had shown up one day and de-clared himself a fugitive from American justice. He was surrendering, he said, and wished to cooperate with American intelligence agencies. Let's make a deal. He'd had a preliminary interrogation by the CIA in Paris, but he insisted on being flown to New York—not Washington—and then he clammed up until his demands were met and he was put on a 747 to JFK. Someone should have smelled a rat, but Asad Khalil was such a high-value defector that the CIA, FBI, State Department Intelligence, and everyone else let their giggles get in the way of their training and com-mon sense.

I and Kate Mayfield had been part of the team sent to JFK to meet Asad Khalil and his two on-board es-corts, an FBI agent and a CIA officer. Also on the meet-and-greet team that day were Nick Monti and

Meg Collins, both murdered by Khalil, along with a civilian government employee, Nancy Tate, who was a nice lady.

The survivors of the meet-and-greet team were me, Kate, FBI agent George Foster, and Mr. Ted Nash of the CIA, who just missed dying that day and barely missed dying on 9/11, but did not miss his date with death at the hands of Kate Mayfield. Life is funny. But that's another story.

I looked closely at Khalil's photo. He was a swarthy man in his early thirties with a hooked Roman nose, slicked-back hair, and deep, dark eyes. The Libyans, I'd learned, were a diverse mixture of people who liked to play with swords—the native North African Berbers, the Carthaginians, the conquering Romans, the barbarian Vandals, and finally the Arabic armies of Islam.

This, I suppose, was all in Khalil's blood and in his features, and he'd been able to pass himself off as Egyptian, Italian, Greek, and even Israeli. His core identity, however, was killer.

He actually spoke some Italian as well as French and German as a result of living and operating in those countries. He also spoke fairly good English, and in my cell phone conversations with him, I was happy to discover that he understood my informal English, such as when I called him a camel fucker and also suggested that his mother was screwing Muammar Khadafi, the Libyan president. Yes, Investigator Miller, I definitely pissed him off. Apparently, he was still pissed. Me too.

I handed the photograph back to the trooper and said, "This man has killed people all over Europe and America, including law enforcement people. He is *very* dangerous and very smart, and he has been known to stay on the scene to finish a job." I added, "His facial features are distinctive and yet he has successfully changed his appearance in the past." I advised both troopers, "What doesn't change is his eyes. If you see those eyes, that may be the last thing you'll ever see. Be very alert."

They both looked at me as though I was a little off my trolley, but they nodded politely.

As I was walking to the surgery waiting room, my cell phone rang, and I saw it was the home number of the boss, Tom Walsh, FBI Special Agent in Charge of the New York Anti-Terrorist Task Force.

I answered, and Walsh said, "John, I'm so sorry. How is Kate doing?"

"Still in surgery." I kept my eye on the doors that lead to the operating rooms.

"My God . . . I can't believe this." He got down to business and said, "I heard your report to Janet." He let me know, "We will devote all the necessary resources and those of our colleagues in local and Federal law enforcement to apprehend this individual."

I thanked him, of course, though I thought that should go without saying.

Tom Walsh is an okay guy, though we've had our run-ins. He's also a political animal, and he tests the winds from Washington about four times a day. Plus, as I said, he's into withholding info and overthinking every operation. His worst fault, however, is underestimating the cops who work for him. He demonstrated that now by asking me, "John, are you sure that this person you saw was Asad Khalil?"

"I'm sure."

"You made a positive ID?"

I thought I just answered that question. I said, "We spoke, Tom. Hanging from our parachutes." I added, "Kate was quite close to him—about six inches, nose to nose—and she IDed him by name. Khalil." I asked him, "Is that positive enough?"

Tom Walsh would not tolerate sarcasm from his FBI agents, but he'd learned that the NYPD on his Task Force could be a bit cranky—especially the contract agents, like me, who could tell him to take his job and shove it.

Having said that, I now needed this job to find Asad Khalil. So maybe I should be nice to Tom.

Walsh said to me, "In your report, you suggested that Asad Khalil has returned to CONUS with the intent of exacting revenge on the people in our Task Force who worked on the original case three years ago."

"That's right."

"And that's why he attacked Kate."

"I think that's a very logical assumption."

"Right . . . but . . . that seems like a very elaborate plan. You know?"

"Psychopaths engage in elaborate rituals, Tom."

"I know . . . but . . ."

Tom Walsh knew he needed to be more patient with me than he usually was. My wife was in critical condition, and I was distraught. He actually didn't care about my emotional state—except as it affected my predictably unpredictable behavior—but he did care about Kate, who was one of his own. He liked her personally and professionally, plus losing an agent was not good for a supervisor's career. Walsh, though, had some cover there because Kate was off-duty when it happened.

In fact, he said to me, "I didn't know you and Kate skydived."

"We were going to surprise you with that."

He changed the subject and said, "You reported that Kate's duty weapon is missing, and so is her cell phone."

"Correct."

He made an intelligent observation: "The Glock in Khalil's hands is a problem, but most likely he already has his own weapon. The real problem is the cell phone."

"Agreed. But it could be an opportunity."

"Correct. The Communication Analysis Unit is running a trace on its signal."

"Good. But I'm sure Khalil turned it off. He's not stupid. The opportunity comes if he turns it on to use Kate's phone directory."

"Right. But assuming he's savvy, he knows he can't keep the phone on for more than a minute or two before CAU pinpoints the signal." Walsh added, "I'm sure he has his own cell phone for long conversations, and since we don't know his number, it can take us awhile to trace his signal if and when he calls one of our phones."

Tom Walsh doesn't exactly talk down to people, but there's a thin line between him stating the obvious and him thinking he's giving you new information. I resisted telling him I really understood the technology and said, "Maybe we'll catch a break."

"Maybe." He reminded me, "Remember that Saudi guy who forgot to turn off his cell phone?"

"I do." I stated the obvious: "The Saudi guy was sloppy and stupid. Asad Khalil is not."

"Most of them are stupid."

There was some truth to Walsh's statement. Most of them were stupid. But even stupid people get lucky, and if the truth be told, sometimes we were more stupid than they were. That's how 9/11 happened—their stupid luck, our stupid heads up our asses. We've got a lot of that straightened out now, but the other side was getting a little smarter. In this case, Asad Khalil started out smart three years ago, and as I said, I didn't think he'd gotten stupider since the last time he was here.

Continuing with the subject of stupid, I said to Tom Walsh, "I assume you sent out a mass text message to all agents regarding this incident."

He replied, "Of course."

I reminded him, "If Kate's cell phone is actually in Khalil's hands, Khalil is now able to read all our text messages."

There was a short silence on the phone, then Walsh said, "Damn it."

I took out my cell phone and saw that I, too, had Tom's text message, though I hadn't heard the chime.

I retrieved the message and read: *NY ATTF—FBI Agent Kate Mayfield criminally assaulted in Sullivan County, NY. Possible suspect, Asad Khalil, a known terrorist, Libyan national. Her medical condition classified. See your e-mail for full details, updates, and operational instructions, or call Ops Center. Amber alert. BOLO and APB sent. Walsh, SAC, NY ATTF.*

So that is what Asad Khalil had most probably read, right from the boss. Walsh was correctly withholding Kate's medical condition, leaving Asad Khalil wondering if he'd had a good day or a bad day. In any case, Khalil now knew that everyone was looking for him—but he knew that anyway.

Walsh said, "We'll cut off the service to that phone immediately."

"Good idea. But before you do that, send out a final text saying, 'Two Libyan informants in NY Metro have come forward with info on suspect Khalil in CONUS. Check e-mail for details and operational instructions regarding apprehending suspect.'" I added, "Or something like that."

Walsh was silent for a few seconds, then said, "Okay. I'll do that."

And take credit for it. I said, in case he didn't fully get it, "That should spook him, and maybe keep him away from his resources here and mess up his game plan."

"Right. Good."

Tom Walsh and I discussed cell phones for a minute, since that was about all we had at the moment.

While I was half-listening to Walsh, I had a thought

that I should have had an hour ago and said to him, "You should also alert George Foster."

"Right . . . we've contacted everyone about the attempt on Kate's life. You saw the text."

"I did. But what I'm saying, Tom, is that Khalil is here for revenge, and George was on the original team assigned to meet Khalil at the airport three years ago, and George worked the case." I added, "Assume Khalil knows George Foster's name."

"Okay."

Tom Walsh wasn't around when Khalil was here with a long list of must-kill people, and Walsh wasn't fully appreciating the nature of the beast. I suggested, "Call George yourself, or have him call me."

"All right."

I wanted to impress on Walsh the serious nature of this problem—and also ruin his day—so I said to him, "You should not think that Asad Khalil hasn't considered killing you as well."

There was silence on the line, then Walsh said, "We have no idea what his intentions are, aside from his attack on Kate." He added, "And by the way, I'm wondering, why didn't Khalil just pull a gun and blast both of you on the ground? You know? This skydiving knife attack really doesn't make much sense."

"Not to you. But it does to him." I suggested, "When you get to the office, pull up The Lion file and see what Khalil did last time he was here, and how he did it."

"All right." He informed me, "We're managing the news on this, John, so be careful what you say, even to the State Police."

"I think I said that in my recorded report."

"Right. Also, there are some agents from Washington on their way there, and I'll assign a detective and an FBI agent from the Task Force."

I informed Walsh, "The guy who is handling the case here is Senior Investigator Matt Miller of the Bureau of Criminal Investigation." I gave Walsh Miller's cell phone number and said, "He seems competent, and he's got the troopers out looking for Khalil."

"Good. We will assist in any way we can."

"He's looking forward to that."

Tom Walsh advised me, "The CIA may also have some interest in this case."

The best reply to that was no reply, and I said, "There's a guy you need to locate. His name is Elwood Wiggins, a.k.a. Chip Wiggins. He was one of the pilots on the Libyan air raid back in eighty-six, and he was on Khalil's original hit list, but we got to him before Khalil did. Wiggins is in our file. Last known address, Ventura, California. When you locate him, have the local FBI office pay him a visit and tell him the Libyan is back." I added, "Also, he needs protection." Actually, I was certain that by this time what Chip Wiggins needed was an undertaker. I said to Walsh, "But we may be too late for that."

Walsh stayed silent for a moment, then said, "All right. I'll let you get back to Kate—"

"She's still in surgery."

"And if you feel you need to take leave time to be with Kate—"

"I will, after we find Khalil." On that subject, I said

to him, "I assume I am the case agent on this investigation."

There was a silence on the phone, then Walsh said, "Well—"

"Tom. Don't mess with me."

"Excuse me, Detective. I believe I am still in charge of this Task Force."

"And I believe I should be the CA."

He replied, "The thing is, John, if Kate . . . takes a turn for the worse, or whatever, then you will want some time off, and I need to assign this case to someone who can stay with it."

"I will stay with it. I am very motivated."

"Yes, but you don't know how you'll feel if Kate— Look, to be quite honest, you may be too emotionally involved to . . . use good judgment in dealing with the Muslim community."

I thought he was going to mention Big Bird's assault on me, but he didn't, so I assured him, "I have very good relations with the Muslim community in New York." That was actually true, though I had perhaps gotten a little rough with a few of them, but that was immediately post-9/11. I've been a lot nicer in the last year or so. Well . . . unless you count Big Bird. But he wasn't a U.S. citizen.

Tom Walsh said to me, "John, I will promise you this—you will be assigned to the case, but I can't promise you that you will be the lead case agent. I'll think about that. Meanwhile, George Foster will lead the FBI end, and you work well with him." He added, "End of subject."

No use arguing and pissing him off, so I said, "All right."

"Good. Meanwhile, I'll speak to Captain Paresi and have him call you." He let me know, "I've asked the hospital to keep me updated. My prayers are with Kate."

"Thank you."

"One more thing. If the State Police apprehend him, and if we don't have any agents there yet, please don't speak to the suspect or do anything that might compromise our case against him."

"Why would I do that, Tom?"

"And keep in mind, John, that Khalil may have a wealth of information that we can coerce out of him."

"I won't kill him."

He didn't respond to that directly and said, "I know you're angry, but don't get yourself in a bad situation." He reminded me, "We don't do revenge—we do justice."

Is there a difference? I replied, "Right."

We hung up, and I walked back to the waiting room. I went to the window and looked out at the countryside and the mountains. The sun was still high above the distant peaks in a blue, cloudless sky. The morning of September 11, 2001, had been a perfect day, like this.

Kate and I had arrived separately at the North Tower, and we each thought the other was inside the building, so when it collapsed, I thought she was dead, and she thought I was dead. That day changed our lives, but it didn't change our careers.

I kept staring out the sunlit window. It was a beautiful world, and ninety-five percent of the people in it were beautiful. I, unfortunately, have spent most of my life with the other five percent, trying to whittle them down to about four percent.

I had mostly gotten over the serve-and-protect thing years ago, and what motivated me for most of my police career was my own ego—I was smarter than any killer who had the audacity to murder someone on John Corey's beat. Then came the Anti-Terrorist Task Force, and I got a little patriotic buzz going, especially after 9/11.

And now it all came down to personal revenge and me asking God to help me kill Asad Khalil. And I was sure that Khalil was right now asking God for the same favor.

Only one of us was going to have his prayers answered.

CHAPTER THIRTEEN

I stood in the empty waiting room, watching the clock on the wall. It had been over an hour since Kate was wheeled into surgery, and I was beginning to think that this might be a good sign. How long does it take to bleed to death? Not very long. How long does it take to repair a severed artery? Maybe two hours.

My phone rang, and I saw that it was the cell phone of Captain Vince Paresi.

I answered, "Corey."

"John, how is she?"

"Still in surgery."

"Mother of God . . . I can't believe this. How are *you* doing?"

"Okay."

He said, "I've been working the phones since I heard from Janet." He assured me, "We're gonna get this scumbag, John."

I allowed myself a small smile at the familiar NYPD profanity. Paresi and I had some issues, but we came from the same mean streets, and we knew a scumbag when we saw one.

Paresi got to the business at hand and said, "I listened to your report, and I spoke to Walsh a few times." He assured me, "I think Walsh and I are on the same page with this."

"That's good." Captain Paresi was in command of the NYPD detectives assigned to the Task Force, and he was my immediate supervisor, while Tom Walsh was Kate's boss and also the FBI Special Agent in Charge of the whole show. That said, I called the Special Agent in Charge "Tom," and I called Paresi "Captain."

Paresi continued, "Tom told me about Kate's cell phone and that some of our texts might have been read by Khalil."

"Right." I asked, "What did you send out?"

"Well . . . I text messaged every detective on the Task Force to report for duty and to immediately begin surveillance on the usual locations where Islamic radicals are known to meet and congregate, including mosques, hookah bars, social clubs, and so forth, with special emphasis on the Libyan community."

"Okay. And that only went to the detectives?"

"Right. So Khalil didn't see that on Kate's phone."

"Good. No use sharing everything with the suspect."

"Right." He continued, "We're waiting for the go-ahead to pull in the usual suspects for questioning, and we'll be contacting our sources inside the Muslim community."

Captain Paresi went through the standard response

drill. I knew all this, of course, but Paresi wanted me to hear it from his mouth.

Terrorism aside, an FBI agent had been attacked, and she was married to a retired cop. That made a subtle difference in the police response. Sometimes not so subtle—as when some uncooperative people got lumped up.

Paresi asked me for some suggestions based on my past encounter with Asad Khalil, and he also asked me what the ATTF knew about Khalil and who he should speak to.

Well, he'd already spoken to Tom Walsh, who apparently had not been helpful or who didn't know too much himself. I had to think about what I could tell Paresi, and what was still classified or on a need-to-know basis.

The file on Khalil had never been closed, of course, and after he had disappeared three years ago, the then Special Agent in Charge of the Task Force, Jack Koenig, had formed a special team consisting of Kate, me, George Foster, and our only Arab-American on the Task Force, Gabriel Haytham, an NYPD detective. The purpose of this team was to follow every lead and tip that had to do with Asad Khalil. Koenig had given us the not very clever code name of Lion Hunters, and we were to report directly to him.

Well, Jack Koenig was dead, as was Captain Paresi's predecessor, David Stein, both killed in the collapse of the North Tower, and over the years the leads and tips from domestic sources and various foreign intelligence agencies and from INTERPOL had gone from a trickle to a dry hole. One theory was that Asad Khalil had met his end in some unknown and unpublicized way—perhaps as a jihadist fighting in Iraq or Afghanistan or elsewhere. We'd also sent word to Guantánamo to see if he'd washed up there, but he hadn't. Another theory suggested that Libyan Intelligence had terminated Khalil for some reason, possibly because he was more of a liability than an asset. My own theory was that Khalil was teaching a course in cultural diversity at Columbia University.

In any case, neither I nor Kate ever believed that Khalil's silence meant he was dead or retired. Unfortunately, we were right.

I said to Paresi, "Regarding what we know . . . the ATTF file on this guy is pretty thin, but you can access it when you get to your computer."

"That's what Walsh said."

"There is another computer file that contains a complete report on what happened three years ago. That file, however, is highly classified and on a need-to-know basis, and only Washington can give you access, and they probably won't."

"Right. Why should they share information with the people who are looking for this guy?"

In truth, there is more information sharing since 9/11, but old habits die hard, and when the CIA is involved, you're lucky if they tell you who you're supposed to be looking for, and anything you give to them gets stamped Top Secret and you can't get it back.

I informed Paresi, "Three years ago, Koenig and Stein assigned me, Kate, George Foster, and Gabe

Haytham to stay with this case. No one ever cancelled that assignment, and we have a paper folder on
Khalil, and Gabe can give it to you." I explained,
"The last time Asad Khalil was here, he was working
for Libyan Intelligence, and his contacts here were all
Libyans. Our folder contains the names, addresses,
photos, and particulars of Libyans living in the New
York metro area who we've spoken to over the years.
That's a good starting point for surveillance." I
added, "As for invitations to come in for a talk, I
don't think we want to tip off the Libyan community
that we're looking for Asad Khalil." I suggested,
"Let's hold off on that. We'll just watch them for
now and also see if anyone comes to us."

"I'll run that by Walsh, and I'll ask Gabe for the
folder." He said, "I assume Walsh has a copy of this
folder."

I didn't reply, which means no.

Captain Paresi asked me a few more questions
about what happened three years ago, and while I
was answering, another thought popped into my
head, which I should have had much earlier, but . . .
well . . . I asked Paresi, "Has anyone called or heard
from Gabe Haytham?"

"I don't know. Why do you ask?"

I replied, "The question is, Does Asad Khalil
know of the existence of Gabriel Haytham, Arab-
American, on the Anti-Terrorist Task Force? If so,
Gabe may be targeted by Khalil, who would consider
him to be a traitor."

"Yeah . . . that's a thought. Okay, I'll give Gabe a call."

I took the opportunity to say, "I'd like you to speak to Walsh about making me the case agent."

He seemed prepared for that and said, "I have to agree with Walsh that you may not be the best man for that job." He reminded me, "You're assigned to the case, and between us, you may be better off not being the case agent." He explained, "You'll have less bullshit to deal with and more freedom to . . . do your own thing. Understand?"

There was a logic to that, and a subtext. I said, "Okay. I understand."

"Good." Paresi changed the subject. "Do you think this asshole has any other mission here? I mean, is this all a personal revenge thing with him? Or is he here to blow up something? Spread anthrax? You know?"

That was a good question, and I replied, "I'm not sure. But my instinct tells me he's here for his own purpose, which is to clip the people who pissed him off three years ago." I added, "Plus maybe a few people we don't know about yet."

Captain Paresi had come from the NYPD Intelligence Unit, so he had some training and background in this world, and he said, "But even if he's not working for Libyan Intelligence this time, somebody has to be backing this guy—like Al Qaeda—and maybe his deal with his backers is that he gets money and resources to come here to settle some personal scores, and in exchange he's got to blow up the Brooklyn Bridge or something."

"That's a thought. What did Walsh think?"

"We didn't discuss theories. Basically, he just wants me to call out the troops and put these people under the eye."

"Right." I informed Paresi, "Khalil is a loner, but it's possible something will turn up. Like a dead body or two." I added, "He kills people who help him kill people."

"Yeah? That's not nice." He asked me, "What's his beef? I don't know how this started."

I replied, "It started on April 15, 1986, when Reagan sent a bunch of fighter-bombers to blow the shit out of Libya. Asad Khalil lost his whole family in that bombing."

"No shit?" He observed, "I guess he's still pissed off."

"Apparently." I advised him, "That's not public information." I explained, "It sort of gives Khalil justification for what he did three years ago—and we don't want to confuse the news media with questions of moral equivalencies."

"Right, whatever." He asked, "What exactly did he do three years ago? I mean, aside from killing his two escorts and three of our people on the ground?"

I asked Paresi, "Did Walsh mention Chip Wiggins?"

"No. Who's that?"

Apparently Walsh didn't want to share this information with his junior partner. And to be fair to Walsh, Asad Khalil's first visit to America was, as I said, mostly classified information, and the need-to-know about that visit was yet to be determined. Nevertheless, I said to Captain Paresi, "Wiggins was one of the F-111 pilots who bombed Tripoli. Khalil came here three years ago with a list of those pilots and he began murdering them."

"Jeez . . ."

"I can't say any more about that, Captain, but I *can* tell you that Kate and I and others stopped Khalil from killing Wiggins."

Captain Paresi thought about that, then said, "Okay, I get it." He asked, "Do we know where Wiggins is?"

"His last known address is Ventura, California."

"I'll bet Khalil knows where he is." Paresi concluded, "Wiggins is already dead."

"Probably."

"For sure. Khalil would take care of unfinished business first. Then . . . Kate." He asked, "Why not Kate *and* you?"

"He wanted me to see her die."

"Sicko."

"Very," I agreed.

"Well . . . maybe we can catch a break here. I mean, think about this—this guy Wiggins, if he's been clipped, was a soft target. He never saw it coming. Same with Kate. Now everybody is a hard target. Including you. Right? The next move that Khalil makes will be his last."

That sounded very optimistic, but I replied, "Hope so."

Paresi said, "Okay. I'm headed right now for the office. I'll call Gabe and have him meet me there and we'll look at your folder."

"Tell him to watch himself. Also, maybe his family wants to take a vacation. He's got a wife, and I think one daughter."

"All right . . ."

I said to him, "I'll get to the office as soon as I can."

"John, don't worry about it. Take care of Kate. We'll stay in touch. And call me if . . . Kate takes a turn for the worse."

That would be a very short turn. I said to him, "There is a chance she won't make it."

There was a short silence, then Paresi said, "She'll make it. She's in my prayers." He added, "She's tough."

We hung up, and I sat on one of the chairs in the waiting room.

Kate was on my mind, but I tried to think about Asad Khalil and get into *his* mind.

Asad Khalil was a showman—a show-off—and like a lot of psychopaths, he enjoyed taunting the authorities. And the authorities were happy to be taunted with phone calls and letters from the guy they were looking for. We call it clues.

Also, Khalil was on a mission of revenge, and revenge and hate distort your judgment and get you caught or killed. That almost happened to him the last time he was here. And I had no doubt that this time Asad Khalil *would* be captured or killed. But I didn't know how many people he'd murder before we got him, or if Kate or I would be alive to see this case closed.

I heard heavy footsteps in the tiled hallway . . . a man, walking by himself.

I put my hand in my gun pocket and watched the door.

CHAPTER FOURTEEN

The door opened, revealing a middle-aged man in green scrubs with a surgical mask around his neck.

We made immediate eye contact, and the next half second lasted an eternity.

"Mr. Corey?"

"Yes."

We walked toward each other, and he put out his hand and introduced himself as Dr. Andrew Goldberg. He put his other hand on my shoulder and said, "She's resting comfortably in ICU."

I closed my eyes and nodded.

He continued, "Her vital signs are stable. Blood pressure and breathing are good."

Again, I nodded.

He steered me toward the chairs, and I had the random thought that he'd been on his feet for over two hours and needed to sit. My second thought was that he wanted me seated for the rest of his report, which might not be so good.

We sat side by side, and he reported in a soft voice,

"The surgery was successful in closing the laceration to her right carotid artery."

Once again, I nodded.

He said, "I noticed a contusion to her face, and her lips were swollen, but the anesthesiologist said there were no loose or missing teeth." He speculated, "That injury may have been a result of her hitting the ground."

Actually, it was a result of Asad Khalil punching her in the face, but I didn't mention this.

He continued, "In any case, it's not significant." He went on, "There were other contusions as a result of her fall, but I don't believe there were any internal injuries, and no internal bleeding, though there may be bone fractures." He assured me, "We'll get her to radiology as soon as possible."

"When will that be?"

"I'm not sure." He continued, "It was a deep puncture-type wound, and there was no other major vascular involvement—no injury to the jugular, or other veins or arteries, and no injury to her trachea." He remarked, "I understand it was a knife wound."

I nodded. It was meant to be a cut across her throat severing everything in its path. But Kate had done something to stop that. I hope she had also kneed him in the nuts.

I asked him, "Prognosis?"

He stayed silent a second too long, then replied, "Guarded."

"Why?"

"Well . . . she lost six units of blood, and we—and

you, I understand—needed to stem the flow of blood
. . . which goes to the brain . . ."

I knew this was coming, and I waited for the
verdict.

Dr. Goldberg continued, "Six units is a significant
loss of blood. Also, her windpipe was swollen, which
may have caused some oxygen deprivation before the
paramedics got a breathing tube down her throat." He
stayed silent a moment, then said, "We just don't know
if there will be any neurological impairment."

"When *will* we know?"

"Shortly after she recovers from anesthesia." He
added, "Maybe in an hour or two."

I did not reply.

He hesitated, then glanced at my bloodstained
jumpsuit and said to me, "I understand that a skydiver
attached himself to her during your skydive and
caused this injury with a knife."

"That's right."

"I assume this was not an accident."

I replied, "You may have noticed the State Trooper
outside the operating room."

He nodded, then asked me, "Any more questions?"

"No."

Dr. Goldberg stood, and I stood also. He said,
"She'll get a complete evaluation as soon as possible,
including a neurological evaluation. In the meantime, you can check in with the ICU nurses' station.
I assume you'll want to stay here until she regains
consciousness."

"That's right."

We shook hands and I said, "Thank you."

He patted my shoulder and suggested, "Some prayers would help." He further suggested, "Take a break in the cafeteria. It will be awhile before we have any further news for you." He assured me, "She's in good hands."

Dr. Goldberg left the waiting room, and I gave him a few minutes to clear out, then I went into the corridor and followed the signs to the ICU.

At the nurses' station I identified myself as John Corey, the husband of Kate Mayfield, who had just arrived from the OR. I showed my creds and also said I was a Federal law enforcement officer. The nurses seemed sympathetic to the former and indifferent to the latter.

In situations such as this, Murphy's Law is in effect, and I couldn't be certain that the ICU staff had gotten the same information as the OR staff, so I said, "My wife was the victim of an attempted murder, and the assailant is still at large and may attempt to gain access to her."

That got their attention. I asked if they'd been told about this, and asked if there were any State Troopers in the unit. They hadn't been told anything, and they said there were no State Troopers in this unit.

I informed them, "You are not to disclose this patient's location or condition to anyone except an authorized medical person, or a law enforcement officer who can show you identification. Do you understand?"

A nurse, who identified herself as Betty, a supervisor, said to me, "I understand, and we will call security."

"Thank you. And also call the OR nurses' station and tell them to have the State Police reassigned here."

One of the nurses picked up the phone to make the calls.

I said to Betty and the other four nurses, "If anyone is looking for Detective Corey, I'll be at my wife's bedside."

Betty was scanning a clipboard—probably Kate's chart—and said to me, "I don't have any orders yet about visitors."

"You do now."

Betty made a note of that on her chart and escorted me toward the ICU.

On the way down the corridor, she informed me, "We're not used to these things here."

"And I hope you never get used to it."

She pushed through a set of double doors and I followed.

Betty, chart in hand, led me toward Kate's bed and said in a quiet voice, "Don't be alarmed by her appearance, or all the monitors and infusion tubes." She added, "She's on a ventilator to help her breathe." She assured me, "Dr. Goldberg is a wonderful surgeon."

But no one, including Dr. Goldberg, knew what was going on, or not going on, in Kate's brain.

We reached Kate's bed, and I stood over my wife and looked at her. Some color had returned to her face, and her breathing, aided by the ventilator, seemed steady. There was a thick dressing around her neck, tubes in her arms, and wires running under the blanket that connected to three different monitors. I looked at the screens and everything seemed normal, though her blood pressure was a little low.

Betty glanced at the monitors and assured me, "Her signs are good."

I took a deep breath and stared at Kate. I could see the swelling around her mouth where Khalil had hit her. *Bastard.* I bent over and kissed her on the cheek. "Hi, beautiful."

No response.

Betty advised me to sit in the bedside chair, which I did, and she said to me, "Press the call button if you need anything." She informed me, "No cell phones." She turned and left.

I took Kate's hand, which was cool and dry, and I could feel her pulse. I kept looking at her face, but it remained expressionless. I watched the rise and fall of her chest, and I glanced at the monitors several times.

Having nearly bled to death myself, I knew what Kate had gone through in those minutes when her blood was pumping out of her body—the very frightening, runaway heartbeat, the falling blood pressure that caused an awful ringing in the ears, the sense of being icy cold on the inside, unlike anything you've ever felt . . . like death . . . and then, the brain becomes cloudy . . .

When I had awoken at Columbia-Presbyterian Hospital, I had no memory of why I was there or what had happened to me. I wasn't allowed visitors, but my partner, Dom Fanelli, had bullied his way in and engaged me in a long, stupid conversation about why the Mets were a better team than the Yankees. Apparently

I didn't agree with him, and he went back to Homicide North and told everyone that I was definitely brain damaged. I smiled at that memory, and the memory of Dom Fanelli, who died on 9/11.

I looked again at Kate and thought, *Too much death on this job.*

I prayed that Kate would come through this as well as I had, against all medical odds. But if there was some impairment, then I'd quit the job and take care of her. After I killed Asad Khalil.

CHAPTER FIFTEEN

I continued my vigil beside Kate's bed, holding her hand and looking for signs of her coming out of anesthesia.

My cell phone was on vibrate, and I'd gotten three calls in the last half hour, which I let go into voice mail.

I listened to the first call from Tom Walsh, who said, "The hospital tells me that Kate is out of surgery and resting comfortably. Glad to hear that. Also, I spoke to Investigator Miller about his search for Khalil. No news there. I called George Foster, and he understands the situation." Walsh had paused, then said, "We can't seem to locate Gabe." Another pause, then, "Or Chip Wiggins in California." He ended with, "Call me."

The second call was from Vince Paresi, who said basically what Walsh said about Gabe Haytham, though Paresi added, "I'm a little concerned about Gabe. We can't get hold of his wife either. I'm sending a patrol car to his house in Douglaston. Glad Kate is doing okay. Call me."

I, too, was a little concerned about Gabe Haytham—and his family. Every agent is theoretically reachable by cell phone or text message, 24/7. But if you're off-duty, you might not be checking your job phone as often as you should. In any case, today was a nice Sunday, and maybe Gabe and his family were at the beach, or at an amusement park, or . . . dead.

As for Chip Wiggins, last I saw him three years ago, he was a cargo pilot. So he could be in the air. Or he could be in the ground.

The third call was from Investigator Miller, who informed me that my vehicle and luggage were in the hospital parking lot and the keys were at the ICU nurses' station.

Inspector Miller also said, "The vehicle and the luggage are clean. We did not find your wife's cell phone in the room or in the vehicle, and the search of the drop zone hasn't yet turned up her weapon or her cell phone." He also advised me, "We checked Sullivan County Airport, and we found an Enterprise rental car in the parking field, and the renter is a man named Mario Roselini, but nothing in his rental agreement checks out. The tire treads on the rental might match the treads we found near the woods. We've taken latex impressions and we're trying to do a match. The car is under surveillance. Also, we checked with the fixed base operators at the airport, and a Citation jet landed there Saturday evening, then took off Sunday about thirty or forty minutes after the incident, destination and passengers, if any, unknown. No flight plan filed. We're following up on this." He added, "Your guy Walsh was not clear if you're the case agent, but call me directly if you need more." He ended with, "The hospital tells me your wife is resting comfortably. Some good news."

I put the phone back in my pocket and thought about Investigator Miller's call. It was fairly obvious how Asad Khalil made his escape—he jetted away. But to where? There was no flight plan filed so it would have had to be a short low-altitude flight.

Another thought was that my colleague, FBI Special Agent in Charge Tom Walsh, hadn't passed on that information to me. But to be fair, I wasn't sure of the timing of all these calls or who was speaking to whom and when.

I turned my attention to Kate and leaned close to her. I tried to see if there was anything in her face that would give me a clue about her mental condition, but her expression revealed nothing.

There are different degrees of mental impairment, as I knew, and I had to prepare myself for anything from mild impairment to . . . whatever.

Another half hour passed, a few nurses came by, and one of them brought me a cup of coffee. I asked for a pen and pad so I could make some notes.

I used the time to recall, in detail, the events of three years ago, and try to apply that unhappy learning experience to what lay ahead. I wished that Kate was helping me with this, and I was sure she had some ideas that we could toss around.

I was about to get up and take a walk in the corridor, but I thought I saw her move.

I stood near her bed and watched her closely. She moved her head, then I saw her right arm move. I was going to press the call button, but I decided to wait.

Every few seconds, she moved an arm or a leg, and her head rolled from side to side.

I leaned closer to her and touched her arm. "Kate?"

She opened her eyes, but kept staring up at the ceiling.

"Kate?"

She turned her head toward me and we made eye contact.

"Kate. Can you hear me?"

She didn't show any sign of recognition.

The breathing tube kept her from speaking, so I took her hand in mine and said, "Squeeze my hand if you can hear me."

After a few seconds, she squeezed my hand. I smiled at her and asked, "Do you know who I am?"

She stared at me, then nodded tentatively.

I said to her, "Squeeze my hand if you know why you're here and what happened to you."

She pulled her hand away from mine.

"Kate? Nod if you know why you're here."

She raised her right arm and made a shaky movement with her hand that looked like a tremor or the beginning of a seizure. I reached for the call button, but then I realized she was pantomiming holding a pen.

I grabbed the pen and pad from the nightstand

and put the pen in her right hand and the pad in her left hand.

She held them both above her face and wrote something, then turned the pad toward me. It said, *Why are you asking me these stupid questions?*

I felt my eyes get moist and I bent over and kissed her cheek.

PART IV

Downstate New York

CHAPTER SIXTEEN

Asad Khalil looked across the aisle at the west-facing window of his chartered Citation jet as it began its descent into Long Island's Republic Airport. In the distance, about sixty kilometers away, he could see the skyline of Manhattan Island. He checked his watch. The flight from Sullivan County Airport had taken twenty-six minutes.

From his window on the port side of the aircraft he could see a vast cemetery with thousands of white crosses and headstones standing in rows across the green fields. In Libya, the dead did not need such fertile land because the Koran promised that their souls would ascend to a Paradise of flowing streams and fruit trees.

His two brothers, two sisters, and his mother, all of whom had died in the American bombing raid, had been buried in simple graves at the edge of the desert, beside his father who had been killed five years earlier by the Zionists. They were surely all in Paradise now, because each of them had been martyred by the infidels. And he, Asad Khalil, had been given a special status by the Great Leader, Colonel Khadafi, as the sole survivor of a martyred family. And with this status came a great responsibility: revenge.

The copilot's voice came over the speaker. "We'll be landing in two minutes, Mr. Demetrios. Please make sure your seat belt is fastened and your seat is in the upright position."

As the aircraft made its final approach, Asad Khalil reflected briefly on his interesting parachute jump. He had two thoughts: one was that he could not be absolutely certain that he had killed the woman; his second thought was that he should have taken the opportunity to shoot the man named Corey.

As for the woman—Corey's wife—she had struck his hand, and he had not been able to complete the cut across her throat. He was not accustomed to women who used physical force against a man, and though he knew this was possible, it had nevertheless taken him by surprise. Still, he had severed her artery, and she undoubtedly bled to death before she hit the ground.

As for Corey, the plan had always been to leave him until the end. Khalil wanted to prolong the man's suffering for his dead wife and to engage him in a game of wits that would end when he, Khalil, delivered to Corey a mutilation of the face and genitals that would be worse than death. And yet . . . something told him he should have changed his plans right there and shot this man as he hung from his parachute—using his wife's pistol.

The Citation touched the runway and the aircraft began to decelerate.

The copilot, whose name Khalil recalled as Jerry, announced, "Welcome to Long Island's Republic Airport."

Why, wondered Khalil, did the pilots always welcome him to a place that had no meaning to them, or to him? They had done the same thing when he had begun his journey from Santa Barbara in California, to the refueling stops in Pueblo, Colorado, and Huntington, West Virginia. And finally, when he had landed at the Sullivan County Airport, he was again welcomed by the copilot, who also said to him, "I hope you have a successful business meeting."

To which Khalil, the Greek businessman, had replied, "I am sure I will."

The Citation taxied toward one of the hangars in the small private airport.

Khalil looked out the window, trying to determine if somehow the authorities had discovered his means of transportation and his destination. When he had landed at Sullivan County Airport on Saturday evening, Khalil told the pilots that he would be flying to Buffalo on Sunday, so he was certain they had filed a flight plan for that city. But when he returned from his business of killing Corey's wife, he announced a sudden change of plans and asked to be taken to Long Island's MacArthur Airport as quickly as possible. The pilots had no problem with this—he was, as they kept telling him, the boss.

The pilots had informed their passenger that no flight plan needed to be filed because it was a clear day, and because they would avoid the New York City restricted airspace zone, and they would also stay below the altitude where a flight plan would be necessary. VFR—visual flight rules—they explained.

Khalil knew all of this, but nodded attentively, and within fifteen minutes they were airborne. Ten minutes into the flight, he made a pretense of using the airphone, then announced to the pilots another change of plans to Republic Airport, which was closer than MacArthur.

So, Khalil thought, the pilots had no time to speak to anyone on the ground at Sullivan County Airport, and there was no paperwork filed as to their new destination. This lack of official involvement in private flights had amazed Khalil the first time he was here three years ago. Even more amazing, he thought, was that a year and a half after the martyrdom of his fellow jihadists on September 11, it was still possible to fly around this country in private aircraft and leave little or no evidence of the journey, or of the passenger on board. All that was required was a credit or debit card that ensured the payment to the charter company.

The only way the authorities could know he was on this aircraft would be if the police guessed that he had arrived at Sullivan County Airport with a chartered aircraft, and departed in the same manner. But no one knew the next destination of this aircraft, though they might radio the pilots. The pilots, however, had appeared completely normal during the short flight, and he was fairly certain they had not received a single radio message.

However, an image of Corey came into his mind. This man had caused him some unexpected problems the last time he was in America. The man was clever, and he seemed to think a step or two ahead, but he had not caught up with Asad Khalil the last time, and he would not do so this time. In fact, it would be the other way around.

Khalil removed a pair of binoculars from his overnight bag and scanned the activity on the tarmac, but he saw nothing suspicious.

He reached into his bag and retrieved the cell phone of Corey's wife. He understood that if the authorities had discovered the phone was missing from her body, they would be continuously searching for the cell phone's signal. His Al Qaeda colleagues who had funded this mission had told him that if he came into the possession of a Federal agent's cell phone, he would have one minute, perhaps two, to access any information on the instrument before the signal was traced to its origin.

He turned on the woman's cell phone, and within a few seconds it chimed, indicating a text message. His sponsors had also told him that a text message could be retrieved without a code. This had surprised him and he was skeptical, but now he would see if this was true. He hit the button marked "OK" and the text appeared on the screen. It read: *Meeting, Monday, 10AM, SAC Office, Subject: Operation Liberty Shield,*

increased surveillance and monitoring of known suspects,
as per Dept Homeland Security. Walsh.

Khalil shut off the cell phone and put it back into
his bag.

This, he thought, was a standard message, sent, according to the time of the message, before he killed the
woman and took her cell phone. And her cell phone
was still in service, so they did not yet know it was
missing from her body. As for this person who sent the
message—Walsh—Khalil knew who he was, and if the
opportunity arose, Walsh would not be sending messages for much longer.

In any case, there was as yet no general alert to all
Federal agents.

The aircraft came to a halt near one of the hangars
and the twin jet engines shut down. Khalil looked
again through his binoculars. His mentor in Libya,
Malik, had recognized in his protégé a sixth sense that
Khalil knew he was born with and which alerted him
to danger. Malik had said to him, "You have been
blessed with this gift, my friend, and if you stay true
to your purpose and to God, it will never leave you."

And it had never left him, which was why he was
still alive, and why so many of his enemies were dead.

The copilot, Jerry, came into the cabin and asked
him, "Did you have a good flight, sir?"

Khalil lowered the binoculars and replied, "I did."
He searched the copilot's face for signs that the man
had been alerted to a problem with his passenger. But
the man seemed as childishly cheerful and fatuous as
most Americans he'd met. If he'd shown any other

facial expression, Khalil would have pulled his pistol and ordered the pilots to start the engines and take off.

There *was* a Plan B, which involved a low-altitude flight below any radar to an abandoned airstrip in the remote Adirondack Mountains, not far from the Canadian border. He had purposely told the pilots that his next destination was Buffalo so that they would take on enough fuel to reach this abandoned airstrip where an automobile awaited him. And that would be the end of the journey for these two pilots.

The copilot glanced at the binoculars and inquired, "Are you being met here?"

"Yes."

"Do you see your party?"

"No."

The copilot swung open the door, which caused a set of steps to descend, and he asked his passenger, "Can I help you with your bag?"

"No, thank you."

The copilot descended the steps to the tarmac, and the pilot, whose name was Dave, came into the cabin and asked, "Do you know how long you'll be here, sir?"

"Yes. I need to leave here tomorrow for my meeting in Buffalo, which has been rescheduled for one P.M."

The pilot replied, "Okay, then we can leave at, say, ten A.M., and that will give you plenty of time."

"Excellent." Khalil unbuckled his seat belt, retrieved his overnight bag from under his seat and put the binoculars in the bag, then stood and moved into the aisle.

The pilot led the way out of the cabin, and Khalil

stayed close to him, one hand in the side pocket of his blue sports jacket that held the .40 caliber Glock pistol of his victim, whom he had known as Miss Mayfield, and who had become Mrs. Corey during his three-year absence. And now she was the late Mrs. Corey.

The pilot and copilot, Dave and Jerry, and their customer, Mr. Demetrios, began walking toward the nearby hangar. The pilot remarked, "A really nice day."

The copilot said, "I've been to Greece. You get some great weather there."

Khalil replied, "Yes, we do."

"Where in Greece did you say you were from?"

Khalil focused on the open doors of the hangar and peered into the darkness inside. He replied as he walked, "Piraeus. The seaport of Athens."

"Yeah. Right. I was there once. Nice place."

Khalil had been there as well, as part of his legend-building, and he replied, "Not so nice."

The pilot changed the subject and asked, "You got a place to stay tonight?"

"I assume my colleagues here have arranged that."

"Right. Well, Jerry and I will get a ride to a motel and meet you here about nine-thirty for our ten o'clock departure. If there's any change of plans, you have our cell numbers."

In fact, Khalil thought, there was already a change of plans. He was not going to Buffalo or anywhere with these men or their aircraft. But it was not their business to know this. In fact, as they would eventually learn, they were lucky to be alive.

They arrived at the entrance of the fixed base operator, who would take care of their aircraft and find the pilots transportation and accommodations.

The pilot asked, "Where are your people meeting you?"

Khalil had not wanted the pilots to see that he had no business colleagues here, and that in fact he had booked a livery vehicle with a driver to meet him in the parking lot. He replied to the pilot, "My colleagues are most likely in the parking area."

"Okay. Any problem, call us."

"Thank you."

The pilots entered the FBO office, and Khalil continued to a wide paved area between the hangars.

If a trap had been set for him, it was at this point, with the pilots safely out of his control, that it would be sprung. He could not escape the trap, but he could send some of his enemies to Hell before he ascended to Paradise. He kept his hand on the butt of his pistol and his finger on the trigger.

He continued between the hangars to the parking area, which was nearly empty. Close to the rear of the hangar he saw a black limousine and approached it.

A driver of enormous proportions, wearing a black suit and tie, sat sleeping in his seat, and Khalil could hear the man's snores through the closed window. A white cardboard sign stuck in the front windshield said MR. GOLD.

Khalil looked around the parking lot, satisfied now that there was no danger. He moved away from the car and the sleeping driver, then opened his bag and retrieved the cell phone that had been in the luggage given to him by the late Farid Mansur in Santa Barbara. Khalil knew this was an untraceable throw-away phone with two hundred prepaid minutes. His Al Qaeda contact in Cairo had assured him, "If you need more minutes, your contact in California can track your usage on his computer and prepay for additional minutes."

Khalil did not think he needed more minutes, and to be certain that he and the phone remained untraceable, he had killed Farid in Santa Barbara. People, too, should be thrown away when their usefulness has ended. Khalil dialed a number.

A man answered, "Amir."

Khalil said in English, "This is Mr. Gold."

After a pause, Amir replied, "Yes, sir."

Khalil switched to Arabic and asked, "Can you tell me if my friends are at home?"

Amir replied in Arabic, "Yes, sir. I have passed the house several times and their two vehicles are still in the driveway."

"And are they alone?"

"I do not know, sir, but I have seen no other vehicles and no visitors."

"Good. I will call you again. Watch the house closely, but do not arouse suspicion."

"Yes, sir." He added, "My taxi would not arouse suspicion."

Khalil hung up and approached the vehicle, which he recognized as a Lincoln Town Car. On his last visit here, he had rented and driven a similar vehicle for his journey from MacArthur Airport to the Long Island Cradle of Aviation Museum where he killed two of the pilots who had bombed Tripoli. He could not know which of the pilots on that bombing raid had dropped the bomb that killed his family, but if he killed them all, it did not matter.

Khalil knocked hard on the window of the black car, and the driver sat up quickly, then lowered the window. He asked, "Mr. Gold?"

"Correct."

Before the driver could get out, Khalil said, "I have only this bag," then he got in the rear seat behind the driver.

The driver removed the sign from the windshield and started the vehicle. He handed Khalil a card and said, "My name is Charles Taylor." He added, "There's water in the seat pocket and I got the Sunday papers up here if you want one. The Post and Newsday."

"Thank you."

The driver asked, "Where we headed?"

Khalil gave him a memorized address in the Douglaston section of Queens, which was a borough of New York City. It was not the actual address of his next victim, but it was very close. The driver programmed his GPS.

Khalil asked, "What is the driving time?"

The driver replied, "It's telling me thirty-two minutes." He added, "It don't tell me about traffic. But it's Sunday, so maybe we can do that. You in a hurry?"

"Somewhat."

The driver pulled out of the parking lot, and within a few minutes they were on the Southern State Parkway, heading west.

The driver asked, "You going back to the airport later?"

"I am not sure."

"I'm yours all day if you want."

"Thank you," Khalil replied, "but it may be a short day for you."

"Whatever."

Khalil marveled at the number of vehicles on the highway, large vehicles, some with only one passenger, many with women driving. And he knew from his last visit that this scene was repeated all over America, every day of the week. The Americans were sucking the oil out of the earth, out of the desert sands, and burning it for their amusement. Someday, the oil or their money would be gone, and they, too, would be gone.

Khalil remarked, "There are no trucks."

The driver replied, "This is a parkway. No commercial vehicles, except like livery cars and taxis." The driver inquired, "Where you from?"

"Israel."

"Yeah? Hey, you didn't come in from Israel at Republic."

"No. I came from Miami by private aircraft."

"Yeah? What business are you in?"

"I am in the candy business. I am known in America as Brian Gold, the Candyman."

"Oh . . . yeah. I think I heard of you."

"Good."

The driver thought a moment, then said, "Brian? Is that a Jewish name? I mean, Israeli?"

In fact, Khalil thought, it wasn't, but it was the name on his forged American passport. Brian Gold. He replied to the driver, "Brian is my American business name." Khalil spoke no Hebrew and no Greek, but he spoke English, so some of the passports he'd found in his luggage were American, with American-sounding first names. His accent and his limited knowledge of America were explained to inquisitive people by saying he had dual citizenship. This was usually sufficient, unless the person became too inquisitive and asked more questions.

On his first visit here, he had found the Americans to be trusting and not suspicious of anything. If they asked him a question, it was out of innocent curiosity or politeness. But since 9/11, according to Malik, some Americans had become suspicious of all foreigners, and they had been told by their government, "If you see something, say something." So now he took extra care and was alert to any hint of curiosity that was not innocent. This driver, however, seemed just talkative, but if he happened to speak Hebrew, or if he had been to Israel and wanted to speak about Israel, then there would be a problem that needed to be solved.

On the subject of business, Charles Taylor informed Mr. Gold, "Just so you know, this trip is prepaid by your company. You just have to sign."

"I understand."

"There's a twenty percent tip included, so you don't

have to worry about that." He added, "Unless you want to."

"I understand." Khalil wondered if he could kill so fat a man with one bullet. He could, of course, if the bullet was fired into his head. But it was Khalil's intention to fire the bullet through the seat, into the man's upper spine, so it would exit from his heart.

The driver asked, "So, are you here for business or pleasure?"

"Both."

"That's the way to do it." He asked, "You like it here?"

"All Israelis love America."

"Right." The driver continued west on the parkway.

Khalil turned his attention to the scene outside. He asked the driver, "Is this place which is called Douglaston the same as I am seeing now?"

"Huh? Oh . . . sort of. Except this is Nassau County. The suburbs. Big taxes here." The driver asked, "You meeting somebody at this address?"

"I am."

"It's a pretty good neighborhood. Some nice houses." He added, "Some Jewish people."

And, thought Khalil, at least one Muslim family by the name of Haytham. But soon there would be one less Muslim family.

His Al Qaeda friends had shown him a photograph of the Haytham house, as well as an aerial view, and told him that the house was located in the borough of Queens, which was part of New York City, though it was a residential area of private homes and middle-class people. They advised him that a stranger might arouse suspicion, but assured him that residents and visitors did arrive by taxi from the train station, and that if he dressed well and acted quickly, he should be able to finish his business and leave without trouble.

They had also advised him to reconsider this business, or at least to do his business elsewhere and not involve the apostate's family. But Khalil had replied, "It is important to send a clear message to others of our faith who work for the infidels. It is the will of Allah that they die, and that their families also pay for their sins." He had added, "It is good that they die at home where they feel safest. That is the message."

Khalil recalled the photograph of the house and asked the driver, "Is it possible that a civil servant . . . or perhaps a policeman . . . could afford to live in this place called Douglaston?"

The driver considered the question and replied, "Yeah, I guess if the wife worked, too, and they don't have a lot of crumb snatchers."

"Excuse me?"

"Kids."

"I see." He had been told that the policeman Haytham's wife was employed outside the home. In Libya, wives did not work, but the police stole money, so they lived well. As for children, the family of Haytham had one daughter, Nadia, who might be at home.

It was not difficult to kill one person, or even two. But three people in the same house caused complications. Most Muslim families had many children, but this policeman, who was Palestinian, had adopted too many American habits. And to add to his sins, he had chosen to work for this group called the Anti-Terrorist Task Force. It was, in fact, an anti-Islamic league of Christian crusaders and Zionists, who were joined in an unholy alliance against Islam. And Jibral Haytham, who called himself by the Christian translation of Gabriel, had committed the worst possible sin against his religion by offering his services and his knowledge of Islam to the infidels.

Khalil's only concern was that someone from Haytham's agency would come to a conclusion that Haytham was also on Khalil's list of victims. The last time Khalil was here on his mission of revenge, he'd had no direct contact with Haytham, though he had known of this traitor and would have killed him then if he were able. But he didn't believe that the FBI would think of this now and be waiting for him. And, according to Amir, who was watching the house, there was no evidence that they were.

Again, his mind returned to Corey. Corey, like Haytham, was a policeman, working with the FBI in this Anti-Terrorist Task Force. It had been Khalil's experience in Europe that the police were often more of a danger to him than the internal security forces or the intelligence agencies. The police thought in a different way, and sometimes came to conclusions that the intelligence agents were not trained to think about.

So it was possible that Corey had not believed Asad Khalil's threat that he himself would be killed next, and perhaps Corey had given some thought to who might actually be the next victim. If so, he might have thought first of the FBI agent, George Foster. Or perhaps Corey was so distraught that he wasn't thinking about anything except his dead wife. In any case, Khalil would know soon enough if they were ahead of him or behind him.

The one person who the FBI would know for certain was on Khalil's list was the late Mr. Chip Wiggins. The last time Khalil was here, the FBI—or perhaps it was Corey—had made some conclusions, and they had been waiting for him at Wiggins's home in California.

This time, however, Mr. Wiggins, who had been last on Khalil's list, had been first. And now, when the FBI began looking for Wiggins after the death of Miss Mayfield, they would discover they were too late to save him this time. *The last shall be first.*

The driver, Charles Taylor, said to his Israeli passenger, "You got some Iranians up in that area, too. You know, people who got out of there and have a few bucks. Maybe some Pakis, too."

"Pakis?"

"Pakistanis. Arabs. People like that." Charles Taylor, perhaps thinking about an extra tip from Mr. Gold, said, "We don't need those people here. Right?"

"Correct."

"I mean, since 9/11 . . . I'm not saying they're all up

to no good, but . . . hey, you got bombings in Israel. Right?"

"Correct."

"Same crap is gonna happen here."

"I am certain it will."

CHAPTER SEVENTEEN

Khalil looked at his watch and saw that twenty-two minutes had passed since they left the airport.

About five minutes later, the GPS sounded a verbal command and the driver exited into a residential area.

Khalil noted that the homes seemed substantial, many made of brick and stone, and that the trees were large and the vegetation was lush and well tended. The traitor Haytham lived well.

Khalil said, "Stop the vehicle, please."

The driver pulled to the curb.

Khalil retrieved the dead woman's cell phone from his overnight bag and turned on the power. Within a few seconds, the chime sounded and he saw on the screen that a text message had been sent. He pushed the button and read: *NY ATTF—FBI Agent Kate Mayfield criminally assaulted in Sullivan County, NY. Possible suspect, Asad Khalil, a known terrorist, Libyan national. Her medical condition classified. See your e-mail for full details, updates, and operational instructions, or call Ops Center. Amber alert. BOLO and APB sent. Walsh, SAC, NY ATTF.*

Khalil shut off the cell phone and dropped it into his bag.

So, he thought, when they sent this message, they still did not know that he had possession of the woman's cell phone—and this message had been delivered to all Federal agents, including the dead one.

Or . . . they knew he had her cell phone and they had not ended her service because they hoped he would be so stupid as to use the cell phone so they could track his movements. Or they would send a false message for him to read.

He thought about the words "criminally assaulted" and "medical condition classified." Could that mean she was not dead? Or would they not announce in a text message that she was dead? This troubled him, but he put it out of his mind and turned his thoughts to his next victim. Would this message alert Haytham to the possibility that he was in danger? Perhaps Haytham had not seen this message, or even if he had, why would he believe that he was in imminent danger?

Khalil's instincts, which never failed him, told him to ignore the possibility that there was a trap set for him at the Haytham house. He could smell danger, but what he smelled now was Jibral Haytham's blood.

Khalil dialed his cell phone.

A voice answered, "Amir."

Khalil said in English, "Mr. Gold. How are things looking there?"

Amir replied, "The same, sir."

"And where are you now?"

"I am parked where I can see the house."

"And there is nothing there that disturbs you?"

"No, sir."

"I will call you again." Khalil hung up and said to the driver, "A small change of plans. I must meet someone coming from the city at the Douglaston train station."

"No problem." The driver punched in the information on his GPS and said, "A few blocks from here."

Within three minutes, the driver pulled into the eastbound side of the small parking lot of the Long Island Rail Road station.

Khalil saw a taxi stand, but there were no taxis on this Sunday afternoon. A few vehicles sat empty in the lot, and the platform was deserted. A sign on a Plexiglas shelter said DOUGLASTON, just as in the photograph Malik had shown him. Malik had many Libyan sources in New York, including taxi drivers and even diplomats from the Libyan mission to the U.N., and Malik had chosen this place, but there were two alternate places if there was a problem here.

Khalil said to the driver, "Park here, beside this van."

The driver pulled into the space beside a large van that blocked the view of the limo from the road.

Satisfied that he could do his business here, Khalil dialed his cell phone and Amir answered. Khalil said, "Meet me in the parking lot of the Douglaston railroad station." He hung up.

The driver asked, "Did he say how long?"

"A few minutes." Khalil took a bottled water from

the seat pocket, opened it, and drank all but a few ounces.

The driver asked, "You want me to pull up to the platform?"

"No." Khalil opened his overnight bag and retrieved the Colt .45 automatic pistol that his late compatriot in Santa Barbara had given him. The other advantage of private air travel was that one could carry firearms on board the aircraft without anyone knowing, or for that matter even caring.

The driver asked, "You want to get out and meet your guy on the platform?"

"No." Khalil pressed the water bottle against the back of the driver's seat lined up with the obese man's upper spine, opposite his heart. He looked around to ensure that there was no one in sight. He was about the pull the trigger, but then dropped the Colt back into his bag and drew Miss Mayfield's Glock from his pocket. Yes, it would be good when the ballistic test showed it was her FBI weapon. He pressed the muzzle of the Glock against the open neck of the bottle.

Charles Taylor said, "I'm gonna step out for a quick smoke."

"You can smoke here." Khalil pulled the trigger, and the Glock bucked in his hand as a muffled blast filled the car.

Taylor pitched forward, then his seat harness snapped him back, and his head rolled to the side. Khalil fired again into the smoke-filled plastic bottle to be certain, and again the man's body jerked forward, then fell back against the leather seat. Khalil drew a long breath through his nostrils, savoring the smell of burnt gunpowder, then put the pistol in his pocket.

He pushed the two shell casings and the smoking bottle under the seat, retrieved his overnight bag, exited the car, and opened the driver's door.

The two .40 caliber rounds had passed through the driver's immense body and lodged in the dashboard. Taylor's white shirt was red with fresh blood, but the well-placed bullets had stopped his heart quickly, and there was no excessive bleeding. A good job.

Khalil found the seat control and lowered the driver's seat to its maximum reclining position. He then reached across the dead man's body and retrieved the two Sunday newspapers from the passenger seat, surprised at their size and weight. He laid the pages of *Newsday* over the driver's face and body, confident that the blood would not seep through. He tucked the *Post* under his arm.

Khalil turned off the engine, took the keys, and closed the door, then locked all the doors with the remote control. It could be many hours or even the next morning before anyone noticed a sleeping livery driver waiting for his customer at the railroad station. He said, "Sleep well."

Khalil walked toward the road at the edge of the small parking area, keeping an eye on the houses across the street, then noting a man and woman fifty meters away walking a dog, and two children on bicycles coming toward him. They had told him in Tripoli that the Christian Sabbath was a quiet day in the residential areas, and this seemed to be the case. After the children passed him, he saw a storm drain and dropped the keys through the grate.

He stood against a lamppost, opened the newspaper, and read an article about suicide bombings in Baghdad. His knowledge of written English was not perfect, but this article was written with simple words, and he could understand it. He did not, however, like the use of the word "terrorist" or the descriptions of "cowardly attacks." It took courage, Khalil knew, to be a martyr, and he admired such men and even the women who martyred themselves for Islam. He, Asad Khalil, did not intend to become a martyr for Islam; he intended to be the sword of Islam. But if martyrdom came, he was prepared for it.

He finished the article, recalling that it was only a few weeks before that the American president had declared an end to the war. He could have told him that this was a war without end, and he wondered why this arrogant man didn't understand this.

A yellow taxi approached slowly, then stopped a few meters from him. Khalil noted that the taxi's off-duty light was illuminated. The driver lowered his window and asked, "Mr. Gold?"

Khalil nodded and got into the taxi behind the driver. He said in Arabic, "Yalla mimshee." Go.

The driver continued down the street, and Khalil said, "Take me to the house."

"Yes, sir." Amir glanced at his passenger in the rearview mirror. He did not know this man, except as a fellow Libyan, a friend of a friend. And this friend had made it clear to Amir that this man, who for some reason was posing as a Jew, was a very important man, and that Amir had been chosen to perform a service to his country by aiding this compatriot. Also, this man would give him a thousand dollars to show his appreciation.

Amir again glanced in his rearview mirror. The man's eyes were black like night, but nevertheless seemed to burn like coal.

"Look at the road. Not at me."

"Yes, sir."

They drove slowly, and Amir made a few turns through the quiet neighborhood.

Yes, Khalil thought, it was a family day, and perhaps the Americans went to church in the morning and then they observed the secular aspects of the Christian Sabbath—going to the park or to the beach where men, women, and children paraded half naked in front of one another. And, of course, there was the Sunday shopping. The Americans shopped seven days a week, morning, noon, and night, including even on their Sabbath and their holy days.

Malik had told him in Tripoli, "There are two hundred fifty million of them, and they are consuming the planet. Money is their god, and spending it is their sacred duty." Malik had added, "The women especially are like locusts in a field of grain."

Khalil turned his thoughts from Malik back to the taxi driver sitting in front of him. He asked Amir, "Have you remained observant here?"

"Of course, sir. And my wife and my six children.

We answer the call to prayer five times each day and read from the Koran each evening."

"Why are you here?"

"For the money, sir. The infidels' money. I send it to my family in Tripoli." He added, "Soon, we will all return to our country, Allah willing." He added, "Peace be unto him."

Amir turned onto a tree-lined street of brick houses and said, "The house is up ahead on this side."

Khalil asked, "Do you have my gift?"

"I do, sir." He took a black plastic bag off the floor and handed it back to his passenger.

Khalil opened the bag and extracted a bouquet of flowers wrapped in green paper and cellophane. He took from his overnight bag an eight-inch carving knife and stuck it blade-first into the bouquet. He said to Amir, "Stop at the house, then park where you can see the whole street. Call me if you see a police vehicle or anyone approaching."

"Yes, sir." Amir stopped in front of a two-story house of brick with a blue front door, which Khalil recognized from the photograph.

Khalil scanned the area around him, but saw nothing that alarmed him. More importantly, he felt no danger. And yet that text message had certainly reached Haytham's cell phone. Perhaps, too, they had called him at his home.

A more cautious man would leave now, but caution was another word for coward.

He exited the taxi quickly with the flowers in his

left hand, the Glock in his right jacket pocket, and the Colt .45 stuck in his belt under his jacket.

He walked straight up the driveway of the house in which two vehicles were parked, and if anyone saw him, they would not be suspicious of a man in a good sports jacket carrying flowers to a friend's house. He could thank his former trainer, Boris the Russian, for the contrivance of the flowers, which according to Boris was a tried-and-tested KGB ruse. Boris had said to him, "A man with flowers and a smile on his face is not perceived as a dangerous man." Yes, and Khalil would thank Boris in person before he cut out his heart. He smiled.

At the end of the driveway was a garage, and the house and garage were connected by a white fence with a gate. Khalil remembered the aerial view of the house and recalled that the rear property was surrounded by a high wall and tall hedges, and there was a patio with furniture and outdoor cooking apparatus. According to Malik, Khalil could expect that the family might be outdoors, and the family had no dog. Khalil now heard music coming from the backyard, Western music, which was not pleasant to his ears.

He took a step beyond the concealment of the house and peered over the low fence as he reached for the Glock. If they were waiting for him, it was here that they would show themselves. But there was no one on the patio, and he opened the gate and moved quickly toward the back door of the house. Then he realized that the music was coming from behind him, and he turned toward a chaise lounge that had been facing away from him. On the lounge was a girl of about fifteen years, lying in the sunlight, nearly naked, wearing only a small white bathing suit such as he'd seen in Europe. On the ground beside her he saw the radio that was playing the music. She seemed to be sleeping.

He stepped toward the girl, whom he recognized from photographs as Nadia, Haytham's daughter. As he moved toward her, he kept glancing back at the house, but saw no one at the windows or door.

He stopped beside the girl and looked down at her body. In Libya, she would be whipped for her near nakedness, and her mother and father, too, would be whipped for allowing this. Her mother might even be executed if the Sharia court ruled against her. No matter, Khalil thought, they would all be dead shortly. He withdrew the knife from the bouquet.

The girl must have sensed his presence or sensed that something was blocking the sun on her body, and she opened her eyes.

The girl did not see the knife; she saw only Khalil's face and saw the bouquet that he extended toward her. She opened her mouth, and Khalil thrust the knife into her bare chest between her ribs and deep into her heart. The girl stared at him, but only a small sound came from her open mouth and her body barely moved. Khalil twisted the knife and let it go, then threw the flowers on her chest.

He spun around, drew the Glock, and moved straight toward the screen door. Khalil turned the handle of the screen door, which was unlocked, and stepped into a rear foyer that was cluttered with shoes and jackets. To the right was an open doorway through which he could see a kitchen, and in the kitchen he saw the back of a woman at the sink. She was wearing short pants, a sleeveless shirt, and she was barefoot. She appeared to be preparing food.

Khalil moved toward the opening, and he could now see the entire kitchen; there was no one there but the woman. He focused on an open doorway that led toward the front of the house, and he heard the cheer of a crowd—a sporting event on the radio or the television.

Khalil pocketed the pistol, stepped into the kitchen, and took two long strides toward the woman.

The woman said, "Nadia?" and as she turned her head over her shoulder, Khalil clamped one hand over her mouth and the other on the back of her head and pushed her hard against the sink. He saw a knife in her hand, but before she could raise it, he twisted her head until she was almost facing him. Their eyes met for a second before Khalil felt her neck snap, and the knife fell from her hand.

She began twitching, and Khalil let her slide gently to the floor, where she continued her spasmodic movements.

Again, they made eye contact, and he watched her for a few seconds, trying to determine if she was going to die or become crippled from the neck down. It didn't matter to him, though he might prefer that she spend the rest of her life in a wheelchair. In a year or two, he thought, her bare legs and her arms would not look so good to a man.

Khalil drew the Glock and walked through the open door, which led into a hallway. Ahead was the front door, to the right was a set of stairs, and to the left was a large opening through which he could hear the sporting event.

He walked down the hall and into the living room with his gun held in his outstretched hand. On the couch opposite him lay a man who he was sure was Jibral Haytham. The man wore short pants and a blue T-shirt, and he was barefoot. He was lying facing the television, which now showed an advertisement for beer. In fact, on the coffee table beside Haytham was a can of beer. Jibral Haytham was asleep, and Khalil thought he should put a bullet in his head and move on to other business. But Khalil had been anticipating some conversation if it were possible—and now it seemed possible.

He walked toward the sleeping man and satisfied himself that there was no gun nearby, though he saw a cell phone on the coffee table—a Nextel, such as he'd taken from Corey's wife. He picked up the phone and saw that the screen announced a text message. Khalil pushed the button and a message appeared— the message from Walsh that he had seen on the phone of Corey's wife. The alert had come in time for Jibral Haytham, but unfortunately for him, he had been sleeping, or he had not appreciated the nature of the message in regard to himself.

There was also a wallet on the table, and Khalil put it and the phone in his pocket. He looked down at Haytham's T-shirt and saw that it had a picture of the Twin Towers printed on it in gold, and the words "NYPD/FBI Terrorist Task Force." Beneath that was written "9/11—Never Forget."

Khalil spat on the shirt, then sat in an armchair that faced the couch. He watched his victim for a few seconds, then looked around the room.

In his country, this house of two levels with its own garden would be the home of a man of some means. Here, there were hundreds, thousands of such houses belonging to common people, with vehicles in the driveway, televisions, and good furnishings. He understood why so many believers from the poorer nations of Islam had immigrated to America—the land of the Christians and the Jews—and he did not condemn them for it so long as they retained their customs and their faith. In fact, America would one day be like western Europe, which Islam now thought of as a bloodless conquest.

Haytham, however, had been corrupted to the extreme by this morally debased nation, living among the Jews and the gentiles, and selling his soul to the enemies of Islam. Khalil recited aloud a Sutra from the Koran. "Believers, take neither Jews nor Christians for friends."

Gabriel Haytham stirred on the couch.

The television returned to the sporting event, which Khalil was able to identify as the American national game of baseball. Truly, this game moved so slowly that it would put anyone to sleep.

Khalil noticed a remote control on the low table beside the can of beer, and he reached for it, examined it, then shut off the television.

Gabriel Haytham stirred again, then yawned, sat up, and stared at the blank screen. He seemed confused, then reached for the remote control and noticed Asad Khalil in the nearby chair.

Haytham sat straight up and swung his legs off the couch. "Who the hell are you?"

Khalil drew the Glock from his pocket and pointed it at Haytham. "Indeed, I am from Hell. Do not move or I will kill you."

Gabriel Haytham focused on the gun, then looked at the intruder. He said, "Take whatever you want—"

"Shut up. You will know what I want when you know who I am."

Haytham stared at the intruder's face, and Khalil could see the recognition seeping into his brain. Gabriel Haytham nodded, then said in a quiet voice, "Where is my wife?"

Khalil knew from experience that if he said the loved one was dead, then the intended victim became irrational and sometimes aggressive, so he replied, "Your wife and daughter are safely secured."

"I want to see them."

"You will. Soon. But first you will answer some questions." He asked, "Has your agency contacted you with the news of my return?"

Haytham nodded.

"If you are telling the truth, why are you sleeping?"

He smiled and said, "You should be more alert." He extracted Haytham's phone from his pocket and read the text message to him, then said, in Arabic, "If you had been awake to read this, then perhaps you would not now be waiting for death." When Haytham did not reply, Khalil glanced at the can of beer and said again in Arabic, "Why do you drink alcohol? It clouds the mind and makes you sleepy. You see?"

Gabriel Haytham again did not reply, and his eyes darted around the room.

Khalil knew that the man was looking for a way out of his situation and that he was judging the distance between them and thinking of an aggressive move. Khalil stood, but before he could back away, Haytham thrust his hands under the coffee table and hurled it toward Khalil, then charged toward him.

Khalil deflected the flying table as Haytham lunged at him, and he fired a single round into the man's chest, missing his heart. Before he could fire again, Haytham got his hands on Khalil's right arm, and they struggled for a few seconds before Khalil felt the wounded man weakening. Khalil broke free and stepped away.

Gabriel Haytham stood unsteadily on his feet, his left hand over the bleeding chest wound and his right hand outstretched toward his attacker. Blood began running from his mouth.

Khalil knew the battle was over and all that remained was to deliver a final damnation that the traitor could take to Hell with him. He said in Arabic, "You have turned away from your faith and you have sold your soul to the infidel. For this, Jibral Haytham, you will die and burn in Hell."

Gabriel Haytham's knees buckled and he knelt on the floor, staring at Khalil.

Khalil let him know, "Your wife and your whore daughter are dead, and you will join them soon."

Haytham cried out in a surprisingly strong voice, "You bastard!" He tried to stand, but fell back to his knees, coughing up blood.

Khalil aimed the Glock at Haytham's face and said, "I will kill you with the gun of your Christian colleague, Miss Mayfield, who you will also meet in Hell."

Blood bubbled between Haytham's lips as he said weakly, in Arabic, "*You* will burn in Hell . . . you, Khalil . . ."

Khalil aimed the Glock at Haytham's forehead, but before he pulled the trigger, the cell phone in his pocket rang. He took Haytham's phone from his pocket and looked at the display window. It read ATTF-3.

He looked again at Haytham, who was still kneeling, now with both hands pressed to his wound, which continued to seep blood between his fingers.

The phone stopped ringing, and a second later a beep sounded.

So, Khalil thought, perhaps this call to Haytham was to warn him, and if that was the case, the police might not be more than minutes away.

He put Haytham's cell phone back in his pocket, then used his own cell phone and called Amir, saying to him, "Do you see any police cars? Any unusual activity?"

"No. I would have—"

"Come quickly."

He hung up, raised the Glock, and fired a single shot into Haytham's forehead, then walked quickly to the front window and looked into the street.

Haytham's cell phone again rang, then a phone in the kitchen also rang. Yes, he thought, they were close to him.

If the police arrived, he could exit from the rear of the house and escape through an adjoining property. Or he would wait for them. If there were only two in a single police car, he could easily kill them as they approached the house. It was always easier to kill than to run.

He waited.

CHAPTER EIGHTEEN

A yellow taxi appeared and stopped at the curb. Khalil left through the front door, moved quickly down the path, and got into the taxi. "Go."

Amir accelerated up the street.

Khalil said, "Do not speed. Continue on this street."

They continued on, and less than a minute later, a blue-and-white police car appeared, coming toward them.

"Sir—?"

"Continue."

The police car was moving rapidly, but it did not have its siren on or the flashing lights.

As the police vehicle drew closer, Khalil could see two uniformed people—a woman driving, and a man beside her. They were speaking to each other, and they seemed neither concerned nor interested in the off-duty taxi.

As the police vehicle drew abreast of them, Khalil turned his head and looked away. He said, "Look in your mirror and tell me what you see."

Amir looked in his rearview mirror, and after a few seconds he reported, "The car is slowing . . . yes, it has come around and it is stopping in front of the house . . ."

"We will go now to Manhattan."

"Yes, sir."

Within a few minutes they were on the entrance ramp to the Long Island Expressway, westbound toward Manhattan.

Khalil took Haytham's cell phone from his pocket. By now, of course, the police had found Haytham dead, and eventually they would discover that his cell phone was missing and they would begin to trace the signal. Therefore it was necessary to turn off the phone. But before he did, he examined the instrument. It was the same as the dead woman's cell phone, as he had noted, and not unlike other cell phones—except that this type, used by the Federal agents, had an additional feature that allowed the user to make two-way radio transmissions to a similar instrument.

They had shown him in Tripoli how to do this, and he accessed the directory, which was different from the phone directory. He scrolled through the directory and saw a series of first and last names, followed by a single- or double digit-number. He noticed the names "Corey, John," and "Corey, Kate," as well as "Walsh, Tom," and thirty or forty other people who he assumed were all Federal agents.

They would soon shut off the service to this phone, so this radio directory would be useless, but to amuse himself, he should make a radio call while he could, and he called Walsh, the chief of this agency.

The man answered almost immediately and said, "Gabe, we were looking for you. Did you get my text about Kate?"

Khalil replied, "Yes." He asked, "What is her condition?"

"She's . . . Who is this?"

"Gabe."

"Who the hell is this?"

Khalil smiled and replied, "This is Jibral Haytham calling you from Hell, sir. I am waiting for you here, Mr. Walsh."

"Where's Gabe? Who—?"

Khalil said in Arabic, "Go to Hell," and shut off the phone.

Yes, he thought, they were looking for Mr. Haytham, and now they have found him and his family.

Khalil and Amir rode in silence, then finally Amir cleared his throat and asked in Arabic, "What is your destination in Manhattan, sir?"

"The World Trade Center."

Amir did not reply.

Khalil instructed, "I do not want to pass through a toll booth."

"Yes, sir. We will take the Brooklyn Bridge across the river."

They continued on, and Khalil examined the contents of Haytham's wallet, finding some money and his driver's license and also his police identification as well as his identification as a Federal agent of the Anti-

Terrorist Task Force. Khalil looked at the three photographs in the wallet: one showed the daughter, Nadia, and one was of the wife, whose name Khalil recalled as Farah, which meant joy. The third was of the family together. He ripped the photographs into quarters and threw them out the window.

The last time he was in America, it had taken the authorities much longer to understand what he was doing here—but this time they understood. And he was glad they did. The game was now more interesting, and much more satisfying.

Khalil turned on Haytham's cell phone again and accessed his telephone directory. He speed-dialed the Haytham home.

After two rings, a male voice answered, "Hello."

Khalil inquired, "Is Mr. Haytham at home?"

"Who is this?"

"This is Mr. Gold. Who are you?"

The man did not respond to the question and said, "Mr. Haytham cannot come to the phone."

No, Khalil thought, *he cannot*. He asked, "Mrs. Haytham, then? Or Nadia?"

"They can't come to the phone. Are you related to the Haythams?"

Khalil smiled and replied, "I am not. And who are *you*, sir?"

"This is the police. I'm afraid there's been a . . . death in the family."

"I am sorry to hear that. Who then is dead?"

"I can't divulge that information, sir. Where are you calling from?"

"I am, in fact, calling from Mr. Haytham's cell phone."

"You . . . what?"

"Please tell Mr. John Corey of the Anti-Terrorist Task Force that Asad Khalil will visit him next. I promise."

Khalil shut off the cell phone and looked at Amir, who was making a pretense of concentrating on the road. Amir had heard every word, of course, and there could be little doubt in his mind about what had happened in the house.

Amir exited onto a southbound expressway. Khalil looked out the right side window and saw the skyline of Manhattan Island in the distance. He inquired of Amir, "Where were they?"

"Sir? Oh . . ." He pointed in a southwesterly direction and said, "There."

Khalil gazed out the window. He now recalled from his last visit where he had seen the Towers while riding in this same vicinity in a taxi that had been driven by another compatriot—a man who had suffered the same fate as Amir would suffer.

Khalil regretted these deaths of his innocent countrymen, but it was necessary to silence anyone who saw his face and how he was dressed. That included the obese driver of the limousine and would have included the pilots of his aircraft if the opportunity had presented itself. And that certainly included Amir, who by now understood what was happening; and if he did not fully understand now, he would when he read or heard the news of the deaths in Douglaston.

Also, Amir had heard Khalil use his own name on the cell phone call to the Haytham house. Khalil knew he needed to watch Amir carefully; the man may have guessed his fate, as Farid Mansur had, and he might attempt to flee—instead of accepting his fate as Mansur had.

Khalil said to Amir, "You are performing a great service to our cause, Amir. You will be rewarded, and your family in Tripoli will profit greatly from your service to our country, and to our Great Leader, Colonel Khadafi, and to Islam."

Amir stayed silent for a second too long, then nodded and said, "Thank you, sir."

Khalil recalled that Malik had always warned him about causing too many incidental deaths. "A murdered man—or woman," Malik cautioned, "is like leaving your footprints on your journey. Kill who you must kill and who you have vowed to kill—but try to be merciful with the others, especially those of our faith."

Khalil respected the advice of Malik, who was an old man who had seen much in his life, including the war fought by the Italians and the Germans against the British and Americans that had left the sands of Libya red with their blood. Malik had said to his young protégé, "Asad, there is nothing so beautiful in this world as seeing the Christians butcher one another while the sons and daughters of Islam cheer them on."

Yes, Khalil thought, *Malik has seen much and done much, and he has killed his share of infidels. But he was*

sometimes too cautious with the Americans and that was
because of the bombing raid.

Asad Khalil's mind returned to that night of April
15, 1986, and he could see himself as a young man on
the flat rooftop of the building in the old Italian colonial fortress of Al Azziziyah in Tripoli. He had been
with a young woman . . . but he could not see her, or
remember her . . . all he could remember was the blur of
the aircraft coming toward him, the hellfire spitting
from its tail, and the deafening roar of its engines . . . and
then the world exploded. And the woman died.

Had the night ended there, it would still have been
the worst night of his life. But later . . . later when he
returned to his home after the bombing, he found
rubble . . . and the bodies of his younger sisters, Adara,
age nine, and Lina, age eleven. And his two brothers,
Esam, a boy of five years, and Qadir, age fourteen and
two years younger than himself. And then he had
found his mother dying in her bedroom, blood running from her mouth and ears . . . and she had asked
him about her children . . . then died in his arms.
"Mother!"

Amir was startled and hit the brakes. "Sir?"

Khalil slumped back in the seat and began praying
silently.

Amir glanced at him in the rearview mirror, then
continued on.

Amir exited the expressway and drove toward the
nearby Brooklyn Bridge.

Asad Khalil gazed out the window and noted a food shop whose sign was in Arabic. He also saw two women walking, wearing head scarves. He asked Amir, "Is this a district of Muslims?"

Amir replied, "There are a few here, sir, but many more south of here, in the district called Bay Ridge." He added in a light tone, "The Americans call it Beirut." He forced a laugh.

Khalil asked, "Where is Brighton Beach?"

"Farther south, sir. That is the Russian district."

Khalil knew that. That was where Boris lived, and where Boris would die.

Amir drove onto the Brooklyn Bridge, and Khalil looked across the river to the towering buildings of Manhattan Island. Truly, he thought, this was a place of wealth and power, and it was easy for the jihadists to become discouraged when they gazed on this scene, or when they traveled through this nation. But he recalled the Roman ruins of Libya—all that remained of the greatest imperial power the world had ever seen. In the end, he thought, the greatest armies and navies were nothing when the people believed in nothing. The wealth of an empire corrupted the people and their government, and they were no match for a people who believed in something higher than their bellies, and who worshipped God, not gold.

Khalil could sense that the American empire was past the height of its power and glory, and like Rome, it had begun its long journey of sickness and death. Khalil did not expect to be at that funeral in his lifetime, but the children of Islam, born and unborn, would inherit the ruins of America and Europe, completing the conquest that had begun with the Prophet thirteen centuries ago.

Khalil looked toward where the Twin Towers had risen. That moment when they fell, he knew, had been the beginning of the end.

The taxi came off the bridge, and Khalil said to Amir, "Take me first to 26 Federal Plaza."

"Sir? That is the building of the FBI."

"I know what it is. Go."

Amir seemed to hesitate, then turned into a quiet street.

There were few vehicles and fewer pedestrians in this quarter of the city that Khalil had been told was the government district. Massive buildings rose into the sky and blocked the sun from the narrow streets.

Within a few minutes, Amir was on a wide boulevard. He slowed and pointed ahead to a building on the left that towered a hundred meters above the sidewalks. "There."

Khalil said, "Park across the street."

Amir stopped on Broadway, across the road from the main entrance to 26 Federal Plaza.

Khalil saw that the building was surrounded with open spaces, and the small street that passed to the south of the government complex was blocked by barriers. Also, a police vehicle was parked there.

Amir, anticipating a question, explained, "Since the great victory of September eleven, that street, Duane Street, has been closed to vehicles."

Khalil watched a man in a suit carrying a briefcase

into Duane Street. He smiled and thought that perhaps Miss Mayfield's death had caused her colleagues to work on their Sabbath day.

It was Khalil's wish to penetrate the security of this building at a time when there were few people at work, and go to the upper floors where the Anti-Terrorist Task Force was located. And then he would kill whoever was in the offices.

Malik had called his plan insane and said to him, "It is acceptable for you to martyr yourself in the cause of our people, but I don't think you will accomplish much, Asad, before you are killed. Or worse, captured."

Khalil had replied, "The greatest heroes of Islam were those who rode alone into the enemy camp at night and cut off the head of the chief in his own tent."

"Yes," Malik agreed, "and if you had a horse and a sword and your enemies were armed with swords and sleeping in their tents, this would be a good thing, and I would approve. But I assure you, my daring friend, you will get no farther than the lobby of that building before you are killed or captured."

Khalil had not argued with Malik, but again he thought that his mentor displayed too much caution. The Americans, in general, were arrogant, and their military and their security forces thought of themselves as invincible, which made them careless. And, he was certain, they had learned nothing on September 11, and nothing in the year and a half since then.

In any case, his Al Qaeda friends had told him they would pick the target, and for security reasons the target would not be revealed to him until the end of his mission.

Amir broke into his thoughts and said, "Sir? Perhaps we should not park here too long."

"Are you nervous, Amir?"

"Yes, sir."

Khalil reminded him, "You are doing nothing wrong, Amir. So do not act like a guilty man."

"Yes, sir."

"Go."

Amir put the taxi in gear and moved slowly south on Broadway. He inquired, "The World Trade Center?"

"Yes."

Amir continued south. He said, "There is an observation platform from which you can see the site." He added, "It has become an attraction for tourists."

"Good. I pray there will be more such attractions in the years to come."

Amir did not reply.

They turned west onto Cortlandt Street, and Amir said, "Straight ahead, sir, is where the Towers once stood. The elevated platform is a block to the right, and if you wish to see the hole in the earth, I will stop near this platform."

Khalil replied, "Yes, good. But first I must go to see the building of the Internal Revenue Service, which I am told is on Murray Street."

Amir did not ask why his passenger needed to see that building, and he turned right on Church Street and passed beside the observation platform.

Khalil could see that there were a number of people

entering and exiting from the long platform, but otherwise these streets were nearly deserted.

Amir turned left into Murray Street, a one-way street of dark office buildings. Khalil noted that there were a few vehicles parked at the curbs, but no moving vehicles except his taxi, and no pedestrians.

Amir pointed to the left and said, "There is the building of the American tax authorities."

"Stop across the street."

Amir pulled to the curb opposite the building.

Khalil said, "I will walk back to the observation platform from here."

"Yes, sir." Amir put the vehicle in park and asked in a carefully worded sentence, "Will I be continuing my service to you, sir?"

"I think not."

"Yes, sir . . . Our mutual friend mentioned a compensation—"

"Of course." Khalil leaned down to the floor and took from his overnight bag a long ice pick, and also an American baseball cap that said "Mets" on the crown. He assured Amir, "You did an excellent job."

"Thank you, sir."

Khalil gripped the wooden handle with his right hand, looked around to be sure they were alone, then glanced up to determine the position of Amir's head and the clearance of the roof. He then brought the ice pick around in a wide, powerful swing. The tip of the pick easily pierced Amir's skull and entered through the top right portion of his head.

Amir's right hand flew back and grabbed Khalil's

hand, which still gripped the ice pick. Amir seemed confused about what had happened, and he was pulling at Khalil's hand and twisting in his seat. "What . . . ? What are you . . . ?"

"Relax, my friend. Do not upset yourself."

Amir's grip on Khalil's hand started to loosen. Khalil knew that the thin length of metal in the man's brain might not kill him immediately, so he had to wait for the internal bleeding to do its work. But Amir was taking his time about dying, and Khalil was becoming impatient. He looked through all the windows of the taxi and behind him he saw a young man entering Murray Street. He was dressed casually, and Khalil did not think he was a policeman, but he could be a problem.

Amir said weakly, "What has happened . . . ?"

Khalil extracted the ice pick, slipped it into his jacket pocket, then pushed the baseball cap over Amir's head and said to him in Arabic, "The angels shall bear thee up to Paradise." He reached over the seat and took Amir's cell phone from his shirt pocket. There were too many calls registered on Amir's phone from Khalil's phone number.

Khalil took his overnight bag and exited the taxi. The man on the sidewalk was now less than thirty meters from him, and Khalil walked toward him. The man had obviously not noticed anything that had happened in the taxi, and Khalil did not want to have to kill him on the street, but it might become necessary. He passed the man on the sidewalk and looked back at him as he approached the taxi.

The man glanced at the taxi but kept walking, and Khalil continued toward the corner of Church Street. He looked back again and was startled to see Amir out of the taxi, still wearing the baseball cap, his arms flailing and his legs trying to propel him forward. The man who had passed by the taxi continued on, unaware of Amir, who now collapsed in the street.

Khalil continued to the corner, cursing his choice of the ice pick, thinking perhaps the Glock would have been a better choice for both of them. In any case, the business was complete without too much difficulty, and as he turned the corner onto Church Street he knew that any danger to himself was past. He dropped Amir's cell phone into a storm drain and continued.

There were a few vehicles and pedestrians on Church Street, and he saw that most of the people were a few blocks ahead near the covered platform that overlooked the place where the jihadists had achieved their great victory over the Americans. He picked up his pace, anxious to see this.

As he walked, he thought about what had happened a few minutes earlier. He learned something every time he killed a man; he learned how men met their death, which was interesting, but not instructive. It was the techniques of death that concerned him—the instrument chosen, the picking of the time and place, the stalking of the victim, and his approach, and, of course, the decisions concerning a quick, painless death or a slow and painful one. Was it business or was it pleasure? He knew that Amir's death would not be immediate, but it should have been quicker and relatively painless. And yet the man had clung to life and caused himself some unnecessary anguish. He recalled that it was Boris, many years ago, who had encouraged him to choose an ice pick in certain circumstances. Boris had told him, "It is easily concealed, it is quick and silent, and it penetrates anything on the body. It is also nearly bloodless, and it is always fatal if delivered into the brain or the heart."

Khalil would have to tell the all-knowing Boris what happened with Amir. Perhaps he would even demonstrate the problem to Boris.

He thought, too, of Corey's wife, and he was pleased with his method, which could not fail to impress Khalil's compatriots and colleagues, and also strike fear into the hearts of his enemies. His only regret was that the woman's death was relatively painless, and perhaps too quick. As for Corey, he would pray for death after Khalil finished with him. Some business, much pleasure.

Khalil reached the area of the platform and saw a set of steps that ascended to the top. He followed a young couple who were dressed in shorts and T-shirts, holding hands. In Europe he'd actually seen men and women entering Christian cathedrals with their legs exposed, and he wondered if anything was sacred to these people.

He climbed the stairs and saw that the platform was covered, and it held perhaps fifty people, most of them dressed as disrespectfully as the young man and woman ahead of him. He noticed, too, that nearly every person had a camera, and they were taking pictures of the vast hole in the earth, and some people posed at the railing with the site behind them.

There were a number of hand-lettered signs stuck in various places and one of them read: HALLOWED GROUND——PLEASE BE RESPECTFUL.

Khalil recalled similar notices in the cathedrals of Europe, asking for silence and respect, and it had struck him that such admonitions should be unnecessary; surely they were unnecessary in a mosque.

Another sign said HERE, NEARLY THREE THOUSAND INNOCENT MEN, WOMEN AND CHILDREN DIED IN AN ATTACK OF UNSPEAKABLE EVIL. PRAY FOR THEM.

Rather, Khalil intended to pray for the ten men on the two aircraft who had martyred themselves here for Islam.

He noticed, too, a number of floral bouquets fastened to the railings, and this made him think of the Haytham daughter. A beautiful young woman, but quite obviously not a modest one. The worst punishment was always reserved for those who had been given the light, and then turned from it. There was no place in Paradise for the Haytham family; there was only the fires of eternal Hell.

Asad Khalil looked now over the vast excavation below him. He was surprised to see that no rubble remained, and the earth was bare, though the sides of the excavation were lined with concrete walls that rose from bottom to top, a distance of perhaps fifty meters. A large earthen ramp led into the excavation, and he saw trucks and equipment sitting motionless at the bottom of the pit.

He looked at where the North Tower had been and recalled the first attack of February 26, 1993: a van, filled with explosives, detonated in the underground parking garage. The damage to the building had been slight, and the number of people killed had not exceeded six, though a thousand were injured. There had been concern among the jihadists that this failed attack would act as a warning to the Americans and that they would understand that the Towers would again be the target. But the Americans had drawn no such conclusions, though Khalil thought that even an idiot should have known what was planned for the next time.

Khalil looked out across the open pit to the damaged buildings that bordered the destroyed area. Then he looked into the sky where the two towers had risen, and he recalled the images he had seen of people jumping from the burning buildings, hundreds of meters to their deaths. The world had seen these images, and everywhere there were public expressions of sympathy, of shock and horror, and much anger. But privately—and sometimes publicly—as he had seen and heard, there were other emotions that were not so sympathetic to the Americans. In fact, there had been much happiness among some people, and not all of them were Muslims. In truth, the Americans were not as loved as they thought they were, or as they wished to be. And when they discovered this, they seemed to be the only ones who were surprised.

A middle-aged man standing near him said to his wife, "We ought to wipe out those bastards."

"Harold. Don't say that."

"Why not?"

The woman seemed to be aware that the man standing close to them might be a foreigner. Perhaps a Muslim. She nudged her husband, took his arm, and moved him away.

Khalil smiled.

He now noticed a small group of young men and women wearing T-shirts that showed the face of a bearded man on the front, and the words "What Would Jesus Do?"

Khalil thought that was a very good question, and although he had studied the Christian testaments, which were holy to all Muslims, as were the Hebrew testaments, he could not satisfactorily answer that question. Jesus had been a great prophet, but his message of love and forgiveness did not speak to Asad Khalil. He much preferred the stern words and actions of the Hebrew prophets, who better understood the true hearts of men. Jesus, he decided, deserved to die at the hands of the Romans, who knew the danger of a man who preached peace and love.

The small group of young men and women were now kneeling at the rail, praying silently, and Khalil had no doubt that they were praying not only for the dead, but also for their enemies and asking that God forgive them. And that was good, Khalil thought; it was the first step toward the victory of their enemies. The Romans themselves became Christians and did more praying than fighting, and they, too, got what they deserved.

The sun was in the western sky, and it shone down into the covered walkways and on the faces of the people who were part mourners and part curiosity seekers. Some of them, Khalil thought, did not comprehend what had befallen them, and some only dimly understood *why* this had happened. Most of them, he was certain, saw this event as a single incident, without context and without meaning. The Americans lived in the moment, without history and thus without prophecy. Their ignorance and their arrogance, and their love of comfort and their disobedience to God, were their greatest weaknesses. The moment in which they lived was passing and there was no future for them.

The sound of sirens brought him out of his thoughts. He glanced back at Church Street and saw two police cars with their flashing beacons moving rapidly in the direction of Murray Street. He assumed they were responding to a call regarding a dead taxi driver. Or perhaps not so dead. But even if Amir survived, he knew less than the police themselves knew by now.

Amir, however, knew how Khalil was dressed, and that he was now on the observation platform of the World Trade Center. So perhaps it was time to leave.

Khalil uttered a silent prayer for the fallen martyrs and ended with his favorite verse from an ancient Arab war song. "Terrible he rode alone with his Yemen sword for aid; ornament, it carried none but the notches on the blade."

CHAPTER NINETEEN

Asad Khalil sat alone on a bench in Battery Park, so named, he understood, because this southern tip of Manhattan Island once held forts and artillery batteries to protect the city. Now it was a pleasant park with views across the bay, and the enemy was inside the city.

He opened a bottle of water that he had bought from a street vendor and took a long drink, then used some of the water to wash specks of Amir's blood from his right hand.

He put the bottle in his bag for possible future use, then retrieved the cell phones of the two dead Federal agents. He turned on the phones and saw they still had service, which surprised him. It was possible, he thought, that the police or the FBI had not yet noticed that the phones were missing. The Americans, in true cowboy fashion, always worried first about the guns.

He accessed the text messages on Haytham's phone and saw one new message, from PARESI, CAPT., ATTF/NYPD.

This was the man, he knew, who was the superior of Corey. Khalil read the message and saw that it was a short command, calling the police detectives to duty, and instructing them to begin surveillance of the Muslim community WITH SPECIAL EMPHASIS ON THE LIBYAN COMMUNITY.

This was to be expected and it did not cause him any alarm. His potential contacts in America were not all Libyans; there were his Al Qaeda friends from other Islamic nations. His only Libyan contacts so far had been Farid in California, and Amir here in New York, and both of them were now in Paradise, far beyond American surveillance.

There were no other messages on Haytham's phone, and he shut it off.

He accessed the text messages on Mayfield's phone and saw a new text from Walsh. It read: TO ALL FBI AGENTS AND NYPD DETECTIVES: TWO LIBYAN INFOR-MANTS IN NY METRO HAVE COME FORWARD WITH INFO ON SUSPECT KHALIL IN CONUS. CHECK E-MAIL FOR DE-TAILS AND OPERATIONAL INSTRUCTION REGARDING APPREHENDING SUSPECT. WALSH, SAC, ATTF/NY.

He shut off Mayfield's phone and thought about this. If this was true, it presented some problems to him and to his mission. In fact, he would not know who to trust.

He realized, though, that if this message from Walsh had been sent to all agents and all detectives, then it should have appeared on Haytham's screen. But it had not. And Walsh did not know at the time he sent his message that he, Asad Khalil, would have

Haytham's phone in his possession. So why was the message not on Haytham's phone? And why was it on Mayfield's phone? She was dead when the message was sent.

Therefore, he thought, this was a false message, sent only to Mayfield's cell phone, which Walsh must now suspect was in the hands of Asad Khalil. And this was why Mayfield's phone was still in service.

He sat back on the bench and stared out at the sunlit water. So perhaps they were being clever. But not clever enough.

Or . . . possibly it was a true message, but not actually sent to *all* detectives and agents despite the heading. Perhaps they did not trust Haytham. Or perhaps Haytham was not included for some other reason.

In truth, Khalil did not know all there was to know about the inner workings of the Task Force, which was not as well known to Libyan Intelligence—or to his new friends in Al Qaeda—as was the FBI, for instance.

In any case, this message had all the tell-tale signs of disinformation, and that was how he would regard it, which would please Boris, who had spent days teaching him about this. Boris had said, "The British are masters of disinformation, the Americans have learned from them, the French think they invented it, and the Germans are not subtle enough to put out a good lie. As for the Italians, your former colonial masters, they believe their own disinformation and act on it." Boris had concluded his lecture with, "But the best disseminators of disinformation in the world are the KGB."

Khalil had not wanted to insult his trainer by challenging him, but he had nevertheless reminded Boris that the KGB no longer existed, and so perhaps the word "are" should be replaced with "were."

Boris had gotten used to Khalil's insults, subtle and otherwise, and only laughed at them between glasses of vodka. Malik had advised Khalil to be easier on the Russian, saying, "He is a lost soul from a lost empire—the godless and godforsaken human wreckage of a sunken ship who has washed up on our shores. Use him, Khalil, but pity him. He will never leave here alive."

But he had left Libya, with the assistance of the CIA, and Boris had then sold himself to the Americans and done for them what he had done for Libyan Intelligence: betrayed secrets for money. And nearly betrayed Asad Khalil. But the day of judgment was now at hand for Boris.

The message from Walsh was undoubtedly a lie, but Khalil had to act as though it might be true. That was what Boris always advised.

As for Mayfield, they had kept her phone alive, but he was certain they had not kept her alive. There was too much blood, and it gushed from her throat as she floated to the earth. He was a good judge of this; he had seen—and caused—bleeding like this, and it always ended in death. And if by chance or Fate it didn't, then the mind was damaged, and that was far worse than the death of the body. He wondered what Allah did with these impaired people whose spirits could neither ascend into Paradise nor be banished to Hell. Perhaps, he thought, there was a place for these souls to dwell while awaiting their ultimate destination—a place where dead minds controlled aimless bodies—a place not unlike an American shopping mall.

Khalil returned to his surroundings. A breeze blew from the water, and the park was filled with people on this pleasant day. He watched them as they walked and ran, rode bicycles, and skated by. A couple sitting on the bench across from him was engaged in an immodest embrace.

On another bench, two men in shorts sat too close, drinking bottled water, talking and smiling. Khalil had seen men like this in Europe but never in Libya, or anywhere in the Islamic world.

Despite his years in Europe, and his brief visit to America, he had not gotten accustomed to this display of public affection, of bare flesh, and of the easy mingling of males and females—or men with men, and women with women. This was not God-pleasing, and it caused him to wonder how such a dissolute people continued to remain wealthy and powerful.

And then he thought again of the Romans. A guide in the Roman Museum in Tripoli had said, "They squandered the hard-won wealth of their forefathers and lived like maggots on the decaying corpse of their empire."

Yes, Khalil thought, and when they could no longer find good men to fill their legions or do the work of the empire, they paid the barbarians to do it for them. And then the gold ran out.

He opened a bag of peanuts that he had purchased from the street vendor, and cracked open a shell and ate the nuts, realizing he hadn't eaten since before dawn.

Pigeons soon began to congregate, and he threw a few nuts at them and they became excited. He watched them as they competed for the food and noticed that some were more aggressive than others, while some simply held back and did not even attempt to compete.

He threw more nuts, these still in their shells, and observed that the birds understood what they had to do to get the nuts and pecked at the shells—but they kept cocking their heads from side to side, looking for the nuts that had been shelled for them. *Their birds, too, are lazy.* He smiled.

Not far from where he sat was Wall Street, the center of American financial power. There was much debate among the jihadists about targeting this street for a future attack. Some said it was necessary, and that it would cripple the American economy. Others said that Wall Street, left intact and functioning, would do more damage to the American economy than a hundred bombs. Still others said it would soon collapse on its own.

Khalil agreed with the last assessment. The nuts were running out.

He took his binoculars from his bag and looked across the bay at the green statue that seemed to stand on the water. This, he knew, was perhaps the most iconic of American symbols; the most recognizable and most representative monument of what was called the American Dream, and the American promise. And he had been told that all Americans, regardless of their political affiliation, or their national origin, or their status in society, revered this statue. This, then, could be the intended target that would be revealed to him shortly.

He continued to stare at the green statue—this woman in robes, holding a torch in her hand—and he saw her toppling off her stone pedestal, falling face-first into the water. Yes, that would be a fitting fare-well—a permanent reminder to the Americans of his visit, and an astounding image to be broadcast around the world.

He lowered the binoculars and extended an open hand filled with nuts, and a pigeon approached cautiously. As the bird lowered its head and took a kernel, Khalil wrapped his hand around the pigeon's head and crushed its neck.

— PART V —

New York City

CHAPTER TWENTY

I slept in the chair in Kate's room, and at dawn I went out to the parking lot, found my Jeep, and collected some clothes from my luggage. Back in ICU, I dressed and sat beside Kate's bed and watched her sleeping. A nurse came in to check her chart, and I asked her to put my bloodstained jumpsuit into a plastic bag and give it to the State Troopers, who probably wanted it for evidence. Maybe they didn't, but I didn't want it, and hopefully I'd never need or see another jumpsuit for the rest of my life.

Kate woke up and she was looking remarkably well for having been at death's door, but the attending physician wanted to keep the ventilator going, so she still couldn't speak, but she wrote me notes. One said, *Find Khalil before he finds you.*

I assured her, "I will."

But in fact, I had not been his next target, as expected. Vince Paresi had telephoned me yesterday afternoon with the news about Gabe Haytham and his wife and daughter. The death of one of our own, along with his family, in his own home, had completely changed this case from an attempted murder of a Federal agent to . . . well, something quite different. I won't say that the hunters had become the hunted, but it certainly looked that way.

I knew Gabe, and I liked him and respected him, and he had been very helpful to me the last time Asad Khalil was in town. I guess Khalil knew that, too—or Khalil simply knew of an Arab-American on the Task Force and decided that Gabe Haytham was a traitor and deserved to die. But why did he kill Gabe's wife and daughter? Because they happened to be home? No, Khalil *planned* it that way. In his world, there were no innocent civilians. Anyway, Paresi had also told me that the crime scene investigator said it appeared that Gabe fought back. Good for you, Gabe.

I suppose I could blame myself for not thinking of Gabe Haytham sooner . . . and when I did, maybe I should have been more forceful with Paresi. But I wasn't going to beat myself up with this; I was going to find Asad Khalil and bring him to justice. Or, as we were saying more and more these days among ourselves, we would bring justice to them.

In any case, I didn't tell Kate about the murder of the Haytham family. I would, but not yet.

Kate wrote me a note. *How are you doing?*

I replied, "Fine. Just a little depressed about missing the next two jumps."

She wrote, *I want to jump again.*

"Great." We'll leave the Libyan terrorist home next

time. I wondered if I could sue Craig for letting Asad Khalil into the club.

Another nurse arrived to check Kate's monitors and IVs and whatever, and I used the time to think about this case.

As for news coverage of the Haytham family's murder, according to Paresi the NYPD, on the strong advice of the U.S. Department of Justice, was investigating the case as a home invasion by a person or persons unknown, motive unknown. We could get away with that for maybe a week before the press got a tip or got nosy. Or until another Federal agent turned up dead. Like me.

Since I've been in Federal law enforcement, however, it's been a little easier to mushroom—keeping the press in the dark and feeding them shit—if there's a national security angle.

Also, since 9/11, the Feds had gotten what amounted to wartime powers under the Patriot Act and other less well-known legislation. And legislation aside, the *attitudes* in the Justice Department had changed, and the people in the field doing the actual work had become more aggressive and more tight-lipped with the news media.

As for media coverage about what happened here in Sullivan County, that was fairly easy to manage. First, it happened in the middle of nowhere, and second, it looked to witnesses like an attack by a psychotic— which it actually was. As for the victim, her name was being withheld by the authorities. End of press release.

On the subject of sharing and disseminating information, I told Kate I'd call her parents and tell them what happened, without worrying them, of course. Something like, "Hi, Mr. and Mrs. Mayfield, your daughter had her throat cut by an Islamic terrorist, but she's fine now."

Kate wrote to me, in her neat handwriting, *No, I will call them when I get this fucking tube out of my throat.*

I said, "Please watch the swearing."

She wrote, *See if you can get me a laptop so I can e-mail and get on the Internet.*

I didn't want her reading about the Haythams, so I fibbed, "No laptops allowed in ICU. They emit microwaves and stuff that will screw up everyone's monitors."

She seemed to buy that, so maybe it was true.

Anyway, Dr. Goldberg arrived to check on his patient and he was all smiles. It's kind of neat saving someone's life, and it probably makes you feel very good inside. As a homicide detective, almost every crime victim I've seen was on the way to the morgue, not the hospital. And to be up front, I've put a few perpetrators in both places, and it never felt good. Well . . . sometimes it did.

On the subject of rough justice, I recalled again my last conversation with Asad Khalil on Kate's cell phone, three years ago. He'd said to us, "I just wanted to say good-bye and to remind you that I will be back."

He had apparently developed a strong personal dislike of me and of Kate as well. And to be frank, we didn't like him either. I mean, the asshole was trying to kill us. Not surprisingly, our professional relationship—lawbreaker and law enforcer—had deteriorated into an unhealthy personal animus. Asad Khalil had given up on his planned mission and I'd given up trying to arrest him; the new game was called Kill the Other Guy. Simple.

So when he told me three years ago that he'd be back, I had replied with enthusiasm, "Looking forward to a rematch."

That's when he said to me, "I will kill you and kill that whore you are with, if it takes me all of my life."

I looked at Kate in the bed, and I recalled that she wasn't real happy with Asad Khalil calling her a whore. And, you know, I don't blame her. On the other hand, there *are* cultural differences to consider, and as I'd explained to her then, she, as a Federal employee, needed to be sensitive to Asad Khalil's more traditional upbringing regarding gender roles. Hopefully we could resolve these differences before I killed him.

Dr. Goldberg was speaking and he seemed happy with his patient's progress. He assured us that Kate could be moved by medical helicopter to the city in about two days, then a few more days in the hospital, then home, and back to duty within a month. Sounded good, but I could tell that Kate thought that was too long.

After Dr. Goldberg left, she wrote to me, *I want to be back to work next week.*

I replied, "Let's get you home first. I need to evaluate the extent of your mental impairment."

She tried to flash me the peace sign, but in her weakened condition, she only managed to raise her middle finger.

I wanted to get on the road and get back to work, but I spent another half hour with her. She scribbled a lot of questions regarding what was going on with the case, and I told her what I knew, except about the death of the Haytham family. I also didn't tell her that her cell phone and gun were missing and probably in the hands of her assailant. That kind of thing really gets to a cop or an FBI agent, and though Kate was not at fault, she'd take it badly. Neither did I want to get into exactly what happened after we stepped out of the aircraft, but I knew from her written questions that she was searching for some kind of reassurance that she had done all she could in regard to Asad Khalil getting the upper hand on her. This was a matter of ego—she felt, like most assault victims, violated. Also her professional pride was wounded. Daddy was an FBI agent and his little girl could hold her own with the big bad meanies and all that.

So I said to her, honestly, "He's bigger and stronger than you. Plus he planned this and he's not stupid. You did all you could, and you saved your own life by deflecting the knife. It's a draw. We'll win the next round."

She nodded to herself, then wrote, *I tried to knee him in the nuts, but he had his legs wrapped around mine.*

"That's why he had his legs wrapped around yours."

I took the opportunity to tell her that the EMS

team had performed spectacularly and that I would send a note to their supervisor.

She nodded.

I certainly didn't want to blow my own horn and tell her about how I had bravely risked my own life to get her into free fall so she wouldn't bleed to death. And neither would I mention that I had quickly and expertly stopped her bleeding for a crucial minute before the EMS arrived. No, John Corey is a modest man and seeing Kate alive and healthy was all the reward I needed for my heroic actions.

I was sure, however, that Kate would want to read my full incident report, in which I was obligated to recount all these things in some detail. Plus, she might want to see the videotape of the jump. Then she would draw her own conclusions about her husband's bravery and quick thinking. And I, of course, would say, "Just doing my job." I might also mention that Craig fainted when he saw her bleeding.

I said to her, "Well, I really have to get to the office so I can write my incident report." Apparently her mind was elsewhere, so I added, "There's a lot to tell."

She nodded absently, then wrote on her pad and showed it to me. It said, *I want to kill him.*

I tore the page from her notepad and put it in my pocket. Even post-9/11, we're not supposed to say—or write—things like that. I assured her, "We will apprehend him and bring him to justice."

She knew, of course, that John Corey had something else in mind, and she made a cutting motion across her throat. I winked.

She began scribbling on her pad again and handed it to me. Her note said, *Khalil, like last time, has contacts here. He kills his contacts. If a dead Libyan turns up, check his cell phone and phone records and see who called him recently and who he called. One of those numbers will be Khalil's cell phone. Get CAU on that phone number.*

I smiled and handed the pad back to her. "Good thinking." All we needed was to find a dead Libyan who owned a cell phone and we'd be in business. I also said to her, "I think you just passed your neurological examination."

She wrote, *Good luck on yours.*

I smiled again and said to her, "I'm heading back to the office. I'll keep in touch with the hospital and we'll get you out of here as soon as possible. Meanwhile, get some rest and follow doctor's orders." I added, "And since you're not doing anything else, think about this case."

I kissed her on the cheek and she grabbed my hand and squeezed it. Then wrote, *Be very, very careful.*

Indeed.

CHAPTER TWENTY-ONE

I went first to the nurses' station and reminded them to be security conscious, though in truth I thought the immediate danger had passed; Asad Khalil was obviously in the New York City area where he'd murdered Gabe and his family. Still, he could easily return here if he thought Kate was alive. She'd be safer in Bellevue Hospital in Manhattan where guarding injured victims, witnesses, or prisoners was an everyday occurrence. I mean, the last time an assault victim had to be guarded in Sullivan County, he had a musket ball in him. Anyway, I arranged a code phrase—Crazy John—that would allow me to get medical updates.

I went next to the elevators where there was a new shift of uniformed State Troopers, and I chatted with them for a few minutes. I was much less worried about Kate so I think I made a slightly better impression on these two, plus I was dressed now in neat trousers and an expensive sports jacket that I had intended to wear to the après-jump party where I was going to push Craig's face in the toilet bowl.

I reiterated to the troopers, "This guy is a good impersonator." A good joke makes a good point, so I said, "If in doubt about someone, ask him if he smokes Camels or rides them."

They smiled politely.

Satisfied that everything was under control here, medically and otherwise, I took the elevator to the lobby and went into the gift shop, where I bought a cute stuffed lion for Kate and asked them to deliver it to her room. I'm a thoughtful guy. And speaking of growling, my stomach was making noises, so I bought some crap snacks and a coffee, then went out to the parking lot and got into my Jeep.

I began the two-hour drive back to Manhattan. It was another perfect day, and the mountains in May are really nice. I could see why Kate sometimes spoke about getting a place up here.

I opened a bag of cheese maggots or something and began stuffing them down my throat. How can they sell this crap in a hospital?

My cell phone rang, and I took the call. I have a hands-off feature for talking while driving—I take my hands off the wheel.

It was Captain Paresi, who asked, "How's Kate?"

"On the road to recovery."

"Good. Where are you?"

"On the road to New York."

"Okay. Look, a body was discovered by a commuter early this morning at the Douglaston train station near Gabe's house. The victim was a livery driver, found behind the wheel of his Lincoln Town Car, with two bullet wounds fired through the back of his seat."

Coincidence? I think not.

Paresi gave me a few more details of the murder, including the reclining position of the body covered with a newspaper.

I asked, "Which paper?"

"Which . . . ? I think Newsday."

"Then maybe he died of boredom."

He continued, "The M.E. says the victim could have been dead since about noon yesterday, give or take a few hours. He'll know better later, but that fits the timeline in regard to the . . . Haytham murders."

"Right." I asked, "Was the victim a Mideastern gentleman?"

"The coroner's report describes him as an obese Caucasian, mid-thirties, name of Charles Taylor." He continued, "Forensics recovered two bullets from the dashboard, and they were .40 caliber. Ballistics is comparing them to the ballistic file on Kate's weapon."

"Okay. We won't be surprised to discover a match."

"No, we won't." He informed me, "They lifted lots of prints from the limo and of course from the Haytham residence." He asked, "Do we have Khalil's prints on file?"

"We do. They printed him at the American Embassy in Paris three years ago."

"Good. So, if we get a match, that nails it all down. The limo driver and the Haytham family."

"Right. Plus, as you mentioned yesterday, Khalil

called the responding officers at Gabe's house from Gabe's cell phone and threatened to kill me next. And, as you also mentioned, someone using Gabe's cell phone, who we will assume was Asad Khalil, called Walsh and inquired about Kate's condition. Also, we have Kate's positive ID of Asad Khalil as her assailant, not to mention my ID of him. So, yeah, we might have a good case against him."

Captain Paresi detected a note of sarcasm in my voice and said, "We need the *forensic* evidence, Detective, to have an airtight case. I don't have to tell you what those defense attorneys can do with eyewitness testimony and circumstantial evidence."

Indeed, I knew what defense attorneys could do, which was why prosecutors needed forensic evidence. A lot of this crap could be avoided if they tried terrorists in a military tribunal instead of Federal court. In this case, however, it was better to skip the trial, pass jail, and go directly to the morgue.

Captain Paresi continued, "They also found two .40 caliber shell casings under the driver's seat and a plastic water bottle with two holes in the bottom."

I informed Captain Paresi, "The water bottle is Khalil's M.O. from last time." I added, "It's not the best silencer, but it's better than nothing, and he seems happy with it."

Paresi speculated, "If the bullets are from Kate's weapon, that could mean Khalil has no weapon of his own."

I replied, "If Khalil has contacts in this country— and I'm sure he does—then he has his own gun." I concluded, "He *chose* to use Kate's gun to say to us, 'Fuck you.'"

"Yeah . . . I guess . . ." He further informed me, "Ballistics confirms that Gabe was also killed with Kate's gun."

Captain Paresi seemed uncomfortable telling me that it was Kate's weapon that killed Gabe, and probably killed the livery driver. I changed the subject and asked, "What else?"

He continued his briefing. "We contacted Charles Taylor's livery company on Long Island and discovered that Mr. Taylor was to pick up a passenger at Republic by the name of Mr. Brian Gold and take him to a destination or destinations as directed by the customer." He added, "The livery company was prepaid by credit card, and we're trying to track down the cardholder, which is a corporation in Lichtenstein . . . where the hell is that?"

"I think it's near Hoboken."

"Yeah, anyway, the corporation is called Global Entertainment, and they have a P.O. box or something."

"Right. Global Entertainment." I advised him, "Tell Walsh not to waste too much time on the money trail. Let the Treasury Department go nuts with that."

"Agreed." He concluded, "We're checking Taylor's GPS for clues."

"Good." I asked, "Okay, so did Charles Taylor take Asad Khalil, a.k.a. Brian Gold, to the Haytham house?" I answered my own question and said, "Not likely. Khalil met up with someone else, probably at the train station after he whacked Taylor." Recalling Khalil's last visit and Kate's advice, I said, "Look for a dead Libyan cab driver."

After a few seconds of awed silence, Paresi informed me, "We got one." He asked, "How did you know?"

"Tell me about it."

"I'll let Walsh tell you."

"All right. But tell me if they found a cell phone on this dead Libyan taxi driver."

"They did not." He let me know, "But we're checking his cell phone records."

"Excellent detective work. So where did *this* body turn up? How was he killed?"

Paresi ignored my questions and said, "Next subject. The medical examiner confirms that Gabe's daughter died of the knife wound, which entered her heart. No surprise there. And the M.E. also says that the wife died of a broken neck." He stayed silent a second, then said, "And those flowers on the daughter's chest . . ." He concluded, "This guy is a very coldhearted killer. Up close and personal."

"Right." Like using Gabe's cell phone to call the cops who'd just found three murdered people in the house. Khalil never missed a chance to stick something up our asses. Can you hear me now?

Captain Paresi went on, "Based on what the M.E. said about the time of death, and what the two responding officers discovered, I think we just missed Khalil by . . . maybe minutes."

I informed him, "Those two responding officers just missed death by minutes."

There was a silence, then Paresi said, "I wish I'd

gotten a patrol car there sooner. Maybe we could have
. . . headed this off." He let me know, "The wife was
actually alive when the police arrived and she died in
the ambulance."

I advised him, "Move on."

Paresi did not reply.

The last time Asad Khalil was here, he had been
either very lucky—he'd say blessed—or very smart.
This time, however, with the murder of Gabe and his
family, Khalil had very nearly made a fatal mistake.
That was a hopeful sign. Or it was simply a one-time
miscalculation on his part—and he learned from his
mistakes.

Paresi took the opportunity to remind me, "You are
likely to be the next person who interacts with him."

"Right. He wants to interact with me next."

Paresi also reminded me, "Walsh and everyone in
Washington want him alive."

"Well, they *think* they do, Captain. But what are
they going to *do* with him? If he's captured in the U.S.,
he cannot be sent to Guantánamo. Do they want this
guy being tried in Federal court in New York where he
can say things that the press and the public shouldn't
hear?" I reminded him, "His whole file is classified."

"I see that. I went into the ACS and the Khalil file
has more Xs than I do."

Vince Paresi had been married multiple times, so
I got the joke and chuckled politely. The Automated
Case System was the FBI's version of Google, and all
you needed was a topic and your ATTF password
and you could access virtually any case—active and

inactive—in the FBI databank. There were, however, internal blocks on restricted files and all you
saw were rows of Xs.

Usually, though, you can get *something* from restricted files, like the date the file was opened, or at least
who you needed to contact about getting access. But
I've seen the Khalil file and there wasn't much there that
you couldn't get from the wanted poster, and there was
no clue about who to see regarding those Xs.

Paresi asked me, "Where is the file that you and Gabe
kept on Khalil?"

I replied, "I'll find it when I get to the office."

"Okay. Where are you now?"

"I'm on scenic Route Seventeen. Maybe an hour
and a half from my desk."

"Let me know when you get here. We have a
meeting at noon in Walsh's office." He informed me,
"We have more info, and I'll let Walsh tell you what
we have."

"Tell me now. I have an hour and a half to kill."

"I don't want to ruin his presentation."

"Who's at the meeting?"

"Your other lion hunter, George Foster, you, and
me." He said, "Walsh wants to keep it small and
focused."

Meaning quiet and restricted. Kate and Gabe
would have been there, too, but the Lion Hunter team
was getting smaller.

Captain Paresi confided in me, "Walsh thinks you're
a loose cannon. So watch yourself at this meeting."

Loose cannon? *Me?*

I poured the last of the cheese maggots down my throat, chewed, and, recalling my last case, reminded him, "Kate and I saved the world from nuclear destruction."

"But what have you done for us lately?"

"Well . . . at the moment, I'm just lion's bait."

"Or his next meal." He hung up.

CHAPTER TWENTY-TWO

I continued along Route 17.

I used the driving time to think about Gabe and some of the insights he'd given me about Asad Khalil three years ago. Gabe had never met Khalil—until yesterday—but he was able to come up with a sort of psychological profile on his co-religionist. He'd explained to me about the blood feud—the obligation of an Arab male to avenge the murder of a family member. This, more than political ideology or religion, was what drove and motivated Asad Khalil; the Americans had killed his family and he was honor-bound to kill those responsible—and also kill those who tried to keep him from his duty. Like me. And Kate. And Gabe. And probably others.

Gabe had also mentioned to me the ancient Arab tradition of the lone warrior, the avenger who is a law unto himself, not unlike the American cowboy hero. Gabe had recited a verse that sort of summed it up. "Terrible he rode alone with his Yemen sword for aid;

ornament, it carried none but the notches on the blade."

Therefore it was very possible that Asad Khalil intended to meet John Corey alone, man to man, with no accomplices, and no purpose other than to see who was the better man—the better killer.

And that was fine with me. I love a challenge.

My cell phone rang, and I answered, "Corey."

It was Investigator Matt Miller, who, after inquiring about Kate and after discovering I was headed back to Manhattan, told me, "We've impounded the rental car that we found in the airport parking lot." He also told me they'd taken fingerprints and fiber samples from it and so forth. No doubt we had enough forensic, eyewitness evidence, and circumstantial evidence to convict Asad Khalil of a variety of crimes. All we had to do now was find him.

Khalil himself wasn't taking any care about covering his crimes, and he didn't give a rat's ass about leaving evidence or announcing his identity. All Khalil was worried about—if he worried at all—was staying one step ahead of us and getting back to Sandland with more notches on his blade. And all I was worried about was making sure that didn't happen.

I changed the subject and asked Miller, "Did you speak to Craig Hauser? The president of the skydiving club?"

"Yes, I spoke to him directly. He really didn't know much about the new sign-on who turned out to be the suspect."

"You sure?"

"Yes . . . why? Do you think he knows more than he's telling?"

I *never* use my police powers to settle a personal grudge, so I shouldn't do that now.

Miller informed me, "He's very concerned about your wife. He wants to visit her in the hospital."

"Book him."

"I . . . what . . . ?"

"Just kidding. Hey, did the club do their other two jumps?"

"No. They weren't able to."

"Right. The jump zone is a crime scene. Good call." I want a refund.

"No, it wasn't that. The old plane they were using had a problem on takeoff. One of the engines caught fire." He added, "Too much leaking oil or something."

Aha! I *knew* it. Wait until I tell Kate.

He assured me, "No injuries or anything."

Fate. I wondered if Cindy did the takeoff. *Ralph, is that engine supposed to be burning?*

He informed me, "We also confiscated the video-tape of your skydive as evidence."

"Good."

He hesitated, then said, "I watched it." He added, "Incredible." He further added, "You're a brave man, Detective Corey."

This is true, but I replied, "You saw what Khalil was capable of."

"I did. But he's not brave—he's psychotic."

I agreed, "He's a little over the top." I told you so.

Investigator Miller assured me, "I got hold of the tape before the cameraman could sell it to the evening news. Also, I distributed a notice to each member of the skydiving club strongly advising them not to speak to the press while this case was under investigation."

I asked him, "Where is the videotape?"

He replied, "The FBI has possession of it."

"Has anyone from the FBI or the Terrorist Task Force mentioned to you any other attacks that may be linked to this suspect?" I asked him.

"No. Why?"

"Just wondering." I advised him, "I think you can assume that Asad Khalil is gone from your jurisdiction."

"Do you think he was on that Citation jet?"

"Maybe. I told you—he used charter aircraft last time."

"Okay. But Walsh seems to think he might still be here."

"It's your call," I said noncommittally. "Anything else?"

"No. But I've also been advised that you are not the case agent and that I need to speak only to whoever is assigned to this case."

"Okay. But let's stay in touch."

"That's not what I just said."

"You just called me," I reminded him.

"This was a one-time courtesy."

Right. Cop to cop. I said, "Well, I hope the FBI extends you some courtesies."

He didn't reply to that, but he did say, "I have a half dozen FBI agents in my headquarters."

I assured him, "They're from the government and they're there to help you." I reminded him, "There are homeland security considerations with this case, so you may be asked to do or say—or *not* do or say—some things that you think you should be doing or saying."

He did not reply.

I said, "As a for instance, do you intend to interview the victim?"

Again, he didn't reply, and I knew that the FBI had already told him to forget about talking to Kate.

He did say, "My new FBI friends in my office say they're moving your wife out of here tomorrow morning."

That was news to me. Obviously, they wanted her out of the jurisdiction of the State Police and back in Manhattan where they could keep a tighter lid on the case and on the information leaks.

We seemed to have run out of things to speak about, so I said, "I appreciate the call."

"Let me know how this turns out."

I couldn't promise that, but I said, "If I find him, I'll let you know."

Investigator Miller added, "And if he finds you, I'll see it on the news."

Not funny, Investigator Miller.

We hung up and I continued along the state highway, then exited onto the New York State Thruway, whose sign promised NEW YORK—50 MILES.

I turned on the radio and scanned a few local channels to see if the psychotic skydiver had made the news, but I didn't hear anything. The newscaster went on to national news, and I was certain now that the skydiving incident would not be mentioned on the news.

I tuned in to a New York City all-news station and listened for any mention of the Haytham murders or the murder of the livery driver, Charles Taylor, in Douglaston, Queens, or the Libyan taxi driver. I waited through the entire news cycle, but none of those murders were mentioned.

So the FBI and the Task Force had done half their job; they'd kept the press in the dark and fed the local police bullshit. Now the Feds could control the search for Khalil and decide for themselves what to do with him if they caught him.

The newspapers, with more space to fill, would have some ink on these murders, but I was pretty sure it would be straight reporting with no speculation and not a clue about any connections.

I crossed into New Jersey and instantly the drivers became insane, weaving in and out, hitting their brakes for no reason, and signaling the opposite of what they were going to do. You're supposed to let your mind wander when you drive in New Jersey, so I took my mind off the road and thought about what Vince Paresi was saying to me.

It occurred to me that this noon meeting in Walsh's

office might actually be less about Asad Khalil and more about John Corey. Apparently I had become a problem.

I don't usually get paranoid about my career because, one, I'm good at what I do, and two, I don't need the job. My old bud, Dick Kearns, formerly of the NYPD, is now a private background investigator, a big growth business since 9/11, and he's offered me a partnership. "Half the work, double the money, and no bosses and no bullshit."

Sounds like a little bit of heaven. But for now, I really needed to stay with the Feds until Mr. Khalil and I interacted one last time.

CHAPTER TWENTY-THREE

As I approached the Holland Tunnel, I glanced at where the Towers once stood across the Hudson River. The geniuses involved with the World Trade Center reconstruction were still arguing about what to build there, and at the rate they were going, it would be two or three more years before the first I-beam was put in place. Meanwhile, the hole in the ground was a top tourist attraction, and a constant reminder of a very bad day.

As I waited in line at the toll booths, a young uniformed Port Authority cop stopped me and said, "Just a security check, sir. Can I see your driver's license?"

Why me? Do I look suspicious? It must be my big blue eyes. Meanwhile, Abdul in front of me is driving an eighteen-wheeler through the frickin' tunnel, filled with God-knows-what, and all he gets is a wave.

"Sir?"

I showed him my NYPD shield and my Federal ID, and he said to me, "Have a nice day, Detective."

"Why me?"

"It's just random. Every sixth vehicle."

"Would you play the horses that way?"

"I just do what I'm told. Have a nice day."

I raised my window and moved into the tunnel. *Well*, I thought, *don't just do what you're told.* I don't. Show some initiative and common sense or you're going to lose that tunnel.

I exited the tunnel and made my way through the busy streets of Lower Manhattan. There were parking spaces reserved for official government business along Broadway, though no parking was allowed in front of 26 Fed since 9/11. But for some inexplicable reason, there *was* parking allowed in front of 290 Broadway, the government building next door—Official Government Business, No Terrorists, No Car Bombs. I found a nice space in front of 290 and parked.

While I was looking to see where Kate hid the parking permit—glove compartment? Under the driver's seat? Behind the sun visor?—a uniformed cop sauntered over and knocked on my window.

I rolled down my window, and he said to me, "Official business only."

"Right. I'm looking for my permit." I handed him my Fed creds and flashed my NYPD detective shield while I rummaged under the passenger seat. Why the hell does she pick a different place every time?

The cop, whose name plate said "Timmons," handed me my creds and said, "Thank you, Detective."

He was about to move off, but I took a shot and asked him, "Hey, do you know anything about the murder of a cab driver? Arab-American guy. Libyan. Happened . . . maybe yesterday."

"Where?"

"I don't know. How many Arab cab drivers have been murdered recently?"

"One. Happened yesterday afternoon on Murray Street." He let me know, "We got a BOLO on the suspect."

"You got a suspect?"

"Yeah. I got a photo in the car."

"Good. Hey, if you were a woman, where would you put the parking permit?"

I thought he was going to say to me, "You're the detective," but he said, wisely, "I don't even want to go there."

"Right. How'd this guy get clipped?"

"Something like an ice pick in his head."

"Ouch." I asked, "What was the victim's name?"

He was wondering, I'm sure, why I didn't ask my boss these questions, and I thought he was going to ask to see my creds again, but he replied, "His name was Amir . . . some Arab name."

"Maybe it's in her purse. Would she put it in her purse?"

"I don't know. But you need it to park here or you're gonna get towed." He reminded me, "High-security zone."

"Right. I work here." Car bomb towing zone. I asked Officer Timmons, "What was the name of the suspect?"

"We don't have a name."

"But you have a photo."

"Right. But no name."

Interesting. I asked him, "Where did the photo come from?"

"I don't know." He said, "But we're looking for another Arab guy." He added, "Last seen wearing a dark blue sports jacket, tan pants, and a light blue shirt."

The last time I saw Khalil, he was wearing a black jumpsuit with a matching helmet. I assumed this description was from the pilots, who were probably the only living people who could ID Khalil's clothing.

I asked Officer Timmons, "Any particulars on the incident?"

He replied, "Homicide Squad says it wasn't a robbery, so it looks like Abdul A knew Abdul B and maybe they had some sort of disagreement."

"Right." I asked him, "If you don't have a name, how can you be sure the suspect was an Arab?"

"That's what I was told." He added, "The guy in the photo is not Irish."

Recalling the wanted poster, I asked, "Dark complexion, slicked-back hair, hooked nose, and crazy eyes?"

"Yeah. I got it in the car. You want to see it?"

"No."

"It's on the floor," Timmons said.

"You should have it on the dashboard."

"No, your parking permit. It's on the floor behind you."

"Really?" I twisted around and sure enough, there it was. Did I put it there?

Anyway, the cop moved off. I retrieved the permit and put it in the windshield, locked the car, and began walking toward 26 Federal Plaza.

It was a really nice day and everyone on the street seemed happy to be alive. Me too. I'll bet even Asad Khalil was happy to be alive. He had a good Sunday. Five dead. Almost six. And maybe a few more we didn't know about yet. Amazing.

Well, assuming Amir the taxi driver was murdered by Khalil the asshole, then that put Khalil in Manhattan yesterday, a few blocks from here. So, first Sullivan County, then Republic Airport, then Douglaston, Queens, and then Manhattan. Like last time, he moved fast.

Three years ago, Asad Khalil had come to America to murder the surviving United States Air Force pilots who had bombed his Tripoli neighborhood in 1986. The names of those pilots were supposed to be highly classified information, and no one in Washington wanted the American public, the American military, or the world to know that American security had been breached, and that American servicemen had been assassinated at home for doing their job overseas. Not good for troop morale or what it said about what we now called homeland security, and certainly not good for the image of American power.

Therefore, Washington had kept a tight lid on those murders three years ago, and they had managed to keep the press from connecting them. The same thing was happening this time.

This time, however, I understood what was happening. So the outcome would be different. Not necessarily better than last time, but different.

CHAPTER TWENTY-FOUR

Outside of 26 Federal Plaza are guard booths, manned by the private firm of Wackenhut Security. This arrangement represents some very advanced thinking from Washington that goes by the name of outsourcing. I mean, why use highly trained Federal law officers who are sworn to duty, when for twice the money you can get a fat guy in a silly uniform who may have trouble getting his gun out of his holster? Call me cynical, but I think I see some people making money on these government contracts. Maybe I should outsource myself.

Anyway, I made it through Wackenhut Security and entered 26 Federal Plaza through the Duane Street entrance.

The big lobby inside was manned by a second echelon of security personnel, in this case an outfit called the FBI Police, who are uniformed officers and whose jurisdiction is strictly confined to Federal property. So if terrorists started shooting from the city sidewalk, theoretically all the FBI Police could do would be to watch from the windows and yell encouragement to the Wackenhut guys. I hoped somebody thought to call the NYPD.

Anyway, I walked toward the security area that surrounded the elevator banks.

Twenty-six Federal Plaza is, as the name suggests, a U.S. government building, and its 44 floors house various tax-eating agencies, most of them filled with civil servants who agonize over how best to serve the American public.

Floors 22 through 29, however, are different; this is where the FBI and the Anti-Terrorist Task Force are located, along with other law enforcement and national security agencies that will go unnamed. Okay, I'll name one—the CIA. Actually, most of their offices are across Duane Street at 290 Broadway, a newer and nicer Federal building, but we are fortunate to have a few of our Comrades In Arms here at 26 Fed. Conversely, we have some ATTF personnel at 290 Broadway. The purpose of this, I assume, is to not put all our eggs in one basket in case a plane or a truck bomb takes out one of the buildings. A worse scenario would be both buildings. Shit happens. That's why we have Wackenhut. And that's why I have a St. Michael medal in my desk drawer.

Anyway, also housed here at 26 Fed is the Bureau of Immigration and Customs Enforcement, who work closely with us to locate illegal aliens who could possibly be national security risks. They do a good job, especially since 9/11, but unfortunately they busted my Costa Rican cleaning lady last month, and I think it was Tom Walsh who tipped them off. Just kidding?

I went up to the thick Plexiglas walls that surround the elevators and punched in my code to open the door. I know most of the FBI Police here and they know me, but to be respectful and proper I held up my Fed creds, and a guy named Walt said, "Sorry to hear about Detective Haytham and his family."

"Me too." I asked him, "Any news on that?"

He shook his head and replied, "Just what's in the papers." He added, "Damned shame. I mean, a cop getting killed by a robber."

"Yeah." Walt didn't mention Kate's encounter with the psychotic skydiver, so I guess the word wasn't out on that yet.

An elevator arrived, and I climbed aboard and pushed the button for the 28th floor where Tom Walsh has his big corner office.

On the way up, I thought about Asad Khalil, who, in a manner of speaking, had called this meeting. This was a unique individual, possessed of some native intelligence and good primitive instincts. I needed to give him credit for his dedication to his mission and his ability to operate in an alien and hostile environment. I mean, the guy was a friggin' camel jockey who probably couldn't tell the difference between an ATM machine and a condom dispenser, and here he was in America jumping out of planes, chartering flights, whacking people in their homes and cars, and making us look stupid.

True, he had been highly trained by Libyan Intelligence, and he had spent some time in Europe. But Libyan Intelligence is an oxymoron, and basically Khalil was an unsophisticated rube from a backward shithole of a country, so none of this was computing.

True, he'd had some resources here then, and I was sure he had resources now, like the late Amir guy whose head Khalil mistook for a block of ice. But local Libyans were only part of the reason for Khalil's success; he had smarts and balls. Worse, he believed God was on his side. Still . . . that didn't explain his James Bond savvy and sophisticated M.O. And then it hit me.

Boris.

I stepped off the elevator and stood in the hallway.

Boris. A former KGB guy, hired by Libyan Intelligence to train Asad Khalil.

Boris had not only trained Khalil in the art of killing, deception, disguises, escape, and evasion; he'd also briefed him on how to get by in the Western world—practical things like making airline reservations, checking into a hotel, chartering a plane, renting a car, and all the other things Khalil had done here three years ago, and was doing now. Plus, Boris spoke nearly flawless English, learned at the old KGB School for American Studies, and he'd tutored his motivated student in the finer points of American English.

And this brought me to my next thought: Khalil wanted to kill Boris.

The first and only time I met Boris was at CIA Headquarters in Langley, Virginia, three years ago, after Khalil had given us the slip. Boris had actually wanted to meet me and Kate, and we spent a pleasant hour chatting about the only thing we had in common: Asad Khalil.

Boris had also indicated that the Libyans intended to terminate his employment—and his life—after he gave Khalil his last lesson. But Boris had gotten out of Libya alive, with a little help from the CIA, and when Kate and I met him, he was spilling the beans about Libyan Intelligence to his new CIA friends, and probably giving up some old KGB secrets while he was at it.

And in return, according to standard CIA procedures, Boris would get an American passport and some other considerations, like maybe a lifetime supply of Marlboros and Stoli, which I recalled he seemed to enjoy.

Boris (no last name, please) was an impressive man, and I would have liked to spend more time with him, but this was a one-shot deal, and he was surrounded by his CIA keepers, who acted like wives, kicking him under the table when he and the vodka said too much. In addition, Kate and I had a few FBI guys with us who also put some restrictions on the conversation. But I did remember that he said he always wanted to see New York, and that perhaps we'd meet again.

I also recalled now the end of the conversation when Boris, speaking of Asad Khalil, said to me and Kate, "That man is a perfect killing machine, and what he doesn't kill today, he will kill tomorrow."

I'd kind of figured that out for myself, but to be contrary, I had replied, "He's just a man."

To which Boris replied, "Sometimes I wonder."

Apparently, Asad Khalil, The Lion, had taken on mythological proportions in the minds of his friends and his enemies—just like Carlos the Jackal had—so if I could get my hands on Khalil and cut his throat, then I'd be known as John Corey, Lion Killer. Better than John Corey, Loose Cannon. Right? Tom Walsh and I would fly to Washington for dinner in the White House. *We're serving pigs-in-a-blanket especially for you, Mr. Corey.*

Or, the people in Washington might not have such a positive response to me killing Khalil. *We're charging you with pre-meditated murder, Detective Corey.* Pre-meditated? I only thought about it three years ago.

Anyway, Boris had ended our tea-and-vodka hour with these words: "I congratulate you both on your survival. Don't waste any of your days."

Thanks for the advice. I hope Boris had taken his own advice. Bottom line on Boris—I liked him, but I didn't like what he'd done, which was to create a monster. And I was sure that Boris was going to regret this himself—if he hadn't already met his monster.

But if Boris *was* alive, then I needed to find him and warn him that his former student was back in the USA to settle some old scores. Of course, I should assume that the CIA had already done this for their defector, but with those guys you never knew who they had no further use for.

Aside from my benevolent motive of wanting to warn Boris, I also wanted to speak to him about how best to find Asad Khalil. Boris should have a few thoughts on that. Probably, though, he'd advise me, "Bend over and kiss your ass good-bye."

And finally, if Boris was not yet dead, then he would make good bait. Better him than me. Right?

Actually, there was a lot of bait out there for The Lion—me, Boris, George Foster, and probably other people we didn't know about. Plus, Kate, if Khalil discovered she was alive.

And of course there was Chip Wiggins, retired U.S. Air Force officer whose bombing mission over Libya had started this unhappy chain of events. I was fairly certain, however, that Chip Wiggins had by now met up with Asad Khalil, and thus had finally met his inevitable fate. *What he doesn't kill today, he will kill tomorrow.* I was sure I'd hear the results of our search for Wiggins at this meeting.

I opened the hallway door with my pass code, and as I walked toward Tom Walsh's office, I thought about forgetting to mention Boris at this meeting. I mean, the FBI does this to me. Right? Like the Iranian diplomat going to Atlantic City. What goes around comes around.

CHAPTER TWENTY-FIVE

Tom Walsh's secretary, Kathy, greeted me and said, "Mr. Walsh will be arriving shortly. Go right in and have a seat."

"Thanks." Forgetting protocol, I asked her, "Where is he?"

She hesitated, then said, "Across the street."

Which meant 290 Broadway, which could mean the CIA.

I walked into Walsh's corner office, where Captain Paresi was sitting at the round conference table across from FBI Special Agent George Foster. They looked grim. I also noticed there were bottles of water on the table—long meeting—and no notepads. Nothing leaves this room.

I shook hands with both men, and George inquired, "How's Kate?"

"Resting comfortably, thank you."

He remarked, "This is unbelievable."

I replied, "George, *you* more than anyone know this is not unbelievable."

He nodded.

George was present at this meeting because he'd been a participant in, and an eyewitness to, the events at JFK three years ago, and as per standard FBI procedure, the Khalil case was his for life—which I hoped was not cut short by the previously mentioned asshole. And as I said, George was part of the ad hoc Lion Hunter team of Kate, me, and Gabe Haytham, who was our go-to Arab guy.

I exchanged a few words with Captain Paresi, and he was a bit cool, which meant that *his* boss, Tom Walsh, had set the tone regarding John Corey. Never mind that my wife was almost killed—she was fine now. And as for me saving the world from a nuclear incident not too long ago—well, as we like to say here, what have you done for us lately?

I said to Paresi, "I am *not* being taken off this case."

He didn't respond directly, but said, "We value your dedication and your prior experience with the suspect."

To further set the tone, I replied, "Bullshit."

I went to one of the big windows. Walsh's corner office faces south, and from here on the 28th floor, I could see most of Lower Manhattan. To the southeast was NYPD Headquarters, a.k.a. One Police Plaza, a tall fortress-like building of red brick, where I did a brief stint many years ago, and which made me crazier than I already was. But I did learn how things work at the center, which has helped me at 26 Fed.

Father east was the Brooklyn Bridge, which crossed the East River connecting Manhattan Island to Brooklyn. About half of the city's relatively small Muslim population lived in Brooklyn, and about ninety-eight percent of them were honest, hardworking citizens who had come to America in pursuit of something that was missing in the place they had left. There was, however, that one, maybe two percent who had problems with the law, and an even smaller percentage who were national security risks.

On that subject, even terrorists need a place to shave, so if I had to guess where Asad Khalil intended to hide out in New York City—actually, I *did* have to guess—I'd say he wouldn't hole up in a Muslim neighborhood in the outer boroughs where we'd be looking for him or where someone might figure out that this new guy was worth a million bucks to the Feds. I mean, Khalil couldn't kill them all, the way he'd killed Amir the taxi driver.

Hiding out in a hotel would be a problem for him because of security cameras and hundreds of guests and staff passing through who might recognize him from the wanted photo that the NYPD would be distributing.

A better bet for Khalil would be a hot-sheet hotel where, if he didn't have so many sexual hang-ups, he could get laid while he was hiding out.

Another possibility was a flophouse, or an SRO—single-room occupancy—that offered daily rates, cash up front, no questions asked.

Or, as I previously suggested, Professor Khalil might have faculty housing at Columbia University.

More likely, though, Asad Khalil would be holed

up in an apartment that had been rented under a corporate name by his backers and was used for colleagues visiting New York. That was standard procedure in the well-financed world of international terrorism, and unfortunately, despite our best efforts, we rarely discovered one of these safe houses—which were usually high-rise apartment buildings in Manhattan—unless we happened to follow some bad guy to the building.

In this case, however, I was certain that Khalil's backers would not put their important killer in a possibly compromised safe house—they'd have a new, clean place just for him.

I looked to the southwest where the Twin Towers once stood. I recalled that Jack Koenig, who had previously occupied this office, had purposely positioned his desk so that he could see the Towers. This reminded him daily of the first World Trade Center attack on February 26, 1993. The bastards got it right on the second try, and Jack Koenig, who'd stared at those towers every workday, died in one of them along with Paresi's predecessor, David Stein, and a few other people from this office who were at a meeting there.

I couldn't see the Trade Center observation platform from here, but Kate and I had been there once, and I could picture the visitors—people from all over the country and the world—staring into the big hole that had been the temporary mass grave of close to three thousand human beings. If you were one of the tens of thousands of survivors who had been in the Towers that morning, or were on your way there, as Kate and I had been, not a day went by that you didn't wonder why you were spared.

On Walsh's office window was a decal that showed a black silhouette of the Towers, and the words 9/11— NEVER FORGET!

To that I would add, *If you do, it will happen again.*

Also a few blocks from here was Murray Street where Amir the taxi driver had dropped off his last customer. Assuming the fare-beater was Asad Khalil, then what was he doing in Lower Manhattan on a Sunday?

Maybe nothing more than killing his taxi driver. But there were better places for that. This reinforced my suspicion that Khalil intended to stay and operate in Manhattan. So what was in Manhattan to attract him here? Well, John Corey lived on East 72nd Street. Vince Paresi and young wife number three lived on Central Park West, and Tom Walsh, like the Coreys, lived on the respectable Upper East Side. And Khalil's other possible targets, such as George Foster, all worked right here.

Hopefully, Khalil did not have our home addresses, but he *did* have our business address, and we all followed a somewhat predictable routine. Well, *I* didn't, but Walsh, Paresi, and Foster did.

Which brought me to the thought that Asad Khalil had some very good intel about Mr. and Mrs. John Corey. How else could he know that we'd be jumping out of an aircraft on Sunday morning? This guy might be acting alone, but he had a big supporting cast here in New York. Like maybe Al Qaeda.

As I turned from the window, Tom Walsh walked into his office. We all shook hands, and Walsh said, "Please sit."

He threw a thick folder on the table and began, "There's no good news, so I'll start with the bad news."

CHAPTER TWENTY-SIX

Before Tom Walsh got to the bad news, he suggested a moment of silence for Gabe, his wife, and his daughter. It was a nice gesture and we all bowed our heads.

I don't know too many Muslim prayers, but I knew what Gabe would want me to pray for, so I prayed that I'd find Asad Khalil and make him pay for what he'd done. Amen.

A brief word about Tom Walsh. He is young for this job—maybe mid-forties—and Kate tells me he's good-looking, though in my opinion he looks like one of those coiffed pretty boys you see in men's clothing ads.

The FBI, as you may imagine, is concerned about their agents' personal lives, and as far as I know Tom Walsh leads a life of exemplary rectitude, though I suspect he wears women's underwear. Yes, just kidding.

The FBI would prefer that their agents be married, with children, but Mr. Walsh has never been married, though he is in a long-term relationship with a lady lawyer. I've seen his significant other at a few office social functions and once at his apartment, and they seem like a good fit—cool, detached, ambitious, and narcissistic. They don't live together, but if they did, they'd need separate bedrooms for their egos.

The moment of silence ended, and Tom Walsh began, "We have located Chip Wiggins."

Since there was no good news, that wasn't good news.

Walsh informed us, "As we suspected, he's dead."

So retired U.S. Air Force officer Chip Wiggins was dead. But Asad Khalil was still here. Another man would have headed home, mission accomplished. But Khalil had a new death list, which included Kate, the Haythams, and others, and might also include my colleagues at this table.

As Walsh consulted his notes, I exchanged glances with Paresi and Foster. Paresi already knew Wiggins was dead, of course, but George Foster looked surprised, and more pale than usual. He took a long drink of water.

Walsh continued, "Elwood Wiggins, a.k.a. Chip, worked as a freight pilot for a company called Alpha Air Freight, based in Santa Barbara, California." Walsh gave us some background on Wiggins, which I already knew.

I also recalled that Chip Wiggins was a nice guy and a free spirit—one could say irresponsible—and not the type of man you'd associate with a jet attack aircraft, dropping bombs on enemy targets. He'd survived that, but he hadn't survived the consequences of that.

Walsh observed, "So, he had a routine, which is not a good thing when someone is looking for you."

Thanks for sharing that with us, Tom. I took the opportunity to remind everyone that I'd worked this case by saying, "Wiggins was also flying for Alpha three years ago when Kate and I met him at his house in Ventura." I informed my colleagues, "We strongly suggested then that he move, or get another job." Which was my way of saying that we had done all we could to get Wiggins off Khalil's radar screen.

Walsh commented, "Well, he should have taken that advice." He continued, "Okay, here's how it went down. The local FBI office in Santa Barbara attempted to locate Wiggins Sunday afternoon, soon after they received the request from us, but he wasn't at home."

Walsh filled us in on the FBI's search for Wiggins, then he cut to the chase. "Later that afternoon, one of the agents, Scott Fraser, drove out to Alpha Air Freight at Santa Barbara Airport. The first thing he noticed was a blue Ford Explorer in the Alpha parking area that matched the description of Wiggins's vehicle, which he then confirmed by the plate number. When Fraser went into the Alpha Freight office, the weekend guy said Wiggins didn't begin work again until Sunday night and the guy couldn't explain why Wiggins's truck was outside. Fraser asked to see the aircraft that Wiggins flew, and they went out to the ramp. After Fraser visually determined that no one was in the cockpit, he entered the cargo cabin."

Walsh, of course, paused here for dramatic effect, and I knew what Scott Fraser was going to find.

Walsh took three e-mail photos from his folder and slid them across the table.

I looked at the photo and there, in color was . . . a man. He was sitting on the floor of the cabin with his back against a wall, wearing black pants and a white shirt, which was red with blood, though you should not make assumptions from a photo. Neither should you assume the subject of the photo is dead, but Walsh said Wiggins was dead, and the face looked like Wiggins. The clincher, though, was that Chip Wiggins's head was sitting in his lap.

I heard Paresi say, "Jesus . . ."

I glanced at George, who was staring blankly at the photo. His face looked whiter than Wiggins's.

Walsh let us study the photos for a few seconds, then said, "It would appear from the crime scene report and the medical examiner's report that Wiggins climbed out of his aircraft after parking it, and he was on the ramp when he was struck four times by a heavy blunt instrument—a crowbar, which if you look closely at the photo, you will see sticking out of Wiggins's neck cavity." Walsh described the location of these blows and concluded, "These injuries, of course, would incapacitate him, but probably leave him conscious or semi-conscious."

Right. You want the guy awake for his beheading. Not to mention being awake for the lecture that Khalil would give to poor Chip Wiggins before he cut his head off. *Mr. Wiggins, one of your bombs killed my two sisters, my two brothers, and my mother. And now, Mr. Wiggins . . .*

Walsh continued the reconstruction of the crime. "After the assailant incapacitated his victim, he carried him into the cabin and there severed his head from his neck with the use of a butcher's saw." He added, very unnecessarily, "Slow and painful."

I thought George was going to pass out, but he took a deep breath and hung in. Paresi was getting himself pissed off and he said, "That bastard."

I looked again at the photograph, and it was easy to work up a whole lot of outrage and hatred for Asad Khalil and his fellow jihadists. But to be honest with myself, if I got the chance, I wouldn't hesitate for one second before cutting Khalil's throat. I'm sure Asad Khalil and John Corey didn't have a lot in common, but at the end of the day, we both knew how to settle a score.

Tom Walsh asked for the photos—you don't want this stuff floating around—and he reminded us, "This is all highly sensitive. Nothing we discuss leaves this room unless I say so."

I said to him, "I do intend to brief Kate on this meeting."

He hesitated, then said, "Of course." He added, "She was on the original case." He advised me, however, "Regarding sensitive information, you should speak to her off the record in the event she's called to testify in any future proceedings."

Tom Walsh was thinking down the road to some end-game scenarios. He was a lawyer, and his bosses at FBI Headquarters and in the Justice Department were lawyers. Therefore, everything had to be legal and correct, even in the war on terrorism. The police and the CIA, on the other hand, were cowboys. One could argue the merits of lawyers and cowboys forever and never resolve the question of who was better equipped to get the job done. But I do know that pre-9/11, the lawyers were in charge. Now the cowboys were getting a little more room to ride.

And to complicate things for Tom Walsh, he was doing a balancing act, on orders from Washington, by trying to apprehend Asad Khalil while denying the existence of Asad Khalil. Meanwhile, the body count had gone from five to six.

Walsh said to us, "There was another murder in California that is most probably related to this case."

Correction. Seven.

CHAPTER TWENTY-SEVEN

Tom Walsh consulted his folder and said, "Before we get to that murder, let me just say that we don't know when or how Asad Khalil entered the country, but it's probable that he took the most direct route and flew into LAX, using a false passport and visa from an Arabic-speaking country." Walsh further informed us, "A man like this, with the right foreign resources, could easily pass muster at passport control."

Correct. The best point of entry would be an airport—LAX—but Khalil would not be traveling as a Libyan national; we had no diplomatic relations with Libya and their two-plane airline didn't fly here. So he'd arrive via some other airline, and on his U.S. entry card and his customs declaration card he'd state the purpose of his visit as tourist—a business trip cover story is too easy to check out. And if he was asked any questions at passport control, he'd keep his answers simple and not go on about his lifelong desire to see Disneyland. Also, he'd have a confirmed hotel reservation with him, though he would not stay at that hotel. The passport control officer, after consulting the computer list of known terrorists, personae non gratae, criminals, and other assholes, would stamp the passport and say, "Welcome to the U.S. Next."

Walsh said, "We are checking video security tapes at a number of airports." He continued, "Our office in Santa Barbara paid a visit last night to Sterling Air Charters at Santa Barbara Airport. This is the company that owns and operates the Citation jet that Khalil used to fly from Sullivan County Airport to Republic Airport on Long Island."

He scanned an e-mail in his hand and said, "At about seven A.M. on Saturday morning, a man who identified himself as Christos Demetrios showed up at the Sterling office. He had a reservation made by his company in Athens, Hydra Shipping. He met his pilot and copilot, and they departed on time, flying first to Pueblo, Colorado, where they refueled and went on to Huntington, West Virginia, for another refueling, then on to their destination at Sullivan County Airport, where they landed at six-thirteen P.M. local time. Mr. Demetrios—who the Sterling employee and the pilots identified from our photo as Asad Khalil—rented a car, and the two pilots went to a local motel with instructions to be ready to fly out the next morning, Sunday, sometime after ten A.M., destination Buffalo."

Walsh thought a moment and said, "Our agents who spoke to these two pilots at their motel last night reported that the pilots found Mr. Demetrios to be somewhat distant, maybe aloof, but that he showed no signs of nervousness at Santa Barbara Airport, or on the way to Sullivan County." Walsh concluded, "Considering that he'd beheaded a man just a few hours before the pilots met him, and that he was on his way to his sky-diving rendezvous with John and Kate, I'd say we are dealing with an extreme psychopath."

And what was your second clue, Tom?

Walsh continued the cross-country odyssey of Asad Khalil. "And when Khalil re-boarded the aircraft in Sullivan County, he'd just . . . attacked Kate, and the pilots said he appeared quite at ease . . . and he was smiling."

Walsh seemed amazed or impressed that Khalil wasn't agitated after his skydiving assault, making me realize that Walsh didn't quite understand the messi-anic nuttiness of Asad Khalil. I mean, the guy was on jihad and he was enveloped in a celestial light or some-thing.

Walsh went on, "The only thing the pilots noticed out of the ordinary was that their passenger no longer had his duffel bag, which we assume held his skydiv-ing gear. Also, he changed the flight plan from Buffalo to MacArthur Airport, then changed it again in mid-air to Republic." Walsh concluded, "He knows how to keep the authorities off his tail."

It's a fact that serial murderers gain more confi-dence after about the third murder. They also get bet-ter at it. But then the learning curve starts to flatten and the level of confidence turns into carelessness. I wasn't sure where Asad Khalil was on this curve, or even if he fit the profile of a common serial killer. So we shouldn't wait for him to make a careless mistake;

we had to get into his head, the way we'd done last time, and be waiting for him. No problem. Right?

So far, the only real mistake that this bastard made was not killing me when he had the chance.

Tom Walsh looked at me, George Foster, and Vince Paresi and said, "Victim seven. A Libyan-born male, name of Farid Mansur." Tom Walsh is a modest man, but sometimes you just have to blow your own horn, and he informed us, "I assumed that Khalil had a local contact in California, and recalling his M.O. of eliminating his contacts, I asked our office in LA to check with every police department in southern California to see if there had been a recent homicide or suspicious fatal accident involving anyone of Middle Eastern background."

Walsh glanced around the table to be sure we appreciated his genius, and we all dutifully nodded at the boss's brilliance.

Walsh continued, "The Ventura County Police reported a body found with no ID under a bed in a Best Western hotel near the Santa Barbara Airport. Also under the bed was men's clothing, covered with blood, which we are in the process of matching with Chip Wiggins's blood." He added, "The room was registered to a Farid Mansur, and the police put this together with a missing person report filed by a Libyan-American lady, Mrs. Hala Mansur, whose husband had gone missing on Friday, and she IDed the body. A background check of Mr. Farid Mansur reveals that he associated with other Middle Eastern immigrants who have come to our attention." He added, "Farid Mansur was strangled with what was probably a piano wire garrote."

Maybe Khalil couldn't find his ice pick.

Walsh said, "We have no idea what Farid Mansur passed on to Asad Khalil, but we can assume it was the usual false IDs, money, weapons, and maybe the skydiving gear, plus some information about Wiggins."

"Don't forget the saw," I reminded him.

Walsh gave me one of those looks, then assured us, "The LA office is following up by questioning Mansur's friends as well as investigating his purchases, his phone calls, and so forth." He concluded, "If we catch a break there, I'll let you know." Walsh asked us, "Any questions? Or comments?"

Paresi asked, "What do you want me to do about the local Libyans?"

Walsh replied, "Stick to the surveillance. No street interrogations and no invitations to come in to talk to us."

I said to Walsh, "Captain Paresi told me about your idea to put out a text message to Kate's phone saying we had some informants in the Libyan community."

Walsh avoided eye contact and said, "Standard disinformation." He added, "Actually, I think that was John's idea."

"No, no," I said. "*You* thought of it."

Tom Walsh moved on to other subjects, and we kicked around a few thoughts, then Walsh looked at us and said, "We must now assume that Khalil is poised to strike again. We don't know where, when, how, or who—but based on Khalil's attack on Kate, his murder of Gabe, and his threat to John, let's recognize that the Task Force has become his target."

George Foster went from white to gray, and even Paresi, who's usually cool and macho, looked a little unsettled. I mean, this was not abstract with seven dead and Kate lying in a hospital.

Walsh looked at me and said, "You are definitely a target. So maybe you should lay low. Like, stay home while Kate recuperates."

I saw that coming and replied, "That's not what I had in mind." I informed him, "Look, Tom, I'm willing to act as bait—if we can come up with a good plan."

Walsh said to me, "We can discuss that later." He remembered to add, "I appreciate the offer." He changed subjects. "We have another murder that may be connected to Asad Khalil." He looked at me and said, "Captain Paresi told you about the Libyan taxi driver."

"Correct."

Walsh asked me, "How did you anticipate that?"

I replied, "As you know, that's Khalil's M.O." I added, "The last time he was here, he used a Libyan taxi driver to take him from JFK to a destination in New Jersey, where he murdered him in much the same way as he murdered"—here was my moment—"Amir on Murray Street."

Paresi said, "I never mentioned the name of the murdered taxi driver, or where he was murdered."

I agreed, "No, you didn't."

He, of course, inquired, "How did you know that?"

I wasn't going to tell him I had a chance chat with a cop on the beat; I wanted to stay on this case so I needed to maintain my aura of being informed and connected in high places, and I replied, "I have my sources."

That did not go over well with my two bosses, and Paresi said, "We'll discuss this later."

Walsh let it go and continued, "No murder weapon was recovered, but the medical examiner says that he found a puncture wound in the deceased's skull, and that the autopsy will probably reveal a deep puncture in the brain consistent with the type of wound made by an ice pick or a similar instrument." He added, "Death was not instantaneous. In fact, the victim exited his taxi and died on the street."

That didn't sound like the Asad Khalil that I knew. I mean, you really don't want your victims doing the zombie walk in the middle of the street while you're trying to put some distance between you and them.

My own brain, which works well enough, retrieved a piece of trivia—Leon Trotsky, an old Bolshevik who had fallen out of favor with his Commie buddies, was murdered in Mexico City by a guy working for the predecessors of the KGB. The weapon used was an ice pick—and Trotsky had lingered for days before dying. So if I was seeing Boris's training here, you'd think Boris would have remembered to tell Khalil, "We love that ice pick, Asad, but you gotta give them two or three pokes."

I made a mental note to discuss this with Boris if I got the chance. Or maybe Khalil.

Walsh continued with his crime scene briefing. "The police found no cell phone on the driver's body or in his taxi. We then attempted to retrieve the murdered man's cell phone records, and his house phone records, but we discovered that he had no house phone, and if he had a cell phone—which he undoubtedly did—it was either not in his name, or it was the paid-minutes type and no records exist." He concluded, "Dead end."

Poor choice of words, perhaps, but not surprising. As I've discovered, most Middle Eastern immigrants come from places where it's not a good idea to create records of your existence—and that mentality had carried over to America, which made my job a little more difficult.

Walsh continued, "We're making the assumption, of course, that it was Khalil who murdered this taxi driver . . . though it *could* be a coincidence."

I offered my unsolicited opinion and said, "Khalil murdered the taxi driver." I added, "That's why you have a BOLO out on Khalil and why his photo is in every police car in the city."

Neither Walsh nor Paresi asked me how I knew that, though by now they had concluded that John Corey was still plugged into the Blue Network. Well, I was, but with each year that passed since my disability retirement, my NYPD sources were fewer, and by now I'd called in most of the favors owed to me. Still, I could flash my shield and talk to a cop on the beat.

Walsh concluded, "NYPD Homicide is investigating this murder and will keep us informed."

Walsh filled us in on a few more odds and ends, including the not-surprising discovery that Global Entertainment in Lichtenstein and Hydra Shipping in Athens were sham corporations. INTERPOL and the national police of both countries were investigating.

In police work, intelligence work, and counterterrorism work, we always say, "It's important to know
who fired the bullet, but it's more important to know
who paid for it."

Indeed. And when you know that, you can guess at
the bigger picture.

Who was backing Asad Khalil? And why? He
could not have pulled all this off by himself. My
knowledge of geopolitics is limited, but I did know
that Libya and its weird president, Colonel Muammar
Khadafi, were being quiet since we bombed the shit
out of them in 1986. And since 9/11, they'd gotten
even quieter. So they wouldn't risk backing their former psychotic terrorist—there was nothing in it for
them except more bombs.

The next usual suspect was Al Qaeda, but I didn't
see their fingerprints on this—unless there was something in it for them. Which brought me to quid pro
quo.

It would appear that a terrorist organization with
some resources had provided Asad Khalil with funds,
sham corporations, passports, and intel about his intended victims—including me and Kate. But Asad
Khalil's mission was *his* mission and not very large in
scale or significant in terms of what it would accomplish
in the war against the U.S. For sure it was insignificant
when compared to 9/11. I mean, whacking Mr. and
Mrs. Corey was not high on Al Qaeda's agenda.

Therefore, Khalil had to return the favor; he had to
take out a big target for his sponsors—a building or
monument, or maybe an important person or persons.

I was thinking about all this while Walsh was going on about this and that, speaking mostly to George Foster now. I was waiting for Walsh to get to the question of who might be behind Asad Khalil, and the possibility of a major attack, using a weapon of mass destruction. But that didn't seem to be on Walsh's agenda memo. Maybe later.

Walsh finished with George, who apparently had just been made the case agent in my mental absence. I had no real problem with that, but I was a little concerned about my future status on this case. *Tom, nice tie.*

Walsh said, "We have a piece of evidence I'd like you all to see." He took a remote control from the table and clicked on the television in the corner. In a few seconds, we were watching a bunch of assholes jumping out of an aircraft.

The first scene was obviously taken by a skydiver as he was free-falling, and it was a bit jumpy, as you can imagine. Nevertheless, I recognized the twenty or so idiots falling through space with their bodies in the Superman position, trying to join up to form a bucky ball or something. I thought I saw Craig flapping his arms and legs like a wounded duck.

Walsh was staring at the screen, and he asked me, "You do that?"

I replied, "Kate and I love it." I added, "You should try it." *I'll pack your chute.*

Walsh fast forwarded. This shot was taken from the ground with a telephoto lens, and I could clearly see a few colored chutes against the blue sky, then Walsh put it into slow motion, and I could now see Kate free-falling with Khalil hooked up to her. Then I saw myself free-falling toward Kate and Khalil, and then Kate's chute opened, and then mine opened.

The room was very silent, but you could hear people on the ground talking, then the distinct voice of a man saying, "Look!"

Walsh froze the picture and said to me, "You don't have to watch this."

I didn't reply and he continued in slow motion.

As the scene unfolded, Walsh asked me to provide a commentary, but I said, "I'll put it in my report."

I saw myself pulling my gun and popping off two rounds at Khalil, but the action was so far away that no one but me knew what I'd done.

Meanwhile, the voices on the ground got louder, and they sounded more excited as they realized something was wrong.

Even in slow motion and with the telephoto lens, it was difficult for the people on the ground, or in this room, to see or comprehend what was happening at that altitude. But I knew the moment when Khalil cut Kate's throat, and I did bring that to everyone's attention.

Then you could see Khalil going into free fall, and I saw his chute opening, and I could see now that he'd steered himself toward the woods.

Khalil was out of the frame, and I looked back at where the cameraman had centered his shot, which was me steering toward Kate. Then our chutes collided and collapsed, and there was a lot of shouting on the ground and someone screamed.

Next you could see my collapsed chute sailing away after I jettisoned it, then Kate's chute, too, sailed off when I released it. And then there we were in free fall again.

It would appear to the uninitiated that Kate and I were falling to our deaths, but the skydivers on the ground understood that a collapsed main chute was actually worse than no chute.

Paresi asked me, "What the hell is happening?"

I explained, "I had to get rid of our main chutes to get us on the ground quickly before she bled to death." I assured him, "Our emergency chutes will open." That's why I'm here.

Paresi mumbled, "Jesus . . ."

Kate and I were free-falling for what seemed a very long time before Kate's emergency chute popped, followed by mine. Even in slow motion I could see now how fast we were falling with the small chutes, and I unconsciously braced myself for the impact. I wouldn't want to do that again.

I saw Kate hit the ground first, then before I hit, the cameraman must have stopped filming, because the next scene was of the ambulance racing toward where we'd landed, then a new scene of me in the distance kneeling over Kate. Then all I could see was the backs of people in jumpsuits running toward where the ambulance had stopped, and I could hear a lot of excited shouting.

The cameraman was now moving quickly through the crowd as he filmed, and I could see brief glimpses of myself and the three EMS people gathered around

Kate. The cameraman seemed intent on working his way closer to where we were trying to save Kate's life, but I don't know if he got that close because Walsh shut off the TV.

We all sat there for a few quiet seconds before Walsh said, "You did a good job."

I didn't reply.

Paresi said, as if to himself, "I can't believe that asshole did that."

Walsh suggested, "Let's take a fifteen-minute break."

I stood and walked out of the room and headed toward the elevators.

I got on the elevator and rode down by myself. I closed my eyes and I was falling through space . . . falling at two hundred miles an hour, and my wife was spurting blood into the airstream, and my heart pounded in my chest.

You bastard. You arrogant bastard.

"You only get one chance at me, asshole. You had it, and you blew it. Payback's a bitch."

CHAPTER TWENTY-EIGHT

I sat at my desk and stared out over the expanse of low-walled cubicles. It was still lunch hour, quiet and empty in Fedland—very unlike an NYPD squad room at any hour of any day.

A few desks away was where Gabe Haytham had worked, and I saw that the human resources people had already packed his desk into nice white boxes—business and personal—and I wondered if Gabe had any family to receive his personal effects.

On the far side of the open space were the cubicles where the FBI agents worked, and I looked at Kate's desk.

Captain Paresi appeared on the floor and walked over to my desk.

I inquired, "Slumming?"

He sat down in my side chair and asked me, "How you doing?"

"Fine."

He said to me, "I think you're experiencing post-traumatic stress."

Apparently Walsh had come up with a good reason for me to ask for some leave time. I didn't respond.

He assured me, "No one here"—he waved his arm to encompass the rows of empty desks—"will think any the less of you if you ask for time to be with your wife." He further assured me, "That's what a man and a husband does."

I wasn't sure if I should take marital advice from a man who's been married three times.

He asked me, "How did you know more about the Amir murder than I told you?"

I replied, "I have my sources."

He changed the subject and said, "I'll take your Khalil file."

I took my keys out of my pocket and unlocked my file cabinet beside my desk. In the bottom drawer was a folder marked "Islamic Community Outreach Program." I pulled the folder and handed it to Paresi, who glanced at the index tab, smiled, and commented, "I hope you read these memos carefully."

"Hey, I organize wet burqua contests at the hookah bars in Bay Ridge."

He opened the folder, flipped through the pages, and asked me a few questions. I briefed him on the efforts of the Lion Hunter team over the past three years and concluded, "No one in the general Muslim community seems to know anything about Asad Khalil. However, the small Libyan community knows of him." I explained, "His father, Captain Karim Khalil, was a big shot in the Khadafi government, and the

Khalil family was close to the Khadafi family." I further informed him, "Captain Khalil was assassinated in Paris, supposedly by Israeli agents, making him a martyr for Islam and a surefire shoo-in for paradise." I added, "Actually, it was Khadafi himself who ordered the hit."

"Why?"

"The CIA says that Khadafi was sexually involved with Mrs. Khalil. Asad's mommy."

"No kidding?"

"It's complicated, but the CIA tried to turn Asad Khalil with this info and have him whack Khadafi."

Paresi thought about that, but did not comment.

"That's all I can say, and all you want to know . . . except keep an eye on the boys at 290 Broadway."

Paresi nodded.

I continued, "Prior to Karim Khalil's residence in paradise, he and his family lived in a former Italian military compound in Tripoli called Al Azziziyah. This was a privileged community where the Khadafis also had a house. It was a nice, quiet neighborhood until the night of April 15, 1986, when four U.S. Air Force F-111s, part of a larger attack group, dropped eight big fuck-you bombs on the compound, killing, among others, Khadafi's adopted daughter and, as I told you, Asad Khalil's entire family—his mother, two sisters, and two brothers."

Captain Paresi processed that, then asked, "How did that bastard survive?"

I replied, "I don't know. But Asad Khalil would tell

you he was spared by God to seek revenge, for himself, and for his Great Leader, Muammar Khadafi."

"Right. Still pissed after all these years."

"I would be, too."

"So, Chip Wiggins was the last of those eight pilots."

"He was," I replied.

"So, time to go home."

"Well, I would. You would. But you know, he's in town anyway, so why not whack a few more people on the way out?"

Captain Paresi observed, "He's got a big hate eating his guts."

"You think?"

Paresi flipped through the folder and asked, "What's in here that I can use to find Asad Khalil?"

I replied, "The names and contact info of people we've worked with around the world—foreign intelligence people, police agencies, INTERPOL, and informants."

"Good. Any Khalil sightings?"

"No. He seems to have totally disappeared for three years." I added, "The serious bad guys usually do that before they resurface for a big mission."

Paresi nodded and said, "I guess he's been preparing for this."

"Or he may have been fighting in Afghanistan or Iraq."

Paresi nodded, then asked me, "How about the million-dollar reward? Any takers?"

"No, but a few interested parties."

"Right. That's how we find ninety percent of the assholes we're looking for. Money talks."

"Except when people are scared shitless. Or if the guy we're looking for has become a legend. How much are we offering for Osama bin Laden?"

"I think it's twenty million."

"Saddam Hussein?"

"That's twenty-five million," he replied.

"How we doing on that?"

"We'll see."

Paresi and I kicked around a few thoughts, and the subject came up regarding where Khalil might be hiding out. We both agreed that he wouldn't be holed up in a Muslim neighborhood where detectives from the Task Force would be looking for him—or where someone might decide that even a measly million dollars was just too tempting.

I said to Paresi, "As we can see, Khalil is well-funded and he has some sophisticated backing, apparently a network or cell here in New York. Whoever these people are, they probably have a few safe houses in Manhattan—apartments rented by XYZ Corporation for visiting colleagues." I speculated, "They could have an apartment in your building."

He forced a smile and said, "Or yours."

"Right. Or Walsh's. Point is, Asad Khalil is not sleeping on cousin Abdul's couch in Bay Ridge or having tea in a hookah bar. He's totally separated from his compatriots—until he needs something from them— then he has one or two cut-outs so he doesn't deal directly with the guy he eventually meets up with. So, for instance, when Farid in California and Amir in New York met Asad Khalil, it was their first meeting—and also their last."

Paresi thought a moment and said, "If Khalil read that text message that Walsh sent to Kate's cell phone, then he may be spooked—which is good and bad. Good because it cuts him off from his Libyan contacts, and bad because we don't have much hope of following some Abdul who could lead us to another Abdul who could lead us to Khalil."

"Right. But I'd rather have Khalil spooked and isolated from his contacts." I reminded him, "We know of three safe house apartment buildings in Manhattan, and you should have around-the-clock surveillance on those buildings."

"We do."

"But I'm fairly sure his sponsors have a never-used place for him to hang out."

Paresi considered all that and concluded, "It won't be easy to find this guy in the usual way."

"No. But we will find him."

"Right. Murderers always leave a trail and sometimes they screw up at the scene."

"Correct. And we have the advantage of knowing at least one person he plans to kill."

Captain Paresi seemed to recall that he might also be on Khalil's list. He said, "We'll discuss personal security in Walsh's office."

I said to him, "Maybe we should discuss now your

thought about what else Khalil is doing here to pay back his sponsors."

He didn't reply for a few seconds, then said, "That would be a very speculative discussion." He added, "We have no information on that possibility."

I pointed out, "We need to think about that and look for evidence of a larger terrorist attack."

He didn't respond directly, but said, "We need to apprehend him quickly so we don't have to worry about that." He added, "When we get him, we can ask him those questions."

Apparently Captain Paresi did not want to pursue this subject that he himself had brought up. At least he didn't want to pursue it with me.

Vince Paresi is a good guy—an honest cop—and he, like me, had entered a different world of criminal justice than the world we once worked in. We had made our adjustments and hoped we were doing the right thing for truth, justice, and the American way. And mostly, I think, we were—except now and then when something weird came up and we were told to back off and shut up. And as proof that we were still outsiders, never once were we asked to do something that was questionable. I mean, I did things like that on my own.

On that subject, Paresi said to me, "I sense that you may be thinking about pursuing this matter on your own time. So here's some advice—don't. But if you do, be careful, and be successful. If you're not successful, you will be brought up on criminal charges. If you're not careful, you will be dead." He added, "That's off the record."

For the record, I didn't reply.

He glanced at his watch and said, "We're a minute late." He stood and walked toward the elevators, carrying my folder with him.

I waited a few minutes, then followed.

CHAPTER TWENTY-NINE

Tom Walsh didn't comment on my lateness or on the fact that George Foster was not there. I also noticed that Paresi had gotten rid of my Khalil folder.

Walsh looked at me and said, "John, let me begin by saying that you've done an outstanding job on this case, and we appreciate your dedication to duty, especially in light of Kate's serious injuries, and the *stress*"— stress on the stress—"that you've been under—"

"Thank you."

He continued, "After thinking about this situation, and after consulting with Captain Paresi, I strongly suggest that you ask for traumatic leave so that you can be with your wife during her convalescence."

I didn't respond.

He sweetened the deal by saying, "This will be paid leave, of course."

I asked, "How long?"

"Thirty days." He added, "Maybe longer."

I informed him, "This will all be over within a week."

He didn't comment on that prediction, and he continued, "I would advise you to stay in your apartment, except for necessary errands and such."

"Can I see a Yankees game?"

"No." He went on, "You'll have ample time at home to write your incident report and to write me a confidential memo regarding everything you know about Asad Khalil and about what happened three years ago."

I glanced at Paresi, fully expecting him to say to Walsh, "Tom, I have a whole folder that John just gave me on that very subject. Let me make a copy for you."

But Captain Paresi did not say that. In fact, Captain Paresi had been screwed so many times by the FBI that he was keeping this to himself. Why share information? No one else does. Paresi's fantasy, of course, was that he and his detectives—sans Detective Corey—would find Asad Khalil without help from the FBI. Competition is good. We're not socialists. And we're really not team players. We're individualists. We're Americans. We're cowboys.

"John?"

I looked at Walsh.

"I said I'd like that report and memo within seventy-two hours."

I had the urge to tell him that seventy-two hours from now, we could all be dead. Then I wouldn't have to write the stupid incident report or the stupid memo. I said, however, "No problem."

He assured me, "Your request for leave will have no negative impact on your career, and nothing of a negative nature will be inferred from your request to be with your wife."

This was getting a little tedious, not to mention silly. I mean, I had no career here. I had a contract. And someday I was going to read it and see what I had to do to get out of here.

By my silence, Walsh may have thought I was wavering or that I didn't believe him about what he'd just said, so he also said, "I will place a letter of commendation in your file thanking you for your service in general, and your outstanding work on this case."

Paresi, in a rehearsed remark, added, "I will do the same."

Thanks, Judas. It seemed that the less I said, the more I got. If I could keep my mouth shut for ten minutes, I'd get a free cab ride home and a Metro-Card. I just wanted to get out of there, so I said to Walsh and Paresi, "I appreciate that."

Walsh reminded me, "This case, like all our cases, is classified and on a need-to-know basis." He further reminded me, "You signed agreements acknowledging that you will not discuss, disclose, or divulge anything that pertains to your duties here."

I glanced at my watch.

He continued, "And I will also ask you not to discuss this case with anyone in this office—or anyone from the State Police or any other law enforcement or intelligence agency, unless authorized by me personally."

"Right."

Walsh reminded me, "Kate is under the same restrictions as you are."

"Okay. Are we done?"

"No." Walsh continued, "There is a news blackout on this case—authorized at a higher level—and it goes without saying that you will not be speaking to reporters."

He went on to the next subject. "I've asked Vince"— he nodded toward Captain Paresi in case I forgot who Vince was—"to arrange for protection for you and for Kate."

Paresi informed me, "There will be SOG personnel in your apartment lobby around the clock."

This is the Special Operations Group, the people I worked with last week on the Iranian dip surveillance. They're part of the Terrorist Task Force, mostly NYPD detectives, but also some FBI agents. Their specialty is not only surveillance, but also countersurveillance, and protective details. They're good at what they do, but I could give them the slip if I had to.

I suggested, "You should both take advantage of that protection."

Walsh replied, "Captain Paresi and I are taking necessary precautions."

"Good. One less thing for me to worry about."

We all thought that was funny and everyone smiled appropriately.

I then let them know, "I do *not* want surveillance people tailing me."

There was a silence, then Walsh said, "You *will* have a team assigned to you when you're mobile."

I reminded both of them, "I can take care of myself. In fact, I have a gun."

Paresi said, "Look, John, we don't want to lose another agent." He smiled. "Not even you." He let me know, "You, me, Tom, George, and maybe a few other people will have SOG personnel assigned to them—that's how we may catch this guy."

On that subject, I said to Walsh, "I'm still willing to act as bait."

Walsh replied, "I think we're all bait now."

"Good point." In fact, Walsh had finally come to the unhappy conclusion that he had no clue about how to find Asad Khalil—except for letting Khalil find us. Officially, we were all under police and FBI protection; unofficially, we were live bait. Thus I was authorized to leave my apartment to go on "necessary errands and such." In reality, and off the record, Walsh and Paresi didn't care where I went—if I agreed to not lose my protective detail.

Good plan, but it wasn't my plan. My plan didn't include being tailed by cops and FBI agents who could scare off Khalil, or arrest Khalil, or even kill Khalil; my plan included only two people: John Corey and Asad Khalil.

Paresi said to me, "John, there can be a role for you in this case, and maybe this is it."

I didn't reply.

Walsh informed me, "It's like the spy who came in from the cold. You're fired—officially off the case, but unofficially, you're bait."

"Got it."

"Good." He asked, "Agreed?"

Better half a loaf and all that. I said, "Agreed."

Paresi informed me, "You'll wear a vest when you go out, and we'll give you a GPS tracking device to wear, and a wire so you can speak to your surveillance team while you're mobile." He added, "You know the drill."

I nodded.

"You can pick those things up at tech before you leave."

"Will do."

That seemed to be the end of that subject, and Walsh said to me, "We have requested the NYPD ambulance helicopter to pick up Kate tomorrow A.M. and bring her here to Bellevue."

"Good. I'll be on the helicopter."

Walsh said, "All right. Someone will text or call you with the lift-off time from the Thirty-fourth Street Heliport."

"Good."

Walsh glanced at his watch, then asked me, "Any questions? Anything that needs clarification?"

"Yes." I said to him, "It seems to me that Asad Khalil needs to pay back the people who financed his trip here and who have provided him with information and logistical support." I asked, "Would you agree with that?"

He replied, "I agree that he has backers. I have no knowledge of how he needs to repay them." He added, "What Khalil is doing may be payment enough."

I replied, "I don't think so."

"Well, you can be sure you're not the first person to think of this, Detective." He let me know, "Washington is aware, and Counterintelligence is investigating."

"Good." I asked, "Is Homeland Security going to raise the alert level?"

He replied, "I have no idea." He advised me, "Check the news tonight."

Walsh was trying to put me in my place, of course. The Big Picture, if there was one, was none of my business, unless and until Tom Walsh or someone higher up made it my business. That was how 9/11 happened.

I looked out the window to where the Towers used to be and I said, "I felt I should mention this."

"Thank you." He assured me, "You're on the record."

I pointed out, "This meeting is off the record."

"This meeting is administrative." He asked me, "Anything further?"

Well, yes, Tom. I want to tell you about Boris, who could be an important resource for us in apprehending Asad Khalil. But you're such a shithead, Tom, that I'll keep that to myself. Or maybe you already know about Boris and you're keeping it to *yourself.* Either way, screw you.

"John?"

"Nothing further."

"Good." He stood, I stood, and Captain Paresi stood.

Walsh said, "Thank you, gentlemen, for your time and your thoughts." Then he gave a little speech. "This is not only a difficult case for us professionally, it is also difficult for us personally."

Right. Someone is trying to kill us.

He continued, "But the best way to resolve this case satisfactorily is to put our personal feelings aside and to follow procedures and directives."

Was he speaking to me?

He went into the pep talk phase. "This is not about us—it is about the security of our country. This is why we're here, and it is what we do." He concluded, "I have no doubt that we, working together with our colleagues in the war on terrorism, will bring this man to justice."

We all shook hands, and both men sent their regards to Kate, then I raced Paresi to the door. I got there first, but I heard Walsh say, "John, I just need a minute more of your time."

Paresi said to me, "See me before you leave."

I returned to Walsh's office, but did not sit.

He said to me, "I have an unofficial complaint forwarded to me through the State Department, regarding an incident that allegedly took place during your surveillance detail last week in the Taj Mahal Casino in Atlantic City."

I replied, "I'm sorry I used my government credit card to buy gambling tokens."

"This actually has to do with someone assaulting an Iranian U.N. diplomat in the men's room."

"Let me check my notes and I'll get back to you."

He looked at me a moment, then said, "You have demonstrated in the past a tendency toward rough justice." He reminded me, "We don't work that way here."

"Right."

He added, "Payback is not what we do. Neither is personal revenge."

"Right."

He changed the subject. "Why do you think this will all be over in a week?"

I replied, "That's my gut feeling."

He considered that reply, then said, "I thought you had some logical reason for that statement."

"All right. It's like this—Khalil began by killing this guy Farid and hiding his body, then he went for Wiggins, Kate, the Haythams, the livery driver, and the taxi driver. This was done so quickly that we had no clue and no time to react. Now we're all awake and waiting for him to strike again. And keep in mind he didn't go for me when he had the chance. Not to overdo the lion metaphor, Tom, but he's playing cat and mouse with me and with us." I reminded him, "The killing is secondary to the game, and he definitely has a game plan, which includes me and maybe you, Vince and George, and others not yet known. But he knows he can't start knocking people off one at a time and expect that his next victim will be sitting around waiting to die. So what's going to happen is that Khalil will make a clean sweep, probably in the course of a single night, and by the time the first body is discovered, the last victim will already be dead." I concluded, "It's all planned and ready to go," then added, "Sorry I can't tell you the night—but I don't think he'll hang around here for more than a week."

Walsh said nothing for a few seconds, then pointed out, "That assumes Khalil does plan to kill more people."

"That's my best guess. But I may be wrong. Maybe he's done—except for me."

He nodded and agreed, "You may be the only reason he's still here."

"We'll find out."

Walsh didn't reply to that and speculated, "But maybe he *is* gone. Maybe it got too hot for him here."

"He's *here*."

"Well . . . good. We want him here."

"*I* want him here."

He walked me to the door and reminded me in an almost offhand way, "If you find him, and if you kill him—and if you can't prove self-defense—you will face murder charges."

I didn't reply.

He also reminded me, "They want this guy alive."

"Why?"

"Obviously, he's worth more to us alive." He added, "Also, we don't murder people. Or even punch them in the groin. We try them in Federal court, as common criminals."

I didn't think that was such a good idea, but I didn't reply.

Walsh assured me, "Asad Khalil will go to jail. Forever."

"We don't know that, Tom."

"Of course we do." He got to the heart of the matter. "You killing Asad Khalil has less to do with protecting yourself and Kate than it does with pure and simple revenge. An eye for an eye. But I want you to consider that incarceration for life is worse than death." He added, "That goes for you as well as Khalil."

I pointed out, "Asad Khalil is more than eligible for the death penalty, but you and I know that the government never asks for the death penalty in these cases, even when the crime is mass murder."

He thought about that and replied, "We don't want to create martyrs for Islam. We want them to rot."

And we didn't want to upset the world community with our primitive death penalty laws. But I didn't want to argue with him—I wanted to cool it, so I said, "I see your point."

He didn't believe me and said, "Think of yourself, of Kate, and of your country."

"I always do, Tom."

"You need to promise me that if you have or receive any knowledge of Khalil's whereabouts, or if he contacts you, you will inform me immediately."

"What else would I do with that information?"

"If you can't promise that before you leave here, then I promise you that I'll do everything in my power to get you put in protective custody." He added, "Ankle bracelet, house arrest, the whole nine yards."

I think that was a bluff. He wanted me out and about with backup people following me. I was his best—and maybe only—chance to grab Asad Khalil. On the other hand, I shouldn't call his bluff if I wanted to stay free.

"John?"

I looked him in the eye and said, "I understand that this is not about me. You can count on me to keep you fully informed, to coordinate with the Task Force, to stay close to my surveillance team, and if I should somehow come into personal contact with the suspect,

I will follow all the rules regarding the use of deadly force." I added, "I promise."

That seemed to make him happy and he said, "Good." He assured me, "That's the right thing."

"I know it is."

We shook on the deal, and I left his office, thinking that he was right and that what I'd just said *was* the right thing, and also the best thing for everyone. Revenge is not justice.

By the time I got to the elevators, however, I was back to where I was when I saw Khalil cut Kate's throat.

It's really scary when you have a moment of temporary sanity.

CHAPTER THIRTY

I went down to the 26th floor to gather a few things from my desk, but before I did that, I went to Gabe's desk to look for his copy of the Khalil folder. In a file storage box I found his folder labeled "Islamic Community Outreach Program."

I noticed another box marked "Haytham—Personal" and opened it. There wasn't much in the box—mostly desk items and grooming aids—but I saw the Koran in Arabic, and also a book of Arab proverbs in English, with tabbed pages. I opened the book to a marked page and read an underlined sentence: "Death is afraid of him, because he has the heart of a lion."

I put the book back in the box and saw a framed photograph showing two smiling, attractive women who must have been Gabe's wife and daughter. I stared at the photo awhile, realizing that these two women were dead—murdered by Asad Khalil in cold blood. I could understand his motives and his sick rationale for the other murders, but even after a decade of homicide work, I was still shocked by motiveless murder—sport killing. And they wanted this guy taken alive?

I closed the box and went to Kate's desk. I took a red marker and wrote on her desk blotter: *Welcome back, darling—Love, John.*

I went to my desk and played my voice mails, skipping through most of them, listening for a message from Asad Khalil. I'd given him my office number three years ago, asking him to give me a call about getting together when he was in town again. Mr. Khalil had not called, but he had Kate's cell phone and Gabe's cell phone, so he now had all my phone numbers, and I was certain I'd hear from him.

I logged onto my computer, checked my e-mails, and printed out a few. I also printed out ten copies of the NYPD Be On The Lookout photo of Asad Khalil and put them in Gabe's Khalil folder.

People were starting to drift back in from lunch to see how the war on terrorism was going, and I didn't want to get involved in conversations with my colleagues, so I locked up and headed to the elevators.

I was supposed to go to the tech squad to pick up my tracking device and wire, but I forgot. I think I was also supposed to see Captain Paresi, but I was under a lot of stress, which made me forgetful.

Out on the street, I got into my Jeep and drove over to Murray Street to see the scene of what I hoped was Khalil's last crime.

I parked across the street from the IRS building and imagined this street on a Sunday afternoon. No one lived on this block, and the offices were closed, so it would be nearly deserted, and Asad Khalil did not pick this street at random. He had some knowledge of the area—either personal knowledge, or more likely someone here in New York had briefed him. What I was seeing with these murders was the end product of a fairly competent and well-informed group living and working in New York. Khalil was the celebrity killer; the others were his advance men, managers, and booking agents.

There were no signs left of a police crime scene investigation—not even a white chalk outline of where Amir had fallen dead in the street. But I pictured Amir getting out of his taxi, probably confused about the pain in his brain, and maybe staggering behind Khalil, who would be moving quickly toward Church Street, or the other way toward West Broadway—and if Khalil saw him, I wondered if he had a moment of fear, anxiety, or even remorse. I think not. The psychopathic killer mentally distances himself from the person whose life he just ended. I understood the head of a killer, but I could never understand the heart of a killer.

I left Murray Street and headed uptown, toward my apartment on East 72nd Street.

My apartment building is a 1980s high-rise, nondescript but fairly expensive, like most apartments on the Upper East Side. After 9/11, rental and sales prices tumbled in Manhattan as they tend to do in a war zone, but after about six months without an anthrax attack or a dirty nuke going off, prices got back to abnormally high.

I pulled into my underground garage and also pulled my Glock. I don't normally arrive at my assigned parking space with a gun in my hand—unless some asshole is pulling into my spot—but things have changed recently, and as an old patrol sergeant once said to me, "The surest way to get your head blown off is to have it up your ass."

I checked out my surroundings, parked, and walked toward the lobby elevator, my left hand holding my folder and my right hand in my pocket with the Glock.

I got off in the lobby and immediately noticed a guy sitting in a chair against the far wall. He was wearing jeans and an orange shirt that had a logo on it—deliveryman. In fact, there were two pizza boxes on the side table.

From where he was sitting, he could see the front doors, and the garage elevator, which went only to the lobby, and he could also see the door to the fire stairs, the freight elevator, and the apartment elevators—but where he was looking was at me.

Alfred, the doorman at the front desk, greeted me, but I ignored him and walked toward the delivery guy, who stood as I approached. *Mario's Pizzeria—Best in NY.* I was ninety-nine percent sure he was a cop, which is good odds for nearly everything in life, but not for things like maybe crossing a busy street, or trying to avoid getting whacked.

As I got closer to him—hand in my pocket—I asked, "On the job?"

He nodded and asked me, "Detective Corey?"

"That's right."

He said, "I'm Detective A. J. Nastasi, Special Operations." He added, unnecessarily, "I've been assigned to your protective detail." He also reminded me, "We've met a few times."

"Right." I know a lot of the Special Operations men and women, but they keep getting new people as the number of Muslim gents who need to be watched grows.

I asked Detective Nastasi, "Do you know why I need protection?"

"I've been briefed."

I took one of the Khalil photos from my folder and asked him, "You know who this guy is?"

He replied, "I have that photo."

"Yeah, but do you know who he is?"

Nastasi replied, "I was told that he's a professional hit man, foreign-born, armed and dangerous, and that he may be disguised."

"That's mostly correct." I also informed him, "He's the baddest motherfucker on the planet."

"Okay."

"You got a vest?"

"Never leave home without it."

"Good. You got real pizzas in those boxes?"

He smiled. "No."

This was not turning out to be my lucky day.

We chatted awhile about procedures, how many shifts there would be, the layout here, my anticipated comings and goings, and so forth. I advised him, "Work with the doormen on duty—they know the residents and some of the usual visitors and deliverymen."

"I'm on that."

I asked him, "Who are you supposed to notify when I leave the building?"

He replied, "Actually, I have some written instructions and contact numbers for you." He handed me a sealed envelope, which I put in my pocket.

I walked over to Alfred, who had remained behind his desk. He greeted me again and asked, "Is there a problem, Mr. Corey?"

"What do you think, Alfred?"

"Well, sir . . . I'm not sure what's happening."

"Well, then I'll tell you." I asked him, "You know of course that I don't work for the Environmental Protection Agency?"

"Yes, sir, I do know that."

"And Mrs. Corey is not a cocktail waitress as she told you."

He smiled tentatively and replied, "I suspected she was making a joke."

"Right. In fact, we are both with Federal law enforcement."

"Yes, sir. I know that."

In fact, on the morning of 9/12, Kate and I had arrived here separately, black with smoke and soot, and Alfred had been standing here with tears in his eyes.

Alfred is a good guy, and he likes me and Kate. He also liked my last wife, Robin, an overpaid criminal defense attorney whose apartment this had been. When Robin split, she gave me the seven-year lease, all the furniture, and some good advice. "Sublease it furnished and you'll make money."

But John the bachelor was a little lazy about moving, plus I liked the neighborhood bars and the south view from the balcony. Kate, too, has gotten to like the building and the neighborhood, so here we are.

Also, it's a secure building, and this was one of those rare times when I appreciated electronic locks, security cameras, and around-the-clock doormen who wouldn't buzz in Jack the Ripper.

On that subject, I asked Alfred, "Are there any apartments in this building with absentee tenants? Like corporate apartments?"

"No, sir."

I put a photo of Asad Khalil on the counter and asked, "Did Detective Nastasi give this to you?"

"Yes, sir."

"Make sure you pass it on to the next doorman."

"I know that."

"Good." I asked him, "Have I had any deliveries? Packages that tick?"

"No, sir. Just Saturday mail in your box."

Wondering if my colleagues had bugged my apartment, or if Asad Khalil's colleagues had gotten into my apartment to pick up my extra set of keys, I asked Alfred, "Has anyone been in my apartment? Phone company? Electrician?"

He checked his visitors' log and said, "I don't show any visitors while you were out." He asked me, "How was your weekend?"

"Interesting." I knew I had to inform him, "Mrs. Corey had a minor accident upstate so she won't be returning here for two or three days."

"I'm sorry to hear that."

I assured him, "She's fine, but we'll both be working at home for a few weeks."

"Yes, sir."

"We are not expecting visitors or deliveries."

Alfred is not stupid, and also he's been doing this for about twenty years, so he's seen it all—cheating spouses, domestic disturbances, maybe some high-priced hookers, parties that got out of hand, and God knows what else. Bottom line on Manhattan doormen, they know when to be alert and when to look the other way.

I said to Alfred, "I have luggage in my Jeep. Please have the porter bring it to my apartment."

"Yes, sir."

I also said to him, "Be certain my Jeep is locked and have the garage attendant give you his set of my keys. I'll get them later."

"Yes, sir."

There are a number of small but important things to remember regarding personal security, and I've advised many witnesses, informants, and others at risk of these commonsense precautions. And now I needed to take my own advice. I mean, if someone *really* wants to get you, they'll get you; but you don't have to make it easy for them. In fact, the best way to avoid an attack is to get the other guy first.

I went to the mailboxes in the outer foyer and retrieved my mail, which consisted mostly of bills and catalogs. The only thing that looked suspicious was an envelope from *Reader's Digest* advising me that I may have already won five million dollars.

I went to the elevators and rode up to my 34th-floor apartment.

When Kate and I rode down this elevator Saturday morning, my biggest concern was weekend traffic to Sullivan County, a possibly crappy motel room, and jumping out of an airplane.

Meanwhile, Asad Khalil was flying across the country in his chartered Citation jet, and we were on a collision course, though only he knew that.

I don't do victim very well, and my usual daily precaution against being one consists of making sure I have a fully loaded magazine in my Glock. I really didn't like being this bastard's quarry and having to look over my shoulder all day. And what *really* pissed me off was that this asshole had the idea that he could threaten me—and try to kill my wife—and live to talk about it.

If Asad Khalil thought *he* was pissed off, then he didn't know what pissed off was.

CHAPTER THIRTY-ONE

Key in my left hand, Glock in my right, I entered my apartment.

I know my own place very well, and within five minutes I'd cleared every room and closet. Fortunately for Asad Khalil, he wasn't there.

I also looked for signs that anyone had been in the apartment, but nothing appeared to be disturbed, though it's hard to tell with Kate's closet and vanity, which always look like they've been burglarized.

My next priority was the bar, where I poured myself a little lunch.

I sat at my living room desk and called the Catskill Regional Medical Center. I identified myself as John Corey and inquired about my wife, Kate Mayfield Corey. The desk nurse in ICU informed me there was no one there by that name, which was the correct response, so I then said, "This is Crazy John."

Silence, then, "Oh . . . yes . . ." She assured me that Kate was resting comfortably.

I asked, "Is she still on the ventilator?"

"She is."

"When will she be released?"

The nurse replied, "I'm showing tomorrow A.M."

"Good. Please tell her that Crazy John loves her and that I'll be there to sign her out."

She replied, "I'll pass that on."

I hung up and opened the envelope that Detective Nastasi had given me. It was basically an ATTF memo informing me of my status as a protected person, plus there were a few names, phone numbers, and e-mail addresses of people to contact in the Special Operations Group regarding my obligation to report my departures and my intended destinations. In addition to the person or persons in my lobby, there would be a surveillance team outside my building, but they wanted at least an hour's notice in order to get a mobile detail in place to follow me. I was to carry my tracking device, wear my wire and vest, and establish wire and cell phone contact with my mobile detail. Someone would call or visit me to go over this.

Regarding these mobile Special Operations teams, they were very experienced in surveillance and countersurveillance—the surveillance team watches and/or follows the subject, the countersurveillance team watches or follows to see if the surveillance team is being watched or followed—but sometimes they assign too many people to the job. I pictured myself walking down the street with a dozen detectives and FBI agents following me, and a half dozen unmarked cars creeping along the curb.

Bottom line on that, even if Asad Khalil was Omar

Abdel-Rahman, the blind sheik, he couldn't fail to notice I wasn't alone.

I mean, if this was simply a protective operation, it would work. But if I was supposed to be bait in a trap, The Lion wouldn't be biting.

I suspected that Walsh and whoever he was answering to weren't entirely clear in their own minds about what kind of operation this was. The police and the FBI often used decoys or undercover people in a sting operation, drug busts, and such, but officially no one ever put a guy out there as a moving target for a known killer. That's not safe for the guy or for civilians who could get caught in a crossfire. As always, there are rules—but there is also reality and expediency.

I knew that Tom Walsh, Vince Paresi, and George Foster were also being protected, but I wondered if it was overt protection—uniformed officers and marked cars, like the mayor gets—or was it covert, like I was getting? That, I suppose, would depend on whether or not those three gentlemen wanted to act as bait, or simply stay alive.

While I was enjoying a mental image of Tom Walsh being driven to work in an armored car, my cell phone rang and I saw it was Vince Paresi.

The temptation not to take the boss's call is overwhelming, but I wanted to demonstrate my full cooperation and good behavior early—it would get worse later—so I answered, "Corey."

He skipped the pleasantries and said, "You were supposed to see me before you left the office."

"Sorry. I'm so stressed—"

"And you were supposed to go to tech support."

"Today?"

"I'll have those items sent to you."

"Great. I'm at home."

"Have you met your SO guy in your lobby?"

"Detective A. J. Nastasi, Mario's Pizza delivery." I told him, "He got here fast. Even before I agreed to go home early."

"He was there, John, to make sure no one got into your apartment to wait for you."

"Good thinking." I asked him, "You guys all protected?"

He informed me, "I don't believe we're targets. But, yes, we are taking necessary precautions."

I advised him, "You should send your wife out of town for a while, Captain."

He didn't reply, and I thought maybe I should specify which wife. Can't send them all. Too expensive.

He asked, "You've read the memo pertaining to your protective detail?"

"Twice."

"Any questions?"

"None."

"Good." He said, "Tom informed me that you understand this is a team effort."

"Right."

"I am your immediate supervisor." He reminded me, "I am responsible for you. Do not screw me up."

I'm the target of a psychotic terrorist and all my boss is worried about is his career. I replied, "We're a team."

"Good." There was a short silence, then he said to me, "John, we may ask you to visit some locations."

"Yeah? Like Paris?"

"Some places that you can walk to, or get to by bus, subway, or taxi."

"Oh, I get it. Places where Khalil could follow me and where you've already positioned a SWAT team."

"Something like that."

"This is not sounding like I'm being protected from harm."

He reminded me, "You volunteered for this."

"What was I thinking?"

"This is your call, of course."

I said to him, "Look, I don't mind being the bait in the trap, but if I'm overprotected, you'll spook The Lion."

"I'd rather do that than have The Lion kill you."

"Are you sure?"

He ignored that and assured me, "The chances are very good that the surveillance team will spot Khalil before he spots us."

I thought about that and replied, "Well, as we both know from experience, it can go either way. But here's something else for you to think about—Khalil is not working alone. He has a network here, people who have prepped his mission for him. So I don't think it will be Asad Khalil himself who will be waiting under the lamppost for me to leave my apartment. It will be people whose faces we don't know, and who will be in communication with one another and with Khalil.

Then when the opportunity arises, Khalil will show up for his date with John Corey."

Paresi was silent for a few seconds, then asked me, "You think he has those kinds of assets here?"

"I do. And I think whoever these people are, they're not new to this game, and they know the territory here." I pointed out, "Think about what Khalil has already done. This is not a man acting alone."

"I know . . . but we're always better and smarter than they are."

Well, almost always.

He continued, "And as always, the countersurveillance team will be on the lookout for *anyone* who seems to be shadowing us—or you."

When you do these kinds of things—tailing people, looking for people tailing you, setting traps, and all that fun stuff—you never know how it's going to go down. So rather than argue with him about the details, I said, "My offer to be red meat stands."

"Good." He moved on to a happier subject and said, "The NYPD helicopter to pick up Kate will leave the East Thirty-fourth Street Heliport at seven A.M. sharp. Kate will be taken to Bellevue." He informed me, "There will be transportation for you in front of your building at six-thirty A.M."

"Thanks."

He advised me, "Don't hesitate to call me with any questions, thoughts, or information that you may recall or receive."

"I will do that."

"And be careful."

"Yourself as well."

We hung up and I refreshed my beverage. I also retrieved my fully charged paid-minutes cell phone from the kitchen counter. It's important to have one of these if you're a drug dealer, a cheating spouse, a terrorist, or just an honest guy like me with a government phone who doesn't want the taxpayers picking up the charges for his private calls.

I took my drink and sat in my La-Z-Boy recliner. This is the real thing—buttery leather, adjustable positions for reading, watching TV, sleeping, or pretending you're dead when the wife wants you to help with the dishes. I chose the half-upright Scotch-drinking position and dialed my prepaid cell phone.

A female voice answered, "Kearns Investigative Service. How may I help you?"

I replied, "This is John Corey. I'd like to speak to Mr. Kearns."

"He's not in. May I take a message?"

"Yes, I'm Mrs. Kearns's boyfriend. I need to speak to him."

"Uh . . . you are . . . ?"

"Mr. Kearns's old friend."

"Oh . . . I thought you . . ." She said, "Please hold."

A recorded voice thanked me for my call and urged me to stay on the line. Then a recorded pitch: "Kearns Investigative Service is staffed by highly trained and qualified men and women who have many years of experience in law enforcement. We offer comprehensive assistance in areas relating to researching the personal and professional histories of prospective employees. Please stay on the line for assistance."

The rousing theme song from *Bonanza* came on, which made me confident I'd called the right people.

Anyway, my old bud, retired NYPD Detective First Grade Dick Kearns, worked briefly for the Anti-Terrorist Task Force, where he learned, among other things, how the Feds operated. He then left the ATTF and started an agency that performed background investigations on people who had applied for work with the Federal government. In the old days this work was done mostly by the FBI, but as I said, outsourcing is the new order of the day—the FBI has more important things to do than vetting some guy named Ramzi Rashid who wants to work for the Transportation Security Agency at the airport.

More importantly for me, Dick Kearns has built up a large database, and he has good contacts in various government agencies, including the FBI, whom he assists and who assist him in his work.

Mr. Kearns himself came on the line and asked, "How long has this been going on?"

"Since you had the midnight-to-eight shift and I had the four-to-midnight."

"You didn't drink my booze, did you?"

"Would I do that to a friend?"

The opening remarks concluded, he asked me, "How's Kate?"

Rather than get into that now, I replied, "She's good. How's Mo?"

"Still putting up with my crap." He asked, "How you doing at 26 Fed?"

I replied, "I'm growing and learning, meeting new challenges with confidence and enthusiasm while developing good work habits and people skills."

"I'm surprised they haven't fired your ass."

"Me too. Hey, Dick, I need a favor."

"Hello? John? You're breaking up."

Everyone's a friggin' comedian. I said, "This is important and highly confidential."

"All right . . . do you want to meet?"

"I'm not allowed out."

"She catch you?"

"Actually, I'm being protected at home by Special Operations."

"Jeez. What the hell did you do?"

"I didn't *do* anything, Dick." I asked him, "Are you bug-free there? Phone and office?"

"Uh . . . yeah. I mean, I check." He asked me, "How about you?"

"I'm on a prepaid-minutes phone, and I'm pretty sure my apartment is clean."

"Okay. But why are we concerned about that?"

"I'm glad you asked. Here's the deal. I'm looking for a guy named Boris. Russian born, former KGB, age about fifty, last known—"

"Hold on. Boris *who*?"

"I don't know. I'm asking you."

"Don't you, like, work for the FBI? I mean, maybe they can help you."

"I'm outsourcing this."

"You mean this is official? I get paid?"

"No."

"*Jeez.* Come on, John. This is risky business."

"Let's say this is a private matter. Like a matrimonial. Maybe a credit check."

"The last two times I did this for you, I was sweating getting caught and losing my license."

"You licensed?"

"And my government contract."

"Last known living in the D.C. area, three years ago. Are you writing this down?"

"You're an asshole."

"After leaving the KGB, this man worked for Libyan Intelligence."

"Who?"

"Then he defected—actually, escaped from Libya—with the help of the CIA and wound up in Washington, where I met him three years ago—"

"I really don't want to touch anything that has to do with the Company."

"I'm not asking you to. My thinking is that when the CIA got through debriefing Boris, he went into this post-Soviet resettlement program that takes care of and keeps tabs on guys like Boris. But the CIA doesn't run this program in the U.S., so these resettled Soviets are usually turned over to the FBI to keep track of. Follow?"

"Yeah."

"So Boris is registered with a local FBI field office somewhere."

"Right." He reminded me, "I checked out a Russian

for you last October. Guy named Mikhail something. He lived in Boston and I—"

"Right. Did you get my check?"

"I had to call the FBI field office in Boston for that one, and they started asking me why I needed this information."

"For your *job*, Dick. And they gave you the info."

"Yeah . . . but . . . it's a stretch."

"Dick, if this wasn't important—"

"Okay. So you have no last name and only a last-seen time and place."

"Right. Ex-KGB. Boris. How many could there be?"

"John, I need something more—"

"He smokes Marlboros and drinks Stoli."

"Oh, why didn't you say so? Let me check my computer."

"Look, I think we have two possible locations on Boris. Washington metro area and New York metro. That's where half these Russians wind up. So you call your FBI sources in both places and say . . . whatever."

"Yeah. Whatever. What the hell am I supposed to tell them—?"

"Wing it. You're doing a background check for a security clearance. That's what the government pays you to do, Dick."

"They usually give me the person's last name, John. Plus other useful information like where he lives, where he's currently working, and everything the guy already put on his government employment application. I do *background* checks on known people—I don't *find* people."

"What happened to the old can-do Dick Kearns?"

"Cut the shit. Okay . . . here's what I can do . . . I can give the Bureau the name of a Russian guy I'm actually doing an FBI background check on . . . and I can say this guy seems to be in contact with a Russian guy named Boris who I need to check out, last name unknown, age about fifty, formerly KGB, worked for Libyan Intelligence, defected here, and was last seen in Washington three years ago."

"Smoking Marlboros. Brilliant."

"Yeah . . . and maybe if the FBI guy I'm speaking to doesn't ask me too many questions about how I already know so much about Boris, and if they don't want to look into this themselves, then maybe they'll come up with a Boris who fits the known information."

"See? Simple."

"Long shot." He asked me, "Where should I try first? D.C. or New York?"

I thought about that and replied hopefully, "New York."

"Good. I have better contacts at 26 Fed than in D.C."

That reminded me to ask him, "Is your job offer still good?"

"No."

"Why not? I have great contacts at 26 Fed."

"It doesn't sound like it."

Dick did not ask me what this was about because

obviously he did not want to know. But he did know that I was off the reservation again, plus, of course, I was under some sort of house protection, not to mention that I was asking about a job. So to give him a little clarification and motivation, I said to him, "Kate is actually not good. She was attacked by an Islamic terrorist."

"*What?* Holy—"

"She's okay. Knife wound to the neck. She'll be in the hospital for a few days, then back home under house protection."

"Thank God." He said, "So . . . the assailant is still at large?"

"He is."

"And he's looking for *you* now?"

"I'm looking for him."

"Right. And this guy Boris, who worked for Libyan Intelligence—?"

"It's related."

"Okay. If Boris is in the U.S., I'll find him for you."

"I know you will." I advised him, "He could be recently deceased."

"Okay. Dead or alive." He asked, "How do I contact you?"

I gave him my prepaid cell phone number and said, "I need this in twenty-four hours. Less."

"If you get off the phone, I'll get on it now."

"Regards to Mo."

"My prayers are with Kate."

How about me, Dick? "Thanks." I hung up and finished my drink.

Dick Kearns had about a fifty/fifty chance of finding Boris. Maybe less. The odds of Boris still being alive were less than that. But if Dick found him alive, then Boris and I could talk about how to solve our common problem.

The alcohol was giving me a little buzz, and I hadn't gotten much sleep, so I lay back in the recliner, closed my eyes, and yawned.

I saw a fuzzy image of me holding Khalil while Boris chipped away at Khalil's skull with an ice pick . . . then Boris was holding Khalil while I demonstrated a surgical incision into Khalil's jugular vein . . . and there was a lot of blood running down my arms . . .

CHAPTER THIRTY-TWO

Dawn is a little darker in the canyons of Manhattan Island, but I could see it was going to be another nice May day—good flying weather.

There was a different Special Operations guy in my lobby, Detective Lou Ramos, who had chosen to be a bagel deliveryman—a good choice at 6:30 A.M., and better yet, he had real bagels in a big bag, and he had a black coffee for me.

I was supposed to stay in the lobby until my car arrived, so I chatted with Detective Ramos, who seemed a little in awe of me for some reason. God knows what they'd told him about me at 26 Fed. *Ramos, you'll be protecting the legendary Detective John Corey, NYPD Homicide, retired on a medical with three slugs in him, and now doing brilliant and dangerous counterterrorism work for us.*

Detective Ramos confided in me, "If something happens to you on my watch, my ass is O-U-T."

"How do you think I'd feel? D-E-A-D."

Anyway, I was enjoying the VIP treatment, though not really enjoying the reason for it.

I sipped my coffee and thought about yesterday afternoon. I'd unpacked our suitcases, doing my own search for electronic devices, but I found nothing suspicious. Maybe I should stop thinking that Asad Khalil was that smart—or that my colleagues were that devious. Paranoia is fun, but it takes up a lot of time. On the other hand, I'm happiest when I get into my paranoid mode. I mean, the thought that my enemies *and* my friends are trying to get me is exquisitely exciting.

Also, yesterday afternoon, my package from tech support had been delivered, and I was now wearing my wire and GPS tracking device to demonstrate my cooperation and ability to follow instructions.

I was also wearing my Kevlar vest under a dress shirt that had been tailored to look good over my bulletproof undershirt, and I had on a sports jacket, also tailored to allow room for the vest and the Glock in my belt holster. I'm not vain, but it's important to look good when you're wearing a gun and armor, in case your picture gets in the papers.

I had used the remainder of the afternoon to read through the Khalil file. There wasn't much in there that I didn't recall, but seeing all our notes—mine, Kate's, George Foster's, and Gabe's—and our memos about our worldwide search for the elusive Libyan asshole made me realize how hard we'd tried for three years, and how completely this bastard had disappeared. I've never seen anything quite like that in my three years with the ATTF. Usually, you get a sighting, or a tip from an informant looking for the reward, or some hard intelligence coming from prisoner interrogations, or electronic intelligence from intercepted communications between terrorist groups or from countries that harbor terrorists. But for three years, we got not a single clue or sighting, and it was as though Asad Khalil had dropped off the planet, or never existed.

I didn't know where Khalil had hid out for the last three years, or what he had been doing, but I knew where he was now, and I knew what he had done, and what he thought he was going to do. So this, I was certain, would be my last chance to kill him.

I'd called the hospital around six to check on Kate—resting comfortably—then I spent some time at my computer, checking personal e-mails and sending a few to friends and family informing them of Kate's minor accident and that we'd be going away for a few weeks and we'd be unable to access e-mail.

There wasn't much voice mail on our home phone—everyone calls your cell phone these days, except for people you actually do want to hear from. Asad? Call John.

Then I began my incident report: *Special Agent Mayfield and I enjoy the sport of skydiving, and we belong to a skydiving club whose president is this shithead named Craig Hauser who wants to fuck Special Agent Mayfield—*

Let's try that again.

May in the Catskill Mountains can be very beautiful, with white doves soaring across an azure blue sky—

Anyway, I didn't get very far on my incident report, so I watched some local news, which reported on the home invasion in Douglaston, Queens, and the tragic murder of an Arab-American family of three. The reporter mentioned that the male victim was a city policeman, but there was no mention that he worked for the Anti-Terrorist Task Force—the "T" word would get people thinking. In fact, the newscaster said, "Authorities are investigating the possibility that this was a hate crime."

Well, it was. But not the kind you'd expect. Not a bad spin, though.

There was no mention on the news of Kate's mishap upstate, nor would there ever be. And no mention of the murdered cab driver on Murray Street and not even a mention of the shooting of chubby Charles Taylor in his limo at the Douglaston Rail Road station. The Feds had a tight grip on this.

I had gone to bed, alone, which I didn't like, and for the first time in a long time, I slept with my gun.

And now here I was in the lobby of my apartment building, eating my buttered bagel and sipping my coffee while waiting for my ride to the heliport.

I was looking forward to seeing Kate, but not happy that she was going to another hospital rather than coming home.

A marked Highway Unit SUV pulled up, and Detective Ramos and I went out to the sidewalk. A uniformed officer, who introduced himself as Ken Jackson, was behind the wheel, and another uniformed officer named Ed Regan opened the rear door for me. I slid in, Officer Regan got in the passenger seat, and off we went.

We got down to the East 34th Street Heliport, on the East River, in about fifteen minutes, and I thanked Ed and Ken and started to leave the vehicle, but Ken informed me that I needed to stay in the car. I was a protected person, and having been on these details my-self long ago, I recalled a few assholes—mostly politi-cians—who made my life and my job difficult, so I was sensitive to that and I stayed put as Officer Regan got out and stationed himself near the car.

Bottom line here was that the police were thinking about a sniper, but Asad Khalil was thinking about trying to cut off my head.

The blue-and-white NYPD helicopter was already on the pad, and I recognized it as the Bell 412, used mostly for air-sea rescue, and also fully equipped as an ambulance.

Bellevue Hospital, where we would be taking Kate, was also on the river, a few blocks south of the heli-port. Bellevue handled what we called sensitive cases— sick and injured prisoners, as well as injured witnesses and victims who were thought to be at further risk, like Kate.

Jackson got the word, and Officer Regan opened my door and escorted me to the waiting helicopter. I thanked Ed, climbed into the cabin, and looked around.

As I said, this was a fully equipped ambulance and rescue craft, so it was packed with all kinds of rescue gear and medical equipment, including a locked-in gurney that looked comfortable, but not as comfortable as my La-Z-Boy.

The engine started and it got loud in the cabin.

In addition to the pilot and the copilot, both NYPD, there was also a SWAT team guy in the cabin, armed with an MP-5 automatic rifle. Were we making an air assault? The SWAT guy greeted me with a wave, then closed the door, which made it a bit quieter.

I noticed also that there was a lady on board, sitting in one of the seats, wearing a blue windbreaker and white slacks. She stuck out her hand and said loudly over the sound of the engine, "Heather. Emergency Services."

We shook, and I said, "John. Door gunner."

She smiled.

She seemed like a nice lady, maybe fifty or sixty years old—maybe younger, like twenty-five, with long flaming red hair, breathtaking blue eyes, and the face of a Norse goddess.

She said, "So, we're going to pick up your wife?"

"Who?"

"Your *wife*."

"Oh . . . right." I'm married.

I took the seat facing her as the helicopter rose off the pad and slipped sideways over the river. We continued our ascent as we headed north, following the East River.

Heather asked me, "Do you like helicopters?"

"I *love* helicopters. How about you?"

"I'm not so sure."

"Can you swim?"

She smiled again.

Heather had the *Post*, and she buried her alabaster white face in the paper and read it with her big, velvety blue eyes.

I turned my attention to the window on my left and watched the towering skyscrapers of Manhattan slide by. We followed the Harlem River until it intersected the Hudson, and we continued north for a while, then turned west toward Sullivan County.

Heather put down the newspaper and asked me, "Who lacerated her carotid?"

I replied, "Some psycho."

She glanced at the SWAT guy and asked me, "You think he's still after her?"

"We're not taking any chances."

She informed me, "She's lucky to be alive. That's usually fatal."

"I know."

Heather observed, "She's getting very special treatment."

I replied, of course, "She's a very special lady." But she doesn't understand me, Heather. Actually, she does.

Heather observed, "You're wearing a vest."

And *she* looked like she was smuggling balloons. I replied, "I am." Why did I spend a thousand bucks on the shirt and sports jacket? As per protocol, I informed her, "And I'm carrying." I added, "NYPD, retired."

"You're too young to retire."

"Disability."

"Mental?"

I smiled and replied, "Everyone asks that."

She laughed.

Realizing that my wife would be on the return trip with Heather, I cooled it and asked, "Can I have part of that paper?"

"Sure."

About thirty minutes into the flight, the engine changed pitch and we began descending. In the far distance, I could see the runway of Sullivan County Airport where all this crap began not too long ago.

Within a minute I spotted the big white building of the Catskill Regional Medical Center, and then I saw the helipad to the side of the building.

A few minutes later, we were on the ground. The engine stopped, the rotary blades wound down, and the door opened.

Heather said to me, very professionally, and perhaps coolly, "Please stay in the aircraft."

She climbed down and moved quickly toward the hospital. The SWAT guy also got out and took up a position between the helicopter and the hospital. I also noticed two uniformed State Troopers near the hospital door, armed with rifles. This might be overkill, but someone had made the safe decision.

I watched from the door as Kate was wheeled out of the hospital and rolled toward the helicopter. She was wearing green scrubs and a white robe, but she had no IVs attached to her and no ventilator, which was a good sight. I saw she was carrying the stuffed lion in her lap. She saw me at the door, smiled and waved. I waved back.

Four attendants lifted her and the wheelchair on board and I stepped aside.

As soon as she was placed on the gurney, I went over to her and said, "Hi, beautiful."

We kissed and she said, "It's good to see you."

Her voice was a little raspy, but I didn't mention it. I said, "It's good to see *you*. You look great." And she did look well. Her lip and cheek were still a little puffy where Khalil had hit her, but she had good color and wore a little makeup to cover the face bruise. There was only a small dressing over her wound, though I could see black and blue marks around the dressing.

One of the attendants gave me a bag that contained her helmet and boots, which I signed for, and I also signed her discharge papers, insurance forms, waivers, and what looked liked a codicil to my will leaving the hospital everything.

The engine restarted and within a minute we were airborne.

I stood beside Kate and held her hand. I could see now that her cheeks looked a bit sunken. She patted the lion and said, "This was in questionable taste."

"It was," I admitted, "but it's the thought that counts."

On the subject of lions, she asked me, "Do we need the SWAT guy?"

I replied, "It's SOP."

Heather came over and said to Kate, "Hi. I'm Heather. ESU. How are you feeling?"

"Fine."

Heather asked Kate a few medical questions, put a

temperature strip on her forehead, took her blood pressure, and said, "Everything's good." She also said, "Cute lion."

Kate replied, "My husband gave it to me," and smiled at me.

I thought Heather was going to say, "Oh, is John your husband?" But she just moved away and sat.

Kate observed, "She's very pretty."

"Who?"

"The nurse."

"Heidi?"

"Heather."

"Yeah?"

Anyway, we chatted awhile, but not about business. Her voice was weak and I urged her not to talk too much, and I helped her sip from a water bottle. She said, "I was able to get some Jell-O down this morning."

What's with the Jell-O? Why do hospitals give sick people Jell-O? When I was at Columbia-Presbyterian after I took three slugs, they kept bringing me Jell-O. Why the hell would I want to eat Jell-O?

Kate said to me, "And you had a poppy bagel for breakfast."

I ran my tongue over my teeth. Was I smiling at Heather with a poppy seed in my teeth?

Kate informed me, "Someone from headquarters, a guy named Peterson, stopped by last night to see how I was doing."

It's not unusual for someone from Washington to call on an agent injured in the line of duty, but I was sure there was more to it than compassion and protocol. In fact, Kate said, "He reminded me not to speak to anyone about the incident—like I need reminding."

I didn't reply to that, but said, "I've been put on traumatic leave so I'll be home while you convalesce."

"That's not necessary." She suggested, "Maybe I'll ask my mother to come for a visit."

Then maybe I'll stand on the balcony with a bull's-eye taped to my forehead.

"John?"

I informed her, "This leave is not voluntary." I reminded her, "No business talk until you're home."

"Okay." She asked me, "Would you jump again?"

"Yes, from the balcony if your mother comes to visit." I didn't actually say that—I said, "I think of little else." I was bursting with the news of what happened with the DC-7B, and this was my opening. I said, "The club didn't want to make the next two jumps, out of consideration for what happened to you, but Craig insisted, saying they'd paid for it, and what happened to you should not spoil their jump." I glanced at her, but I couldn't tell if she was buying this. So I got down to the true part of the story. "Well, they took off, and—you're not going to believe this—but one of the engines caught fire and they had to make an emergency landing."

"Oh my God."

"The engine that had the oil leak. The one I was concerned about."

"Really?"

"That's what a State Trooper told me." I added,

modestly, "I have a nose for trouble. A sixth sense for danger."

"Was anyone hurt?"

"No, but Craig got hysterical and had to be sedated."

She seemed a little skeptical about that, but said, "I don't blame them for going ahead with the jump. We planned it for months."

"Well, next time pick a better plane."

To get me off the subject, she conceded, "You're very smart, John. I should listen to what you say." She smiled and asked me, "So, how do you feel about this helicopter?"

Heather was back, and before I could reply she piped in, "John says he loves helicopters."

Kate inquired, "Really?"

Heather took Kate's blood pressure again and found it slightly elevated.

Anyway, the flight back was smooth, fast, and without incident—no ground fire, no surface-to-air missiles, and no pursuit aircraft.

As we approached the heliport, I looked out the window and saw police highway units in position to close down the FDR Drive so that the waiting ambulance could make a straight shot to the Bellevue E.R. entrance in about one minute.

Kate said to me, "I'd really rather be going home. I feel fine."

"You'll be home in a few days."

Heather informed us, "I do visiting nurse work if you need somebody."

Yes.

Kate said, "Thank you, but my mother will be visiting."

Actually, she wouldn't be. Not under the present circumstances. But I didn't get into that.

I looked at Kate, then I looked out the window at the city. The bastard who had tried to kill her in Sullivan County was now here. But he wasn't leaving here.

CHAPTER THIRTY-THREE

The NYPD had stationed a uniformed cop directly outside the door of Kate's private room. Actually, half the floor is basically a secured zone, and most of the patients are guests of the FBI, the NYPD, or the Department of Corrections, and they will be discharged into a paddy wagon or a hearse. It's an interesting floor.

Kate didn't bring up the subject of Khalil's attack on her, but I'm sure it was on her mind, and it's best not to repress the trauma, but rather to talk about it. So I said, "I saw the videotape of the jump."

She stayed silent, then asked, "What could you see?"

"You need to see it yourself. And read my report."

She advised me, "Don't puff yourself up like you usually do."

"I can tell you're getting back to your old self."

She smiled, took my hand, and said, "I know you saved my life."

I said, "We can talk about all that when you're home." Or now, if you'd like.

She changed the subject to the business at hand. Kate, like Heather, had noticed my extra bulk, and we discussed some of what was happening in regard to my status—and her status—as a protected person, though I didn't mention that I might be taking some long walks at night.

I didn't bring up the subject of the two murders in California, or the five murders in New York. I would, but murder is a conversation stopper, so we discussed some ideas, theories, and possible strategies.

Kate, with time and motivation to think about all this, had come to some of the same conclusions that I'd come to, and that Paresi and Walsh had eventually reached, to wit: Khalil was the worst type of person to be looking for—a highly trained, disciplined, and motivated loner with no close accomplices, no friends or family in the area, and no usual or suspected places that he would frequent.

Kate also agreed that Khalil most probably had resources here, people who had no prior or direct connection to him, but who would provide logistics and information.

We also discussed the possibility that Khalil might have some fireworks planned for his finale. Kate said, "He might, but like last time, he will take care of personal business first." She thought a moment, then said, "Like Chip Wiggins." She asked me, "Has anyone done anything about that?"

"Actually, yes. Khalil has."

"Oh . . . my God . . ."

"Right. Last week in Santa Barbara." I told her

about the murder of Chip Wiggins, and I didn't spare her the details of his beheading. I said, "Khalil picked up where he left off." I also told her about the Libyan-American, Farid Mansur.

She nodded, then said, "Chip was a nice man."

"Khalil didn't think so."

I also told her about the murder of Amir on Murray Street, and I said, "You'll recall last time that Khalil knocked off a Libyan cab driver."

She nodded, and correctly concluded, "Khalil is in the city."

Her next thought was that I, John Corey, was the man most likely to next see Asad Khalil—assuming I saw it coming.

She said to me, "John, I hope they have you completely covered."

"Of course."

"Be careful . . . and don't volunteer to . . . trap Khalil."

"Of course not."

It was time to tell her about Gabe, but first I said, "We're thinking that Khalil may be targeting the Task Force, so there may be others on Khalil's list—like George Foster, or even Vince or Tom."

Kate nodded and said to me, "I suppose Khalil does have some knowledge of the inner workings and command structure of the Task Force." This brought her to another thought, and she said, "Also Gabe. He's an Arab-American, and he's on the Lion Hunter team."

I took her hand and said, "Gabe is dead."

She didn't respond.

I told her what happened to Gabe and his wife and daughter, and again, I didn't spare her any of the reported details, which she would soon have access to, but I did not tell her that Gabe had been killed with her gun. I concluded, "The police are calling it a home invasion, or a possible bias crime." I made sure to let her know, "By the appearance of the crime scene, we know that Gabe fought back." I also filled her in about the murder of the limo driver near Gabe's house.

She stared up at the ceiling with tears in her eyes. Finally, she said, "What did those poor women do to . . . die like that?"

She seemed tired and her voice was getting weaker, so I said, "I'm going to let you rest."

She looked at me and said, "Get me out of here tomorrow."

"I'll try."

I told Kate I'd be back that evening if I could. We kissed and I went to the nurses' station and told the duty nurse that Mrs. Corey wanted to be discharged the next day.

The nurse consulted her chart and informed me that Mrs. Corey first needed to be medically evaluated. Also, there was a flag on her discharge.

"Meaning?"

"Meaning it is not purely a medical decision."

"Meaning?"

"Meaning we need to notify certain people before she can be discharged."

Meaning that Walsh and whoever he was taking orders from had decided to keep Special Agent Kate

Mayfield in Bellevue where they could keep her under wraps, and also keep her away from her husband whom she loved dearly, but who the FBI needed to borrow for a special assignment, namely, live bait.

The people at 26 Fed and in Washington sometimes impressed me with their thinking. I say that whenever they think like I do.

The nurse wasn't going to tell me who "certain people" were, and she didn't know herself, so I said, "See if Mrs. Corey would like a sedative." I thanked her and left.

CHAPTER THIRTY-FOUR

Back in my apartment, I managed to get half of my incident report typed—being careful not to embellish the facts, and letting my actions speak for themselves. And keeping in mind that Kate would be reading this, I made her look good, describing how she grappled with her assailant and so forth. I even gave her that knee to Khalil's nuts.

At five o'clock I watched the local news that had dropped the story about the home invasion and murders in Douglaston, Queens. This was yesterday's news, and it wouldn't be news again unless there was an arrest in the case, or if the media decided to cover the funeral. Gabe would get a full inspector's funeral, and I needed to find out the funeral arrangements.

The scroll at the bottom of the TV screen reported the alert level at yellow, where it seemed to have been stuck for many months. It would never be green, and it hadn't been orange in a long time. I personally like orange—it gets everyone's attention and gives people something to talk about over cocktails.

On that subject, it was now cocktail hour, and I had time for a small one before I was picked up by my chauffeur and shotgun rider for my hospital visit.

As I was trying to decide if I wanted vodka (odorless) or Scotch (my usual), my prepaid cell phone rang.

Not many people have that number, but it could be Kate.

I picked up the phone from the coffee table and answered, "Corey."

Dick Kearns's voice said, "May I speak to the man of the house?"

Dick obviously had good news. I replied, "Yes, ma'am. I'll get him."

He laughed at my quick wit and said, "Hey, John, I think I found him. Right here in New York."

"Alive?"

"Yeah . . . I guess. The guy I got this from in the New York field office didn't say he was dead."

"Okay." But the FBI wouldn't necessarily know immediately if one of their registered defectors had gone missing or had an accident.

"Ready to copy?"

I had a pad and pencil on the coffee table and said, "Shoot."

"Okay. Boris Korsakov." He spelled it for me and said, "He fits your description of approximate age and former KGB employment. The FBI guy I spoke to didn't say anything about Libyan Intelligence, or past addresses, but he did say that Boris was here under the post-Soviet resettlement program."

"Okay . . . I guess that's close—"

"You saw this guy—right?"

"Right."

"So, go to your computer. I e-mailed you the photo the FBI e-mailed me."

"Hold on." I went into the spare bedroom that Kate and I had made into a home office—*not* a guest room for Mom—and logged onto my computer.

Dick asked me, "How's Kate?"

"Much better."

I retrieved Dick's e-mail, and staring back at me on the screen was Boris. My Boris.

"You got it?"

"I do. That's him, Dick. You're a genius."

"I am a total bullshit artist. I had this FBI guy in the palm of my hand."

Dick went on a bit, and I listened politely and patiently. Dick Kearns, who hadn't been so sure he could or should do this for me, now assured me that it was a piece of cake. But then he caught himself and said, "I busted my butt getting to the right guy, and convincing him I had clearance and need-to-know."

I kept staring at the photo of Boris. This was a tough-looking hombre, and I recalled that Kate and I had been impressed with him—he not only talked the talk, he walked the walk. Could Asad Khalil have gotten the upper hand on this guy? I wouldn't have thought so three years ago when I'd met Boris, but . . .

"John? I said, I have an address."

"Good."

"He lives at 12–355 Brighton 12th Street, Brighton Beach—along with half the Russians in New York. Apartment 16-A." Dick added, "He's been there almost three years."

"Okay." Boris got his wish to be resettled in New York, and he'd picked a neighborhood where he wouldn't get too homesick, and where ex-KGB guys got together over a bottle of vodka and reminisced about the good old days when they were young and hated.

"I couldn't get Boris's cell or home phone from the FBI, but I did get his business phone."

"Good enough."

Dick gave me Boris's business number and I asked him, "Where's he work?"

"Okay, here's the part that could be a little fun for you, so I saved it for last—"

"You better not tell me he works in a Russian bath house where he scrubs men's asses."

"Funny, I was going to say that. But here's the deal. Boris owns and operates a Russian nightclub in Brighton Beach. You remember, we went to a few of those places with Ivan the crazy Russian when we were single, and—"

"*I* was single. You've been married thirty years."

"Whatever. Anyway, remember that place . . . ? What was the name? Rossiya. Those tall, blonde—"

"Do you have a name for *this* place?"

"Yeah. It's Svetlana. I don't think we were ever there. It's right on the boardwalk at Brighton Third Street."

"Okay . . . and this place is owned by Boris?"

"Well, with these Russkies, who knows who the silent partners could be? It's all Russian Mafia. Right? Maybe Boris is the front guy."

"Maybe. But maybe the CIA gave him a loan."

"Yeah? Hey, maybe we should defect to Russia and see about opening an American nightclub."

"You go first. I'll stay here and run your business."

"We can talk." He asked me, "What do I do now with Vasili Rimski?"

"Who?"

"The guy I'm doing the background check on. He put in an application to work for the General Accounting Office—he's an accountant. Low-level background check. But I just told the FBI that he consorts with an ex-KGB guy named Boris Korsakov. Should I mention that in my report?"

"Do what's best for the country, Dick."

He laughed and said, "Hey, let me know how this turns out."

"Okay—"

"Why haven't I seen anything in the papers?"

"It's under tight wraps." I hesitated, then asked him, "Did you see that story about the home invasion and murders in Queens?"

"Yeah. A cop and his family."

"Well, that cop worked for the Task Force."

Dick was silent for a moment, then said, "Jeez." He asked me, "And that's related to the attack on Kate?"

"Yeah."

He was silent again and asked, "Is that why you're under house protection?"

"You should be a detective." I said to him, "Okay, I owe you big time for this. I'm off to see Kate—"

"Watch yourself."

"Thanks for reminding me. I'll call you next week."

I hung up and printed out the color photo of Boris, and I wrote on it, "Svetlana Nightclub, Brighton Beach," then I wrote a note to Kate saying, *Tell Vince and Tom they need to see Boris, and tell them why.*

It occurred to me that I was leaving notes around as though I didn't expect to be around myself.

Before I left the apartment, I poured myself a little Stolichnaya, to celebrate appropriately, and to wish Boris a long life. Or at least long enough to be alive when I got there.

CHAPTER THIRTY-FIVE

The high-security floor at Bellevue is the worst of two bad worlds—a hospital run like a prison. My name was on the authorized visitor list, and my NYPD shield and Fed creds got me through the security checkpoint with only minor hassles. On the positive side, Asad Khalil was not getting onto this floor.

Actually, Asad Khalil should have no idea that Mrs. Corey was alive, well, and here. I wondered, though, if his friends in New York were looking at the obituaries or checking the public records for Kate's death. Not to be too paranoid, but if Khalil knew or suspected that Kate was not dead, then his local friends would probably guess that this was where she'd be. We could, as we'd done in the past, plant a fake obit, but then my phone would be ringing off the hook, and half the single women in my building would be knocking on my door with casseroles. So, no obit, but I made a mental note to tell Walsh to get a phony death certificate issued and recorded.

Sitting now beside Kate's bed, I let her know that she needed to stay in the hospital for a while, but she'd already discovered that, and she wasn't happy about it. Kate, though, is career FBI, and she does what's best for the Bureau, the team, and the mission. I, on the other hand, would by now be climbing out the window on knotted bed sheets.

I noticed that she had the stuffed lion hanging by its neck from the window-blind cord, and I asked her, "Have you had your mental evaluation yet?"

She smiled and said, "I'm trying to get into the nut ward so we can be together."

We chatted awhile and Kate told me she'd gotten a call from Tom Walsh, who, she informed me, was the only person at 26 Fed, aside from Vince Paresi, who knew she was in Bellevue Hospital. She told me, "I asked Tom to send me my cell phone, and I also asked him who was holding my gun."

I didn't respond to that.

She continued, "Tom said my gun and cell phone were missing and possibly in the possession of my assailant."

I replied, "The State Police are still searching for those items."

"That's what Tom said . . ." She didn't speak for a while, then told me, "I don't remember . . . but I think he may have grabbed my gun . . ."

"Don't worry about it. He's got lots of guns."

She replied, "But if he has my cell phone, then he has my phone directory." She looked at me and said, "He's going to call you."

"I hope so." I changed the subject and asked her, "Is there anything I can bring you?"

"My discharge papers."

"Soon."

She said to me, "I told Tom about my idea to check that murdered taxi driver's cell phone records to see who called him and who he called, but there's no record of this man's cell phone."

"Right. Good thought, but dead end."

She stared up at the ceiling awhile, then said, "I feel so helpless here . . . so useless."

I tried to make her feel better by saying, "You may be the only person on this planet who fought back against Asad Khalil and lived to tell about it."

She forced a smile and reminded me, "Twice. He missed me—missed both of us—three years ago."

"Right. And he's going to regret that."

She asked me, "Why didn't he . . . try to kill you this time?"

Kate was obviously starting to think about all this, and I said, "He had his hands full with you."

She looked at me. "I think he wanted you to see me die."

To get her off unpleasant subjects, and to put her mind at ease, I told her about how I was surrounded by Special Operations teams wherever I went, and that our apartment building was under tight security.

Kate nodded absently, and I could see her mind was elsewhere. She looked at me and said, "We let Khalil get away, John."

I didn't reply, and she continued, "We had a chance to kill or capture him three years ago, and we—"

"Kate, I don't want to go through that again—what we could have done or should have done. We did the best we could at the time when the bullets were flying."

She didn't reply, but I was actually glad she'd raised the topic and got it out in the open. The fact was, Kate and I were the last people to interact with Asad Khalil—though we never actually saw him; he was target shooting with a sniper rifle and we were the targets. And even though he had the advantage in firepower, there were a few things we—I—could have done to nail his ass. And I guess that still bothered her—and me.

I reminded her, however, "No one else raised that point. There was never anything said. So don't be harder on yourself—or on me—than our bosses were."

Again, she didn't reply, but I wasn't sure that what I said was actually true. The fact was, we never saw the Khalil case file, and we never would. And it was not a stretch to imagine that John Corey and Kate Mayfield made convenient scapegoats. And maybe that's what Walsh read.

In police work, the one that got away is the one you think about more than your successes. And you think about it even more when the guy who got away comes back.

She said to me, "We have a chance now to . . . finish this."

"Right." I reminded her, "As I said to Khalil on the

cell phone three years ago—looking forward to a re-match."

I realized I had to say something about Boris before Kate thought of it, and before she mentioned Boris to Tom. I began by asking, "When you spoke to Tom, did you mention to him our trip to Langley after Khalil escaped?"

She stayed silent for a few seconds, then said, "No . . . I'd forgotten about meeting Boris. I'll tell Tom—"

"No, you will not."

"Why not?"

"Well . . . I'd like to take the credit for that piece of information." I reminded her, "I need all the credit I can get."

She thought about that and came to another conclusion. "I hope you're not pursuing that on your own."

"What do you mean?" I asked her innocently.

"You *know* what I mean, John." She reminded me, "You do this every time."

"That's not true." I only do it when I can.

"You have this need to keep something to yourself, which you think gives you some power or something, and then you'll spring it and show everyone—"

"Hold on. I'm not the only one at 26 Fed who keeps things to themselves."

"That's not the point. The point is, it's your *duty* to share with your supervisors whatever you know—"

"And I will do that." But not today. I said, "First, I'm not sure if Boris can add anything to the resolution of this case. And two, I—and you—know nothing about Boris, not even his last name, so how could I possibly find him on my own? Therefore I will certainly turn this information over to Tom Walsh, who can have Boris found in a few hours—if he's still alive."

She thought about that and said, "All right. I'll trust you to speak to Tom about Boris."

"I will do that."

She thought again, then said, "Khalil will go for Boris."

"Right." I added, "That may already be a done deal."

She nodded. "I remember our conversation with him . . . I had the impression that Boris realized he'd created a monster."

I agreed and said, "Boris had a lot of material to work with."

Kate was still processing all this and said, "We could use Boris to entrap Khalil."

"We could."

An orderly came by and dropped off a dinner menu. Kate checked off some items, then passed the menu to me and suggested, "Get something."

I saw that it was fusion cooking—prison and hospital. I said, "The unsolved mystery meat looks good."

"Not funny."

Lockdown lettuce?

I passed on the dinner, and we watched a little TV and talked until her meal came.

Medically, she could be out of here in a few days, but Walsh would try to keep her here until her husband and her assailant had their final meeting.

Russian nightclubs start late, and I would have stayed with Kate until visiting hours were over, but she

NELSON DeMILLE

said she was tired—or tired of me—so I kissed her good-bye and said, "Try to get some rest."

"What else can I do here?"

"Think about what else Khalil might be up to."

"I'm thinking." She asked me, "Where are you going now?"

"The only place I'm allowed to go. Home."

"Good." She smiled and said, "Don't go out clubbing."

Funny you should say that.

"Be careful, John." She squeezed my hand and said, "I love you."

"Me too. See you tomorrow morning."

I left her room and chatted with Kate's NYPD guard, a lady named Mindy who assured me that she was aware that Kate's assailant was not a common dumb criminal, and she also assured me that not even Conan the Barbarian could get on this floor—but if he did, he wasn't getting past Mindy Jacobs.

I was not as concerned about Conan the Barbarian as I was about Asad the Asshole having himself delivered here in a crate of enemas or something.

I said good night to Mindy and walked through the ward, noting the closed and bolted room doors and the uniformed and armed men and women from the Department of Corrections.

If I were Asad Khalil, how would I get in here and get to Kate? Well, I'd start by getting myself thrown in jail, identity unknown, then faking a serious illness, which would get me sent to Bellevue, behind a bolted door. After that, Asad Khalil would have no difficulty getting out of that room and into Kate's room.

But I shouldn't give him supernatural powers. And he didn't even know that Kate was here.

I took the elevator down and met my escorts in the lobby—still Officers Ken Jackson and Ed Regan, who must be as tired of me as I was of them.

Within fifteen minutes, I was back at my apartment building on East 72nd Street.

There was a custodian in the lobby who looked very much like Detective Louis Ramos, the bagel deliveryman. I stopped and chatted with Ramos a moment, then went to the desk where Alfred was reading a newspaper.

He put down his newspaper—the *Wall Street Journal*; tips must be good—and inquired, "How is Mrs. Corey?"

"Much better, thank you." I said to Alfred, "I forgot to pick up my car keys."

"I have them right here." He opened a drawer and produced my keys.

I told him, "I need to get some things out of storage, so if you don't mind, I'll borrow the key for the freight elevator."

"Yes, sir." He retrieved the key to the freight elevator and put it on the desk, and I held it in my hand with my car keys in case Detective Ramos was watching. I wished Alfred a good evening and walked to the apartment elevators.

The other way out of here without going through the

lobby was the fire stairs, but each staircase had surveillance cameras, and the monitor was sitting on the doorman's desk where Ramos or anyone could see who was on the staircase—or see the videotapes afterward. The freight elevator, however, was not monitored, and it went down to the garage where I would be going shortly.

I rode up to my apartment, where I'd already picked out my Russian nightclub outfit.

CHAPTER THIRTY-SIX

I had laid out a dark gray suit and gray tie that I usually wear for weddings and funerals, plus a silk shirt and diamond cufflinks that my ex had given me. My shoes were real Italian Gravatis and my watch was a Rolex Oyster that an old girlfriend had bought on the street for forty bucks and might not be real. To complete my outfit, I slipped into my Kevlar vest, though this time I forgot my wire and tracking device. I finished dressing, not forgetting my Glock, and checked myself out in the mirror. Russian Mafia? Italian Mafia? Irish cop dressed funny?

I put one of the photos of Asad Khalil in my jacket pocket, left my apartment, and walked to the freight elevator located in a far corner of the 34th floor. The apartment elevators all stopped in the lobby, and you then needed to walk across the lobby to the garage elevator. But the freight elevator was sort of an express to the underground garage, and for security reasons you had to ask for the key, which I had done and which I now used to summon the elevator.

The detectives who would have cased this building before I arrived home must have figured out the freight elevator escape route, but even if they did, they weren't looking at me as a flight risk; I was a colleague who was under protection—not house arrest. Not yet, anyway.

The doors opened, and I got into the big, padded car and pushed the button for the garage level. The freight elevator bypassed the lobby and continued down to the parking garage, where truck deliveries were made.

The doors opened, and I stepped out of the elevator into the underground garage. So far so good.

Or was I now trapped in the garage whose entrance would be under surveillance by the Special Operations team on the street? Obviously, I couldn't walk up the parking ramp or drive my green Jeep out onto 72nd Street without getting busted. Actually, if I was running this job, I'd also have a surveillance guy down here. And maybe there was one, and I'd meet him in a minute. If not, then I'd found an easy way out of my building.

I walked over to the parking attendant's window, and there was an older gent in the small office who I didn't recognize. He was watching TV and I said, "Excuse me. I need a ride."

He looked away from the TV—Mets game—and asked me, "What's your number?"

"No," I explained, "I don't need my car. I need a ride."

"I think you got the wrong place, Bub."

"I'll give you fifty bucks to take me down to Sixty-eighth and Lex." I explained, "I have a proctologist appointment."

He looked at me and asked, "Why don't you walk?"

"Hemorrhoids. Come on—what's your name?"

"Irv." He advised me, "Call me Gomp."

"Why?"

"That's my name. Irv Gomprecht. People call me Gomp."

"Okay, Gomp. Sixty bucks."

"I don't have a car."

"You have two hundred cars. Pick one." I assured him, "You can listen to the game on the radio."

Gomp looked me over, silk shirt and all, and decided I was a man to be trusted—or Mafia—and he said, "Okay. But we gotta move fast."

I threw three twenties on the counter, and he snatched them up, then picked a key off the board, saying, "This guy ain't used his car in two months." He added, "Needs a run."

Anyway, within a few minutes I was in the passenger seat of a late-model Lexus sedan, and Gomp was driving up the ramp. He confessed, "I do this for the old people once in a while, but nobody never paid me sixty bucks."

"You're making me feel stupid, Gomp."

"Nah. I just meant I usually—hey, whaddaya doin'?"

"Tying my shoes."

"Oh . . ."

I stayed below the dashboard and felt the car turn

right onto 72nd Street. I waited until we stopped at the light on Third Avenue before I sat up.

I looked in the sideview mirror and didn't see any of the usual makes or models that the Task Force used. It would be really funny if Lisa Sims was on this detail and she busted me. Maybe not so funny.

Gomp asked me, "You live in the building?"

"No." I volunteered, "I live on East Eighty-fourth." I put out my hand and said, "Tom Walsh."

Gomp took my hand and said, "Good to meet you, Tom."

"My friends call me tight-ass."

"Huh?"

God, I hope the FBI interviews this guy tonight.

With that in mind, I asked him, "Are you a surveillance cop? FBI?"

He thought that was funny and said, "No, I'm CIA."

Not funny, Gomp.

The light changed, and he continued on 72nd, while tuning in to the Mets game. He asked me, "Are you Mets or Yankees?"

"Mets," I lied.

Gomp was an old New York icon, accent and all, and I realized there were fewer of them every year, and I was missing the old days when life was simpler and stupider.

Within a few minutes we were at the corner of Lexington and 68th Street, and I said, "I'll get out here."

He pulled over and said, "Anytime you need a ride, Tom, look for me in the garage."

"Thanks. Maybe tomorrow. Urologist."

I got out of the car and descended the stairs to the Lexington Avenue subway entrance. I consulted the transit map, used my MetroCard at the turnstile, and found my platform.

For Manhattanites, Brighton Beach is somewhere this side of Portugal, but the B train went there, so that's how I'd get there.

The train came, and I got on, then got off, then got on again as the doors closed. I saw this in a movie once. In fact, some asshole I was following five years ago must have seen it too.

To make a long subway ride short, less than an hour after I'd boarded the train, I was traveling on an elevated section of the line, high above the wilds of Brooklyn. I recalled taking this line from my tenement on the Lower East Side to Coney Island when I was a kid, when Coney Island was my magic summer kingdom by the sea. I remembered, too, spending all my money on arcade games, rides, and hot dogs, and having to beg a cop for subway fare home.

I still don't handle money very well, and John Corey still screws up, but now the cop I go to when I need help is me. Growing up is a bitch.

I got off at the Ocean Parkway stop and descended the stairs onto Brighton Beach Avenue, which ran under the elevated tracks. After all this escape-and-evasion, and a long subway ride, Boris had damned well better be alive and at his nightclub—or at least in his apartment, which wasn't too far from here. The good news was that if the FBI had been following me, they'd still be at the 68th Street station trying to get their MetroCards in the turnstile. And if an NYPD detective from my surveillance detail was following me, I'm sure I'd have picked him out.

I haven't been to Brighton Beach in maybe fifteen years, and then only a few times, with Dick Kearns and the Russian-American cop named Ivan who'd been born here and who knew the turf and spoke the language. Of all the interesting ethnic enclaves in New York, this is one of the most interesting and least touristy. I'd say it was real, but there was something unreal about the place.

I walked east along the avenue and checked it out. Lots of cars, lots of people, and lots of life on the street. A guy was selling Russian caviar from a table on the sidewalk for ten bucks an ounce. Great price. No overhead and no middleman. No refrigeration either.

I got to Brighton 4th Street and headed south toward the ocean, which I could actually smell.

The people on the street seemed well fed. No famine here. As for how they were dressed . . . well, it was interesting. Everything from expensive suits, such as I was wearing, to fake designer clothing, and lots of old ladies who'd brought their clothes with them from the Motherland. Despite the balmy weather, a few guys wore fur hats, and a lot of the older women wore babushkas tied around their heads. Also, the air was thick with unfamiliar smells. Did I take the subway too far east?

About now, I was wondering if this was a good

idea. I mean, it *seemed* like a good idea when I thought about it back in Manhattan. Now I wasn't so sure.

My first concern was that I might be screwing up a good lead. It's okay to do that when you're on the job and things just go bad. But when you're in business for yourself, if you screw up an investigation, a fecal storm will descend on you so fast, you couldn't dig your way out of it with a steam shovel.

My other concern, which was not really a concern, was that Asad Khalil might be on the same mission as I was tonight. I certainly didn't need help in dealing with Khalil, mano a mano, but it's always good to have backup in case you're outnumbered. On the other hand, if Khalil was alone, then I wanted to be alone with him.

As I approached Brightwater Court, I could see the lighted entrance to Svetlana in a huge old brick building with bricked-up windows that ran a few hundred feet back to the boardwalk.

I continued past the building and onto the boardwalk, where I saw, as I'd expected, a boardwalk entrance to Svetlana.

I also noticed a cloud of gray smoke outside the nightclub, and if I looked through the smoke I could see tables and chairs, and lots of men and women puffing on cigarettes. It's good to get out into this healthy salt air.

I went over to the railing and looked out at the beach and the Atlantic Ocean. It was a little after 10 P.M., but there were still people on the beach, walking or sitting in groups, and I'm certain drinking some of the clear stuff from Mother Russia. The night, too, was clear and starry, and a half moon was rising in the east. Out on the water I could see the lights of cargo ships, tankers, and an ocean liner.

JFK Airport was about ten miles east of here, on the bay, and I stared at the string of aircraft lights heading into and out of the airport. One of the things that still sticks out in my mind after 9/11 was the empty skies—the lights and the noise stopped, and it was very eerie. I remembered the night when I was standing on my balcony and I saw the first aircraft I'd seen in four days. I was as excited as a kid from Podunk who'd never seen a jetliner before, and I called Kate out to the balcony and we both stared at the lights as the lone aircraft made its descent into Kennedy. Civilization had returned. We opened a bottle of wine to celebrate.

I turned and looked up and down the long boardwalk. There were hundreds of people promenading on this warm, breezy evening, and I saw parents pushing strollers, families walking and talking, groups of young men and women engaged in pre-mating rituals, and lots of young couples who one day would also be pushing baby strollers.

Indeed, it was a good world, filled with good people, doing good and everyday things. But there were also the bad guys, who I dealt with, and who were more into death than life.

I slipped off my wedding band—not so I could pass as single to the babes at the bar, but because in this business you don't give or advertise any personal information.

I took a last look around to be certain I was alone, then I walked across the boardwalk toward the red neon sign that said SVETLANA.

CHAPTER THIRTY-SEVEN

How can I describe this place? Well, it was an interesting blend of old-Russia opulence and Vegas nightclub, designed perhaps by someone who had watched *Dr. Zhivago* and *Casino Royale* too many times.

There was a big, horseshoe-shaped bar in the rear with a partial view of the ocean, and a better view of the patrons. I made my way through the cocktail tables and squeezed myself in at the bar between a beefy guy in an iridescent suit and a bleached blonde lady who was wearing her daughter's cocktail dress.

Most of the male patrons at the bar were dressed in outfits similar to mine, so I was not in a position to be critical.

Anyway, my attire notwithstanding, I don't think I look particularly Russian, but the bartender said something to me in Russian—or was he a Brooklyn native and did he say, "Whacanigetcha?"

I know about six Russian words, and I used two of them: "Stolichnaya, pozhaluista."

He moved off and I looked around the cocktail lounge. Aside from the slick suits, there were a lot of guys with open shirts and multiple gold chains around their necks, and a lot of women who had more rings than fingers. The no-smoking law seemed to be observed, though there was a steady stream of people going out to the boardwalk to light up.

I heard a mixture of English and Russian being spoken, sometimes by the same person, but the predominant language seemed to be Russian.

My Stoli came and I used my third Russian word. "Spasibo."

The bartender asked, "Runatab?"

"Pozhaluista." Can't go wrong with "please."

I could see the restaurant section through an etched glass wall, and the place was huge, holding maybe four hundred people, and nearly every table was filled. Boris was doing okay for himself. Or Boris *had* done okay for himself before Asad Khalil cut off his head.

At the far end of the restaurant I could see a big stage where a four-piece band was playing what sounded like a cross between "YMCA" and "The Song of the Volga Boatmen." The dance floor was crowded with couples, young and old, plus a lot of pre-teen girls dancing with each other, and the usual old ladies out on the floor giving the hip replacements a workout. In fact, this scene looked like any number of ethnic weddings I'd been to, and I had the thought that maybe I'd crashed a wedding reception. But more likely this was just another night at Svetlana.

I should say, too, for the sake of accurate reporting,

and because I am trained to observe people, that there were a fair number of hot babes in the joint. In fact, I seemed to recall this being the case the last time I was at Rossiya with Dick Kearns and Ivan.

Anyway, the lady next to me, who might have been one of those hot Russian babes fifteen years ago, seemed interested in the new boy. I could smell her lilac cologne heating up, and without sounding too crude, her bumpers were hanging over my Stoli, and they could have used a bar stool of their own.

She said to me, in a thick accent, "You are not Roosian."

"What was your first clue?"

"Your Roosian is terrible."

Your English ain't so hot either, sweetheart. I asked her, "Come here often?"

"Yes, of course." She then gave me the correct pronunciation of "spasibo," "pozhaluista," and "Stolichnaya"—I was stressing the wrong syllables—and made me repeat after her.

Apparently, I wasn't getting it, and she suggested, "Perhaps another voodka would help you."

We both got a chuckle out of that, and we introduced ourselves. Her name was Veronika—with a k—and she was originally from Kansas. No, Kursk. I introduced myself as Tom Walsh, and I briefly considered giving her Tom's home number. Maybe later.

I bought us another round. She was drinking cognac, which I recalled the Russkies loved—and at twenty bucks a pop, what's not to love? And I couldn't even put this on my expense account.

Anyway, recalling Nietzsche's famous dictum—the most common form of human stupidity is forgetting what one is trying to do—I said to her, "I need to see someone in the restaurant, but maybe I'll see you later."

"Yes? And who do you need to see?"

"The manager. I'm collecting for Greenpeace."

Veronika pouted and said, "Why don't you dance with me?"

"I'd love to. Don't go away."

I told the bartender, "Give this lady another cognac when she's ready, and put it on my tab."

Veronika raised her glass and said to me, "Spasibo."

The tab came, and I paid cash, of course, not wanting any record of this on my government credit card, or on my Amex card, where I'd have to explain Svetlana to Kate.

I promised Veronika, "I'll see you later."

"Perhaps. Perhaps not."

I made my way through the cocktail lounge and into the restaurant. It really smelled good in here and my empty tummy rumbled.

I found the maître d's stand and approached a gentleman in a black suit. He regarded me for a moment, decided I was a foreigner, and addressed me in English, asking, "How may I help you?"

I replied, "I'm here to see Mr. Korsakov."

He seemed a bit surprised, but he did not say, "Mr. Korsakov had his head cut off just last night. Sorry you missed him." He asked, "Is he expecting you?"

So, Boris was alive and here, and I replied, "I'm an old friend." I gave him my card, and he stared at it. I assumed he read English, and I assumed, too, he didn't like what he was reading—Anti-Terrorist Task Force and all that—so I said to him, "This is not official business. Please take that to Mr. Korsakov and I will wait here."

He hesitated, then said, "I am not certain he is in, Meester . . ." He looked at my card again. ". . . Cury."

"Corey. And I'm certain he is in."

He called over another guy to hold down the fort, and I watched him make his way toward the back of the restaurant, then disappear through a red curtain.

I said to the young guy who was filling in for the maître d', "You ever see Dr. Zhivago?"

"Please?"

"The scene in the restaurant where the young guy shoots the fat guy—Rod Steiger—who's been screwing Julie Christie."

"Please?"

"Hey, I'd take a slug for her. I took three for less than that. Capisce?"

A group came in and the maître d' trainee escorted them to a table.

So I stood there, ready to escort the next group to their table.

Meanwhile, I looked around the cavernous restaurant. The tables were covered with gold cloths on which sat vodka bottles, champagne buckets, and tiered trays filled with mounds of food, and the diners were doing a hell of a job getting that food where it belonged. The band was now playing the theme song from *From Russia with Love*, which was kind of funny.

The wall behind the stage rose up about twenty feet—two stories—and I noticed now that in the center of the wall near the ceiling was a big mirror that reflected the crystal chandeliers. This, I was certain, was actually a two-way mirror from which someone could observe the entire restaurant below. Maybe that was Boris's office, so I waved.

Three female singers had taken the stage, and they were all tall, blonde, and pretty, of course, and they wore clingy dresses with metallic sequins that could probably stop a .357 Magnum. They were singing something in English about Russian gulls, which I thought strange, and it took me awhile to realize they were saying, "Russian girls." In any case, they had good lungs. Kate would like this place.

I guess my attention was focused on the gulls, because I didn't see the maître d' approaching, and he came up to me and said, "Thank you for waiting."

"I think that was my idea."

He had a big boy with him—a crew-cut blond guy with a tough face who wore a boxy suit that barely fit over a weight lifter's body.

The maître d' said to me, "This is Viktor"—with a k?—"and he will take you to Mr. Korsakov."

I would have shaken Viktor's hand, but I need my hand, so I said, "Spasibo," in Veronika's accent, but several octaves lower.

I followed Viktor through the crowded restaurant, which was like following a steamroller through a flower garden.

Viktor parted the red curtain with his breath, and

I found myself in a hallway that led to a locked steel door, which Viktor opened with a key. We entered a small plain room that had two chairs, another steel door on the opposite wall, and an elevator. The only other item of note was a security camera on the ceiling that swiveled 360 degrees.

Viktor used another key to open the elevator doors and he motioned me in. I guessed that the steel door beside the elevator led to a staircase, and I noticed that the door also had a lock.

So, if I was Asad Khalil . . . I'd pick someplace else to whack Boris.

As we rode up, I said to Viktor, "So, are you the pastry chef?"

He kept staring straight ahead, but he did smile. A little humor goes a long way in bridging the species gap. Plus, he understood English.

The elevator doors opened into an anteroom similar to the one below, including another security camera, but this room had a second steel door—this one with a fisheye peephole and also a sliding pass-through like you find in cell doors.

Viktor pushed a button, and a few seconds later I heard a bolt slide and the door opened.

Standing in the doorway was Boris, who said to me, "It is so good to see you alive."

"You too."

CHAPTER THIRTY-EIGHT

Boris motioned me to an overstuffed armchair, and he sat in a similar chair opposite me. He was wearing a black European-cut suit and a silk shirt, open at the collar. Like me, he sported a Rolex, but I suspected his cost more than forty bucks. He looked like he was still in decent shape, but not as lean or hard as I remembered him.

Viktor remained in the room, and he took a cocktail order from the boss—a bottle of chilled vodka.

Boris poured into two crystal glasses, raised his glass and said, "Health."

I replied, "Na zdorov'e," which I think means "health"—or does it mean "I love you"?

Anyway, the vodka, whose label was in Cyrillic, had traveled well.

Boris was waiting for me to say something—like why I was here—but I enjoy a few minutes of companionable silence, which sometimes throws the other guy off while he's thinking about an unannounced visit from a cop. Also, Viktor was still there, and Boris needed to tell him to leave. But Boris was a cool customer and the silence didn't unsettle him. He sipped his vodka and lit a cigarette—still Marlboros—without asking me if I minded, and without offering me one.

So these two Russian guys go into a bar, and they order a bottle of vodka and they sit and drink for an hour without saying a word. Then one of them says, "Good vodka," and the other guy says, "Did you come here to drink, or did you come here to bullshit?"

I looked around the big windowless room, which was more of a living room than an office. The parquet floors were covered with oriental rugs, and the place was filled with a hodgepodge of Russian stuff—maybe antiques—like icons, a porcelain stove, a silver samovar, painted furniture, and lots of Russian tchotchkes. It looked very homey, like Grandma's living room if your grandma was named Svetlana.

Boris noticed my interest in his digs, and he broke the silence by saying, "This is my working apartment."

I nodded.

He motioned to a set of double doors and said, "I have an office in there and also a bedroom."

I had the same deal on East 72nd Street, and we were both going to be holed up in our working apartments for a while, though Boris didn't know that yet.

As I said, his English was nearly perfect, and I'm sure he'd learned a lot more words since I'd last seen him—like "profit and loss statement," "working capital," and so forth.

Boris, I'm sure, was not used to being jerked around, so he said to me, "Thank you for stopping by. I've enjoyed our talk." He said something to Viktor, who walked to the door, but did not open it until he looked through the peephole. Maybe this was normal precaution for a Russian nightclub. Or paranoia. Or something else.

Boris stood and said to me, "I'm rather busy tonight."

I remained seated and replied, "Viktor can leave."

Boris informed me, "He speaks no English."

"This isn't a good time for him to learn it."

Boris hesitated, then told Viktor to take a hike, which in Russian is one word.

Viktor left and Boris bolted the door.

I stood and looked out the two-way mirror that took up half the wall and had a sweeping view of the restaurant below, and also the bar beyond the etched glass wall. Veronika was still there. On the rear wall of the restaurant above the maître d's stand were high windows that offered glimpses of the beach and the ocean. Not bad, Boris. Beats the hell out of Libya.

Directly below was the stage, and through the banks of overhead lights, prop pulleys, and other stage mechanicals, I could see two trapeze artists—a male and female flying through the air with the greatest of ease.

Boris asked me, "Were you enjoying the show?"

Obviously, he'd seen me waiting at the maître d's stand.

I replied, "You put on a good show."

"Thank you."

I turned from the two-way mirror and said to him, "You've done well."

He replied, "It is a lot of work and worry. I have

many government inspectors coming here—fire, health, alcohol—and do you realize most of them don't take bribes?"

"The country is going to hell," I agreed.

"And I have to deal with cheating vendors, staff who steal—"

"Kill them."

He smiled and replied, "Yes, sometimes I miss my old job in Russia."

"The pay sucked."

"But the power was intoxicating."

"I'm sure." I asked him, "Do you miss your old job in Libya?"

He shook his head and replied, "Not at all."

At this point, he may have thought that I'd come here to talk about the one thing we had in common—and he'd be correct. But I'd said this wasn't an official visit, so to stay true to my word, I'd let Boris ask me about our favorite subject.

He offered me another drink, which I accepted. How many vodkas was that? Two that I paid for, and this was my second freebie. My on-duty limit is five. Four, if I think I may have to pull my gun.

On that subject, I was certain I wasn't the only one here who was carrying, though Boris may have stashed his piece if he wasn't licensed. Ah, for the good old days in the USSR when the KGB ruled. But money is good, too. Though money and power are the best.

Before Kate and I had met Boris three years ago at CIA Headquarters, we hadn't been fully briefed about his rank or title in the old KGB, or what Directorate he'd been in, or what his actual job had been. But afterward, an FBI agent had confided to us that Boris had been an agent of SMERSH, meaning licensed to kill—sort of an evil James Bond. If I'd known that beforehand, I'd still have had the meeting with him, but I don't think I'd have found him as charming. As for Kate . . . well, she always liked the bad boys.

I suppose I didn't actually care what Boris had done for a living in the Soviet Union; that was over. But it bothered me that he'd sold himself to a rogue nation and had trained a man like Asad Khalil. I'm sure he regretted it, but the damage was done, and it was extensive.

Since I was standing anyway, I took the opportunity to walk around the big room and check out the goods. Boris was happy to tell me about the icons and the lacquered wooden boxes, and the porcelains, and all his other treasures.

He said to me, "These are all antiques and quite valuable."

"Which is why you have such good security," I suggested.

"Yes, that's right." He saw me looking at him, so he added, "And, of course, the most valuable thing here is me." He smiled, then further explained, "In this business one can make enemies."

"As in your last business," I reminded him.

"And yours as well, Mr. Corey."

I suggested, "Maybe we should both look for another business."

He thought about that and said, correctly, "The old business will always follow you."

This was my opening to say, "Regarding that, I have some bad news, and some even worse news," but I wanted to get a better measure of this man first. I mean, I wasn't here to simply give him a warning; I was here to get some help with our mutual problem.

I thought back again to my and Kate's hour with Boris at CIA Headquarters, and I recalled that I had trouble reconciling this nice man with the man who had trained Asad Khalil for money. Kate and I were products of our upbringing and backgrounds—middle class, cop and FBI agent—and Boris's morally weightless world of international intrigue, double-dealing, and assassination was not how we lived or worked. The CIA, on the other hand, seemed to have no problem with Boris's past. He was part of their world, and the CIA made no moral judgments; they were just happy to have him as their singing defector.

Boris asked me, "What are you thinking about?"

I told him, "Our meeting in Langley."

"I enjoyed that." He added, "I was sure I would see you again—if nothing happened to you."

"Well, nothing too fatal has happened to me, and here I am."

I let that hang and continued my walk around the room. On one wall was an old Soviet poster showing a caricature of Uncle Sam, who looked less Anglo-Saxon and more Jewish for some reason. Sam was holding a money bag in one hand and an atomic bomb in the other. His feet were planted astride a globe of the world, and under his boots were the necks of poor native people from around the world. The Soviet Union—CCCP—was surrounded by American missiles, all pointing toward the Motherland. I couldn't read the Russian caption, and the iconography was perhaps a bit subtle for me, but I think I got it.

He saw me studying the poster and said, "A bit of nostalgia."

I replied, "Nostalgia is not what it used to be." I suggested, "Let me get you a Norman Rockwell print."

He laughed, then said, "Some of my American friends still find that poster offensive."

"Can't imagine why."

He reminded me, "The Cold War is over. You won." He informed me, "Those posters, if they are original, are quite expensive. That one cost me two thousand dollars."

I pointed out, "Not a lot of money for a successful entrepreneur."

He agreed, "Yes, I am now a capitalist pig with a money bag in my hand. Fate is strange."

He lit another cigarette but this time offered me one, which I declined. He asked me, "How did you find me?"

"Boris, I work for the FBI."

"Yes, of course, but my friends in Langley assured me that all information about me is classified."

I replied, "This may come as a shock to you, but the CIA lies."

We both got a smile out of that one.

Then he got serious again and said, "And any information about me is on a need-to-know basis." He took a drag and asked, "So, what is your need-to-know, Mr. Corey?"

I replied, "Please call me John."

"John. What is your need-to-know?"

"Well, I'm glad you asked." I changed the subject and my tactics and said, "Hey, I'm drinking on an empty stomach."

He hesitated, then replied, "Of course. I have forgotten my manners."

"No, I should have called." I suggested, "Don't go out of your way. Maybe call for a pizza."

He went to the phone on a side table and assured me, "No trouble. In fact, you may have noticed this is a restaurant."

"Right." Boris had a little sarcastic streak, which shows intelligence and good mental health, as I have to explain often to my wife.

Boris was speaking on the phone intercom in Russian, and I heard the word "zakuskie," which I know from my pal Ivan means appetizers. Some words stick in your mind. Of course, Boris could also be saying, "Put knockout drops in the borscht." Before he hung up, I asked, "Can they do pigs-in-a-blanket?"

He glanced at me, then added to his order, saying, "Kolbasa en croute."

What?

Anyway, he hung up and said to me, "Why don't you sit?"

So I sat, and we both relaxed a bit, sipping vodka

and enjoying the moment before I got down to what he knew was not going to be pleasant.

Boris said to me, "I have forgotten to ask you—how is that lovely lady you were with?"

In this business, as I said, you never reveal personal information, so I replied, "I still see her at work, and she's well."

"Good. I enjoyed her company. Kate. Correct? Please give her my regards."

"I will."

He smiled and said to me, "I had the impression that you and she were more than colleagues."

"Yeah? Hey, do you think I missed a shot at that?"

He shrugged and gave me a hot tip. "Women are difficult to understand."

"Really?" For fun, I said, "I think she married a CIA guy."

"A poor choice."

"That's what I think."

"As bad as a KGB guy."

I smiled and asked him, "Are you married?"

He replied without enthusiasm, "Yes."

"Russian gull?"

"Excuse me?"

"Russian girl?"

"Yes."

"Kids?"

"No."

"So, how did you two meet?"

"Here."

"Right. I'll bet this is a good place to meet women."

He laughed, but didn't respond. He asked me, "And you?"

"Never married."

"And why is that, if I may ask?"

"No one ever asked me."

He smiled and informed me, "I think you are supposed to ask them."

"Well, that's not going to happen."

Boris said to me, "I am remembering now your sense of humor." He hesitated, then said, "If you wish, I can send a woman home with you."

"Really? Like, take-out?"

He was really enjoying my humor, and he laughed and said, "Yes, I will put her in a container with your leftovers."

This generous offer—sometimes known as a honey trap—was serious and needed a reply, so I said, "Thank you for your offer, but I don't want to take advantage of your hospitality."

"No trouble." He added, "Let me know if you change your mind."

It occurred to me that Boris actually had *another* good reason for all this security, beyond personal safety and works of art: Mrs. Korsakov's unannounced visits.

Boris finally broached the subject of my attire and said to me, "You look very prosperous."

"I just dressed for the occasion."

"Yes?" He commented, "That watch is . . . I think ten thousand dollars."

"It didn't cost me anything. I took it off a dead man."

He lit another cigarette, then very coolly said, "Yes, I have some souvenirs as well."

It was time, I thought, to move the ball down the field, so I asked him, "Did the government give you a loan for this business?"

"Why do you ask? And why don't you know?"

I didn't answer either question, but asked him another: "Have you heard from your friends in Langley recently?"

He asked me, "Are you now here on official business?"

"I am."

"Then I should ask you to leave, and I should call my attorney."

"You can do that anytime you want." I reassured him, "This isn't the Soviet Union."

He ignored that and said, "Tell me why I should speak to you."

"Because it's your civic duty to assist in the investigation of a crime."

"What crime?"

"Murder."

He inquired, "What murder?"

"Well, maybe yours."

That called for a drink, and he poured himself one.

I said to him, unnecessarily, "Asad Khalil is back."

He nodded.

"Are you surprised?"

"Not at all."

"Me neither."

A few musical notes sounded—Tchaikovsky?—
and Boris stood, went to the door, and looked through
the peephole. I wondered where the monitor for the
security camera was located.

Boris opened the door, and a waiter entered pushing a cart, with Viktor bringing up the rear.

Viktor closed and bolted the door, and the waiter
unloaded three tiered trays of food onto a black lacquered table. Boris seemed to have forgotten about
my bad news and busied himself with directing the
waiter.

The table was now heaped with food and bottled
mineral water, and the waiter was setting the table with
linens, silverware, and crystal from a sideboard.

Boris said to me, "Sit. Here."

I sat, and Boris followed the waiter and Viktor to
the door and bolted it after them, then sat opposite
me.

He asked me, "Do you enjoy Russian food?"

"Who doesn't?"

"Here," he said, "this is smoked blackfish, this is
pickled herring, and this is smoked eel." He named
everything for me and I was losing my appetite. He
concluded with, "The pièce de résistance—pigs-in-a-
blanket."

The pigs-in-a-blanket were actually chunks of fat
sausage—kolbasa—wrapped in some kind of fried
dumpling dough, and I put a few of them on my plate
along with some other things that looked safe.

Boris poured us some mineral water and we dug into the chow.

The kolbasa and dough were actually very good—fat and starch are good—but the jury was out on the pickled tomatoes.

As we dined, Boris asked me, "How do you know he is back?"

I replied, "He's killed some people."

"Who?"

"I'm not at liberty to tell you, but I will say he completed his mission from last time."

Boris stopped eating, then said, "I want you to know that when I trained him, I did not train him for a specific mission—I simply trained him to operate in the West."

"And to kill."

He hesitated, then said, "Well . . . yes, to kill, but these are skills that any operative needs to know . . . in the event it becomes necessary."

"Actually," I pointed out, "Khalil was not an intelligence operative who might have to kill. He was, in fact, a killer. Trained by you. That's why he was here."

Boris tried another approach to the subject. "Understand that I had no knowledge of Khalil's mission in America. The Libyans certainly were not going to tell me about that." He added, "I explained this to the CIA, and they believed me because it was logical and it was the truth. And I am certain they passed this on to you before we met."

I didn't reply.

He asked, rhetorically, "If the CIA believed I knew that Khalil was going to kill American pilots, would they have gotten me out of Libya? Would they have let me live?"

That was a good question, and I had no good answer. What I did know for sure was that the CIA and Boris Korsakov had struck a devil's deal: they saved his life, and he spilled his guts. There may have been more to the deal, but neither Boris nor the CIA was going to tell John Corey what it was. Officially, Boris Korsakov, former KGB operative, and quite possibly an assassin himself, had sold his services to a rogue nation and trained one, or perhaps more, of their jihadists in the art of killing. But Boris himself had no blood on his hands—according to Boris—and he was welcome in America as a legitimate defector. Aside from the moral ambiguities here, Boris was doing well financially—not to mention having a great life—and the rest of us who were still in this business were not eating caviar, surrounded by wine, women, and song. Hey, life is not fair, but neither is it supposed to reward treachery or pay a lousy salary for loyalty.

On the other hand, we all make our choices and we live—or die—with the consequences of those choices.

In any case, Boris was trying to rehabilitate his reputation, such as it was, and I should have moved on, but I said to him, "I assume the CIA fully briefed you on what Khalil did here three years ago."

"Not fully." He added, "I had no need-to-know."

"But you said you knew he murdered American pilots."

"Yes . . . they did tell me that."

I suggested, "Boris, the bullshit is getting a little old."

"For you, perhaps. Not for me."

"Right." I wasn't trying to get at any truth with these questions—I just wanted to put him on the defensive, which I'd done, so I said, "All right. Let's move on. You eat, I talk." I pushed my food aside and said, "Khalil has been in this country for maybe a week. He killed the last pilot who had been on the Libyan raid—a nice man, named Chip—then he killed a few more people, and he didn't go out of his way to hide his identity. So, yeah, we know he's here. In fact, right here in the city."

Boris didn't look over his shoulder or anything, but he did stop chewing. I mean, this is a tough guy, but (a) he trained the killer in question so he knew how good he was, and (b) Boris had undoubtedly gone a little soft—mentally and physically—in the last three years. Meanwhile, Asad Khalil had undoubtedly gotten a little tougher and better at his job.

I continued, "It has occurred to me that Khalil has some scores to settle with you. If I'm wrong, tell me, and I will get up and leave."

Boris poured me more mineral water.

So I went on, "Quite frankly, I didn't expect to see you alive."

He nodded, then said to me, of course, "I'm surprised *you* are alive."

"You're *lucky* I'm alive. Look, I know we're both on his must-kill list, so we need to talk."

Boris nodded, then said, "And perhaps your friend Kate is also in danger."

"Perhaps. But to give you more information than you need to know, she is now in a location that is more secure than yours. We did this," I lied, "to reduce the number of potential targets." I gave him the happy news. "So I think it's just you and me left."

He took that well and joked, "You can sleep on that couch tonight."

I said, "You should also stay here."

"Perhaps."

"Your wife will understand."

"I assure you, she will not." He thought a moment, then said, "In fact, she will be going to Moscow tomorrow."

"Not a bad idea."

Boris poured himself a cognac and poured one for me, then said, "I assume you have a better plan than hiding."

"Actually, I do. My plan is to use you as bait to trap Khalil."

He replied, "I am not sure I like that plan."

"Works for me."

He forced a smile, but didn't respond.

Actually, being bait was my new job, and I had no problem with that. In fact, I wanted to be the only person in a position to kill Asad Khalil. But Boris Korsakov was also a target, and I had an obligation to tell him that, and I also needed to put my own ego and anger aside in favor of the mission. I wouldn't be thrilled if it was Boris who nailed Khalil, but the bottom line would still be Khalil in a casket.

Boris asked me, "Do you have any actual information that he knows where I am?"

I replied, truthfully, "We don't. But why don't we assume he does know where you are?" I added, "He had three years to find you. Plus he has friends in America."

Boris nodded, then smiled and informed me, "I have actually been mentioned in some publications that write about food, or about the Russian immigrant community."

"I hope they didn't use your photo, Boris."

He shrugged and replied, "A few times." He explained his security lapse by saying, "It is part of my business. And to be truthful, I didn't mind the publicity, and I was not thinking of personal security."

"Apparently not." I asked him, "And that's your real name?"

"It is." He further explained, "The CIA urged me to change my name, but . . . it is all I have from my past."

"Right." And that's the name they'll use on your tombstone. Well, I guess Boris Korsakov felt safe in Brighton Beach, Brooklyn, despite the fact that he'd pissed off Libyan Intelligence, Asad Khalil, and maybe his old KGB buddies. But he couldn't be feeling completely at ease about the past, so add another reason for those locks and bolts on the door.

I said, "So let's assume that Khalil knows you are the proprietor of Svetlana, and that you have a wife and an apartment on Brighton Twelfth Street. You can run, you can hide, but you can also sit here and wait for him, and I'll have people waiting with you."

He replied, "Well, I will think about that. In the meantime, you and your organization should think about some other way to capture him—or kill him."

I pointed out, "I think you know him better than the Feds."

He thought a moment, then said, "He will be difficult to find. But he *will* find you."

"Boris, I know that. I'm not hiding." I reminded him, "He's probably already found you. The question is, How do I find *him*?"

Boris sat back in his chair and lit another cigarette. He stared off at a point in space and spoke, almost to himself: "The Soviet Union, for all its faults, never underestimated the Americans. If anything, we tended to overestimate you. Khalil, on the other hand, is from a culture that underestimates the West, and especially the Americans. And this perhaps is his weakness." He thought a moment, then continued, "He cares nothing for money, women, comfort . . . he has no vices, and he thinks those who do are weak and corrupt."

He thought a moment, then continued, "They call him The Lion because of his courage, his stealth, his speed, and his ability to sense danger. But in this last regard, he often misses the signs of danger because of his belief that he is strong—physically, mentally, and morally—and that his enemies are weak, stupid, and corrupt." He looked at me and said, "I warned him once about this, but I did not bother to warn him again."

Boris was on a roll, reminiscing about his student, so I didn't respond.

Boris continued, "Khalil had a mentor, an old man called Malik, who was somewhat of a mystic." He informed me, "Malik, like me, tried to teach Khalil caution, but Malik also convinced Khalil that he was blessed—that he had special powers, a sixth sense for danger, and a sense for knowing when his prey was close. Nonsense, of course, but Khalil believed it, and therefore he does stupid things, but seems to get away with his stupidity, which only reinforces his rash behavior." He speculated, "Perhaps his luck is running out."

Not so you'd notice, but I said, "Maybe." In truth, the few murderers I've come across who thought God was in their corner had been a problem; they certainly were not blessed by God, but they *thought* they were, and that made them unpredictable and more dangerous than the average homicidal nut job.

Boris took a drag on his cigarette and said, "He was an excellent learner—very quick, very intelligent. And also very motivated—but what motivated him was hate." He looked at me and said, "As you know, the Americans killed his entire family."

I did not reply.

Boris said, correctly, "Hate clouds the judgment."

Again, I didn't respond, but I did think about this odd couple—Boris Korsakov and Asad Khalil—teacher and student from opposite ends of the universe. I was sure that Boris had done a good job training his young protégé to kill and escape, but at the end of school, Asad

Khalil was the same deranged person as he'd been at the beginning.

Boris continued, "He is what you call a loner. He does not need friends, women, or even colleagues, though he will use people and then dispose of them. So, how do you find such a man? Well, as I said, you will not find him—he will find you. But when he does, he is more likely than most professional assassins to make an error—an error in judgment, and thus an error in tactics. And by this, Mr. Corey, I mean that he will pass up an opportunity to safely blow your head off at two hundred meters, and he will attack you in a most personal way—the way a lion attacks, with his teeth, and his claws. He needs to taste your blood. And like a cat playing with a mouse, he often plays with his victim and taunts him before killing him. This is important to him. So if you survive the initial assault, you may have a chance to respond." Boris concluded, "This is all I can tell you that may be of help."

Well, aside from Malik the mystic, there wasn't too much there that I didn't know, and in fact Kate and I recently had some personal experience with Khalil's modus operandi. But it was good to have my own thoughts and observations confirmed. I said to Boris, "So we should bend over and kiss our asses good-bye?"

He smiled and, being a good host, complimented me by saying, "I feel that you can handle the situation if it should arise." He added, of course, "And so can I."

Maybe I shouldn't have cancelled my gym membership. I returned to my previous suggestion. "Another way to catch or kill a lion is to leave bait in a trap."

He'd apparently given some thought to my suggestion and replied, "Yes. If you want the lion alive, you put a live goat in a cage, and when the lion enters the cage, the door closes. The lion is trapped, but the goat gets eaten. Or if you want the lion dead, then the goat is tethered to a tree, and as the lion is killing him, the hunter shoots. In either case, the goat is dead. But goats are expendable."

"Good point." I assured him, "But we know you're not a goat and we will ensure your safety."

He wasn't so sure of that, and frankly, neither was I. Boris said to me, "*You* try it first."

"Okay. I'll let you know how I make out."

"Yes, if you can." He did say, however, "It is an interesting idea, and it may be the only way you will capture or kill him. But be advised—John—even as you are setting a trap for him, he may be doing the same for you."

"Right."

To continue the lion thing, he said, "And you would not be the first hunter to follow the lion's spoor, only to discover the lion has circled around and is now behind you."

"Hey, good analogy. I'll remember that."

"Please do."

My next question wasn't really important to the subject, but I had to know. "Did you teach Khalil how to kill with an ice pick?"

He seemed at first surprised, then a bit uncomfortable with the question. I mean, it was not an abstract question. He hesitated, then replied, "I believe I did." He then inquired, "Why do you ask?"

"Why do you think I asked?"

He didn't reply to my question, but let me know, "That idiot had never seen an ice pick, and when I showed it to him, he was like a child with a new toy."

"I'll bet."

"So, did the victim die?"

"Oh yeah. But I think it took awhile."

"How many stabs?" he asked.

"Just one."

Boris seemed annoyed, maybe frustrated with his old student, and said, "I told him two or three."

"Kids don't listen."

"He is not a kid. He's . . . an idiot."

I asked him, "Hey, what's with the Russkies and the ice pick? Didn't you guys whack Trotsky with an ice pick?"

Boris seemed interested in this subject and replied, "Well, as you can imagine, there are a lot of ice picks in Russia, and so they become the weapon of convenience, especially in the winter."

"Right. I should have thought of that."

Boris regarded me a moment, wondering, I'm sure, if I was having some fun with him. He played along by picking up a sharp knife on the table, saying, "If you do not know what you are doing with this, you will not deliver a fatal wound. You will get this stuck in a bone, or in a muscle, or you will deliver a few non-fatal wounds, and the other person will have an opportunity to run or attack. Even a deep abdominal wound is not fatal unless you hit the artery." He explained, "The knife is good mostly for the throat"—he put the blade to his throat—"the jugulars here, or the carotids. That is fatal, but it is a difficult cut to make if you are facing your opponent. You need to come up behind him for a proper throat cut. Correct?" He put the knife down and concluded, "But the ice pick will easily penetrate the skull from any angle, and it will also penetrate the breast bone into the heart, even if the victim is wearing heavy winter clothing, and it will, in either case, cause a fatal wound, though not instantly fatal."

He seemed to realize that he'd gotten carried away with this subject, and he forced a smile and said, "Perhaps not good dinner conversation."

"I brought it up. You just ran with it."

"Try that cognac."

I took a small sip to be polite. Boris, for all his alcohol consumption, seemed alert—maybe it was the sobering thought that he was marked for death that kept his mind focused. In any case, he said to me, "You must take care of him this time. If you do not, you will never have a day of peace."

"Neither will you."

He ignored that and asked me, "How did he get away last time?"

Boris had some skin in the game, so this was not simply a professional or academic question. I replied, "I certainly can't tell you more than your CIA friends told you three years ago. If you don't know, they don't want you to know."

And since the CIA was my next subject, I asked him, "What did the CIA tell you about their interest in Asad Khalil?"

He stayed silent for a while, then replied, "Very little. But I had the impression—based on my own training and experience—that the CIA's interest in Khalil was not the same as the FBI's interest."

"Meaning?"

"Meaning, of course, that the CIA wanted to use Khalil for their own purposes."

"Which were?"

He shrugged and said, "If you don't know, then they don't want you to know."

Time to stir up some poop, so I pointed out to Boris, "The CIA must certainly know that Asad Khalil is back in America. So has anyone in Langley called you and said, 'Hey, Boris, your old pal is back and he probably wants your head in his overnight bag. But we're going to protect you'?"

Boris had thought about that within one second of me telling him Khalil was back, and he'd been thinking about it ever since. He stayed silent awhile, then said to me, "My relationship with them is complicated. In fact, it is nonexistent since my last debriefing. They have turned me over to the FBI, and that is why I have not heard from them, and why it is you who are here."

Actually, that was not why I was here—I was freelancing. As for the FBI being Boris's nursemaid, there was often a disconnect between the FBI and the CIA in the post-Soviet resettlement program. Sometimes it was just a glitch, sometimes it was simply indifference on the part of the FBI. Boris had no value to the Bureau, or to anyone, and he was now in limbo. But if someone in the CIA or the FBI realized that Boris Korsakov had become lion's bait, then they'd be all over him. The problem with the system, as always, was faulty communication, firewalls between the agencies, and bad institutional memories. So that left John Corey having pickled beets with Boris Korsakov. Or . . . it was possible that the FBI and the CIA were already on this, and half the clientele of Svetlana were Federal agents, but they weren't telling Boris, as I had, that Khalil might come calling. Well, I'd know very soon if my visit here was captured on film by my colleagues.

Boris said to me, "I assume that my unwillingness to become bait, as you call it, will not be held against me."

"Of course not. We protect all citizens—hey, are you a citizen?"

"No."

"Oh, well, then . . . gee . . ."

"But I hold an American passport."

"Me too." I suggested, "Maybe you and I should go to Moscow with your wife."

He informed me, "I would rather be in New York with Asad Khalil than in Moscow with my wife."

I let that go, and reassured Boris, "If you don't want to be actual bait, we can still work out some sort of protective detail for you."

He had another thought and said, "You know, I am very safe here, and I have no plans to leave here . . . until Khalil is killed, captured, or flees . . . so I am not sure I need your protection." He added, "In fact, I pay very good money for my own protection."

There was a subtext here, and I thought that Boris was realizing he did not want the NYPD or the FBI hanging around Svetlana for a variety of reasons, some legitimate, and some maybe not so.

It occurred to me, too, that Boris was coming to some of the same conclusions that I had come to—he wanted to kill Asad Khalil without police or FBI interference. And his reasons went beyond my simple reasons of revenge and permanent peace of mind. Boris, I suspected, wanted Asad Khalil dead because Khalil knew too much about Boris. And what Khalil knew might not comport with what Boris had already told the CIA three years ago, about his not knowing that Khalil was coming to the U.S. to kill American pilots. Therefore, Boris did not want Khalil captured alive and interrogated by the FBI and the CIA. Boris would not be the first defector—a non-citizen—to be shipped back to the old country. I may have been wrong about that, but it was certainly a reason for Boris to want to get to Khalil first.

Another reason, possibly, was the reward, which he may have known about. I said to him, "There's a million-dollar reward for Khalil's capture—dead or alive. Did you know that?"

"I would assume that." He added, "Not a lot of money for this man . . . but I am not thinking about capturing him . . . I am saying I will protect myself."

"Come on, Boris. I know what you're thinking. And if anyone can capture—or kill—Asad Khalil, it's you."

He did not reply.

I advised him, "But don't get overconfident. Khalil

hasn't spent three years running a nightclub and drinking vodka."

This annoyed him, as I knew it would, and he leaned toward me and said, "I have no fear of this man. I taught him all he knows, and it would be a good thing if I was able to teach him one last lesson."

"There you go." I reminded him, "You taught that young punk everything he knows, and you can still kick his ass."

Boris had no response.

I said, "Well, I'll pass on your statement that you don't want protection." I informed him, officially, "It is your right to decline police protection, and you certainly don't have to volunteer to act as bait. But you can't stop a surveillance of your premises, or your movements." I added, "However, it might be easier and better for everyone if you cooperated and coordinated with us."

He informed me, "I have . . . former colleagues who I trust to assist and protect me."

"You mean like old KGB guys who know how to take down a punk like Khalil and know what to do with him in a back room here when they get him?"

Boris lit another cigarette and replied, "No comment."

I advised him, "If you should somehow capture him alive, call me first."

"If you wish."

Well, Boris was getting less talkative and it was time for me to leave. The next thing I had to do was report this meeting to Walsh and Paresi. I could get away with what I'd done so far—cops and agents often take a shot at something without telling the boss everything they're doing. But if you don't make a quick and full report of something like this, you are in big trouble.

On the other hand . . . I wasn't even supposed to *be* here. I mean, I think Walsh was pretty clear about my limited duties and limited movements, and about carrying my GPS tracker. Another reason for not reporting this was that Boris and I seemed to be on the same page with this. Khalil did not need to be apprehended—he needed to be killed.

I stood and said, "We may speak more tomorrow."

But Boris seemed not to hear me, and he was deep in thought.

Boris, as I said, is not stupid, and in the old days he played games that were more dangerous and more deceitful and convoluted than this one. And I could tell that his KGB brain was awake and working. No doubt he was getting interested and excited about being back in the old business. He looked at me and asked, "Does anyone know you are here?"

Well, Veronika does. Viktor. You. That was not the question I wanted to hear. And I had a good, strong reply. I said, "What do you mean?"

"I think you know what I mean." He asked me, "Why are you alone?"

"I work alone. Like James Bond."

He shook his head and said, "You should have an FBI agent with you." He added, "I don't mean to be disrespectful, Mr. Corey, but you are a New York City detective—as I was told three years ago. Where is your FBI counterpart?"

"She's at the bar."

"No. I believe you are pursuing this matter on your own and I understand why."

"Believe what you want. Tomorrow I'll be back with my team."

He thought about that, then looked at me and said, "Give me a week. Give yourself a week. One of us, I think, will resolve this problem in a way that is best for *us*."

I replied, of course, "This is not just about us. It is about the law, and justice, and national security."

Again, he shook his head and said, "No. It is about us."

I didn't want to continue on this subject, so I changed it. "You have my card." I also said, "I need your phone numbers."

He took his card and a pen from his inside pocket, wrote on the card, and handed it to me, saying, "Please keep me informed."

I took Khalil's photograph from my pocket, handed it to him, and said, "To refresh your memory."

He took the photograph but did not look at it, and replied, "My memory needs no refreshing."

"Well," I suggested, "copy it and give it to your people."

"Yes, thank you." He informed me, "He is very good at changing his appearance."

"Right. And that's three years old, though I have

information that he looks the same. And the eyes never change."

Boris glanced at the photograph and said, "Yes . . . those eyes."

I moved toward the door and said to him, "I can let myself out."

"I am afraid not." He stood, went to his phone, hit the intercom and said something in Russian, then said to me, "Let me ask you a question which may be important to you and to me."

I like questions that are important to me, so I replied, "Shoot."

He asked me, "Do you have any idea if Khalil is acting alone, or if he is working for Libyan Intelligence, or perhaps some other group?"

"Why do you ask?"

"Well, obviously it makes some difference in his . . . capabilities. His ability to discover what he needs to know about us." He added, "And perhaps in his mission, as well."

"Right. Well, I can't answer that question directly, but I will say he seems to have help."

Boris nodded and informed me, "Then you can be sure he will do something here that is different from what he has been doing."

"I'm losin' ya, Boris."

Boris looked at me and said, "He is going to detonate a bomb. Or perhaps it will be a biological attack. Anthrax. Or a chemical device. Perhaps nerve gas."

"You think?"

"Yes. He must repay those who assisted him in his

mission of personal revenge. Have you not thought of this?"

I admitted, "It has crossed my mind."

"But I believe it will not happen before he finishes his business with you and with me."

"Right." I don't make a habit of discussing things like this with people like Boris, but he did have some history with Khalil, and this was once his business, so I said to him, "Think about that and let me know what you come up with."

"I will."

Tchaikovsky filled the room, and Boris walked to the door, looked through the peephole, then unbolted the door and opened it.

Viktor stood aside for me, and as I walked to the door I said to Boris, "If you look through a peephole, you can get a serious eye and brain injury if there's a gun muzzle looking back at you. Or an ice pick."

He seemed annoyed at my critique of his security procedures and said, "Thank you, Detective."

I asked, "Where's your security monitor?"

"There is one in my office, and there is a television in that armoire that has a security camera channel."

"You should use it."

"Thank you, again."

"And thank you for your time and your hospitality." I started through the door, then I did one of my neat turnarounds and said, "Oh, FYI—the pilot who Khalil killed. Chip. Khalil cut off his head."

Boris kept his cool and said, "I never taught him that."

I suggested, "Maybe he has a new teacher."

I walked out of Boris's apartment, and as the door closed I heard the bolt slide home.

Poor Boris—holed up in his place of business without his wife, and with nothing to do except eat, drink, look out his two-way mirror, maybe watch some Russian TV, listen to music, and possibly enjoy the company of a lady or two. But even that gets old after a few days. Well . . . maybe a few weeks.

Viktor indicated the elevator, but I said to him, "Let's take the stairs."

"Please?"

"Come on, Viktor. You teach English at Brooklyn College." I walked to the steel staircase door and Viktor opened it with a key.

This was basically the fire escape staircase, and fire marshals don't like to see a lock or a bolt, but Boris must have told them, "Look, boys, there are a lot of people who want to kill me, so I gotta lock myself in." Or he removed the doors when the inspectors came around.

I let Viktor go first and I followed. The door at the bottom of the staircase was also locked, and Viktor used his key to open it.

We entered the small room with the security camera, then Viktor unlocked the door to the hallway, and I followed him through the red curtain and into the restaurant.

Well, I thought, the security was good, but too much depended on human involvement and two keys—one for the elevator and one for all the steel doors. Also, the door to Boris's apartment had to be bolted manually.

Boris needed a code padlock for all the doors between the outside world and him, plus he needed easier access to his security monitors.

There may have been some security features that I didn't see, such as a panic button, or maybe a safe room, but the real bottom line with personal security was vigilance and a large-caliber gun.

Viktor escorted me through the restaurant, which was half empty now, and I said to him, "Someone wants to kill your boss. Keep your head out of your ass."

He didn't reply, but he nodded.

"You got a gun?"

Again, he didn't reply, but he tapped the left side of his jacket.

I suggested, "Work on your pronunciation."

Anyway, I skipped the bar and Veronika and walked out the rear door. It was almost midnight, and the boardwalk and the beach were nearly deserted.

If I'd been followed by my surveillance team, it was now that someone would approach me. And if I'd been followed by Khalil's team, this was as good a time and place as any for Khalil and Corey to meet.

I stood there for a minute, but no one seemed interested in me.

I walked to the front entrance of Svetlana where a few cabs were parked.

On the way back to Manhattan, crossing the Brooklyn Bridge, I again had the thought, reinforced by Boris, that Asad Khalil was indeed planning something big for his finale—something that would please his backers and get him another line of credit for his next mission—and all that stood between him and that big climax to this mission was Boris Korsakov and John Corey.

So, yes, Boris was right; it was about us—him, me, and Asad Khalil. And it was about the past following us, and catching up with us.

CHAPTER THIRTY-NINE

The taxi from Brighton Beach had let me off in my underground parking garage, and also left me forty bucks poorer, which is cheap for life insurance.

I'd taken the freight elevator up to my apartment, and no one from the surveillance team seemed to have noticed my absence. I didn't want to get these guys in trouble, so I'd be certain to never get caught leaving home without them.

Anyway, it was now 7 A.M. Wednesday morning, a short seventy-two hours since Kate and I had woken up in the High Top Motel in Sullivan County, excited about jumping out of an airplane. Little did we know, as they say, how exciting it was going to be.

I didn't have anything specific planned for the day, reminding me that the problem with doing nothing is not knowing when you're done.

I did take the opportunity to go through my daily dozen exercises, being motivated not by vanity but by health concerns, meaning in this case, I needed to be in good shape if Khalil and I got into a wrestling match. Boris was right—Khalil's attacks were up close and personal, and if you could survive the initial surprise assault you had a chance to turn it around. This was why Kate was still alive.

As I was getting ready to visit Kate at Bellevue, my cell phone rang and it was Paresi. I answered, "Corey."

Captain Paresi inquired, "What did you do last night?"

Uh-oh. Time to come clean. I said, "I visited Kate in the hospital."

"I know that. What did you do afterward?"

Time to come clean. "I was driven home."

There was a silence on the phone, then Paresi said, "The surveillance guy in your lobby, Ramos, reported that he called your apartment phone and your cell phone and also had the doorman buzz your intercom, but you didn't answer."

Time to really come clean. I replied, "I was dead to the world by ten P.M." Or was I having a vodka with Veronika? I asked, "What did Ramos want?"

Paresi replied, "Nothing. Just a commo check and a situation report."

Bottom line here, Paresi had no evidence that I'd actually gone out, so I got a little huffy and said, "Captain, I'm a cop—not some Mafia informant who needs watching twenty-four/seven—"

"Your life is in danger, Detective Corey." He added, "You have agreed—"

"I didn't agree to sleep with my surveillance guys."

There was a silence, then Paresi said to me, "All

right." He informed me, "As it turns out, we know where you'll be tonight."

I didn't reply, and I didn't ask.

He continued, "But first, some housekeeping. Gabe's funeral and that of his wife and daughter was yesterday. It was a private religious ceremony, but we will have a memorial service for him and his family sometime next week if possible." He added, "Depends on what happens."

Right. Depends on our own funerals. I said, "Okay."

Paresi asked me, "How is Kate?"

"Well enough to get out of the hospital, but Walsh is keeping her there, and neither of us is happy about that."

He replied, "She's safer there, and you're better off not having her home."

I didn't respond to that and said, "There's something you need to do—have a death certificate issued and recorded in Sullivan County ASAP, and have the Catskill Medical Center alter their records accordingly."

"Okay . . . if you think someone would actually be checking on that."

"Let's assume that Khalil is obsessed with his confirmed body count."

"All right. Will do." He asked me, "Have you received or recalled anything I should know about?"

This was basically my last chance to come clean about Boris, and I'd weighed the pros and cons of reporting my contact with Boris Korsakov. Boris, however, had correctly determined that I was acting on my own, and he'd asked me for a week of no police or FBI interference—a week to see if Khalil attempted to whack him on his protected turf at his nightclub. Boris's purpose, of course, was to silence Asad Khalil forever, though I didn't really care what Boris wanted— he wasn't running this operation. But his best interests might coincide with mine. This was a tough call.

"John?"

"I'm thinking."

On the other hand, Boris may have sobered up by now, and smartened up, and he might call me and say he'd changed his mind and please send the police to protect him. Or for all I knew, Boris, the devious KGB man, might now be hightailing it to Moscow with his wife—or the French Riviera without his wife. I wouldn't blame him if he did.

"Hello? John?"

I replied, "I can't think of anything." I changed the subject and asked him, "Has Special Operations seen anything unusual at the bad guy safe houses?"

"No."

"Are we trying to find any other safe houses that we don't know about?"

He replied, "We're checking with rental agents about corporate rentals that they may have thought were suspicious—but that's very time-consuming and a very long shot."

"Right." I said to him, "I had a thought that if I was Khalil's pals in New York, I'd have rented a place on my street—an office or an apartment—and mounted a mini camcorder in the window, and I'd be keeping an eye on my front door from a monitor located in that office or apartment."

Paresi stayed silent awhile, then replied, "That's a good thought . . . but your street is lined with high-rises—like thousands of apartments and offices—"

"Right. I live here. I can see them." I said to him, "You should get some manpower on that, Captain."

"Right." He advised me, "You should stay off your balcony."

"I was going to invite you over for drinks on the balcony."

Paresi sometimes appreciated my dark humor, but this was not one of those times. He said to me, "I have to tell you, we're spread pretty thin, but I'll see if I can get the FBI field office and One P. P. to give us some people."

Recalling my unproductive surveillance of the Iranian dip, I suggested, "Pull people off the U.N. assignments." I pointed out, "This case is high priority."

"I know. But you have no idea how many tips, threats, and leads we've gotten in the last few months that we have to follow up on."

I thought about that and said, "It's possible these are planned distractions."

He stayed silent a moment, then replied, "Maybe." Then he said, "I never thought we'd be overwhelmed . . . you know?"

"The world," I reminded him, "has changed."

"Yeah. But we're staffing up." He joked, "That's why you still have a job."

Funny. I asked him, "Any hits from CAU on Kate's cell phone or Gabe's cell phone?"

He replied, "As you know, we've discontinued service on both, but CAU is watching to see if anyone turns them on to use their phone directories."

"Okay. Are the surveillances of the Muslim neighborhoods turning up anything?"

"No."

"I assume you've cancelled all leave and that everyone is putting in extra days and hours."

"Goes without saying. In fact, John, let me assure you that despite personnel shortages, the Task Force, the FBI, and the NYPD are on top of all this. And let me remind you, you are not part of the investigation. You are on leave."

"Then why are you asking me questions?"

He informed me, "We ask you questions—you do not need to ask us questions. Or give us advice."

Well, I had been wavering about telling him about Boris, but I wasn't wavering anymore. Hey, I'm not part of the investigation.

"John?"

"I understand."

In a more kindly tone, he said, "We want you to focus on remembering the past, and anything from the past that can help us this time."

I said to him, "My car and driver are waiting. Anything else?"

"Yes, the reason I called. You're going trawling tonight."

That was exciting news, and I said, "Good. What's the plan?"

He began, "At about ten P.M., you will leave your apartment and go on foot along Seventy-second Street and enter Central Park—"

"I could get mugged."

He ignored that and continued, "We're using the park because we all know it and we've all trained there for surveillance and countersurveillance."

"Right." I got lost once.

He continued, "You'll meet a Special Operations Group supervisor in your lobby at ten, and he will give you your route and your various destinations in the park. Then you will establish communication with the surveillance teams outside your building, and off you go."

"Sounds like a plan." I reminded him, "I don't want a parade behind me or a brass band in front of me."

"Right. You're covered, but not overprotected."

"I'll let you know what I think when I see it."

"Okay. We're willing to learn. Trial and error."

"No errors, please." I asked him, "Have you notified the Central Park Precinct?"

"We have. They know what's going down and we'll keep in contact with them."

"Good." The CPP had a strong presence in the park at night, including mounted police, undercover cops, and marked and unmarked cars. In fact, too much presence. I said to Paresi, "Keep them away from my route."

"Understood." He went on with his mission briefing. "At your various destinations in the park, there will be backup people—SWAT teams—concealed with night-vision devices and sniper rifles."

"Don't forget to tell them what I'm wearing."

Without even a chuckle, he continued, "The places where you will stop and linger are waterside spots—the Kerbs Boathouse, then a prearranged spot on Belvedere Lake, and then maybe up at the Reservoir." He informed me, "The surveillance and SWAT teams want to use waterside locations because that limits the possible avenues of approach for Khalil, and it also narrows down the area that needs to be covered by the SWAT team, and by the surveillance teams." He added, "In other words, you're covered on one side by the water." Then a joke. "Can you swim?"

"No. But I can walk on water." I asked, "What am I supposed to do at these locations at that hour, other than look like I'm bait in a trap?"

"Good question. And I don't have a good answer, but I'm thinking you just lost your wife . . . and you can just be taking a long walk. You know? Head down, sit on a bench, put your face in your hands . . . or maybe carry a bottle of booze—not real, of course— and act a little drunk. You know how to do that."

"Maybe I should look like I'm going to drown myself in the lake."

"Yeah . . . you can do that . . . I guess. Anyway, what you won't do is jog. You'll walk slowly, and follow the planned route and listen to instructions on your earphone." He added, "You'll go through this with the Special Operations boss in your lobby."

"Right."

"And remember, John, as you said, if anyone is watching your building and waiting for you to come out, it might not be Khalil himself. So if the bad guys are on the street, or in vehicles, or as you suggested in a building overlooking your street, it could take some time for them to get hold of Khalil while they're following you." He again assured me, "The countersurveillance team will pick up anyone tailing you, and we'll know if we've got a game going. Okay? And remember, the most critical part of this, if it's going to work, is them picking you up as you leave your lobby. Right? So, linger without being obvious."

"Obviously."

"Any questions?"

"Nope."

Then the pep talk. He said, "This is above and beyond, John, and we appreciate your willingness to put yourself in harm's way. You may feel alone tonight, but rest assured, you will not be alone. Tom and I, and everyone on the Task Force and in the Special Operations Group, will be thinking of you and praying for your safety and your success."

"Thank you." I inquired, "Where will you be thinking of me and praying for me?"

"I'm home on call." He reminded me, "I'm on Central Park West, and I can be in the park within minutes."

"Good. We can both pose for photos with the dead lion."

He also reminded me, "We want to take him alive, if possible."

"Of course." I asked him, "Where will Tom be?"

"Also home, waiting to hear."

"Where's your wife, Captain?"

"Out of town."

"Good." I would have asked him where Tom's girl-friend was, but she wasn't in any danger. Why not? Well, she's a barracuda, and Khalil would not harm her out of professional courtesy. Should I share this with Paresi? Maybe not.

Anyway, we seemed to have covered all the points, and I said, "I'm off to the hospital."

"Give my regards to Kate. We'll speak later before you go out."

I hung up and, ignoring Paresi's advice, walked out to the balcony and looked at the buildings across the street. Indeed, there were thousands of windows that all had a good view of me and my balcony, and also the front doors of this building, plus there were dozens of rooftops, many of them higher than my balcony. A very easy way to kill John Corey was to have a sniper on a roof or in any of those apartments or offices—and he didn't even have to be a particularly good shot. But if that was going to happen, it would have already happened.

From here, I could see Central Park at the end of 72nd Street, over eight hundred acres of open fields, woods, ponds and lakes, park structures, and lots of dark spaces at night. It was a good place for this game—but maybe too obvious.

Like the lion for whom he was named, Asad Khalil *could* smell danger, but a hungry lion will take a risk for a meal, and by now, The Lion must be very hungry.

CHAPTER FORTY

Alfred was on duty, and I wished him good morning and confessed, "I can't find the freight elevator key."

"Oh . . ."

"I'll keep looking, but in the meantime . . ." I pushed five twenties across the counter. "If you need to have one made . . ."

"Yes, sir. I do have a spare, but if you can't find it, I'll see a locksmith."

"I'm sure I'll find it, but you keep that for your trouble."

"Thank you, sir."

"Don't mention it." And I mean don't mention it.

I saw there was a new surveillance person in my lobby, a female this time, sitting in an armchair reading the *Times*, with a Bloomies bag beside her.

I didn't know her, and I went over and introduced myself. She introduced herself as "Kiera Liantonio, Special Operations."

She was an attractive, well-dressed woman in her

mid-twenties, maybe older, but I can't tell anymore. In any case, she was too young to be an NYPD detective, so I asked her, "FBI?"

"Does it show?"

"I'm afraid it does." Where do they get these kids? Well, right out of law school and Quantico. Like Lisa Sims. I suppose this kind of assignment was good on-the-job training for a rookie FBI agent. Why assign a pro to guard my life?

I said to Special Agent Liantonio, "I'll probably be out for two or three hours. You can take a break if you want."

She nodded.

FYI, it's never a good idea to ask a female cop or agent if they're wearing a vest—it's like asking them if they're pregnant, and they might take it the wrong way. But I'm slick, and I said to her, "Why aren't you wearing a vest?"

She replied, "I am."

"Oh . . . good." See?

Anyway, she seemed very self-assured, the way most of these new agents are when they get out of Quantico—the way I was when I got out of the Academy. I mean, you're in great physical shape, you listened in class, and you have a gun that you know how to use and a badge or shield that carries authority. The only thing you don't have is a clue.

I said to Ms. Liantonio, "My wife is with the Bureau."

"I know."

"Do you know where she is, and why she's there?"

"I've heard something."

"Good. She doesn't need or want a roommate." I added, "Stay alert. This is a very bad guy."

She didn't reply, but she nodded.

I left the building and stood under the canopy with my shotgun rider—Ed Regan again—while the Highway Unit SUV pulled up closer.

I got in the vehicle and off we went. The driver was someone new, and his name was Ahmed something. I mean, there's like fifty Mideastern cops on the whole thirty-five-thousand-person force, and I get one of them.

We all chatted as we made our way down to Bellevue, and Ahmed was a good guy, and he made some good jokes, like, "I'm kidnapping you." Well, if you're a Muslim on the NYPD, post-9/11, you *really* need a sense of humor.

Ed Regan demonstrated his interest in Ahmed's culture by asking him, "What's the definition of a moderate Arab?"

Ahmed replied, "Someone who ran out of ammunition."

I knew a couple of good ones, but I didn't want to be perceived as culturally insensitive. Well, okay, just one. I asked, "How do you blind an Arab?"

Ahmed replied, "Put a windshield in front of his face."

Anyway, Ahmed drove a lot better than a Pakistani taxi driver, except now and then he did some weird things, but I knew he was trying to see if we had a tail.

Also, I knew we had a trail car somewhere, as we'd had for every trip to Bellevue. Bottom line on this, if the bad guys were watching and if they saw I was making regular trips to Bellevue Hospital, they might conclude that (a) I was getting much-needed psychiatric counseling, or (b) I was visiting a patient. And we didn't want them thinking about that.

Anyway, with all due respect to the driving abilities of certain foreign-born people, most of those gentlemen couldn't follow a car even if they were tied to the bumper.

We got to Bellevue without mishap and without company, and I got out and said, "I'll call you."

Kate's physical appearance was better, but she told me she was going a little stir crazy and wanted out.

I could have reminded her that being in the hospital was better than being dead, but I wanted to be sensitive to her state of mind, so I said, "Think of this as a tough assignment that you can handle."

"Get me the hell out of here."

"You should talk to your jailer."

Anyway, Kate had gotten a loaner laptop from 26 Fed, and she told me, "I'm writing my incident report."

"Good. Write mine, too." I reminded her, "We shared the same incident."

She moved on to another subject and informed me, "Mom and Dad want us to come visit as soon as I'm able to travel."

"I don't really want to go to Montana."

"Minnesota, John. Where we got married."

"Right. Whatever."

She changed the subject and asked me, "What did you do last night?"

"Last night . . . ? What did I do? I looked through our wedding album."

She moved on to the next question. "What are you doing tonight?"

"Sailing paper planes off the balcony."

"Has Tom asked you to . . . go out and see if Khalil follows you?"

Good question, and I needed a nuanced reply. I said, "Well, we've discussed that with Paresi. But only as a last resort—if we can't find Khalil using standard methods and procedures."

She stayed silent for a while, then said, "You don't *have* to do that. That's not in anyone's job description."

I reminded her, in case she forgot, "We have a *personal* interest in apprehending Asad Khalil."

She stayed silent again, then said, "Why don't you wait until I get out of here? Then I can be part of that operation."

She's a big girl, and she's in the business, so I said, bluntly, "Why do you think you're still here? You're here so you're safely out of the way while Khalil and I see who finds who first."

Again she stayed silent, then asked me, "Do you have a good plan?"

Well, I thought the plan seemed okay, and I trust the surveillance teams, and I know that my execution of the plan will be, as always, flawless. But as an old Army guy once told me, even the best battle plans rarely survive the first contact with the enemy.

"John?"

"It's a standard and safe surveillance and countersurveillance, with a SWAT team added in case an arrest is not possible." In fact, I would make sure an arrest was not possible.

She asked, "When are you doing this?"

I really didn't want her losing any sleep over this, so I lied, "I told you—when we've exhausted everything else."

She nodded and said, "Let me know."

"I will."

She informed me, "If I'm not out of here by Sunday, I'm going to call my lawyer and get a habeas corpus."

"Get one for me, too. And a pepperoni pizza." I advised her, "Don't screw up your career."

Anyway, it was lunchtime and Kate insisted I have lunch with her. I looked at the menu and said, "I'll have the prison-striped bass with the stir-crazy vegetables."

She smiled, which was a good sign.

Over lunch, which wasn't too bad, I filled her in on most of what had happened in the last day or two, and she asked me, "Have the State Police found my gun and cell phone yet?"

"Still looking."

She said, without mincing her words, "Khalil could kill you with my gun."

"No, I'll kill him with *my* gun." Actually, I wanted to use my knife. Maybe my hands.

She said, "If he calls you, I want you to pass on a message for me."

"I can't. You're dead," I reminded her.

"Well . . . when we capture him, I want him to see me alive. I want to interview him . . . I want to see him strip-searched."

Obviously, Special Agent Mayfield was still pissed off, and that was a healthy attitude—though a few days ago she wanted Khalil dead. Now she'd toned down her revenge fantasy and wanted him humiliated and incarcerated for life. I'd like to help her fulfill this wish, but I was still on Plan A—kill him. I said to her, however, "That would be fun to watch."

She nodded, then asked me, "Have you told Tom about Boris?"

I knew I couldn't lie because she'd check with Walsh, so I replied, "I have not."

"Why not?"

Good follow-up question. And I couldn't finesse this, and I didn't want to tell her the truth, so I retreated into the last refuge of husbands and boyfriends and said, "Trust me."

"What is that supposed to mean?"

"Trust me."

She looked at me, and after a few seconds she said, "You're going to wind up either dead or in jail."

"Neither."

She then asked me, "Have you called Dick Kearns like you always do when you're going around the FBI?"

I didn't reply.

We made eye contact and she said, "Tell me about Boris."

I took a deep breath, and told her about my trip to Brighton Beach and Svetlana, leaving nothing out—

except Veronika. I concluded with, "Boris convinced me to give him a week, and I agreed. And now I want you to do the same." I added, "He sends his regards."

She processed all this very quickly and asked me, "Are you crazy?"

"Yes, but that's not relevant."

She retreated into some deep thinking, then said, "I did not hear this."

I nodded.

She advised me, "Call Tom."

I stood and bent over to kiss her, and she took my head in her hands and gave me a long, hard kiss, then said, "I know you'll be looking for Khalil tonight. Be careful. Please. We have a long life ahead of us."

"I know we do." I squeezed her hand and said, "I'll call you later."

Back in my apartment, I spent the rest of the afternoon doing paperwork.

I spoke to Paresi again, who didn't have much new to say except, "Everyone is revved up about tonight."

"Let's not get too excited."

"Yeah . . . but at least we're *doing* something—not just reacting."

"Right. The best defense is a good offense."

I'd noticed that Tom Walsh wasn't calling me, and I guessed that he wanted to distance himself from me, or from this operation, in case it went south. If, however, I nailed Khalil tonight, Walsh was waiting in his apartment with a car running outside so he could share the moment with me.

I said to Paresi, "If it goes well tonight, I'll see Tom with his photographer in the park."

Paresi did not respond to that, but said, "Good luck and good hunting."

At 5 P.M., I cleaned my Glock and took three extra magazines of 9mm rounds. I also cleaned my off-duty weapon, which is an old .38 Smith & Wesson Police Special. The high-performance automatics like the Glock sometimes jam, and though I've never had a jam, it was possible, so the second weapon should be a basic revolver, which is less likely to go *click, click* when you want to hear *bang, bang.*

I rummaged through my closet and found some clothes for my walk in the park, then I found an old Marine K-bar knife that's been in my family since Uncle Ernie served in the Pacific. The knife, according to Uncle Ernie, had drawn blood, so it was not just any knife; it had been baptized.

It also needed sharpening, which I did with a honing stone from the kitchen drawer. And while I was sharpening the big knife, I understood a little of how ancient warriors must have felt on the eve of battle—or modern soldiers, who sharpened their bayonets before an attack. The sharpening of the steel was less about the cutting edge of the blade than it was about the cutting edge of the soul and psyche;

it was an ancient communion with every man who ever faced battle and death, and who stood with his comrades, but stood alone, with his own thoughts and his own fears, waiting for the signal to meet the enemy, and to meet himself.

CHAPTER FORTY-ONE

At 10 P.M., I went down to the lobby where a Special Operations supervisor, FBI Special Agent Bob Stark, was waiting for me. I knew Bob, and he was one of the good guys.

I was wearing khaki pants, white running shoes—but no flashing lights on them—and a white pullover jersey. It was drizzling on and off, so I had on a tan windbreaker and a tan rain hat. It was kind of a dorky outfit, and I hoped I didn't run into anyone I knew. Except, of course, the Libyan guy. More importantly, I hoped that Khalil or his pals didn't realize I was dressed to be seen in the dark.

Stark and I went over the assignment, and I took a park map from him in case I got lost, which I sometimes do in the park. I did a commo check on my wire, and we made sure my GPS was up and running.

I had my Kevlar vest on, of course, and my Glock in a hip holster and the S & W stuck in my gun belt on the left side for a quick crossover draw.

Stark noticed the sheathed K-bar knife on my gun belt, but he didn't comment on that.

I also had my cuffs with me, as per regulations, but I seriously doubted I'd get to use them.

On the subject of bringing him back alive, Bob offered me a can of Mace, and I said, "Thanks, but I forgot my purse."

Satisfied that I was good to go, he said to me, "Okay, I'll be in a commo van, and I'm SO One, and you are Walker—"

"Hunter."

"It doesn't . . . Okay, you are Hunter. As you know, the wire is an open channel, so when you speak, everyone on the surveillance teams, countersurveillance, and SWAT can hear you. But to keep wire traffic at a minimum, my teams will speak to me via cell radio, and I will relay to you—though if something is urgent, you will hear directly from a surveillance person on your wire."

"Understood."

He said to me, "Good hunting, Detective."

I said to him, "If it gets late and the weather gets bad, will you let me know if the FBI guys went home?"

He smiled and advised me, "This is not a good time for you to make FBI jokes."

"Good point."

So off I went.

I stepped outside and stood under the lights of the apartment canopy, then moved toward the curb and stood there a moment, feigning dejection or indecision.

This was the only place where I could be picked up by the bad guys, so I lingered, without being obvious.

East 72nd Street is a wide, multi-lane road that runs both ways, and it's a busy street, so it would be hard for me to tell if anyone was watching me from the street or from a vehicle—but the surveillance team would have picked that up by now, and Stark wasn't talking to me on my earphone.

Remembering that Khalil had planned this for years, and that he had local assets here, my best guess, as I'd told Paresi, was that Khalil's friends had rented an apartment or an office on this street. And as I also told Paresi, these guys would be keeping my front door under 24/7 surveillance with a mini camcorder mounted in one of these thousands of windows. That was a fairly standard method of safe-distance surveillance, and all it took was money, manpower, and guys who didn't mind staring at a monitor all day and night, looking at an image of my front door. If you're going to kill someone, it's good to know where they are and where they're going.

I turned to my right and headed toward Central Park. By now, if I'd been seen, Abdul was calling Amin who was calling Asad.

I walked slowly along the sidewalks, which were still crowded with people despite the hour and the drizzle.

Now that I was actually doing this, it occurred to me that if Khalil was not holed up in this immediate area, it might take him awhile to get to the park and to make contact with his friends who were following me. And if they weren't pros, then they might lose me before Khalil showed up.

Therefore . . . if they did have an apartment or office on East 72nd Street, it could be not only their surveillance post, but also where Khalil was living and hiding out. There goes the neighborhood.

I continued on, and Bob Stark's voice in my earphone said, "Hunter, SO One here—you read?"

I spoke to my condenser mic under my shirt, "Hunter five by five."

"Okay, we're with you, but I think you're alone."

"All right. But I'll stop at the park entrance and you'll see if anyone seems interested in me."

"Right. We have two people there—a man and a woman—right inside the park."

He described their clothing, and I said, "Try to keep your people away from me once I get deep into the park. I do *not* want you to spook any tails."

"We're pretty good at this."

"I know. I'm just saying I can protect myself."

"Good. Next time you can go by yourself."

I replied, "Don't get pissy."

"Copy."

FYI, if you're walking along the street in New York talking to yourself, no one notices—except maybe other people who are talking to themselves.

Anyway, I crossed Fifth Avenue and stood near the low stone wall that surrounds the entire park. There were still a few pushcart vendors around the park entrance, and remembering that I needed to linger here, I took the opportunity to buy a chili dog. In fact, make it two. Hey, this could be my last meal.

I sat on a wet bench and ate my hot dogs, trying to

look like a dejected widower, which is not easy when you have two magnificent dogs in your hands.

Anyway, I finished dinner and walked into the park.

I spotted the surveillance couple sitting on a bench, looking for all the world like lovers—not husband and wife, because they were holding hands and talking. Okay, that was not nice. More importantly, they did not look at me, and I sensed they were pros.

I kept walking, and as I got deeper into the park, away from Fifth Avenue, I was struck by how the mood and feeling changed—it was almost as though I'd stepped back in time to when Manhattan Island was all forest, meadows, and rock outcrops.

You can, however, see the lighted skyscrapers around the park, and in the park are paved paths lined with ornamental post lights. I followed one of those paths north toward my first stopping point, which was the Kerbs Boathouse.

The drizzle had kept the big crowds of promenaders away, and also kept people off the lawns. In fact, there weren't many people around tonight, and this was good.

I made my way north, then followed a sign and a path that took me toward the Kerbs Boathouse on the pond.

I tried to spot my surveillance people, but other than the couple, who were walking fifty yards behind me holding hands, I couldn't ID anyone.

I also tried to spot anyone else who was following me, but no one looked particularly interested in me.

In fact, a voice in my ear said, "Hunter, this is SO One—you seem to be alone. Copy?"

I replied, "Copy."

And that was it. Nothing more to be said.

I got to the boathouse, which was used to house model boats for geeks, and I stood on the stone patio between the house and the pond and looked out over the water.

Somewhere across the pond was a SWAT team with sniper rifles, and they could shoot the chewing gum out of a guy's mouth and not chip his teeth. But it seemed that I was the only one here.

There were benches near the shore and I sat on one of them, looking despondent, which isn't hard to do when your ass is wet and the rain is getting colder.

I gave it ten minutes, and I was about to move on when Stark said, "Someone approaching from the north."

"Copy."

I drew my Glock and held it in my lap.

I heard footsteps coming from my right and I glanced at the far corner of the boathouse.

A male figure—tall—stood in the glare of a lamp-post. He was watching me, then took a few steps forward and walked slowly across the patio toward me.

He wore a long black topcoat that was too heavy for this time of year, and he was carrying a big bag, the way homeless people do, and as he got closer I could start to make out his features.

I kept an eye on him as he approached, but it was not Asad Khalil—though it could have been one of his pals.

He sat on the bench next to mine and said to me, "How ya doin'?"

"My wife is dead and I'm going to drown myself in the pond."

"Yeah? Sorry 'bout that, man." He added, "Hey, it ain't that bad."

Stark said to me, "Who are you talking to?"

I replied, "I don't know. Hold on." I asked the gentleman, "What's your name?"

"Skip. What's yours?"

"Tom Walsh. Hold on." I said to my condenser mic, "It's Skip."

"Skip who?"

Before I could ask Skip for more info, he asked me, "Who you talkin' to?"

"Myself. Don't you talk to yourself?"

"Hell, no. Crazy people talk to theirselves."

"Hunter," asked Stark, "who *is* that?"

I asked Skip, "Are you an Arab terrorist?"

He replied, "Yeah. I'm an Arab terrorist."

I said to my mic, "He says he's an Arab terrorist."

"What the hell are you doing? Get rid of that guy."

"Ten-four." I said to Skip, "You gotta leave."

"Says who?"

"The voice in my head."

"Can you spare a few bucks?"

I said to Stark, "I'll give him a few bucks, but you might want to check him out when he leaves." I added, "Get my money back."

I heard a few laughs from the surveillance team in my earphone.

Skip asked again, "Who ya talkin' to, man?"

"Aliens." I pulled two dollars out of my pocket, but Skip was up and gone.

I decided to do the same, and I said, "SO One, Hunter is mobile."

"Copy."

I headed toward another body of water, Belvedere Lake, which was about a third of a mile farther north and west.

I walked slowly across the area called the Ramble, which is heavily treed, and a good place for an ambush, though I seemed to be the only person around. But, you know, sometimes you get that feeling you're being watched.

I reached Belvedere Lake, and Stark said to me, "Take a walk around the lake."

So I took a slow walk around Belvedere Lake, also known as Turtle Pond, or perhaps tonight as Sitting Duck Lake.

I completed the walk without meeting anyone interesting, and I stopped near a building called Belvedere Castle, where I sat on a wet bench and looked at the pond.

I said, "Hunter at rest."

Stark replied, "We have visual." He added, "No one followed you. But sit awhile."

So I sat for fifteen or twenty minutes, then Stark said, "We're thinking that if you had company, we'd know by now. So maybe we'll cancel the Reservoir."

I replied, "I'm having too much fun."

I thought I heard a few groans in my earpiece, then Stark said, "Your call."

I stood and replied, "Hunter mobile." I asked, "How do you want me to go?"

He replied, "Around the Great Lawn, to the west."

"Copy."

I began walking, skirting the Great Lawn along a path that passed beside a treed area. There was no one around except a guy on a bicycle coming toward me. I kept walking and as he got closer I could see he was looking at me, and I put my hand on the Smith & Wesson.

A voice in my earphone said, "Hunter, I'm the guy on the bike."

"Ten-four."

He passed me, gave a quick nod, and continued on.

I, too, continued on. Off to my left, in the trees, I saw a guy walking his dog. The dog was sniffing around, the way dogs do when they're supposed to be taking a crap, and the guy was talking on his cell phone, probably saying to his wife or significant other, "Why do *I* have to walk the dog every time it rains? It's *your* dog." And so forth. Been there, done that.

I continued on, but I glanced back at the dog walker to be sure he and the dog were not terrorists.

I could see the apartment buildings on Central Park West, and I pictured Vince Paresi sitting in his nice warm apartment having a glass of vino and trying to remember what was happening tonight that was keeping him on call. Actually, Paresi had a base station in his apartment, and he could monitor all radio traffic, including my wire, so I said, "Captain, I can see your house from here. Wave."

There were a few chuckles in my earpiece, but no response from the boss.

Anyway, it was now about 11:30, and the drizzle persisted. It was getting colder, and I was wet, and the only thing that would make me happy now was Asad Khalil. And on that subject, I was fairly certain I could filet his throat before the surveillance teams could interfere.

I crossed Transverse Road at 86th Street, and to my right I could see the lights of the Central Park Precinct, which sits in the park. This was not bad duty if you like the outdoors. On the other hand, there is winter. No job is perfect. Not even this one.

Anyway, up ahead I saw the Reservoir, which is a large body of water, nearly a half mile across. There is a running track that circles it, and I saw two people jogging together. I mean, who jogs in the rain at midnight?

Stark said, "Hunter, we have some people up there at the Reservoir, and they report that there are only a few joggers, and no one has followed you, so I think it's time to call it quits."

I replied, "I'm going to jog around the Reservoir."

Again, a few groans, but more this time and louder. Hey guys, I'm the one trying to get mugged by a terrorist.

I got on the jogging track and began running in a counterclockwise direction, which is the rule. My running shoes and socks were wet, and I could hear squishing coming from my feet.

The track is about a mile and a half around, and after about five minutes I was starting to enjoy it, which is the first creepy step toward becoming a jog-ger zombie.

By now, of course, I'd given up any hope of meet-ing up with Asad Khalil, but if one of his goombahs was watching, he'd be calling Khalil now saying, "This man will die of pneumonia or a heart attack before you can kill him. Come quickly."

Anyway, I circumnavigated the Reservoir in about twenty minutes, which is not too bad, and I was so jazzed, I took a deep breath and said to Stark, "I'm go-ing to do that again."

Stark replied, "Hold on—I'm trying to talk the SWAT team out of shooting you."

"Come on. Just one more—"

"It's over. The operation is over. Surveillance and countersurveillance all report no sightings. Time to go home."

"All right . . . but I'll walk back through the park." I gave him my route along the east side of the park and began my two-mile walk back to my apartment.

I headed south, along a path that took me past the rear of the Metropolitan Museum of Art, which was on my left, and the Egyptian obelisk on my right. I looked up at the towering stone obelisk, which was about 3,500 years old, and a profound thought took hold in my mind, which was, "That's pretty fucking old."

Anyway, I continued on, disappointed, but also strangely elated. It was like Paresi said—we were doing something, which was better than doing nothing; bet-ter than waiting around for that asshole to make his next move.

Tonight's operation was over, but I was still alert and I hoped my team hadn't gone home while I was still in the park.

I said, "SO One, Hunter here. You guys still with me?"

Silence.

"SO One, Hunter. Hello?"

Stark said, "I think everyone left."

"Joke, right?"

"Joke. Hey, pick up the pace. Everyone wants to cut out."

I don't really like jokes in serious situations unless I'm making them.

I said, "Hey, do me a favor—call Bellevue, get through the switchboard, and have someone on the security floor go into my wife's room and tell her I'm heading home."

"Will do."

I continued on, still thinking that there was a chance of making contact with the enemy. But the enemy was either oblivious that I was here in the park or they'd seen me, reported to Khalil, and he'd smelled a trap. But I was game to do it again, tomorrow night, and every night for as long as Walsh and Paresi believed this could work, and as long as they wanted to commit manpower to it. In fact, this was all we had. The only other way that we'd find Khalil was to wait until he sprung his own plan on us.

Up ahead was the Alice in Wonderland sculpture, and I stopped and looked at it. The Mad Hatter reminded me of Tom Walsh.

I continued on, then exited the park at Fifth Avenue and 72nd Street and began the walk home. The street was quiet at this hour, and the rain was a little heavier.

Stark said, "We'll try another location tomorrow night."

I said to everyone, "Thanks. Good job."

About eight or nine voices acknowledged.

I walked into my lobby, and Special Agent Lisa Sims, of all people, was on duty. She asked me, "How'd it go?"

"A good trial run."

She nodded and said, "Sorry to hear about your wife."

"Thanks. She's okay."

"Good." She took something out of her pocket and handed it to me. It was a silver dollar token from the Taj Mahal. She said, "For luck."

I smiled. "Thanks." I added, "It worked last time."

She smiled in return and said, "You look like you need a good night's sleep."

"Yeah. But *you* have to stay awake."

"Right . . . well, if you get insomnia . . . I'm here."

How shall I take that?

I wished her a good evening, walked to the elevator, got on, and drew my Glock.

I entered my apartment, gun in hand. I'd left all the lights on and they were all still on. I swept the rooms, returned to the door, and bolted it.

The bolt itself was good, but not great, though I had never worried about it. But if someone had a door ram with them, they could take out the lock *and* the bolt with one or two hits.

I wasn't getting paranoid or skittish—I was just thinking about worst-case scenario.

The bad guys could sometimes be clever and smart, but smart people also know when not to be clever and when to use brute force. Speed, surprise, and frontal assault—and I'd be falling thirty-four floors from the balcony, without a parachute, and Khalil would be waving good-bye and calling to me, "Your last free fall, Mr. Corey!" *Splat.*

That called for a drink, but it also called for being cold sober. So I had half a drink. I *really* hated this bastard.

I dragged the couch into the foyer and shoved it against the door.

Then I changed into dry clothing and sat in my La-Z-Boy. I turned on the TV and found a great old John Wayne movie—*Danger Rides the Range*—and when the Duke got into a gunfight with the bad guys, I aimed my revolver at the screen and helped him out. *Bang, bang.* Watch out, Duke! *Bang.*

At about 2 A.M., I went to bed. The bedroom door has a good lock, as I'd found out the hard way from two wives and one girlfriend, and for the first time it was me who locked the bedroom door.

I was completely pissed off that I had to live like this; this went against my training and my natural instincts to be the guy playing offense. But sometimes you just had to wait for the other guy to make his move, and when he did, the game would be over quickly.

I fell into an uneasy sleep and had a dream that Khalil and I had entered a big arena from opposite ends and were walking toward each other. It was night, and the stadium was empty, and it was very quiet, and only a few of the stadium lights were on, and there were dark shadows across the field, and we both passed through light and dark as we approached each other. And finally, we stood face-to-face, a few feet apart in a circle of light. We both nodded, and he drew a knife from his belt, and I saw it was covered with blood—Kate's blood. And he licked it. I drew my knife—the K-bar—and held it up so he could see it. He nodded again, and we moved toward each other. The stadium lights suddenly went out . . . and I could hear his breathing in the dark. Then he was close enough for me to smell him, and I heard him say, "I saved you for last."

I lunged at his voice in the dark, and felt warm blood on my chest, but I didn't know if it was his blood or mine—or both.

I woke up in a sweat, breathing hard. I sat there in bed, staring into the dark, and pictured his face, and I said to him, "I saved you all for myself."

CHAPTER FORTY-TWO

Thursday morning. The weather was better than yesterday, which I took as an omen that today I would kill Asad Khalil. Maybe that's a stretch.

I spoke to Captain Paresi and we discussed the previous night's operation, but there wasn't much to say except that it ran well, and everyone—especially me—did a good job. The target of the operation, Asad Khalil, however, did not show up. And that's when we'd find out how good we really are.

Paresi said he got some manpower to check the apartment houses and office buildings on East 72nd Street, starting across the street from my building. He informed me that it would take at least ten days to accomplish this—unless, of course, they got lucky before that.

Then he said to me, "Are you up for another night of walking?"

"Anything that gets me out of the house."

"Okay, we're going to try something different tonight. I want you to come to 26 Fed at about six P.M.

Take a taxi, and maybe you'll be followed by Sandland Taxi Service. But even if you're not, we're going to assume, or hope, that 26 Fed is being watched from the street or from a surrounding building. Okay?"

"You mean *we* could be under surveillance? Is that legal?"

"Actually, it probably is. Okay, then about nine P.M. you leave the building and proceed on foot to the area of the World Trade Center construction site. It's pretty quiet down there after dark and you'll just wander the area—sad, lonely, contemplating life and death. Then at some point you'll walk down to Battery Park." He added, "We'll play it by ear and see what looks good as the hour gets later."

"Okay." I asked him, "Where will you be?"

"I'll stay at 26 Fed so I can be close."

"Good. And Tom?"

"Same."

I said to him, "I want to pick the place for tomorrow night."

He replied, "We're not running this operation over the weekend. Too many people out and about."

That made sense, but it didn't make me happy. I said, "Try to rethink that." I reminded him, "This is all we have unless we find him the old-fashioned way."

"Right. In fact, we're going to use the manpower we save on you this weekend to knock on doors in your neighborhood."

"All right, but—"

"Also, John, the other possibility is he will find you."

"Right. But I need to make myself available to him."

He pointed out, "You're also available at home. Maybe he'll try that this weekend."

I didn't want to argue with him, and I was already thinking about giving my protective detail the slip and going out on my own to see if The Lion was stalking me.

Paresi said, "Let's see what happens tonight." He speculated, "Khalil may have skipped out."

"He's here."

I called Kate and she said to me, "A nurse came in last night about one and said she had a message for me." Kate informed me, "I thought you were dead."

"I wouldn't leave you a message like that."

"This is not funny."

"Sorry, but I can't get through the switchboard after midnight."

"Tom sent me a new cell phone this morning, so you can call me direct now."

"Good."

She then asked me, "Where did you go last night?"

"A walk in Central Park." I added, "I'm a despondent widower, thinking about drowning myself in the lake."

She had no comment, but she may have thought that was not a bad idea.

I said, "I was covered. Maybe too covered. And maybe Khalil and his pals are on to our game."

She didn't respond for a while, then said, "He's come here with his own game."

"Right."

She asked me, "Are you going out tonight?"

"Yeah. I'm starting at 26 Fed, then the WTC site, then Battery Park, then . . . maybe I'll do a hookah bar crawl."

She said, "I'd give anything to see John Corey drinking tea with Arabs in a hookah bar."

"Somebody has to do it."

Kate stayed silent awhile, then said, "It's a little disturbing to think there could be cells living and working here—I mean, real cells with competent and dangerous people."

"Right." We'd never discovered any such organized activity here in New York, but there were a number of individuals and small groups of suspects who were so incompetent and outright dumb that we just kept an eye on them, hoping they'd lead us to someone or some group that was actually dangerous. But Asad Khalil, if he had help, would not be using the gangs that couldn't shoot straight that we'd been watching for years.

In fact, Kate said, "It would be good if all this led to a real cell—maybe Al Qaeda—that we could round up." She reminded me, "That's why we need to take Khalil alive."

"Right." But Khalil, if taken alive, was not going to talk—unless, of course, the CIA took him out of the country and interrogated him in an enhanced manner. But there was no guarantee that would happen. And if it did, we would never know what Khalil said. Also, I'm not comfortable with using torture to get information. So my plan was still the best—cut his fucking throat.

But I'm also not a big fan of cold-blooded murder . . . so it would be good if Khalil put me in a position where I had no choice—or the choice wasn't so clear. I mean, he wasn't thinking about taking *me* alive.

"John?"

"Right. We need him alive."

On the subject of sticking to the letter of the law, FBI Special Agent Kate Mayfield asked me, "Have you spoken to Tom about Boris?"

"I'm drafting a memo."

"Call him."

I informed her, "Tom has done a disappearing act on me."

"He has a phone."

"Kate, I will handle this. Subject closed."

She changed the subject. "Do you think that Tom, George, and Vince are in danger?"

I asked her, "What does Tom think?"

She replied, "He's not discounting it, but he's also not totally believing he could be a target."

"Right." The cemeteries are full of people like that. I said to her, "Tell Tom you want a gun."

She didn't reply for a few seconds, then said, "There's a uniformed officer outside my door twenty-four/seven."

"Even cops have to take a leak. Get a gun. If Tom says no, I'll give you one. They don't count guns on the way out."

"All right."

I told her, "I can't come tonight—I need to be at 26 Fed at six."

"I understand." She gave me her new cell phone number and said, "Call me tonight with good news."

Well, if it was bad news, I wouldn't be the one calling.

Back in my apartment, I worked on my incident report, then I began drafting a long memo about this case, starting from the beginning three years ago. The memo contained all I knew that was classified, and also my own thoughts and theories about things like the CIA's involvement in the original case. I had no idea who this memo was addressed to—but maybe it was addressed to posterity; to whoever worked this case in the event of my death.

Under the heading of "Khalil II," I revealed my recent meeting with Boris Korsakov, which reminded me that I hadn't heard from him since I'd left him at Svetlana contemplating a reunion with his star pupil. This might mean that he was dead, but I think I might have heard about that on the news, or maybe through official channels. More likely Boris had nothing more to say to me. Or, as I said, he'd skipped town, which was the smart move, but maybe not what an egotistical former KGB guy would do. And as I'd discovered long ago, the most common cause of death among alpha males was ego. I should know.

I used my ATTF cell phone to dial Boris, hoping he'd recognize the number that I'd given him and that he'd take the call. Or another voice would answer, "Khalil here."

Boris Korsakov answered. "Good afternoon, Mr. Corey."

"And to you." I asked him, "Where are you?"

"Where I was when I last saw you."

Of course he could be anywhere, and I said to him, "I thought I heard a Swiss yodeler in the background."

He laughed and replied, "No, you are hearing the Red Army Chorus singing 'Kalinka.'"

"No kidding?" I suggested, "Tell them to take a break."

"Hold on."

The Red Army Chorus packed up and left, and Boris said to me, "One becomes nostalgic as one gets older."

"Right. I've got an old German deli guy down the block who misses the hell out of the Third Reich. So, what have you been up to?"

"Nothing. And you?"

"Same. And where is Mrs. Korsakov?"

"Moscow."

"Lucky girl. Look, I'm rethinking what I said to you about not having your place put under surveillance. What do you think?"

Without hesitation, he replied, "You promised me a week."

"Boris, I made no such promise, or if I did, I've come to my senses and I hope you have, too."

He informed me, "We both came to the right decision about this. You should not rethink it."

"Well, I am." I asked him, "What do you think you'll accomplish by locking yourself in your office?"

"Maybe nothing more than staying alive while you find Khalil. But we will see."

I said, "He's not going to come for you if he knows you're barricaded in there. In fact, that's a tip-off to him that you know he's here."

He informed me, "I often spend days living in my office when my wife is not here. So this is not unusual."

"Yeah? What do you do all day?"

"Come visit and you can see."

He laughed and it was *that* kind of laugh. Men are pigs.

I got back to the subject and said to him, "Look, Boris, you don't have much chance of killing or capturing Khalil. I'm thinking you need my help. I want to put your place under surveillance, and I also want you to let me set up a trap." I explained, "You leave your fort there, go back to your apartment, take long walks on the boardwalk, go about your normal business, and I'll have people around you who can protect you and also grab Khalil if he makes an attempt on your life." I assured him, "I've done this a thousand times. Haven't lost anyone yet." Not even myself.

He seemed to be thinking about that, then said, "I will consider that."

I knew he was stalling so I asked him, "Why do you want to kill him?"

He replied, "I did not say I wanted to kill him."

"Okay, so you want to reason with him?"

"There is no reasoning with that man."

"So, what's your goal? Your objective?"

"To defend myself until you capture him. Or I may capture him here."

"And then you'll turn him over to the police or the FBI."

"Correct."

"But if you do that, then he'll sing—and it won't be Kalinka."

"I am not following you."

"All right. Let me be more clear." I said to him, "Your story about your involvement in and your knowledge of Khalil's mission here three years ago and Khalil's story about that are probably not the same story."

No response.

I continued, "You knew damn well that he was coming here to murder U.S. Air Force pilots, and that's what you trained him to do. But you bullshitted the CIA, and they believed you—"

"They never believed me. But they found it convenient to say they did."

"Okay . . . so they *think* you were involved with, and had knowledge of, these murders. But if Khalil is captured and interrogated by the FBI, he *will* implicate you in those murders, and the best you can hope for from the Justice Department is a forfeiture of all your assets and a one-way ticket out of here." I added, "The worst would be an indictment for accessory to murder."

He thought about that and replied, "They would not let that happen."

"Who?"

"My friends in Langley."

"You think?" I asked him, "Have you heard from them?"

He replied, "If I have, I could not tell you."

"Try."

"This is a closed subject."

"Okay, then I'm going to have surveillance put around your club and your apartment."

This was not what I really wanted to do, of course— I wanted to find Khalil myself. But I couldn't pass up this opportunity to set a second trap for him, and the first trap, with me as bait, didn't seem to be working. Also, I had a legal—and maybe moral—obligation to call Tom Walsh about Boris.

Boris said to me, "May I ask you a question?"

"Sure."

"Why did you come here alone?"

Good question. I replied, "Well, I was on my way to Coney Island, and out of the blue I had this thought that Boris Korsakov could be living in Brighton Beach."

"That sounds very improbable."

"Right. Okay, your club and apartment will be under surveillance in the next hour or so, and you'll be followed if you decide to come outside for some fresh air. Also, I'd like you to consider cooperating with this surveillance, and let us put a few people inside your club. Okay?"

He didn't respond to that and said, "You came

alone because you want to kill him. Not capture him, Mr. Corey, but *kill* him."

"I don't remember saying that."

"Oh, but you did." He further informed me, "You'd like to do it yourself, of course, but you would accept me doing it. The important thing for you—and for me—is that he is killed."

"Boris, I think you were in the KGB too long."

"Long enough to know how to solve a problem." He continued, "We understand each other, so you don't have to say anything, but please think about what you were thinking about when you arrived here . . . unofficially."

"Well, to be honest with you, I've rethought that."

"No. You are trying to make yourself feel better about your unorthodox method of dealing with Asad Khalil."

Boris had a point there, but I replied, "I didn't call you for psychotherapy."

He replied, "We are both men who have seen some of the world, and we understand how things are done." He informed me, "In Langley, they told me a little about your involvement with Khalil when he was here last, and I have concluded from that and from what you yourself said to me three years ago that you have some personal reasons for wanting Khalil dead. And he feels the same about you—as he feels about me. So why don't we leave others out of this, and also leave our conversation where it was when you walked out of my office?"

I thought about that. I mean, what was the downside to letting Boris try to kill Khalil? None. But there was a big downside for Boris if Khalil killed him instead. That, however, was not a downside for me—in fact, hate to say it, but Boris would get just what he deserved at the hands of the monster he helped create.

But if Boris killed Khalil, then, yes, I'd have to accept it wasn't me who did it. But Khalil would be just as dead.

"Mr. Corey?"

"Okay. I said a week. That's Tuesday."

"Good. That is the correct decision for both of us."

"I hope you still feel that way when you find Khalil sitting in your office."

Boris did not comment on that, and he said to me, "As I mentioned, I would not be surprised if Khalil intends to kill your friend, Ms. Mayfield. So you should warn her."

"Let me worry about that." I then asked him, "Have you thought about what else Khalil might have planned, aside from whacking me and you?"

He stayed silent awhile, then replied, "Well, as I said, he must need to repay someone for his trip to America. But I can tell you that when Khalil was last here, he had not been trained in explosives or in handling chemicals or biological materials."

"Well, that's good news." I asked him, "You didn't have time for that?"

He replied, "That is not my area of expertise."

"Right." I said, "But he could have learned something new in the last three years."

"Of course. But I want you to know he did not learn from me."

"Right. So if we all start keeling over from nerve gas or anthrax, you had nothing to do with that."

"Correct. And if there is a large explosion—"

"Not your fault."

"Also correct."

"Okay, but . . . do you have any thoughts, any theories about a possible target—is there anything this asshole might have said to you? Like, 'Gee, Boris, I hate to see women shopping in department stores.' Follow?"

"Yes, I do." He stayed silent awhile, then said, "He did have what I would call an anti-materialistic opinion. So perhaps he would target something like a department store, but . . . what real damage would that do?"

"Are you kidding? Boris, this is New York. Have you seen all the ladies on Fifth Avenue?"

He laughed, then said, "I wish I could be helpful in guessing a possible target . . . but this man has so many hates." He informed me, "He did not like women, though he is not gay. He was a . . . puritan. He would, like his leader Khadafi, go into the desert for weeks at a time to pray, and live on bread and water. He rejected all comforts and material objects, except his clothing and his weapons."

"Not a fun guy."

"No. In fact, a rather boring man. But regarding

a hated target . . . his biggest hate was simply America, and everything about America, so he has many targets."

"Right."

"He considers America corrupt, decadent, and weak."

"What's he have against decadence?"

Again, Boris laughed and said, "He considered me decadent. Can you imagine that?"

Well, yes, but I said, "Maybe he needs a night in Svetlana."

"It would be good for him," he agreed. Then he said to me, "Khalil had a favorite expression—'the Americans know too much of gold, and they have forgotten steel.'"

Well, there could be some truth there. But rather than tell Boris that, I said, "Let me ask you a more specific question about the CIA and Khalil, and you don't have to answer this, but if you don't, I might have to pull the plug on you."

No reply, so I asked him, "Did the CIA have any involvement with Asad Khalil?"

Again, no reply.

I waited.

Finally he said, "This is not something you want to know."

"Then why did I ask?"

Finally, he replied, "You understand that my friends in Langley were not giving me too much information during my debriefing. They were asking *me* questions.

But as a trained interrogator yourself, you know that one can learn much from the questions."

"What did you learn?"

"I learned . . . the CIA and the KGB have much in common."

I didn't reply and waited for more.

I pictured Boris lighting a cigarette and sipping vodka. Then he said, "I have no idea if Khalil and the CIA had any sort of understanding then—or now. But I will tell you this—when a country is attacked, the people rally to the government. You saw this on 9/11. But when a country is *not* attacked—or has not been attacked in . . . let us say almost two years—then people forget. And perhaps they become critical of the government, and critical of the methods used by the government in fighting the enemy. In America especially, people resent any loss of their liberties. Correct? So what is the solution of the government? To hand back the power to the people? No. The solution is another attack."

Again, I didn't respond, but I completely understood what he was saying. Boris, though, was . . . well, a Russian. A KGB guy. And these guys loved their conspiracies. And they loved to speculate about secret plots and all that. So when I asked him to speculate, I'd hit his X-Files button.

"Mr. Corey?"

"Sorry, I was making notes for a movie script."

"Is there anything else I can help you with?"

"Not at this time," I assured him.

"Thank you for your call. And for the week."

"You're quite welcome, and don't forget to call me if you should happen to kill him in self-defense."

"My attorney first, then you."

"You're a real American, Boris."

"Thank you." He stayed silent awhile, then said to me, "Whatever he has planned for you, Mr. Corey, is not going to be pleasant."

"Right. You too. And probably you first."

He didn't reply to that and we hung up. I got a beer and sat on the balcony.

Well, I might now know a little more about Khalil's head, but I wasn't any closer to finding him. And I wasn't any closer to figuring out what else he had planned here. But I *was* a little more certain that he had *something* planned—something chemical, biological, or, God forbid, nuclear. Something given to him by his backers.

As for Boris's CIA conspiracy theory . . . well, Boris wasn't the first person to think that there were people who would welcome another attack. But welcoming an attack and conspiracy to instigate one were very different things.

My other thought was that I shouldn't be conspiring with Boris Korsakov, former KGB assassin. But sometimes you have to partner up with a bad guy. As the Arabs say, the enemy of my enemy is my friend. Plus, I doubled the chances that Khalil would wind up dead before he could set off a weapon of mass destruction. Or kill me. And that was the goal. I'd worry later about explaining all this to Tom Walsh if I had to.

I finished my beer and looked out at the buildings across the street. If Khalil was there, then I was a tempting target. But I recalled my dream, which came to me as the sum total of everything I knew about this man, how he'd killed before, and who he was. So we'd meet—probably at a time and place of *his* choosing, not mine—but we'd definitely meet.

CHAPTER FORTY-THREE

At 5:30, I took a taxi to 26 Federal Plaza.

I spent a few hours at my desk, catching up on e-mails and memos and listening to voice mail. There was nothing pertaining to Asad Khalil, which reinforced my conclusion that this was a very tightly controlled case. As for all the other cases that I—and Kate—had been working on, it appeared that they'd been parceled out to other detectives and agents. So, was I still working here? I guess I was until the Khalil case was settled, one way or the other.

I didn't see Tom Walsh, which reinforced my suspicion that he was distancing himself from me and from the operation—but not so far that he couldn't be on the scene if I killed or captured the wanted Libyan terrorist. I wondered, though, if he'd show up if I got whacked and Khalil got away. No photo op there. In any case, if I'd seen him, I'm sure I would have told him about Boris. Unless it slipped my mind.

At 8 P.M., I met with Paresi and Stark, and we went over the operation in detail.

At 9 P.M. I left 26 Federal Plaza, pretty much as I'd been dressed the night before, except this time I had a Yankees cap on—so if I ran into Khalil, he could shout, "Die, Yankee!"

I made the short walk down to the Trade Center site, and noticed that the observation platform had a locked gate at the entrance, and the surrounding area—which had been devastated when the Towers collapsed—was deserted at this hour.

I did a complete walk around the site, which was about a third of a mile on each side, and I stopped a few times to look down into the huge excavation, which was partially lit by stadium lights. At the bottom of the deep pit was construction equipment and piles of building material. Virtually all of the rubble was gone, but now and then human remains still turned up. *Bastards.*

On the Liberty Street side of the big hole was the long earthen ramp that went down into the construction site. The ramp was blocked by two high chain-link gates that were locked. On the other side of the gates I could see a house trailer that was a comfortable guard post for the Port Authority Police who manned this single entrance to the excavation. Parked near the gates was a Port Authority Police vehicle that was used by the two PA cops in the trailer.

Well, I didn't expect to see Asad Khalil here near the guard post, so I moved onto West Street, which runs between the World Trade Center site and the buildings of the World Financial Center site, which had been so heavily damaged by the collapse of the Twin Towers that the area was blocked off by security fences. This place was like a war zone—which it actually was.

On the opposite side of the excavation I could see the lighted observation platform, and it occurred to me that Asad Khalil would not have missed this tourist attraction while he was in New York. I pictured him standing there, looking down into this abyss, trying to hide his smile from the people around him.

Stark's voice in my earpiece said, "You are alone."

"Copy."

I walked down to Battery Park, which was about a half mile south of Ground Zero. Battery Park at night is quiet, though not desolate. You get some romantic types who sit and watch the water and look at the Statue of Liberty, or take a ferry ride to Staten Island. Cheap date. Done it.

It was a nice evening, so there were a few people in the park, including the surveillance team couple I'd seen in Central Park, sitting on a bench again, holding hands. I hoped they at least liked each other.

I said into my mic, "This is not promising."

Stark replied, "Maybe it's too early. Let's take a walk on some dark, quiet streets. Then we'll come back here later."

I liked the way Stark used the plural pronoun as though *he* was walking. No, *I* was walking, and half the surveillance team was walking, and the other half was in unmarked vehicles. As for the SWAT team, they were transported to various locations, and they stayed mostly in their unmarked van so they wouldn't scare anyone.

As I walked through the quiet streets of the Financial District, I called Kate to put her mind at ease, and she answered and said, "I've been waiting for your call. Where are you?"

"Stepping over drunk stockbrokers."

"Be careful, John."

"Love you."

Being married to someone in the business has its advantages. You worry about the other person, but it's informed worrying. And the less said, the better.

I continued the walk through the nearly deserted streets of Lower Manhattan, then back to Battery Park, then back to the Trade Center.

At about midnight, we all agreed that no one was following me, and I found a taxi near 26 Fed and headed home.

On the way, I called Kate's cell phone, and said, "No luck. I'm in a taxi, heading home."

"Good." She advised me, "Don't do this again." She said, "I don't think my nerves can take another night of this."

Well, there goes my theory about being married to someone in the business. I said, "I've got the weekend off. Get some sleep. I'll see you tomorrow."

Me being lion bait did not seem to be working. Which could mean that Khalil and his local contacts had no idea I was out and about. Or they knew, but they smelled a trap. Or Khalil was gone.

No. He was here. I *knew* he was here. And as Kate suggested, and as I suspected, Khalil had his own plan for John Corey. He hadn't come this far with that much hate in his heart to let me live.

Back in my apartment building, I spoke to the two surveillance guys in the lobby, said good evening to the night doorman, got in the elevator, drew my Glock, and so forth.

My apartment was terrorist-free, and I made myself a Scotch and soda and collapsed into my La-Z-Boy.

I decided not to barricade my door tonight—I am available at home. I swiveled my recliner so it faced toward the foyer, put my Glock in my lap, and fell into a half-sleep.

I had a recurring dream that the door burst open, and in some of the dreams I was pumping rounds at the dark figures silhouetted in the hallway light. In other dreams I couldn't find my gun. One time, my gun jammed.

Where does this stuff come from? I used to dream about sex.

Friday morning. The sun came through the balcony doors and it looked like it was going to be another nice day. Today would also be a good day to kill Asad Khalil.

The shower is a dangerous place, as everybody knows who saw *Psycho*. I mean, you're naked and defenseless, and you can't hear anything with the shower running. So I took a nice bath, with my Glock, which will fire when wet.

I visited Kate at Bellevue, and she'd had a bad night and had made up her mind that she was breaking out today.

She said, "I am *not* spending the weekend in this place."

I really didn't want her back in the apartment yet, so I said, "Tell you what. If something doesn't happen by Monday, you and I will fly out to . . . where your parents live . . ."

"Minnesota."

"Right. But just hang in here a few more days."

She didn't reply.

I *really* didn't want to go to East Cow Meadow, Minnesota, but maybe I could deposit Kate with her parents and get back here. Her father has a small arsenal in the house, and her crazy mother is a skeet shooter who can handle a shotgun better than most men. Also, of course, Khalil didn't know Kate was even alive. To the best of my knowledge.

On that subject, I asked her, "Did you ask Tom about a gun?"

"I did. It's against hospital regulations for a patient to have a gun."

"That's a silly rule. I mean, maybe the convicts on the floor shouldn't have a gun, but why can't everyone else have their own gun?"

"John . . . please."

I took my revolver out of its holster and slid it under

her pillow. I said, "You'll sleep better with Mr. Smith and Mr. Wesson."

She nodded, but didn't reply.

I put her laptop on the bed and said, "Get into the Sullivan County Medical Examiner's Office."

She hesitated, then logged on and found the site, and discovered that Katherine Mayfield Corey had died in the Catskill Regional Medical Center. The cause of death was listed as homicide.

She stayed quiet awhile, then said, "I guess your point is that I shouldn't complain about being here."

"Better here than downstairs." Meaning the city morgue.

"Okay . . . Monday."

I stayed for lunch—broiled stool pigeon with plea bargain peas—and as we dined, Kate asked me if I was going out again Monday night, and I replied, "I haven't heard."

She said, "It's a waste of time."

"What would you suggest?" I asked.

"I don't know, but . . . Khalil's not going to fall for an obvious trap."

"It's not that obvious." I added, "It's good for everyone's morale and it makes the bosses happy. Plus, you just never know."

She took my hand and said, "John . . . Khalil has obviously thought this out. I told you, he has his own trap. For you."

"I hope so."

"Don't hope so."

"Look, Kate, I can spot a trap, too."

"I know you can. And I also know that you'll walk right into it because you think you can turn it around." She suggested, "You have a big ego."

Leading cause of death among alpha males.

She said, "Monday, two tickets to Minneapolis."

"I thought you wanted to go to Minnesota."

She said, "I'm looking forward to getting out in the country. It will do us a lot of good."

"Right." Should I remind her about what happened last Sunday when we got out in the country? Probably not.

I stood and said, "Okay, I have to go."

"I'll go online and book the trip."

"Great." Actually, of course, I wasn't going with her. Unless Asad Khalil was dead by Monday. And if I was dead by Monday, then I certainly wasn't going to Minnesota. That would be redundant. I reminded her, "You have a revolver under your pillow."

"Maybe that will improve the service here."

"See you tonight."

She suggested, "Take the night off, John. I'm fine here."

"Are you sure?"

"I'll see you in the morning."

"Okay . . . I'll call you later."

She also suggested, "Do not give your protective detail the slip and go out to see if Khalil is waiting for you."

Wives become mind readers. Or maybe I was predictable. I replied, "I wouldn't do anything that dangerous."

"Of course, you wouldn't." She suggested, "Let's talk every hour."

"Right."

We kissed and I left.

I spent the afternoon on paperwork and thinking, and also working out. A sound mind in a sound body. The body is easier to work on.

I had eaten my last can of chili, and there was nothing left in the apartment except things in bottles. So at 6 P.M. I called down to my protective detail and ordered a pepperoni pizza, which is good for the soul.

At seven, my intercom buzzed and the SO guy said, "Pizza coming up."

I unlocked the door and left it ajar, then drew my Glock and moved back into the foyer. If the pizza had anchovies, the delivery guy was dead.

There was a knock on the door, then it opened, and there was Captain Vince Paresi carrying a pizza box. I wished I had a camera instead of a gun.

Paresi noticed me holstering the Glock, but didn't comment.

He said to me, "I thought I'd keep you company tonight."

That sounded like it could have been Kate's idea. Or Walsh's. Or Paresi had the same idea himself— Corey needed company and needed to be watched. I'm flattered.

I said, "That's very thoughtful of you."

"Yeah. Take the pizza."

I took the box and noticed that Paresi also had a bottle of red vino under his arm.

I suggested, "Let's dine al fresco."

He reminded me, "You're not supposed to go out on your balcony."

"Live dangerously."

I took the pizza out to the balcony and set it on the café table. Paresi remained in my living room while I went back into the kitchen and collected a corkscrew, glasses, a few napkins, and a bottle of Scotch.

At my urging, he joined me on the balcony, and we shared his wine and my pizza. It was a nice night, and below on the street the city was coming alive on this Friday evening.

The wine wasn't bad and the pizza was okay, and the conversation was sort of strained. Also, Paresi kept looking at the buildings up and down the street. Vince was not a good date.

Finally, he said to me, "Those bastards could nail both of us up here."

"Don't be paranoid. More wine?"

He suggested, "Let's go inside."

"It's nice out here." I let him know, "If Khalil wanted to whack me with a sniper rifle, he'd have already done it." I added, "He has something else planned for me."

Paresi replied, "I was thinking about *me*." But not wanting me to think he was any less brave or crazy than I was, he produced two cigars and we lit up.

He poured himself the last of the wine and informed me, "CAU got a hit on Kate's cell phone just a few hours ago." He flipped his ash and continued, "A seven- or eight-second signal lock. Then it was gone, like someone was accessing the phone's directory, then shut it off."

"Where did the signal come from?"

"Well, the cell tower that logged in her phone has coverage between Forty-fourth and Forty-third streets."

"Okay . . . did you send cars there?"

"We did, but I'm guessing the signal came from a moving vehicle."

"Right. Sandland Taxi Service." I said, "Well, at least we know that Kate's cell phone is in Manhattan."

"Right. And I hope that means Khalil is in Manhattan." He nodded toward the city below and said, "He's out there."

"Maybe you'll get a call."

"More probably you." He reminded me, "Let us know within five seconds if you get a call from him."

"You and Tom do the same."

He nodded.

I looked again at the towering apartments and office buildings up and down my street. Some windows were lighted, some were dark, and I suspected one of those windows was looking back at us.

I asked Paresi, "How's it going on Seventy-second Street?"

He glanced out at the buildings and replied, "Lots and lots of doors to knock on." He informed me, "Some buildings don't even have a doorman or security guard that we can speak to—"

"Check the lobby directories for Terrorist Safe House."

He ignored that and said, "Half the doors we bang on don't even answer." He added, "Even some of the offices didn't answer during normal business hours."

"Kick the doors in."

He ignored that, too, and said, "I think we've cleared about half the apartments and maybe eighty percent of the offices." He then asked me, "Do you actually think they have a safe house—an observation post on this street?"

"Makes sense to me. That's what we'd do so that's what they'd do."

He nodded, but said nothing. Then he said, "It would have been good if that cell signal came from across the street."

I informed him, "They're not that stupid."

He disagreed. "They are."

"They *were*, Vince. But they're getting smarter." I advised him, "They might not have our technology, but they know what we have, and they know how to get around it."

He shrugged.

I further advised him, "Don't underestimate them. And do *not* underestimate Asad Khalil."

"Right. How's the cigar?"

"Better than the wine, but not as good as the pizza."

"How's your Scotch?"

"Older than the kids you've got watching my lobby."

He smiled and reminded me, "We're understaffed. Especially on weekends."

Right. And we might be more understaffed before this weekend was over.

Kate called and was very happy to find me home with my date. She inquired, "Have you been drinking?"

"No. We're *still* drinking."

"Good night, John. I love you."

"Love you, too."

Vince and I finished a half bottle of Scotch, and he left before midnight.

I wasn't sure if he had a protective detail with him, and I didn't want to ask. Macho guys don't ask or answer that kind of question.

Anyway, having tempted fate and finding out that fate wasn't interested in me tonight, I left the balcony and went to bed.

A quiet night. But I had that feeling I sometimes get when nothing happens that something is going to happen.

CHAPTER FORTY-FOUR

Saturday. Light rain today and showers forecast for Sunday. Good weather to kill a Libyan terrorist.

I called for my government vehicle at 10 A.M., and visited Kate at Bellevue.

She seemed in a good mood, knowing she'd be out soon.

I asked her, "Is Tom okay with you leaving?"

"He is," she informed me, "as long as I go to my parents' place."

"Okay. Does he know that you want me to go with you?"

"Yes. He's fine with that."

That was a surprise, and I asked, "Are you sure?"

"Yes. I convinced him that you shouldn't be doing what you're doing."

"I *like* doing what I'm doing."

"Well, *I* don't." She informed me, "I had a very frank talk with Tom—a tough talk. And I told him that, one, he couldn't keep me here against my will, and two, Washington might not approve of him using you—a contract agent—as live bait to trap a terrorist. If something happened to you—"

"Hold on. I volunteered for this."

"*I* didn't. And you never consulted me."

I seem to remember my life and job being simpler before I got married—both times.

She also informed me, "Tom doesn't believe this is working anyway, and it's taking a lot of manpower and resources that could be better used elsewhere to find Khalil." And then the clincher. "In fact, if something happened someplace in the city, and it came out that half the surveillance teams were watching our apartment and following you around, Tom would have a lot of explaining to do in Washington." She also informed me, "Tom would like us—including you—out of here and on a plane to Minneapolis on Monday."

Kate is a smart lady, and she knew how to play Tom Walsh better than I did. In fact, I was sure that Walsh would rather have his FBI agents kill or capture Asad Khalil so he didn't have to pose for photos with me.

Kate said, "Don't sulk." She assured me, "I'm doing this for us."

"Well . . . I'm touched . . . but this is not the old gung-ho Special Agent Mayfield I used to know."

She replied, "John . . . I just had a near-death experience. That changes a person."

"Yeah . . . I nearly bled to death myself once. But I got over it."

She took my hand and said, "If you love me, you won't want to put yourself in danger—"

"Of course I love you. But I don't want us looking over our shoulders for the rest of our lives."

"John, there are *hundreds* of people, here and around the world, who are now looking for Asad Khalil. They will find him without your help."

Kate was apparently having a weak moment; it happens. But knowing Kate, it wouldn't last long. After two days with her mother, she'd be back in New York kicking down doors in Bay Ridge.

She informed me, "We are booked on a Monday night flight to Minneapolis." And more bad news. "I also called your parents and told them we'd be visiting them in Florida, right after our visit to my parents." She instructed me, "Plan to be gone for two months. We're on administrative leave."

"Two . . . *months*. With your parents and mine?"

"Isn't that wonderful?"

"Can I borrow your gun?"

She took my hand again, looked at me, and said, "You've become obsessed with this, and that's not healthy. You need to get away from here."

I didn't reply.

She said, "I'd like to leave tomorrow, but the doctors won't let me travel until Monday, so Tom wants me to stay in the hospital until then. He feels I'm safer here, and he doesn't want me back in the apartment. The staff and the neighbors could see me, and that could leak out to the wrong people, who think I'm dead."

"Right." Plus, Tom didn't want me deprogramming

her. I think it's called divide and conquer. Tom is an asshole.

Kate made sure I understood all this and said, "It's a done deal. In fact, it's an order, Detective." She switched to the honey trap. "John, I love you. You saved my life, and this is how I'm repaying you."

I must have missed a link in that chain of logic. I needed to speak to Walsh, and also Paresi, but in the meantime, I said, "Okay. Monday to Indianapolis."

"Minneapolis."

"Right. Okay, I have to go."

"You have no place to go. Stay for lunch." She smiled and said, "The dessert today is early release dates."

She must have been thinking about that all morning. I smiled, but I guess it wasn't a sincere smile because she said, "Be happy, John." She assured me, "You'll be a new man in a week."

I kind of liked the man I was, even if nobody else did.

So it was a long afternoon in the hospital room, but I managed to look happy and share Kate's happiness.

Before I left, Kate said to me, "I feel so much better knowing you won't be out tonight."

"Me too."

"And before we leave, you will call Tom and tell him about Boris."

"Yes, ma'am."

"And make sure you're all packed Monday morning so we have time."

"For? Oh . . . yeah. *Yeah.*" Finally, a plan I could approve of.

"See you tonight."

We kissed and I left.

Well, I had less than forty-eight hours before I was on my way into exile. I might have one, maybe two plays left before then.

Or I wasn't fully appreciating the fact that I'd been boxed in by the boss and the wife—the perfect one-two punch. This sucked.

Back in my apartment, I called Paresi to bitch about this turn of events, and to see if he'd go to bat for me. But my call went into his voice mail, so I left a message that was a nice balance of professional concern and personal disappointment. Plus, I threw in a few unspecified threats and ominous predictions of disaster. That usually gets the bosses rethinking what's best for the case, and what's best for themselves.

I then called Tom Walsh, but it was Saturday and apparently Tom wasn't taking business calls—not mine, anyway. I left a message that addressed his concerns, and I made a convincing argument for continuing the operation, or at the very least letting me back into the office to work the case. I was doing pretty well until I said, "And I'd appreciate it in the future if you'd speak to me before you spoke to my wife." I didn't want to end on a sour note, so I said, "Give me a call, and we can discuss this, man to man, instead of you going behind my back—" Whoops. "Call me."

I hung up.

I would have told him about Boris if he'd taken the call, and if he agreed with me that I needed to stay here, on the case. In any event, I'd tell him Tuesday, when Boris's time was up to see if Khalil tried to whack him. Unfortunately, I might be making that call to Tom from a cow pasture.

As I was getting ready for my evening visit to Bellevue, my house phone rang, and the Caller ID said "Blocked."

No one on the ATTF, including Paresi and Walsh, would normally call that number, and Kate's new cell phone wouldn't say "Blocked." So maybe it was my parents. Or hers. But they never came up "Blocked"— they came up "Nuisance Call."

Well, the best way to find out . . . I answered and said, "Corey."

Silence. I knew who it was.

A voice with an accent said, "It is me."

I didn't reply.

"Mr. Corey? It is Asad Khalil."

I replied in an even tone, "I've been expecting your call."

"I know you have." He said, "I found your number on your wife's cell phone, so I am calling to express my condolences on her death."

"That is really sick."

"And the death of your friend and colleague, Mr. Haytham."

"You also killed his wife and daughter. What kind of man are you?"

"I don't understand your question."

"You are going to burn in hell."

"No, *you* are going to burn in hell. I am going to live forever in Paradise."

I didn't respond. There was a silence on the phone, and I could hear traffic noises in the background. Then he said, "I told you three years ago that I would return, and you saw that I kept my promise." He added, "I am an imperfect man, Mr. Corey, and I do not keep all my promises, but when I promise to kill someone, I kill them."

Again, I didn't respond.

He reminded me, "You had more to say to me the last time I was here. Well, I know you are mourning the death of your wife, and that makes one . . . less talkative. And perhaps less arrogant and less insulting."

Again, I didn't respond, and let the silence continue.

CAU was not listening in on my calls, but they were monitoring my number, and they could trace any incoming calls to their source—which in this case, I was certain, was a cell phone.

As if he knew what I was thinking, he said to me, "I am now in a moving vehicle and soon this phone will be out the window." He added, "I have many phones, Mr. Corey. You will not find me that way."

"But I *will* find you. And kill you. I promise."

"You are not clever enough to find me, nor are

you man enough to kill me. But I will find *you* and kill you."

"I'm not hiding, asshole. You know where I live, and where I work. If you had any balls, you'd have already tried. Instead, you kill defenseless women and murder men who have done nothing to you, and you also kill your countrymen who trust you. You're a fucking coward."

He didn't respond to that, and I thought he'd hung up, but I could still hear background noise.

Finally he said, "Did you think I was a coward when we all jumped from that aircraft? In fact, it was *you* who looked frightened."

"No, asshole, it was *you* who looked scared shitless when I popped off a few rounds at you. Did you piss your pants?"

He didn't respond directly to that, but he said in a less cool voice, "I told you I would kill that whore, and I did. And you watched her die, bleeding like a frightened lamb with her throat cut." He told me, "And I tasted her blood."

I took a deep breath and said, "Enough of your bullshit. We need to meet—"

"Unfortunately, we cannot meet this time. However, I promise you that I will be back. And I will kill you."

"Why are you running away?"

"I am not running away. I have finished my business here, except for you, and you can wait. And think about your fate."

"Are you frightened of me?"

"Mr. Corey, do not try to provoke me as you did

last time. You made me angry, and that is why your wife is dead. And why you are as good as dead."

"We need to meet and finish this. Now. I will come alone—"

"Please. You are not speaking to an idiot. When we meet, I will pick the time and place, and I will be certain you are alone."

"Did you come all this way to tell me you're leaving?"

He replied, "For all you know, I am already gone. Or I could still be here, and I may change my mind and see you before I leave."

This was starting to sound like bullshit. He wanted me to believe two things—one, he was gone and I could relax, and two, he was still here and I should be very worried.

I said to him, "You should have tried to kill me when you had the chance, stupid."

"It is *you*, Mr. Corey, who is stupid if you think I would kill you so quickly, as I killed your wife. In fact, I have a more interesting death planned for you." He asked, "Would you like me to tell you?"

"If it makes you feel better about running away."

"Well, let us see if you feel better when you hear what I have planned for you." He told me, "First, I intend to cut off your genitals. Then I will cut off your face. I will peel it from your skull." He said, "The Taliban do that in Afghanistan, Mr. Corey. Have you seen those photographs? The man is alive, but he has no face—only two eyes staring out from his skull. So, of course, we cannot see his fear or his pain—but he can see his own skull in the mirror that we hold up to his eyes. And then we feed his face and his genitals to the dogs, and the man is left to kill himself. And they all kill themselves. Or they ask someone to kill them. Life would not be good without genitals or a face. Don't you agree? And that, Mr. Corey, is what I intend to do to you. The next time we meet. And I look forward to that. So, until then—"

"Hold on. I want to remind you again that your *mother* was a whore, and she was fucking your great asshole of a leader, who you know had your father killed so he could keep fucking your mother."

I could hear him breathing on the phone, and I think he was a little pissed off at me.

Finally he said, "We will meet. Good-bye, Mr. Corey."

The phone went dead.

Well, that was a good conversation. No beating around the bush. That's what I like about psychopaths. They give it to you straight.

But did I piss him off enough to make him stick around and take a run at me? Would I get face time with him? Was that a poor choice of words?

I was now supposed to call Walsh or Paresi, but . . . I dialed Boris's cell phone. If Boris was alive, I'd tip him off that I'd heard from Khalil, and advise him to stay awake tonight. In fact, maybe I could get over to Brighton Beach and keep him company. That might be my last and best hope to find Khalil.

My call went into voice mail, and I said, "Corey. I just got a call from our Libyan friend. Call me ASAP."

I then dialed Svetlana to see if the place was closed because of the death of the owner.

A man with a Russian accent answered, and I could hear music and loud talking in the background.

I asked for Mr. Korsakov, and the man said he was not available, but he would take a message. I told him, "Have him call Mr. Corey. It's important."

I hung up. Well, Boris was apparently still alive, and Boris, I thought, was the canary in the coal mine; if Boris was dead, could John Corey be far behind?

Bottom line here was that Asad Khalil was not going anywhere until he finished his business. I don't know who he hated more—Boris or me—but I was sure that Khalil himself knew who was next on his list.

Back at Bellevue, Kate was still in high spirits, and we sat in the only two chairs in the dismal room and watched some television. The History Channel had a special about Saddam Hussein, comparing him to Adolf Hitler, who was Hussein's hero. I mean, if your role model is Adolf Hitler, you've got a problem.

So we watched TV, but my mind was elsewhere.

In fact, I *had* seen photos of anti-Taliban fighters in Afghanistan who'd had their faces completely peeled from their skulls, which were red with blood and shredded muscles and ligaments. And Kate had seen this, too, in an info session we'd attended at 290 Broadway, hosted by the CIA, who thought we needed to see the type of enemy they were fighting in Afghanistan. A picture is, indeed, worth a thousand words, and we all got the message and got a little queasy in the stomach, too. And then, of course, it was lunchtime. The CIA are great jokesters.

Anyway, it sounded like Khalil had been hanging out for the last few years in Afghanistan with the Taliban. It was a wonder they could stand him.

I thought about telling Kate that I'd gotten a phone call from Asad Khalil. *Oh, by the way, Khalil and I spoke today, and he wants to meet me to cut off my genitals and my face. What do you mean I can't meet him? I can't run away. I'll lose face.*

Regarding reporting this phone call to the bosses, I think the five seconds for me to do that had passed.

Of course, I would have reported Khalil's call if there was any useful intelligence to be learned from what he'd said. But other than the face thing, all he said was that he was leaving—or had already left— New York. And that was bullshit. But Walsh might not think so.

Meanwhile, I still hadn't heard from Boris.

"John?"

"Yes, darling?"

"I said, will this bother you?"

Kate had taken the dressing off and there was a four-inch purple scar across her throat.

I assured her, "I think it's sexy."

"It's ugly."

Would Kate still love me if my face was cut off? I knew she would—and she wouldn't have to complain about me not shaving. But how about the family jewels? That could be a problem.

I said to her, "It's what's inside that counts." I suggested, "Use makeup."

I stayed for dinner—Saturday night special—and Kate said we were not going to discuss one word of business; we were going to start decompressing and turn our thoughts to happy things, like berry picking and canoeing on the bug-infested lake near her parents' house.

I reminded her, "Your father tells FBI stories for hours on end."

"I'll speak to him."

"And he doesn't drink."

"My parents don't approve of alcohol."

"Neither do I. I just drink it."

She reminded me, "You are under orders to accompany me to Minnesota. Make the best of it."

I nodded, but my mind returned to my phone conversation with Asad Khalil.

He never asked me where I was because he knew where I lived. And I had no doubt that he would not leave here until he finished what he'd come here to do. So all I had to do was wait for him to make his move, on his terms, and at his time. And that's the way it was always going to be.

Therefore, I needed to be here when that time came. No Montana, no Michigan, no Minnesota—just here.

CHAPTER FORTY-FIVE

Sunday morning. My Special Operations keepers offered to accompany me to church if I was so inclined. Last Sunday, I was threatened with death by a skydiving terrorist, so I gave this some serious consideration before opting to watch a little of the televised Mass from St. Pat's, in my bathrobe. But I was there in spirit.

At noon, I made my pilgrimage to Bellevue.

Kate was in a jolly mood, and I was reminded of prisoners I'd seen on the eve of their release date.

She asked me, "Have you packed yet?"

"All packed and ready to go." Not.

Kate asked me, "Anything new on the case?"

"Not that I know of. What do you hear from Tom?"

"Nothing." She informed me, "I think he's away for the weekend."

"Really?" So the Special Agent in Charge of the New York Anti-Terrorist Task Force was out of town while the baddest terrorist on the planet was in town.

I said to Kate, "Tom *should* relax. Nothing bad ever happens on a weekend."

Because it was Sunday, the ward was busy with chaplains making their rounds, offering communion and God's message of love to those who needed it most—murderers, rapists, drug dealers, and other felons capable of salvation, except convicted politicians, who have no souls to save.

I was not in as jolly a mood as Kate, and she sensed this, but dealt with it by ignoring it. Happiness, she thinks, is as contagious as the syphilitic druggie in the next room; just kiss and you'll get it.

The highlight of my visit, though, was the Catholic priest who walked into the room. He looked like a nineteen-year-old kid, and his name was Father Brad. He was standing between me and the door, so I eyed the window. Could I survive a nineteen-floor jump? Worth a try?

Anyway, he turned out to be a good guy, and we all chatted, and he knew, of course, that I was a Catholic—they can tell within five seconds. Kate told him she was Methodist, so I pulled out my old joke: "He didn't ask you what kind of birth control you use."

Father Brad got a chuckle out of that, but I thought Kate was going to faint.

Father Brad was happy to discover that Kate was not a felon—she seemed like a nice girl—and he was happier to discover that I'd gone to Mass at St. Patrick's earlier. I didn't actually *say* that, but that's what he assumed from something I may have said.

I had a bunch of great pope jokes that I thought he

might find funny, but he needed to get on to tougher cases, so he blessed us both. And to be completely honest, that made me feel better for some reason. Maybe my prayers to find and kill Asad Khalil would be answered.

Kate spent the next few minutes critiquing my behavior with Father Brad, but I was now filled with the Holy Spirit, so I just smiled. Also, I was thinking about a Bloody Mary when I got home.

Kate reminded me, "I'm being picked up here tomorrow at four P.M. I need an hour to pack."

Two. Three.

"So," she said, "that gives us time to cuddle."

I thought we were going to have sex. I suggested, "Cuddle first, then pack."

"Well . . . okay."

I did a little dance around the room.

I stayed for Sunday lunch, which was actually not bad, especially the pat-down de foie gras.

The visit ended on a bittersweet note, with Kate saying to me, "You are a brave man, John, and I know you don't want to leave this problem for others to solve. But if something happened to you . . . my life would be over. So, think of me. Of us."

If something happened to me, my life would also be over, but I replied in the spirit of the sentiment and said, "We have a long life ahead of us." Unless I drop dead of boredom at a Mayfield family dinner.

I left Kate in a good mood—hers, not mine—and met my driver in the lobby.

I had only one FBI guy with me—it's Sunday, a day

of rest for the FBI and the terrorists—and his name was Preston Tyler, or maybe Tyler Preston, and I wasn't sure he was old enough to drive a non-farm vehicle. Anyway, we got on the road, and he asked me, "Did Captain Paresi get hold of you?"

"Nope."

"He didn't want to call while you were in the hospital, but he said he'd text you."

"Okay." I looked at my cell phone and sure enough there was a text message from Paresi that I'd missed. I think it came as I was being blessed by Father Brad, and I must have thought the vibration I felt . . . well, anyway, I pulled up the message, which said: *A new development. Call me ASAP.*

I saw the hand of the Holy Spirit at work here. Or maybe some good detective work.

I called Paresi's cell phone and asked, "What's up?"

He replied, "Well, we may have found the safe house—or *a* safe house."

"Where?"

"Where we thought—across the street from you."

We? I thought that was my idea.

Paresi continued, "At ten-eighteen this morning, the Command Center got an anonymous phone call from a male who said he had observed suspicious activity at 320 East Seventy-second Street—an apartment building—and he said there were, quote, 'Suspicious-looking people, coming and going at all hours.'"

That sounds like half the apartment houses in Manhattan. But this one was apparently different.

He asked me, "Where are you now?"

"I'm about five minutes from there."

"Good. I'm here. Apartment 2712."

I hung up and said to Preston, who was not from around here, "Drop me off at 320 East Seventy-second."

"Where's that?"

Mamma mia. I'd be better off with a Pakistani cab driver. Even a Libyan. I said, "Between First and Second."

"Avenues?"

"Correct."

He found the address, which was a nice pre-war building, about thirty stories high. I'd passed it a million times, but for some reason it never occurred to me that there could be terrorists in Apartment 2712.

I got out of the car and looked west, across the street at my building, which is between Second and Third avenues. I could see my balcony from here, and from Apartment 2712—on the 27th floor of this building—it would be no problem for a sniper to shoot my cocktail glass out of my hand.

I entered the foyer of the building and the doorman buzzed me in.

There were four NYPD detectives in the ornate old lobby—in case the terrorist tenants showed up—and we did the ID thing, and one of them called upstairs on his radio, and another detective accompanied me up the elevator and escorted me to Apartment 2712. He rang the bell for me, and the door was opened by Captain Paresi, who said, "Wipe your feet."

The joke here was that the apartment was not neat—

it was, in fact, filthy, as I could see and smell from the doorway.

I walked in, and Paresi, who was the only person in the room, asked me, "How's Kate?"

"Happy and healthy."

"Good. The country air will do her a world of good." He added, "You too."

I put that subject on hold for later and asked, "What do we have here?"

He replied, "As you can see, we have a squalid apartment—a one-room studio in a good building in a declining neighborhood." He thought that was funny and smiled.

He also informed me, "We actually knocked on this door twice in the last two days, but no one answered." He added, "The name on the lease is Eastern Export Corporation, with headquarters in Beirut, Lebanon." He further added, "They've had the lease for two years."

I asked, "And we've never seen any bad guys coming or going here?"

"No. It's not a safe house on our list."

I also asked, "What does the doorman say?"

"He says there were three or four guys—he can't be sure—foreign-looking, and they showed up only about two or three weeks ago. He barely saw them and they were quiet."

I pointed out, "That doesn't square with the tipster who called and said there were suspicious-looking people coming and going at all hours."

"No," he agreed, "it doesn't."

I looked around the studio apartment, which had a galley kitchen and two open doors—one that led to the bathroom, and one for a closet that was empty.

The white-painted walls were bare, and the only furniture was three ratty-looking armchairs and four unpleasant-looking mattresses on the floor, with sheets that may once have been white.

Also in the room were two floor lamps and a big television on a cheap stand.

Paresi said to me, "There's some stuff like food, towels, and toiletries, but there's no clothing or luggage, so it looks like they pulled out."

"Right." I asked, "Any camel milk in the fridge?"

"No, but it's mostly Mideastern-type food."

I surmised, "So these foreigners were not Norwegians." I asked him, "When do we get forensics here?"

"Soon. I'm waiting for a search warrant." He added, "We entered under exigent circumstances with the super's passkey on the suspicion that there could be a dead or dying person in here."

"Who said that?"

Paresi replied, "The anonymous tipster and the super."

Neither of them said that, of course, but you have to explain why you're in the apartment without a warrant. It's easier with a corporate tenant, but even if the lease said "Al Qaeda Waste Management," you need a search warrant.

I looked around again, and there was nothing in the apartment to suggest that it was anything but a druggie shooting gallery, or maybe a crash pad for illegal aliens.

But not in this neighborhood. And not, coincidentally, within sight of my building.

Paresi said to me, "There's a wet sponge in the sink, so . . . how long does it take for a sponge to dry?"

"What color is it?"

"Blue."

"Six hours."

I walked around the mattresses and went to one of the two windows, which I opened. I looked to the left and saw my building, and I spotted my balcony. Easy shot. Also, close enough to mount a video surveillance camera here somewhere, pointed at my front door.

I stepped back and looked at the windowsill.

Paresi said, "Over here."

I went to the second window and looked at the wide, painted sill. There was a layer of dust on most of the sill, but in the center was a spot where the dust had been disturbed. I speculated, "This is where they set the wine bucket down."

"Yeah. And the lead wire from the wine bucket ran to the TV."

We both walked to the television, a fairly new model, and though there were no video wires attached, the TV was equipped to accept a video camera input. The John Corey Show. Reality TV.

Paresi said, "So, if these guys were here to watch you, then they saw you leave your apartment on your walks." He added, "And they watched us having wine and pizza."

"Right." And they chose to do nothing about that. Because Khalil has his own plan. Also, they saw me getting in a vehicle a few times a day, but I couldn't know if I'd ever been followed to the heliport, or to Bellevue. But I really think the trail vehicle would have picked that up. Still, it was kind of disturbing and creepy.

Paresi was thinking and he said, "Okay, so we got three or four foreign-looking guys who enjoy Mideastern cuisine, and they happen to have a view of your building, and we know that Asad Khalil is trying to kill you. So can we assume that the people who were living here were Arab terrorists watching you? Or is this just a coincidence?"

"The coincidence," I agreed, "is suspicious. And here's another coincidence—the tip came just before these guys pulled out. I draw your attention to the wet sponge. Therefore—follow me on this—the tipster was one of Khalil's guys."

"That's brilliant, John. And now we're supposed to believe that Khalil and his pals have gone back to Sandland."

"Correct." I added, "And why would this tipster call the Terrorist Task Force and not the cops or the FBI field office? Makes no sense."

He reminded me, "I told you these people are stupid."

"They do often miss the subtleties of deception," I agreed, "but they have now put some doubts in our minds."

He nodded and said, "As much as this looks like a ruse to make us think Khalil and his pals are gone, we have to take it into consideration, and act accordingly."

This might be the time to tell Captain Paresi that I'd recently chatted with the scumbag in question, and the scumbag had also hinted that he was leaving town. But did I want to reinforce that possibility?

Also, I was supposed to report that in a timely manner—just as I was supposed to report my contact with Boris Korsakov when it happened. So now I had a problem, albeit of my own making, but this was not the time to come clean; I'd do that when I was in the wilds of Minnesota where being threatened with disciplinary action would be a welcome relief.

Plus, if I came clean now, I'd be removed from the case immediately for misconduct. And I still had about twenty-four hours before I was exiled.

On that subject, I said to Paresi, "You didn't return my call yesterday."

He asked, "Which call was that? The one where you were pissy about being sent out of town?"

"That's the one."

He looked at me and said, "John, I have to agree with Walsh that this is best for us, and best for you, and especially best for Kate."

"Vince, it is not best for the investigation. It is not best for the war on terrorism, and not best for the country or the American public."

He suggested, "You have a very high opinion of your importance."

"Indeed, I do." Well, apparently my fate was sealed, but I said to Paresi, "Obviously you want to keep me informed, and that's why I'm standing here."

"I was getting a little bored here by myself, and you

were in the neighborhood." He added, "Plus, this seems to have something to do with someone who wants to kill you."

"Right. So why don't we stay in touch while I'm enjoying a few weeks' rest? And I'll make myself available for a quick trip back to New York if you think you're on to something."

He thought about that and replied, "I'll take it up with Walsh." He informed me, "Subject closed."

We poked around the apartment awhile, being careful not to touch or disturb anything that would throw the forensic people into a fit, and I reminded Paresi that we did have Khalil's prints in the FBI databank, along with some of his DNA that was collected in Paris three years ago at the American Embassy.

Paresi commented, "By the looks of this place, there's enough DNA here to create life and arrest it."

Good one, Vince. Wish I'd thought of it.

In any case, forensic people like dirty houses, and I was fairly certain that they'd be able to establish the presence of Asad Khalil here.

Paresi asked rhetorically, "What the hell did these people do here all day and night?"

Good question. I was going stir crazy in an apartment about five times this size, filled with creature comforts, a balcony with a view, and a well-stocked bar. These people, however, were not interested in comfort or entertainment; they were patient, single-minded, and on a holy mission. This did not necessarily make them better equipped for this fight—they lacked freedom of thought and they underestimated *our* dedication and willingness to fight—but they *were* proving to be tougher than we thought.

I replied to Paresi's rhetorical question, "They sat here and watched my apartment building on TV, twenty-four/seven, they prayed, they discussed politics and religion, and they read from the Koran."

"What did they do for fun?"

"I just told you."

"Right." He suggested, "They should have had a house-cleaning contest." He checked his watch, and again asked a rhetorical question. "How long does it take to get a fucking search warrant?"

"It's Sunday," I reminded him. "Did you go to church?"

"I was on my way when I got the call. How about you?"

"Saint Pat's." I asked him, "Where's Walsh?"

"He and his lady went upstate for the weekend."

"Skydiving?"

He said under his breath, "Let's hope." He then assured me, "He's reachable."

Unless his Caller ID comes up "John Corey."

We chatted for a few more minutes, then a Task Force detective, Anne Markham, showed up with a search warrant. Anne took a look around and said, "I want this pigpen cleaned before the forensic team gets here."

Funny. Anyway, two FBI guys from the Evidence Recovery Team arrived—they don't want to be left out—and a few minutes later the NYPD forensic team arrived and kicked everyone out.

Down in the lobby, Paresi said to me, "You know, John, Khalil really may be gone. So don't feel too bad about going on vacation."

I replied, "I'm fairly certain this is a ruse. Sometimes known as a trick. And the purpose of the trick is to make us all drop our guards and scale down our manhunt. Get it?"

"Yeah, I get it. But maybe it just got too hot for them with us knocking on doors." He informed me, "We'll have a supervisors' meeting tomorrow A.M. to discuss it."

"What time should I be there?"

"How about never? Is never good for you?"

I had some advice for him, and I said, "Don't drop your guard, Vince."

He had no reply to that, but he did extend his hand and said, "Thanks for being bait." He also said, "Have a good trip. Take it easy. Regards to Kate. We'll stay in touch." He added, "See you in a few months."

If not sooner.

Back in my apartment, with my Sunday afternoon Bloody Mary in hand, I went out to the balcony. They were gone—right? But a stupid ruse is often a cover for a smart ruse.

Or were they and Asad Khalil really on their way back to Sandland? Mission accomplished? Mission aborted? Or mission continues?

Asad Khalil came halfway around the world to

cross names off his list, and he hadn't gotten to my name yet. Or Boris's.

And what happened to that big finale we were expecting? Have they already poisoned the water supply? Have they spread anthrax? Is there a bomb ticking somewhere?

This is one of those cases where the silence is deafening.

I looked down the street at the window that had looked back at me for two or three weeks. They weren't there any longer—but where were they? Where was Asad Khalil?

I didn't have much time left, so the ball was actually in his court. Make a move, asshole.

I spent the late afternoon packing, which made this trip finally real for me.

Time was slipping by, and I thought about working the phone, which is another way of saying bugging people who had less information about Asad Khalil than I did—and who didn't want to be called on a Sunday by an obsessed nutcase whose wife was in the hospital and who was under house protection with nothing to do.

Nevertheless, I decided to call Tom Walsh, hoping he'd come to his senses, or maybe he'd gotten eaten by a bear, clearing the way for me to come back to work Monday morning.

I started to dial his cell phone, but then I pictured

him in some romantic lodge upstate with his girl-friend, trying on her clothes while she was napping, so I decided to text him: *Discovery of safe house on E. 72nd changes the situation—let's discuss new strategy Monday A.M.*

Sounds good. If I was a supervisor, I'd bite on that.

I also thought about going to 26 Fed to work the Automated Case System, and to see if there was anything new there in the Khalil file—something other than his name and rows of Xs. This is called clutching at straws.

Mostly, though, I waited for my phone to ring, hoping that something would break.

At about 5 P.M., I decided to call Boris again on the theory that if he was still alive, that meant that Khalil hadn't begun his final cleanup operation.

Boris didn't answer his cell phone, but neither did Asad Khalil nor a homicide detective, so I left another message with the maître d' for Boris to call me. This time I said "urgent." I pictured Boris with some *de-vitsa*—that's a girl, right? Not a guy. And he was plying her with champagne and impressing her with his KGB exploits while the Red Army Chorus set the mood.

About ten minutes later, my house phone rang, and it came up "Anonymous Caller" so I answered it.

A familiar male voice said, "John, we are so delighted that you and Kate are coming to visit."

I said to Mr. Mayfield, "Hold on, sir, I'm just putting my gun in my mouth."

Actually, I said, "We're looking forward to it."

He inquired, "How does Kate look to you? Is she really feeling well?"

"I've never seen her looking better." I'm okay, too. And so forth.

About twenty minutes later, my parents called from Florida—they were all in on this together—and it was my mother who was on the line, and she let me know, "It's hot and humid here, and it's going to be worse when you get here. Bring comfortable clothes. We have plenty of suntan lotion. You know how easily you burn. And you're going to eat healthy here—lots of fish and vegetables."

I reached for my Glock.

"Do you and your wife play Bingo?"

I chambered a round.

My father, in the background, yelled out, "Tell him I have plenty of Scotch."

I put the gun down.

At 6 P.M., I called for my ride to Bellevue.

—PART VI—

Brooklyn and Manhattan

CHAPTER FORTY-SIX

Asad Khalil sat in a taxi in front of Svetlana. A text message appeared on his cell phone, and Khalil read it, then got out of the taxi and said to the driver, a fellow Libyan named Rasheed, "Wait here."

Khalil, wearing a suit and tie, and also a drooping mustache and glasses, entered through the front door of the nightclub, where he was greeted by a maître d', who asked him in Russian, "Do you have a reservation?"

Khalil replied in the passable Russian he'd learned from Boris, "I am going only to the bar."

The maître d' took him for a native of one of the former Asian Soviet Republics—a Kazakh, perhaps, or a Uzbek. The maître d', Dimitri, did not like these people, and he would have turned him away if the man wanted a table. But it was more difficult to turn away someone who wanted to sit only at the bar to watch the floor show. The bartenders could deal with the man.

Dimitri motioned wordlessly toward the open doorway behind him and turned his attention to an arriving group.

Asad Khalil walked through the doorway and down a long corridor that was brightly lit and decorated with large photographs of past events at Svetlana—weddings and other happy occasions—accompanied by advertisements in Russian and English urging people to book their special events here.

He stopped at one of the group photographs that had caught his eye. Standing in the group was Boris Korsakov, whose smile, Khalil thought, was not sincere. "So," Khalil said to himself, "the great KGB man has sunk to this." Also he thought Boris had gained some weight.

Khalil continued on, and the corridor opened out into the big restaurant, where he could see the bar and lounge farther toward the rear. The restaurant, he noted, was half full on this Sunday evening at 6 P.M., and the stage was empty.

Khalil had never been here, but he felt he knew the place from the photographs and information given to him a few days earlier by a fellow Muslim, a man named Vladimir, a Russified Chechen who had been instructed a month ago to find himself a job here.

Khalil stood at the entrance to the restaurant for almost a minute, knowing that a security person would notice him, then he walked deliberately to a red-curtained doorway and entered the short corridor that led to a locked door.

Almost immediately, he heard footsteps behind him, and a man's voice in English said, "Stop," then in Russian, "Stoi!"

The man put his hand on Khalil's shoulder, and

Khalil spun around and thrust a long carving knife into his throat, severing his windpipe.

Khalil held the man and let him slide into a sitting position against the wall, then withdrew the knife. He went through the dying man's pockets and found a keychain, and also a Colt .45 automatic pistol and a radio phone.

The man was still alive, but he was drowning in his own blood, and his larynx was severed, so he made no sound except for the gurgling in his throat.

Khalil glanced at the red curtain. No one had followed them, and he hefted the dying man over his shoulder, then went to the locked door, tried a key, then another, and the door opened.

Khalil found himself in a small room that contained an elevator and a steel door that Vladimir had told him led to the staircase. Vladimir had also texted Khalil that the other bodyguard, Viktor, was now sitting in the anteroom above, outside Boris's office, while Vladimir set the table for Boris and a lady who would be arriving shortly.

Khalil relocked the door to the corridor, then unlocked the steel door to the staircase and threw the bodyguard, who now appeared very close to death, onto the stairs. He relocked the staircase door and made his way quickly up the stairs.

At the top of the stairs was another door, and Khalil put the key in the lock with his left hand and held the long carving knife in his right hand. He opened the door quickly and burst into the small room.

Viktor jumped to his feet and his hand went inside

his jacket for his gun, but Khalil was already on him, and he thrust the long knife into Viktor's lower abdomen while pulling him closer in a tight hug with his left arm so that Viktor could not draw his gun. He withdrew the knife quickly, then brought it around and thrust the blade into Viktor's lower back at a downward angle so it would puncture his diaphragm and leave him unable to make a sound.

Viktor tried to break loose from his attacker, and Khalil was surprised at his strength. Khalil held him tightly and brought his knife around again and buried the blade into Viktor's abdomen, then made a long, deep angular cut that severed the abdominal artery.

Khalil withdrew the knife and held Viktor in a bear hug. Khalil could feel the man's heart pumping, and his breathing becoming more labored and shallow. He also felt the warm wetness of Viktor's blood on his skin.

Viktor's head tilted back and they made brief eye contact, then Viktor's eyes widened and his body arched and shook in a series of death throes, before going limp.

Khalil lowered the dead man back into his chair and retrieved Viktor's gun from his shoulder holster, noting that it was also a Colt .45 automatic. He stuck the gun in his belt next to the gun of the other dead bodyguard.

· Khalil looked at his watch. It had been just nine minutes since he'd entered this place. He dialed Vladimir's cell phone.

* * *

Boris Korsakov sat in his armchair, sipping a cognac, smoking, and reading a local Russian-language weekly that was filled with news of the immigrant community—births, deaths, marriages, some gossip, and many advertisements, including a full-page ad for Svetlana, which Boris studied. Perhaps, he thought, his ads should put less emphasis on the floor show and more on the food. Less breasts, more borscht. He smiled.

The busboy, Vladimir, was taking his time setting the table with chilled caviar and champagne for two. Boris was expecting a lady at 6:30, and it was already 6:15, and the stupid busboy—who was only a few weeks on the job—seemed nervous or unsure of what to do.

Boris looked over his shoulder and said to the busboy in Russian, "Are you not done yet?"

"I am just finishing, sir."

Vladimir knew that for all appearances he was an ethnic Russian, but in fact his name, his speech, and his Russian ways had been forced on him from birth by the Russian occupiers of Chechnya—and though he was Russian on the outside, in his heart he hated everything and everyone who was Russian, and he especially hated the former KGB and its successor, the FSS, which had arrested, tortured, and killed so many of his fellow Muslims in his homeland.

Vladimir looked at Boris Korsakov, sitting with his back to him, drinking, smoking, and giving him orders. Soon there would be one less KGB man on this earth.

Vladimir felt his cell phone vibrate in his pocket. It was time.

Boris put down his newspaper and said to Vladimir, "Just leave everything and go." Boris stood to walk to the door and look out the peephole for Viktor, and to show the busboy out.

But Vladimir was already at the door, without his cart, and with his hand on the bolt.

Boris shouted across the room, "Stop! You idiot! Stand away from that door!"

Vladimir slid the bolt open, stood aside, and the door swung open.

Vladimir left quickly as Asad Khalil entered with a pistol in his hand. Khalil bolted the door and looked at Boris Korsakov.

Boris stood absolutely still, his eyes fixed on the man who stood less than twenty feet from him.

The man had a mustache and glasses, and perhaps his hair was more gray than Boris remembered and not combed back as he recalled, but he knew who his visitor was.

Boris also noted, almost absently, that the man's dark suit and white shirt were covered with fresh blood.

Khalil took off his glasses and peeled off his mustache, then said in Russian, "Are you not happy to see your favorite student?"

Boris took a deep breath and replied in English, "Your Russian is still as bad as the stench of your mouth and your body."

Khalil did not respond to that, but said, "I would advise you now to reach for your gun so I will be forced to give you a quick death. But . . . if you prefer to live a few minutes longer, we can share a few words before you suffer a painful death. The choice is yours."

Boris reverted to Russian and said, "Yob vas." Fuck you.

Khalil smiled and said to Boris, "Still arrogant." Then he said, "So, your CIA friends are not protecting you."

Boris replied, "They are."

Khalil again smiled and said, "Then where are they? They used you like the whore you are, and they put you here in this place filled with other whores and drunken pigs."

Boris's eyes darted around the room, looking for a way to save his life.

Khalil said to him, "Look at me. Why don't you understand that you are dead?"

Boris took another deep breath and said, "Then do it."

"You must reach for your gun. This needs to be interesting for both of us."

Boris looked at his former student and said, "What did I teach you? Kill quickly. You talk too much."

"I enjoy the talk."

"I assure you, your victims do not."

Khalil seemed annoyed and said to Boris, "I had to listen to you for one year insulting me, my country, and my faith. And I had to smell your stinking cigarettes and your stinking alcohol." He stared at Boris and said, "And look at you now. Who are you? And how clever are you? Who is holding the gun? Not you. And you should be more careful who you hire. Vladimir is a Chechen and he would pay me if I let him cut your throat. And you should also know, before you die, that your two former KGB bodyguards are now waiting for you in Hell."

Boris's mind was racing, thinking of a way to save himself. The girl, Tanya, would be escorted here by a security man, and that man would notice . . . something. A body. Blood on the floor . . .

Khalil, who knew exactly what his old teacher was thinking, said, "Vladimir is cleaning up my mess. And he has called downstairs to have the girl sent away—on your instructions." He added, "You will not be having champagne and caviar tonight, and you will not be fornicating after I cut off your testicles."

Boris did not reply, and his mind was still searching for a way out.

Finally, Boris realized that there was only one move he could make—he had to go for his gun. That would either save him, or end it quickly. He looked at Khalil for a sign that the man's attention was not fully focused—they sometimes let their eyes dart around to take in their new surroundings, or to look for signs of danger, and their guns tended to drift in the direction they were looking. But all Boris saw was Khalil's black eyes staring straight at him, and the black muzzle of the gun—aimed as accurately as Khalil's eyes.

Again, Khalil knew what Boris was thinking, and he said to him, "My advice is to go for your gun. That will make you feel more of a man as you are dying." He added, "You do not want to be shot like a dog." He further advised Boris in Russian, "Courage. Show me some courage, boy. Do something."

Boris took another deep breath and in his mind he was reaching inside his jacket for the gun on his hip as he dove to the side, rolled, and fired.

Khalil said, "No, I would not suggest a floor roll. I would suggest a step back—your armchair is behind you—a backward roll over the chair. That will give you a moment of concealment, but unfortunately not cover from my bullets that I will fire through the chair. Still, you will have drawn your gun during your backward roll and you may be able to return fire before you are hit." He asked, "Have I given the correct advice, Mr. Korsakov? Have I correctly evaluated the situation, sir?"

Boris stared at Khalil, then nodded and said, "That is the only move possible."

"Then make the move. Do not just stand there. And do not think you can surprise me by diving to the right or the left. You will be dead before you hit the floor . . . though I may let you get your hand on your gun as you roll."

Boris continued to stare at Khalil. He understood that this man needed to mock him and torment him before he killed him. But he also understood that he could not expect a quick death with a bullet from Asad Khalil's gun. Boris realized that no matter what he did—rolled, dove, even charged at Khalil—this man would shoot to wound him, then he would finish him off in a way that Boris did not want to think about. Or worse, Khalil would not kill him—he would mutilate him and leave him as a freak, a half-man with no genitals, no eyes, no tongue . . .

Boris felt his heart beating wildly in his chest, and a cold sweat chilled his body.

Khalil seemed impatient and said, "Have you forgotten everything? Or was that just classroom talk? I have done all that you taught me. And more. So now you must show your student what you will do in this situation. I am waiting and curious."

Boris thought if he could keep Khalil talking, there was a chance that someone would come up the stairs or the elevator and see that something was not right. He waited for the doorbell to ring—a few notes of Tchaikovsky that would distract Khalil for half a second. That's all Boris needed. A half second to draw his gun.

Boris cleared his throat and said in a confident voice, "This building is under surveillance by the police and the FBI."

Khalil replied, "They do not seem to be any more competent or alert than your stupid bodyguards."

"You will not get out of this building alive."

"It is you who will not get out of this building alive."

Khalil had not moved far from the door, and now he stepped back and put his ear to it, then turned to Boris and said, "Someone is coming."

Boris took a deep breath, and prepared himself to go for his gun.

Then Khalil smiled and said, "Perhaps I was hearing things." Then he laughed.

Boris was enraged and shouted a string of half-remembered Arabic obscenities, then he shouted in English. "You fucking bastard! You piece of shit! Your mother was a fucking whore!"

Khalil aimed his gun—the Glock he'd taken from Corey's wife—at Boris's midsection, and Boris could see that Khalil's arm was shaking in rage. Boris waited for the bullet, hoping it would either miss him or hit his heart.

Khalil took a deep breath, then reached under his jacket and pulled out the long carving knife that he'd used to kill the two bodyguards.

Boris stood completely still and watched as Khalil gripped the blade, holding the knife in a throwing position.

Khalil's arm cocked back, and he flung the knife toward Boris, who flinched as the knife stuck in the carpet at his feet.

Boris stared at the knife with the bloody blade. He understood what was coming.

Khalil said to him, "You may have the knife—in exchange for your gun."

Boris looked at Khalil, but did not respond.

Khalil said, "You have chosen not to draw your gun. So I am offering you this instead." He added, "This is very generous of me—though it will be more painful for you." He asked Boris, "Have you been practicing with the knife since I last saw you?" He smiled and added, "Or perhaps just the knife and fork."

Boris weighed his options, which were reduced now to two—go for his gun and hope for a quick bullet in the head or heart; or engage Asad Khalil in a knife fight. He could win that fight, but if he didn't, he knew what Asad Khalil would do to him with the knife.

Khalil said to him, "You seem to be unable to make a decision today. So I will make it for you." He crouched into a shooting stance and steadied his aim.

Boris shouted, "No!" He raised both hands, then slowly lowered his left hand and pulled back his jacket, revealing his gun and holster on his belt.

Khalil nodded.

Boris grasped the gun butt with his thumb and index finger and pulled the gun out of his holster, then slid it across the rug toward Khalil.

Khalil stepped forward and retrieved the gun, which he saw was a Browning automatic. He removed the magazine and threw it across the room, then moved to the dining table and dropped the gun into the glass bowl heaped with black caviar.

He said to Boris, "I would take your word that you have no other gun—but perhaps you can show me."

Boris nodded and pulled up his trouser legs to show he had no ankle holster, then he turned his pockets inside out. He slowly removed his jacket and turned completely around and faced Khalil again.

Khalil said to him, "I am surprised you have not taken your own advice about a second gun."

Boris replied, "Even if I had a second gun, I would prefer to cut your throat."

Khalil smiled and said, "That is also my preference for you."

Khalil drew the two Colt .45s from his belt, removed the magazines, and stuck both guns in the champagne bucket. Then he removed the magazine from his own gun, put it in his pocket, and laid the Glock on a table napkin. He then drew a short, heavy hunting knife from his belt and flung it to the floor where it stuck in the carpet.

He looked at Boris and asked, "Are you ready?"

Boris did not reply, but he took off his tie, shoes, and socks, then wrapped his jacket around his left arm.

Khalil smiled approvingly and did the same.

Both men stood about fifteen feet apart and stared at each other, the knives stuck in the floor a few feet in front of them.

For the first time since Khalil walked into the room, Boris believed he had a chance to kill this man. He knew that Khalil could have a second gun, but it didn't matter—he would prefer a bullet to losing this fight.

They stood watching each other, waiting for the other to make a move.

Boris made the first move, running straight at Khalil and snatching the knife as he continued toward him.

Khalil dove forward, grabbed his knife and rolled to the right, then sprang up and went into a crouched defensive position with his wrapped arm in front of him and his legs spread wide.

Boris stopped short, wheeled around, and came at Khalil.

Khalil held his position, and Boris feinted left and right, stepped in, then stepped back, then in again. He remembered Khalil's strengths and his weaknesses, and Khalil's major weakness was too much aggression, and too much impatience, which led him to an impulsive and ill-timed attack. But now, Boris saw, Khalil had apparently learned when to defend and when to attack.

Boris decided on another strategy and he backed away, putting nearly twenty feet between them.

Khalil came out of his defensive position and strode directly at Boris, who held his ground and was surprised to see Khalil stop.

Boris was beginning to think that Khalil had either learned caution or had realized that he should not have gotten into this situation with the man who taught him how to fight with a knife.

Boris took the offensive again and moved in, causing Khalil to move back. Then the two men silently circled each other in the middle of the large room.

Boris watched Khalil's movements. He knew that the Libyan was more agile and in far better shape than he was, but Boris had more bulk and believed he was still physically stronger than Khalil.

Khalil again dropped into a half crouch, with his legs spread and his coat-wrapped arm in a horizontal position—a defensive position that Boris did not think was called for with ten feet still separating them. Khalil, Boris thought, had misread his movements, or he was becoming anxious, which made Boris more confident.

Boris moved in quickly—a feint that he hoped would cause Khalil to backpedal and lose his defensive posture. But instead, Khalil unexpectedly charged forward and met Boris's forward movement as Boris was in mid-stride.

Khalil came in low under Boris's knife hand and

under his wrapped arm and delivered an upward thrust that caught Boris below his left rib cage.

Boris let out a startled cry of pain, then pivoted away from the probing knife and delivered a high kick to Khalil's lowered head.

Neither man pressed the attack and both of them retreated to a safe distance.

Khalil nodded and said, "Very good."

Boris cautiously felt his wound and determined that it was a narrow puncture wound, perhaps deep, but not bleeding profusely, and not mortal.

Khalil watched the blood forming on Boris's white shirt and came to the same conclusion, saying, "You won't die from that."

Boris also determined that he wasn't going to win this fight—he was already out of breath, and the wound would bleed more quickly with further exertions and eventually weaken him.

Also, Boris admitted, Khalil was the better knife fighter—Khalil remembered the skills, but more importantly he remembered the tricks, and had learned some new ones. Boris also knew that Khalil possessed the will and the courage to face a man with a knife, and Boris was not sure that he himself possessed that will any longer.

Out of desperation, Boris said to Khalil, "It is over. You have won."

Khalil laughed. "Yes? Are you dead already? May I go now?"

"Asad—"

Khalil said, "There is another man who is going to

die in this way tonight—so I had hoped you would be good practice for me. But now I see you are a poor opponent—too old, too slow, and too frightened."

Boris did not reply. He tried to think of another way out of this, and thought of the door. If he could work his way closer to the door . . . he began circling so that Khalil would circle too, and not be between him and the door.

But Khalil kept his position and said, "If you wish to run out of the room, I have no objections. But I must tell you, all you will find out there is a locked elevator and a locked staircase door. But perhaps you prefer a smaller room for this fight." He smiled and said, "I don't care where I slaughter you."

Boris took a deep breath and said, "You have made your point." He lowered his knife and said, "I have done nothing to you. I have taught you—"

"Shut up." Khalil took a few steps toward Boris, and as Boris moved back, Khalil said, "We have not finished this lesson. Do you not want to show me how you will disarm me and throw me against the wall as you did once? Do you think I have forgotten your knee in my testicles? Or perhaps the great Russian assassin has dirtied his pants, and he wishes me to leave to spare me the smell."

Boris felt the anger rising in him again, and he pulled the jacket from around his arm and snapped it at Khalil as he moved forward with his knife extended in his right hand.

Khalil stepped back and lost his footing on the loose area rug, then fell to the floor, losing his knife.

Boris charged him, and realized too late he'd again been drawn into a ruse, as Khalil raised his legs and caught Boris in the abdomen and hurled him into the air, headfirst into a china cabinet, which shattered in a loud crash.

Khalil snatched up his knife, jumped quickly to his feet, and watched as Boris pulled himself away from the cabinet.

Boris stood unsteadily, his face bleeding from glass cuts and his eyes blinded with blood. He had lost his knife, and he wiped his eyes with his hands as Khalil moved in for the kill.

Boris, his back to the shattered china cabinet, side-stepped along the wall, and Khalil followed him, then realized what Boris was doing.

Boris seized a floor lamp with both hands and swung the heavy base at Khalil's head.

Khalil ducked, and Boris missed, but then Boris pivoted in the direction of his swing and came around again with the base of the lamp now lower, and he caught Khalil's outstretched arm in a glancing blow that knocked the knife from Khalil's hand.

Khalil backpedaled quickly, and Boris, knowing this was his last and only chance to kill this man, charged forward with the floor lamp.

Khalil feinted right, then moved left and kicked Boris's leg out from under him. Boris crashed to the floor, losing his grip on the lamp, and Khalil was on Boris's back, with his knees straddling the big Russian and his right arm locked around Boris's throat.

Boris tried to rise on his hands and knees, but Khalil

kept his full weight on the weakening man while tightening his chokehold.

Boris felt himself blacking out, and he gave one last upward heave with his body, then twisted with every ounce of strength he had left. He found himself on his back, staring up at the ceiling, which was dark and blurry. He felt his abdominal wound throbbing and he knew it was gushing blood now.

He knew, too, he should do something, but everything around him seemed quiet and peaceful, so he lay there and closed his eyes, his chest rising and falling, and his lungs filling with air.

He heard a voice say, "Get up."

Boris remained still, keeping his eyes shut and feigning more injury and exhaustion than he felt. He was vaguely aware that Khalil was close by, standing over him, then he felt a kick in his right side that knocked the air out of his laboring lungs. The second kick came, as he hoped it would, and Boris swung his legs and body around and knocked Khalil's legs out from under him.

Boris was on his feet, but it took him a second too long, and before he could react, Khalil was already up and delivered a powerful kick into Boris's groin.

Boris doubled over, and Khalil came around him and delivered a running kick to his rear that sent him sprawling.

Khalil dove on Boris's back and knocked the remaining air out of him, then put him in a headlock that again constricted his airway.

Boris remained still, hoping for another opportunity. His mind was cloudy, but his survival instincts had been aroused and his will to fight for his life had become stronger as he faced death.

Khalil's head was close, and Boris could feel the man's warm, steady breath on his neck. Then Khalil whispered into Boris's ear, "I underestimated you, and for that, I apologize."

Boris could not reply.

Khalil said, "And I thank you, Mr. Korsakov, for sharing with me all your skills and your knowledge." He asked, "Are you proud of me?"

Boris lay perfectly still, not wanting to provoke the man because he felt a small glimmer of hope—not hope that Asad Khalil would spare his life out of compassion; the man had none. Nor would Khalil spare his life out of respect for a worthy opponent. But Khalil might spare his life, Boris thought, because he was satisfied with humiliating him—killing his bodyguards, beating him in a fight, and heaping abuse on him. Khalil, he knew, would not spare any other man's life for those reasons, but Boris knew that he was a special case, and that Khalil understood that the most satisfying conclusion for Asad Khalil would be to leave him a broken man. Yes, Khalil knew that . . .

Khalil said to him, "You taught me well, so I will not mutilate you or cause you a painful death."

Boris tried to nod his head, but Khalil tightened the pressure around his neck.

Khalil said into Boris's ear, "But you gave me some bad advice . . ."

Boris saw something in front of his blurry eyes, and

he could not identify it at first, though he could see Khalil's free hand gripping something. Then he knew what he was seeing—the long, thin shaft of an ice pick.

"No!"

Khalil put the tip of the ice pick into Boris's left nostril and pushed it back into his brain.

Boris screamed again, but this time it was an unintelligible, animal scream.

Khalil withdrew the pick, which glistened with Boris's blood and brains, then positioned the tip into Boris's right nostril, and again pushed it up into his brain and kept pushing until the handle flattened Boris's nose and the tip of the ice pick came up through his skull.

Khalil left the pick where it was buried, then slid off Boris and rolled him over onto his back.

He watched him for a few seconds and saw the dark red blood beginning to trickle out of his nostrils. Then Boris began to convulse, small spasms, accompanied by a very strange sound coming from deep in his throat—almost, Khalil thought, like the moaning sound of the southern wind, the Ghabli, coming out of the great desert.

Khalil retrieved his knives, then walked to the dining table, retrieved his gun, and pushed the magazine into the butt. He peeled off his bloody clothes and washed himself with the linen napkins and mineral water on the table.

On the bottom shelf of the serving cart under a tablecloth was a dark shirt, dark trousers, and a black windbreaker that Vladimir had laid there for him.

Khalil dressed quickly, put on his shoes and socks, then took a linen napkin from the table and stuffed it in his pocket.

He then texted Vladimir: *It is finished.*

He walked toward the door, looked through the peephole, and was about to slide open the bolt, but then a thought came into his mind.

Khalil walked to the large two-way mirror and looked down into the restaurant. It was more busy now, mostly families with children having their Sunday dinner. Directly below him on the stage were three women in tight dresses, and they appeared to be singing, though he could hear only the muted sound of the three musicians on the stage.

Khalil returned to Boris, who was twitching now, though the moaning had ceased. He dropped to one knee and lifted the big man in his arms, then raised him up over his head, took two long strides, and flung Boris through the glass.

The sound of the shattering glass died away, and there was a momentary silence, followed by a loud thumping sound, and then the screams of the people below.

Khalil drew his gun, then went back to the door, opened it, and exited into the anteroom, noting that Vladimir had disposed of the bodyguard's body and the blood. He opened the elevator door with his key and rode down to the basement. On his way down, he wrapped the linen napkin around his right hand and his gun, then put his hand in the side pocket of his windbreaker.

Vladimir met him in the basement at the elevator and escorted him through the dark storage area to a flight of concrete steps, which they both ascended.

Vladimir pushed on a metal door that opened to an alleyway between the buildings, filled with trash cans and plastic garbage bags, two of which, he understood, contained the corpses of the bodyguards.

Vladimir said to him, "God has blessed you, my friend."

"And you."

Khalil pulled his hand out of his pocket, and Vladimir thought he was extending his hand in friendship, but as he reached for Khalil's hand, he saw that the hand was wrapped in a bloodstained table napkin, and he hesitated.

Khalil fired a single bullet into Vladimir's forehead.

The man fell back into a pile of garbage bags, and Khalil tossed the smoking cloth on his face, pocketed the gun, then threw garbage-filled bags over him to cover his body.

Khalil walked up the alleyway to an iron gate, which he unbolted and exited onto the sidewalk of Brightwater Court.

There were a number of pedestrians on the sidewalk, and he glanced at the front entrance of Svetlana and saw that people were streaming out the doors. Some women and children were crying and some men were shouting excitedly.

Khalil moved through the crowd and saw his taxi-cab, which was now surrounded by people, one of whom was trying to get in the vehicle, but the driver had locked the doors.

Khalil did not regret throwing Boris through the window, but his act of self-indulgence had now created a small problem.

Khalil pushed through the crowd, banged on the driver's window, and shouted, "Rasheed!"

The driver unlocked the doors as Khalil pushed aside the man holding the rear door handle. Khalil opened the door and jumped in the rear, pulling the door shut as Rasheed moved away from the curb.

The taxi gathered speed as it moved into the traffic of the avenue.

Rasheed asked in Arabic, "What has happened there?"

Khalil replied, "A fire." He looked at his watch and said to Rasheed, "The Brooklyn-Battery Tunnel. Hurry, but do not speed."

Asad Khalil sat back and looked out the window. He said to himself, "And now for Mr. Corey."

CHAPTER FORTY-SEVEN

Rasheed drove his taxi through the long Brooklyn-Battery Tunnel and exited in Manhattan at West Street, near the site of the World Trade Center.

Asad Khalil made a cell phone call, spoke for a few seconds, then hung up and said to Rasheed, "Rector Street."

Rasheed continued on for a minute, then turned into the narrow one-way street. Parked on the short and quiet street, near the large Battery Parking Garage, was a tractor-trailer, and Khalil said, "Wait here."

Khalil exited the taxi and walked toward the large truck.

Painted on the side of the long trailer was CARLINO MASONRY SUPPLIES with an address and phone number in Weehawken, New Jersey. This company, Khalil was told, existed, but this was not one of their vehicles, and what was inside was not masonry supplies.

Khalil approached the tractor, and he saw the face of a man looking at him in the large sideview mirror. Khalil held up his right hand and made a fist.

The door opened, and Khalil climbed up the step and swung into the rear compartment of the big cab.

This large windowless compartment appeared to be a sleeping area, and also in this compartment was a burly man with a crew cut, dressed in jeans and a green T-shirt with the masonry company's logo on the front. In the driver's seat was another man, wearing a baseball cap, and in the right front seat was the man who had opened the door for him, who also wore a cap, jeans, and a blue team shirt that said "Mets."

These three men, Khalil understood, were European Muslims, Bosnians, and they had all fought in the war against the Christian Serbs, so they were not strangers to danger or killing. They all claimed to have lost relatives in the massacres, and they had undertaken this mission, according to Khalil's Al Qaeda contact in New York, not for the money—which Khalil knew was substantial—but as mujahideen in the holy war against the infidels.

Khalil was not so sure of their motives, and he would have preferred to be meeting Arabic speakers whom he could fully trust. But this part of his mission—the part that would end his visit here in mass destruction and death—was controlled by others, who felt that these Western-looking men were well suited for what needed to be done.

Each man introduced himself in English by his first name, and these were strange-sounding names to Asad Khalil—not good Arabic names, but names that he thought were some corruption of the Turkish language.

Khalil said to them, "You may call me Malik," using

the name of his spiritual advisor in Libya—a name that meant "master," or even sometimes "angel," though these men would not know or appreciate that.

The driver, Edis, said to him, "We were stopped at the entrance to the Holland Tunnel."

Khalil did not reply nor did he want to know more—they had obviously gotten through the tunnel.

Edis continued, "The policeman asked to see my license, and it was good that I had gone to school to obtain a commercial driver's license for a vehicle of this size."

Again, Khalil did not respond.

Edis glanced back at Khalil and told him, "Two policemen made us open the doors." He paused, then said, "But all they could see were the stacked bags of cement, and they did not look further." He added, "They are lazy."

The man in the passenger seat, Tarik, corrected Edis and said, "We are good bluffers."

Khalil did not recognize that word, but he recognized their motives in telling him this—they wanted approval, or more likely more money, or perhaps another job.

Khalil had no way of knowing if they had actually been stopped, and what he did not see with his own eyes he did not believe. In fact, he trusted these three men even less now; he did not fully trust even Arabs who came to live in the West, and he felt less favorable toward these three who were Europeans and had most probably been corrupted by their Christian neighbors.

In any case, they would be dead in a few hours.

Khalil said, "Tell me what you have here."

Tarik in the passenger seat replied, "We have fertilizer." He laughed, and the other two men laughed with him. Khalil did not laugh, and the men became quiet. None of them particularly enjoyed working with the Arabs. The Arabs were almost without humor, and they did not enjoy a drink or a cigarette, as the Bosnian Muslims did, and they treated their women—all women—very badly.

Khalil asked again, "What do you have?"

Tarik replied, this time in a flat tone of voice, "Ammonium nitrate fertilizer, liquid nitromethane, diesel fuel, and Tovex Blastrite gel. It is all mixed in fifty-five-gallon drums—eighty-eight of them—and half the drums are connected to electrical blasting caps." He added, "It took us two years to amass these chemicals in this quantity without arousing suspicion."

Khalil asked, "And how do you know you have not aroused suspicion with these purchases? Or were they stolen?"

It was Edis who replied, "Everything was purchased." He said to Khalil, "All of these chemicals are legal for their intended use, and they were purchased in small quantities by others who had legitimate uses for them, and then resold to us at a criminal price." He smiled and said, "What is not legal is mixing them together."

Bojan and Tarik allowed themselves a small smile, but they did not laugh. Edis added, "Or attaching blasting caps to the mixture and blowing it up."

Even Khalil smiled, so Edis also added, "The most

expensive ingredient at today's prices was the diesel fuel."

Bojan and Tarik laughed, and Edis said to Khalil, "The Arabs are going to bankrupt this country with these oil prices."

The three Bosnians all laughed, and Khalil thought they were idiots—but useful idiots who had apparently accomplished their task. Khalil said, however, "The FBI are not like the police in most countries. They do not make an arrest when they see an illegal activity. They watch, and wait, and keep watching until they are certain they know everyone and everything there is to know. They have been known to wait for years before making mass arrests—sometimes only hours before an operation is to begin."

None of the men replied, but then Tarik said, "They would not have waited this long—for all they know, this truck can be detonated in seconds."

Khalil again nodded. There was some truth to that.

Edis reassured their Arab friend, "Since September 11, the authorities have kept better track of certain chemicals, but with the proper authorizations for legitimate use, and in small quantities—and with patience—one can amass the ingredients for a very large bomb."

Khalil asked, "How large is this?"

Tarik, who seemed to be the expert, answered, "Behind us is 45,000 pounds of explosive." He wasn't sure the Arab understood, so he added, "As a comparison, the bomb that was detonated in Oklahoma City was only 4,800 pounds in a small truck. And that bomb created a crater that was ten meters wide and three meters deep, and it destroyed or damaged over three hundred buildings and killed 168 people."

Khalil nodded, though he knew nothing of that explosion, and he wondered who had set it and why.

Tarik continued, "The explosion that will result from this quantity of chemicals will be the equivalent of 50,000 pounds of TNT." He added, "This explosion, if it was detonated in midtown Manhattan, would cause death and destruction for a mile in all directions, and it would be heard and felt for over a hundred miles."

Khalil thought about that, and he wished that the bomb would be detonated in midtown Manhattan, among the skyscrapers and the hundreds of thousands of people on the streets and in the buildings. But those who had planned this operation had decided on something else—something not as destructive or deadly, but a symbolic act that would shock the Americans and open a recent wound. An attack that would shake American confidence and morale and strike a blow at their arrogance.

The man next to him, Bojan, lit a cigarette and Khalil said, "Put that out."

Bojan protested, "The ingredients are inert—not volatile. They are safe until detonated—"

"I do not like the stink of your tobacco." He was tempted to tell them all that he had just killed a man whose cigarettes offended him, but he snapped, "Put it out!"

Bojan threw the cigarette on the floor and ground it out with his heel.

Khalil asked Tarik, "How is this detonated?"

Tarik replied, "It is electrical. There are fifty blasting caps in the drums—more than enough—which I have connected by wires to a standard twelve-volt battery. The current from the battery must pass through a switch, and the switch will make the electrical connection when the electronic timer reaches the hour I have set it for." He asked Khalil, "Do you understand?"

In fact, Khalil did not fully understand. His experience with explosives was limited, and the roadside bombs he had seen in Afghanistan were called command detonated—a person with a handheld detonator chose the time to explode the bomb. Or a suicide bomber initiated the explosion with a simple device.

Khalil did not completely trust this method of a timer—he would have preferred a martyr in the back of the trailer, who he thought would be more trustworthy than an electronic timing device. But this idea for the bomb was not his idea—he was in America to kill with the knife and the gun, the way a man kills, the way a mujahideen kills. His jihad, however, needed to be paid for, and so he had agreed to assist with the bomb. But he had made certain that his mission and the mission of his Al Qaeda backers came together on this last night of his visit.

Khalil looked at his watch and said, "I have much work to do tonight. You will hear from me at approximately ten P.M., and until then, you will move this truck every half hour and you will do nothing to attract attention or arouse suspicion."

No one replied, and Khalil continued, "If a policeman is inquisitive, and he asks you to open the trailer, you will do as you did at the tunnel. If he becomes more inquisitive, you must kill him."

This time, each man nodded.

Khalil addressed each of them by name and said, "Edis, Bojan, Tarik, are you all armed?"

Each man produced an automatic pistol with a silencer, and they made certain that Khalil saw the guns.

Khalil nodded and said, "Good. You are not being paid to buy chemicals, or to drive a truck. You are being paid to kill anyone who is a threat to this mission." He added, "I will be with you later to assist you in the killing of the guards. Then you are free to leave." In fact, they were not going to leave—they were going to die. But Khalil did not think they suspected this. And even if they did, they were stupid and arrogant enough to believe that three former soldiers with guns were safe from harm. But Khalil had killed better men than these in Afghanistan, men who were better armed and better trained than these three, whom he considered mercenaries for hire, not mujahideen who fought for Islam.

Khalil would have liked to give his final encouragement to them in Arabic, the language of the Prophet, which was beautiful and sonorous, but he said in English, "In the name of Allah—peace be unto him—the most merciful, the most compassionate, I ask his blessing on you and your jihad." He ended with, "May God be with us this night."

The three men hesitated, then responded in English, "Go in peace."

Tarik opened the door, and Khalil climbed out of the cab. Bojan said in Bosnian, "Go to hell."

The men laughed, but then Edis said, "That man frightens me."

No one had anything to add to that.

━ PART VII ━

Manhattan

CHAPTER FORTY-EIGHT

Bellevue. I'm gonna miss this place.

I'd brought Kate some clothes that she'd asked for, plus makeup and whatever so she'd look good when they wheeled her into an ambulette the next day, and good when she walked through the lobby of our building.

Kate, however, was exhibiting the classic symptoms of short-timer anxiety—like, something is going to go wrong, I'm not really getting out of here, and so forth.

I reminded her, "You have a gun. We'll get you out."

She asked me, "Anything new?"

Well, yes, our apartment building has been under round-the-clock surveillance by terrorists for maybe three weeks. But that might send her into a tailspin, so I replied, "Nope."

She asked me, "Have you spoken to Tom or Vince?"

"Nope."

She moved on to family matters. "My parents were going to call you today."

"They did. Didn't I mention that? Your father

wants to know why I didn't shoot the terrorist who attacked you."

She seemed a little embarrassed and said, "I explained that to him."

"I'll explain it again." Or, with luck, I'll cut off the terrorist's head before our flight and bring it to him in my overnight bag. "Here he is, Mr. Mayfield. He won't be cutting any more throats. This calls for a drink."

Kate said, "Your mother told me she was going to call you."

"She did."

"What did she say?"

"Eat more fish."

"She asked me why I'm not pregnant yet."

"Eat more fish."

Kate and I watched some TV—a History Channel documentary about the earth being wiped out by a meteorite, which, if it happened tonight, would put the Minnesota trip on hold for a while. God?

Visiting hours ended at 9 P.M., and Kate and I kissed good-bye, and she said, "I'll see you tomorrow. Get here an hour early and get me checked out." She added, "This is the last time we have to say good-bye here."

"Get some recipes before you go."

Officer Mindy Jacobs was on duty outside Kate's door, and I said to her, "Kate's being discharged tomorrow."

"That's good news."

"Right. So if you're superstitious—"

"I hear you." She assured me, "If I don't recognize a

nurse, a doctor, or an orderly, I get someone I know to ID them before they get past me."

"Good."

I wished her a nice quiet evening and left the ward.

My FBI driver was still Preston Tyler, who was putting in a long day. He informed me that there would be no driver on duty until morning, but he assured me, "Your surveillance and protective detail is still in place."

"Terrific."

There were no messages on my home phone, no e-mail, and my cell phone was silent. Maybe everyone was dead from anthrax. Nerve gas?

I thought about calling Boris again, but then I thought about just sneaking out of here and making another unannounced visit to Svetlana. Maybe I'd spend the night on Boris's couch and see if Khalil turned up. But maybe Khalil would come for me here, and I didn't want to miss him.

I decided to wait a half hour, and if nothing happened here, then I'd go see Boris.

At 10:15, as I was watching another History Channel documentary about possible doomsday scenarios—earthquakes, supervolcanoes, meteors again, gamma-ray bursts, and an avalanche of fourth-class junk mail that could bury entire cities—my cell phone vibrated.

It was a text from Paresi that said: *Urgent and confidential. Meet at WTC site, PA trailer. ASAP.*

I stared at the text. Was this the break I'd been waiting for?

I wasn't sure what Paresi meant by confidential, and he wasn't going to say in his text, "This is cop-to-cop," but that was the implication. Maybe he was finally getting his head on straight.

I texted him: *20 minutes.*

I called down to the parking garage and was happy to get Gomp on the phone. I said, "Gomp, this is Tom Walsh."

"Hey, Tom, how ya doin'?"

"Swell. I need a ride down to Sixty-eighth and Lex again."

"Sure thing."

"I need you to meet me at the freight elevator."

"Freight elevator?"

"Right. Two minutes. And mum's the word." I added, "Fifty bucks."

"Sure thing."

I hung up and strapped on my gun belt and hip holster. On the belt, in a sheath, was Uncle Ernie's K-bar knife that I'd taken with me on all my walks in the park. I put on a blue windbreaker and left my apartment.

As I was speed walking toward the freight elevator, I realized my vest was packed in my luggage. I don't normally wear a vest, so it's not second nature, like my gun, or my shield, or leaving the toilet seat up. I hesitated and looked at my watch. The hell with it. I got in the freight elevator, hit the garage button, and down I went.

The elevator doors opened, and there was Gomp sitting in a nice BMW SUV. I was glad he hadn't stolen my green Jeep.

I came around the car and said to him, "I need help with something in the elevator."

"Sure thing."

He got out of the BMW and moved toward the freight elevator as I jumped in the driver's seat.

Gomp shouted, "Hey! Tom! Where you—?"

I hit the accelerator, drove up the ramp, and turned right onto 72nd Street. I caught the green light at Third Avenue and continued on.

I looked in the rearview mirror. There wasn't much traffic at this hour on a drizzly Sunday night, and I didn't see any headlights trying to keep up with me. That was easy.

Subways are faster than cars in Manhattan, but the closest station to the World Trade Center has been damaged and closed since 9/11, and the other stations in the area were a five- or ten-minute walk to Liberty Street where I had to meet Paresi at the Port Authority trailer. Also, subway service to that devastated part of the city was subject to changes, meaning delays. So I'd drive. It was a nice car.

Crosstown traffic wasn't too bad on this Sunday night, and I drove through Central Park at the 65th Street Transverse Road, then got over to the West Side Highway and headed south along the Hudson River. Traffic was moving and within fifteen minutes I was on West Street driving between the dark, devastated sites of the World Financial Center and World Trade Center.

Pre-9/11, a footbridge spanned West Street at Liberty, and I saw the remnants of the structure and turned left. I parked the BMW near the chain-link gates and got out.

I'd expected to see a few unmarked cars or cruisers here, but the only vehicle around was the Port Authority cruiser parked near the fence.

I walked quickly to the gates and saw that the heavy chain and lock were in place, but there was a lot of slack in the chain and I squeezed through and walked quickly to the trailer.

I knocked on the door, then tried the handle. The door was unlocked, so I took my creds out, opened the door, and called inside, "Federal agent! Hello? Coming in."

I stepped up into the trailer and saw that the front area—an office with two desks, a radio, and maps—was empty. An electric coffee maker was on in the galley kitchen, but the TV on the counter was turned off.

There was a narrow hallway that led to a bathroom and a bunk room where the PA cops could catch a few winks or whatever, and I called out, "Anybody home?" but no one answered.

My cell phone buzzed. I looked at the text message, which was from Paresi: *We're down in the pit. Where are you?*

I replied: *PA trailer. 1 minute.*

I left the trailer and started down the long, wide earthen ramp that went into the deep pit.

The excavation site was huge, covering sixteen acres,

and it would have been pitch-dark except for some lights strung along the remains of the deep concrete foundation, and a dozen or so stanchion-mounted stadium lights that illuminated some of the desolate acreage.

There were pieces of equipment scattered around— mostly earthmoving equipment and dump trucks, plus a few cranes. I also saw some construction office trailers, and one big tractor-trailer parked near the center of the site.

About halfway down the ramp, I stopped. I looked into the pit, but I didn't see anyone. The stadium lights didn't cover the entire site, and large areas were in darkness or in shadows cast by the equipment.

I texted Paresi: *Where?*

He replied: *Center, big semi.*

I looked at the tractor-trailer I'd seen, about two hundred yards away, and I saw someone pass from light to darkness.

I continued down the hard-packed earth ramp.

Okay, so why did Paresi want to meet here? Something to do with the big tractor-trailer? Who else was here? And where were the Port Authority cops? Down in the pit? And what's with the cell phone silence?

The drizzle had stopped, but at the bottom of the ramp the softer earth had turned muddy, and I wished I'd changed out of my loafers. I also noticed deep, fresh tire marks made by what was probably an eighteen-wheeler that had come through not too long ago. Assuming these were made by the big semi in the center of the site, I followed the tread marks.

I was passing in and out of darkness, and the banks of stadium lights to my front were shining in my eyes.

I saw the tractor-trailer—CARLINO MASONRY SUPPLIES—about fifty yards ahead, but I didn't see Paresi or anyone else.

I took another few steps and stopped. I was getting a weird feeling about this. Something in the back of my mind . . . the stadium lights . . . the shadows . . .

I pulled my Glock and stuck it in my belt, then moved more slowly toward the tractor-trailer.

My cell phone buzzed loudly in the quiet pit. I looked at the text from Paresi: *I am to your left.*

I stopped beside a big dump truck and looked to my left. About ten yards away, I could see something moving in the half-light. As my eyes adjusted, I could see an object swinging from the cable of a crane . . . and it took me a few seconds to realize it was a person . . . and then I realized I was looking at the face of Vince Paresi.

I grabbed my gun out of my belt, and as I was dropping to one knee, I heard a high-pitched scream from the top of the dump truck behind me, and a fast-moving shadow flitted across the light, then something slammed into my back with such force that I was driven face-first into the wet ground. The wind was knocked out of me, and I saw my gun lying in the mud a few feet in front of me. I lunged for it, but something hit me in the back of my head, and then a foot kicked the gun away.

I jumped to my feet and realized I was wobbly, and as I caught my breath and tried to get my bearings, I saw someone in dark clothing standing about ten feet from me. I took a deep breath and stared at The Lion.

Asad Khalil had a gun in his hand, but it was at his side. I could cover the distance in about two seconds, but it would take him one second to aim and fire, and he didn't have much aiming to do at this distance.

Finally, he said, "So, we meet again."

He wanted to talk, of course, so I replied, "Fuck you."

He informed me, "That is the second time tonight someone has said that to me. But the last man said it in Russian."

Well, I knew who that was, and since Khalil was standing here, I knew that Boris was not standing anywhere. And Vince . . . my God . . . I felt a rage rising inside me, but I knew I had to keep it under control.

He said to me, "I know you are alone, and I want you to know that I, too, am alone." He said, unnecessarily, "It is just us. As you requested, and as it should be."

I nodded.

He nodded in return and said, "I saved you for last, Mr. Corey."

I replied, "I saved you for myself."

He smiled, and it wasn't a nice smile. He said, "I didn't feel a bulletproof vest when I knocked you to the ground."

I didn't reply.

"No matter. I am not going to shoot you in the heart." He held up his gun and said to me, "This is the gun of your deceased wife. I am looking forward to shooting off your manhood with this gun."

He had a few more things to say before he did that, and I thought about a few moves I could make, but none of them seemed promising.

Without moving my head, my eyes darted around at what was nearby. My gun was too far away, and there was nothing close by that I could use. I quickly scanned the top of the distant foundation walls. The observation deck was closed, and even if someone was walking by at street level, they couldn't see this far into the dark pit.

Khalil said, "Look at me. There is no one here to help you." He let me know, "They are all dead. The two policemen in their comfortable trailer are dead. And as you can clearly see, your superior officer is close by, but he cannot help you." He held up a cell phone and said, "His final message to you is this— Asad Khalil has won."

Again, I felt the rage and anger taking over—this psychotic piece of shit, this cold-blooded, murdering—

"Did it not occur to you, Mr. Corey, that this was not as it seemed?"

I looked at him and I thought about that. Maybe it did occur to me, way deep down inside . . . so deep that I just left it there because . . . it didn't matter to me if it was Paresi or Khalil.

He said to me, "I have dreamed about this moment. Have you?"

I nodded.

He looked at me and said, "It was fated that we

meet, but often we must help fate." He smiled again and said, "Both of us have helped fate tonight, and it is my fate, Mr. Corey, to cut off your face."

I assumed he brought his own knife for that, and I said to him, "Try it. Put the gun down and try it, asshole."

He ignored my invitation and glanced around. He said to me, "Here we are, where three thousand of your countrymen died."

I reminded him, "There were hundreds of Muslims who died in the Towers."

He ignored that, too, and said, "This, I think, is a good place for you to die as well." He asked me, "Did I choose well?"

I didn't reply, and I wondered if he somehow knew that Kate and I had actually come within minutes of dying here on 9/11. But I didn't die here then, and I wasn't going to die here now.

In fact, he said to me, "But I will not kill you unless you force me to. I will, however, shoot you in the groin, then slice off your face as I promised."

I had no reply to that.

He reached behind his back and produced a long, wide knife. He said, "This is what I will use, and you will be alive to feel it and to see your face being pulled from your skull."

He was into taunting, which was part of the ritual for most pleasure killers. And they get so deep into their fantasies that they forget to be careful.

Khalil, however, was also a trained killer, and he asked me, "Do you have another gun?"

Well, I did, but I loaned it to Kate. I didn't reply.

He looked at me, then said, "I didn't feel one . . . but . . ." He stuck his knife back in his belt, and then he surprised me—or maybe not—by also sticking his gun—Kate's gun—in his belt at his right side.

He stood perfectly still, looking right at me. His legs were slightly parted and bent at the knees, and his arms were away from his sides. Did he learn that from Boris? Or too many cowboy movies?

As though he read my mind, he said, "You are a cowboy—no? Is your gun hand faster than mine? Please. Reach for your gun."

Well, if I had one, asshole, the first and last thing you'd see was the flash of the muzzle. It also occurred to me that Khalil would rather not fire a shot that could be heard . . . or maybe he simply preferred the knife.

He straightened up and said, "You either have no gun, or you are a coward."

Well, I had no gun, but I did have a knife he didn't seem to know about. I said, "I can't hear you. Step closer."

He drew his knife again and moved toward me, saying, "I once flayed a man's flesh from his chest, and I could see his ribs, his lungs, and his beating heart."

As he came closer, I could see his face more clearly, and he looked exactly like the photograph in the wanted poster—deep, dark, narrow-set eyes, separated by a hooked nose that gave him more the appearance of a bird of prey than a lion.

He kept coming closer, brandishing his long knife, a big smile on his face.

I stepped back, and he smiled wider. He was really having fun.

He moved closer, slicing the air with his knife.

I stepped back again, and he closed the gap.

He let me know, "If you turn and run, I will shoot your legs out from under you, then butcher you."

"I'm not running."

"No, but you are stepping backward. Come to me. Fight like a man."

"You have the knife, asshole. Put it down."

He flipped the knife into the air, then caught it by its handle and smiled again.

He was really enjoying this, and to be honest, I was not. I knew this guy could slice me up if I made a move toward him, so I again backed off. It was time to end his fun, so I reminded him, "Your mother was a whore."

He screamed something and charged at me.

I turned, took a running step, pretended to slip in the mud, then drew my knife and spun around on my knees and let him run into the K-bar, which caught him in his groin.

He let out a surprised scream and backpedaled away as I charged in for the kill before he went for his gun.

He had his knife hand over his groin and his other hand was reaching for the Glock as he backpedaled, and he lost his footing in the mud and fell backward.

The only move I had was to dive on him to keep him away from the Glock, and I made a running jump and landed full on his chest as he was starting to raise his legs to catapult me into the air.

I saw his arm coming around, and I felt his knife cutting into the back of my shoulder blade, scraping across the bone.

His arm was rising again for another stab, and I grabbed his wrist. I kept the full weight of my body on him as he struggled to get me off him and get his knife hand free.

My knife hand was free, and his left hand was free, but instead of reaching for his gun, he made the right decision to grab my arm before I got my blade into his face or throat.

He got a tight grip on my wrist, then lifted his head and got his teeth into my cheek and bit down hard on the maxillary nerve, which sent flashes of pain through my head.

He was still holding my wrist, but I managed to get my arm up, and I brought the butt end of the heavy K-bar down on the top of his head.

He released his bite on my cheek, and I twisted my hand to bring the business end of the knife into the top of his skull, but he was incredibly strong and he pulled my arm away and held it.

So we were locked together, neither of us able to use our knives, and this would go on until one of us weakened, or did something unexpected—or desperate.

He was in very good physical shape, and he didn't seem to be tiring as we each tried to break free from the other's grip.

He tried a few times to get his knee in my groin, but he had no leverage, and I kept my full weight on him. Then he tried to get his teeth into my face again, but I kept my head tilted back.

I had no idea where I'd stuck him. Genitals? Thigh? Lower abdomen? But I knew the wound wasn't bleeding enough to weaken him. My own wound felt warm and wet, but I didn't think he'd done too much damage.

We made eye contact and stared at each other. I said, "You're going to die."

He shook his head and said, "You."

His voice was still baritone so I guess I'd missed his nuts.

As we struggled, I realized he wasn't weakening at all, but I was, and he knew that, so he was waiting me out. Time to do something.

I gave him a head butt, but it didn't cause him any more pain than it did me. He retaliated by trying to get his teeth on my face again, which is what I wanted him to do. I clamped my teeth on his big hooked nose, and I bit down as hard as I've ever bitten on anything. Before he screamed, I felt his cartilage cracking under my teeth and I tasted the blood oozing out of his nose and into my mouth.

He was in real pain now, so he barely noticed that I'd released my bite on his nose. I spit blood into his left eye, and when the eyelid closed, I got my teeth on it and ripped at it.

I spit more blood in his eyes and said quietly, "I'm gonna eat *your* fucking face."

He spit back at me, then managed to get a bite out of my chin.

A man in great pain and great danger has super strength—adrenaline-charged muscle power—and Khalil arched his body up with me on top, which gave him the leverage he needed to go into a rolling motion, trying to reverse our positions and get on top of me. I lost my grip on his knife hand, and he immediately brought his knife down into my back again, slicing into my rib cage.

He would have stabbed me again, but I suddenly relaxed my muscles, and he found himself going through the rest of his twist and roll without resistance, and this put him unexpectedly face-first into the ground with me on his back. His knife hand was free, but he couldn't use it from that position, and he tried to scramble away, but I came down heavy, and he collapsed on his chest and stomach. Both my hands were free now, and I pulled his head back by his long hair and slashed his throat, then pushed his face into the mud. He didn't make a move or a sound, but my instincts said he wasn't finished.

In fact, his arm slid under his body, and I knew he was going for his gun. I got there first and snatched the gun out of his belt, and because you don't want a gun in play this close, I jumped off him and stepped back.

I stood there, breathing hard, keeping my eye on him.

The stadium lights were shining in my eyes, and my stocking feet were buried in the mud. A worse problem was that the wetness was spreading over my back, and it felt warm in the cool night air.

I realized that Khalil's second stab had gone deeper than I thought, and I was losing blood.

My head was getting light, and I felt my knees giving out, then I found myself kneeling on the ground.

Khalil was moving now, and I watched as he rose slowly to his feet.

His back was to me, but I saw him wiping his face with his hands, then he turned around, saw me, and began walking toward me.

His face and clothes were covered with mud, but I could see the blood on his throat and his shirt, and I realized that the blood wasn't gushing the way it should have if I'd hit his jugular or carotid.

He spotted his knife on the ground, picked it up, and kept coming toward me.

Die, you sonofabitch.

I stood too quickly, and I felt light-headed again. I thought I was going to pass out, but I took a few deep breaths and kept still so my heart wouldn't start pumping more blood out of me.

Khalil kept coming, holding his knife in front of him.

When he was less than ten feet from me, he said, "Your face."

Well, I didn't want him to deface me, and as far as I was concerned, the knife fight was over. So I raised Kate's Glock and pointed it at him. My arm was unsteady, and again I thought I was going to black out.

I said, "Drop the knife."

I noticed that the Glock was totally covered with mud, and I wasn't sure it was going to fire, and neither was he. I said, "Drop it, asshole," but I didn't really want him to drop it. I should have had no trouble just pulling the trigger, but . . . I couldn't do that; I wanted him to earn his bullet.

He took a few more steps, then sunk to his knees.

It was over, but it's not over until it's over—and he was still holding his knife pointed at me.

I would have waited it out, but I was starting to get that old bleeding-to-death feeling that I remembered too well, so I had to put the final nail in this bastard . . . I aimed at his head and squeezed on the trigger, but then I stopped and looked at him. I lowered the gun and shoved it in my belt.

Again, Khalil stood, and he did the zombie walk with his knife pointing the way toward me.

I took a deep breath, then lunged at him with my knife, parrying his arm away as I brought the K-bar up in an underhand motion. The blade sliced through the bottom of his chin, through his mouth and into his palate, where it stuck. I let go of the knife and stepped back.

His eyes widened, and he tried to speak or scream, but I think the blade must have passed through his tongue, and he just made a few unintelligible sounds as blood ran out of his mouth.

He started choking, then amazingly he took another step toward me, and we made eye contact, not three feet apart.

I looked into his eyes. One eye was filled with

blood where I'd ripped his eyelid, but the other was bright and burning, and it stared at me.

The handle of my K-bar knife was stuck up to the hilt under his chin, and he looked like he'd sprouted a strange goatee.

I said to him, "My wife is alive. I am alive. You are dead."

He kept staring at me, then he shook his head.

I saw weird green-and-yellow stuff oozing out of his mouth and nose—maybe mucus from his sinus cavity, or maybe this guy was from outer space.

Asad Khalil was dead, but he wasn't finished dying, and I wasn't feeling so well myself.

So we both stood there, a few feet apart, our eyes fixed on each other, and I had the sense that this was a contest of wills—who was going to drop first?

Well, it wasn't going to be me. I managed to keep standing, even though my head was starting to spin.

Khalil suddenly seemed aware that he had a problem, and his right hand came up and grabbed the handle of the knife stuck under his chin.

Well, nobody but me touches Uncle Ernie's combat knife, so I hauled off and smashed him in the face.

He went down, and I knew he wasn't getting up again, so I let myself fall to my knees.

Then I crawled over to Khalil, turned, and dropped my head and shoulders on his chest to keep my wounds elevated.

I could feel his chest still rising and falling.

I stared up at the sky and felt a light drizzle on my face, which felt good.

I found my cell phone and called 911. I said to the dispatcher, "Ten-thirteen . . ." Officer in trouble. I IDed myself and gave her my shield number, then using cop lingo to make this sound real, I said, "I need a bus, forthwith," an ambulance—now. I gave her the location and had to repeat it, then I said, "Look for the . . . big semi . . . Carlino Masonry . . . yeah . . . let's be quick."

I closed my eyes and tried to control my breathing and my beating heart. This was going to be close.

Within five minutes, I heard sirens up on Church Street, then a minute later I felt Khalil's chest heave and stop.

I turned my head and looked at Vince Paresi dangling from the big crane. I took a deep breath and said to him, "It's over, Captain—we won."

CHAPTER FORTY-NINE

I didn't want to go to the closest hospital—I wanted to go to Bellevue, so that's where the EMS ambulance headed.

I had pressure bandages on my wounds and two saline drips in my arms, and I was feeling terrific. Let's do that again.

Actually, I was sort of drifting in and out, but I remember getting to Bellevue and I remember letting the emergency room staff know that my wife was a patient in the security ward—then I don't remember much.

The sun was coming through the window, and hanging from the window cord was a stuffed lion.

I was pretty sure this wasn't a dream, and the room definitely looked familiar.

Someone was squeezing my hand, and I turned my

head to see Kate standing beside my bed. She was wearing the white blouse and blue skirt I'd brought her, and it took me a few seconds to process that.

She smiled and asked me, "How are you, handsome?"

I didn't know how I was, but I replied, "Not bad." I added, "You should see the other guy." *He's dead.*

She forced a smile and said, "You're going to be fine."

"Good." *But I can't go to Minnesota.*

She had tears in her eyes, and she bent over and kissed my cheek—right where Khalil had bitten into my nerve. *Ouch!*

I put my hand there and felt a bandage, then another bandage where the asshole took a bite out of my chin. Then, not quite being able to separate what happened from a bad dream, I did the guy thing and felt for the jewels. One, two, exclamation mark. One more time—one, two—

"Are you okay? What hurts there?"

"Nothing." I found the bed control and raised myself into a sitting position.

I had tubes and wires attached to me, and I checked out the monitors, which looked okay. I was starting to experience that euphoria you get when the Grim Reaper just missed you, and I leaned forward and said, "I want to get out of here."

Kate informed me, "The doctor said three or four days—but I told him a week."

Not funny.

She further informed me, "You lost some blood, but they gave you a refill." She added, "I told the neurologist you were mentally impaired before the blood loss, so he shouldn't expect much when he evaluates you."

What did I do to deserve this sarcasm?

Kate held a cup of ice water to my lips and I took a sip. I noticed now that her bed was still in the room, and I asked her, "You staying?"

"No, *you're* staying. I'm leaving."

"Yeah?" I lay back on the bed, and even with the painkillers, I could feel where I'd taken the two knife cuts. In fact, my whole body ached. This sucked.

I stared up at the ceiling for a while, then I said, "Khalil's dead."

"I know."

"Vince Paresi is dead. Khalil killed him."

A silence, then, "I know."

She was crying again, and to be honest, I felt a little lump in my throat. I had no idea how Khalil had killed Vince, but I hoped it was quick.

She pulled up a chair, took my hand, and we sat there for a while.

Finally, she said to me, "Tom is at the . . . crime scene. He's coming to visit later."

"I'm not receiving visitors named Tom."

"John . . . he wants to see you, and . . . congratulate you."

"No photos."

She didn't reply to that, but said to me, "When you're ready to talk about it . . . I want to know what happened."

I was ready to talk about it now, but I knew I'd be telling the same story at least twenty times to half the

Justice Department—not to mention Tom Walsh—so I said, "When I get home." I added, "You can help me with my incident report."

She smiled and said, "Don't puff yourself up."

I smiled.

I was actually hungry, and I asked her, "What's for breakfast?"

"Jail-O."

"What happened to the hard labor boiled eggs?"

She squeezed my hand tight, stood and gave me a teary kiss on my forehead—right where I head-butted the asshole. *Ouch!*

She looked at me and said, "I want you home with me."

"Me too." I asked, "Where are my clothes?"

She replied, "Probably in an evidence bag."

"Where's my gun?"

"Tom said they have it, and they recovered my gun, too."

"Good." I was going to ask her where Uncle Ernie's knife was, but the last time I saw it, it was sticking out of Asad Khalil's chin—so by now it was downstairs in the morgue where the medical examiner was tugging at it, trying to decide if he should pull it out before or after he cut open Khalil's skull.

Kate and I chatted a bit, and we agreed that I needed a few weeks at home so I could recuperate quietly. I expressed my deep disappointment that we couldn't see her parents or mine in the foreseeable future, and she knew I was full of crap, but she couldn't say that to a man in my delicate condition. I also informed her, "The E.R. doctor said no skydiving for five years."

Breakfast came at about 7:30, and apparently I was on a liquid diet that didn't resemble my usual liquid diet.

Kate chowed down on pancakes and sausages. She asked me, "Would you like more confine mint tea?"

This wasn't as funny as I'd thought when *she* was lying here.

Anyway, I sat in bed thinking about Vince Paresi and even Boris, who I liked on some level. Boris and I had agreed that he was capable of handling Asad Khalil, but obviously we'd been wrong about that— and we both should have known we were wrong. And on that subject, what the hell was I thinking when I thought I wanted Asad Khalil all for myself? Well, it worked out . . . barely.

I asked Kate, "Have you heard anything about Boris?"

She shook her head and said, "Why do you ask?"

"I think Khalil killed him."

She didn't respond, but she was probably thinking what I was thinking—I should have reported my contact with Boris to Tom Walsh. Not only would Boris probably still be alive, but if the surveillance team had grabbed Khalil in Brighton Beach, I could have saved myself some excitement at the WTC site—not to mention a few days in the hospital.

Also, Vince Paresi would still be alive.

Well, in this business, you call it like you see it, and as I said, you live—or die—with the consequences.

I wasn't going to beat myself up with this any more than I was going to beat myself up for not thinking about Gabe Haytham in time to save him and his family. The bad guy here was Asad Khalil, and people like him, and those who helped him, and everyone who celebrated death and not life.

Bottom line here—I killed Asad Khalil, so he wasn't going to trial or to prison, and he wouldn't be haunting our dreams anymore. But there are more of them.

I asked Kate, "Did you hear anything about the Port Authority cops? The ones who were in the PA trailer?"

She replied, "Tom mentioned that there were two of them—a male and female—but they haven't been found." She added, "I don't want to talk about this now."

I nodded, but this was still on my mind. My mind, however, was in happy pill land, and I needed to focus on something that was bothering me about this.

It was certainly possible that someone like Asad Khalil could get the drop on two cops who weren't expecting trouble. But what did he do with the bodies?

It would make sense that Khalil had help at this critical moment—maybe one or two other guys to kill the cops and to get rid of the bodies . . . and hang Vince from the crane.

But when I saw Khalil, he was alone. So if he had accomplices, where were they? Disposing of the bodies? Or did Khalil, true to his M.O., kill them, too?

And all of this brought me back to what had been on my mind all week. Did Khalil have something else planned? Based on just what I saw in the apartment on 72nd Street, Khalil obviously had accomplices and resources here, so he probably had a favor to repay. And what was it? And was it still in the works?

Kate interrupted my thoughts to ask me what I was thinking about.

"Khalil's big finale."

She stayed quiet awhile, then said, "If . . . *if* there was supposed to be a finale . . . maybe whatever was going to happen is not going to happen now that he's dead."

I'd thought about that, and it was possible. But if something big was going to happen—like a car bomb or an anthrax attack from a crop duster—and if somebody like Al Qaeda was behind it, did they need Asad Khalil to pull it off?

Kate said, "I think we talked ourselves into this possibility."

"Do you really think so?" I said to her, "Boris thought it was possible."

"Why don't you get some rest?"

A nurse came in with painkillers. I didn't like these things the last time I was in the hospital with daylight coming through three holes in my body, so Dom Fanelli would bring me a colorless and odorless painkiller made in Poland, which did the trick. But I didn't argue and I put them in my mouth, drank some water, then when she left I spit them out.

Kate said, "You have to take those."

"No pain, no brain."

I started to realize that maybe I should have asked

the asshole himself what was up. He wasn't going to tell me when I was beating the shit out of him—but he might have told me when he thought I was as good as dead. He would have said, "I am glad you asked me about that, Mr. Corey. And I will tell you because"— big laugh here—"dead men tell no tales."

Okay. *What?*

I raised my bed a little more and could feel the sutures pulling in my back. I closed my eyes and got my brain in gear. Something had struck me as odd—or out of place—at the WTC site, and it was now coming back to me.

The tire marks. They were fresh.

That semi had been driven into that site sometime on Sunday. Do they make deliveries to a security zone on a Sunday? I recalled late one night—maybe during the week, maybe a weekend—seeing trucks parked with the drivers bedded down in their sleeping compartment, waiting for the gates to open.

Therefore . . . why would the PA cops let this tractor-trailer through the gates on a Sunday night? Well, maybe because they were dead.

CARLINO MASONRY SUPPLIES.

The masonry supply thing wasn't quite right either. They weren't pouring concrete yet, and there were no cement mixers on the site. And if they were delivering something like steel mesh or rebars, they'd use a flatbed truck. So what was in that big trailer?

And why did Khalil choose the WTC site to meet me? Well, for the symbolism, as he'd said. I get it . . . but . . .

I sat up. "Holy shit."

"John? Are you all right?"

"No."

"What's the matter?"

"Hold on." I was pretty sure I knew what was in that trailer—and I knew, too, it hadn't blown yet, because if it had, I'd have heard it, and even felt it, here, three miles away.

I reached for the phone on the nightstand, and Kate asked me, "Who are you calling?"

"The Ops Center—no, Walsh. He's probably still at the site."

"John—"

Walsh's cell phone went into voice mail—he didn't recognize the number, or it came up "Bellevue" and he knew only two people there, and he probably didn't want to speak to one of them.

I was about to dial the Ops Center, but I got into crazy mode and pulled the tubes and wires out of me. Kate went a little nuts and started yelling, then tried to push the nurse's call button, but I pulled it out of her hand, slid out of bed, and said to her, "Let's go."

"What—?"

I took her arm, and as I moved her toward the door, I said, "You're getting me out of here."

She pulled her arm back and said, "No. John—"

"Trust me. I'll explain. Come on."

She looked at me, then said in a calming voice, "Stay here, John, and I'll get you some clothes."

I looked at my watch, but it was gone. I asked her, "What time is it?"

She glanced at her watch and said, "It's 8:05. You stay here—"

"Kate, at 8:46 A.M., the time when the first plane hit the North Tower, a very large bomb will detonate at the World Trade Center site."

She stared at me, and she looked frightened—not about the bomb, but about me.

So to get this moving, I lied, "Khalil told me this when he thought he was going to kill me."

"Oh my God . . ."

"Let's go. You got your cell phone?"

She grabbed her purse, and we hurried out the door.

The other side of the ward was for the criminally insane, and I didn't want to wind up there, so I tried to look nonchalant as we passed quickly through the ward filled with guards from the Department of Corrections.

We got to the security checkpoint and almost got through, but a big DOC guy stopped us. It must have been my hospital pajamas and slipper socks that caught his attention.

Kate went into full FBI mode, flashed her creds, and made it clear to the guy that this was none of his business.

He backed off, and we were out in the corridor.

We got on an elevator and she asked me, "Where are we going?"

"Ground Zero. Let me have your phone." I dialed Walsh. I knew he always took Kate's call, but he got me instead, which confused and disappointed him.

He said, "John . . . good to hear from you. I was going to—"

"Tom, listen to me—"

"We are so sorry about Vince—"

I lost the call in the elevator, and I said to Kate, "When we get outside, commandeer an ambulance."

She nodded.

The elevator reached the lobby, and Kate moved quickly toward the First Avenue exit as I redialed Walsh and followed her.

Tom answered again and said, "Kate told me you were resting comfortably and I just want to say—"

"Tom, shut up and listen to me." That shut him up, and I said, slowly and clearly with calm urgency in my voice, "Asad Khalil, when he thought he was going to kill me, told me that there was a bomb planted at the WTC site—"

"What?"

I could hear engine noises in the background, and I asked him, "Are you still there?"

"Yes."

"I think the bomb is in the big semi there—Carlino Masonry Supplies. Do you see it?"

"I'm . . . standing next to . . ."

"You might want to move. But before you do that, call the Bomb Squad ASAP. Then get everyone the hell out of there—that is a *very* big truck."

Silence.

I walked out of the lobby, and the guard at the door said to me, "Hey! Where you goin'?"

Walsh asked, "John . . . are you sure about this?"

Very good question. And the answer was no, but I said, "Yes."

The guard was speaking to me, but I waved him off. Where the hell was Kate?

Walsh was saying, "The trailer is locked."

By now, Tom Walsh was probably thirty blocks away, so I wondered how he knew that. I said, "Yes, it would be locked, Tom." I hesitated, then said, "I *think*—think it's set to—"

The guard had another guard with him now, and they wanted me to go inside with them. I said to them, "I'm waiting for an ambulance." I said to Walsh, "It's set to go off at 8:46 A.M."

He didn't ask why I thought that, because that time is burned into everyone's mind.

There was another silence on the phone, and I thought I'd lost him, but then he said, "That's thirty-one minutes . . . I don't think we can evacuate this area—"

"Try. Meanwhile, evacuate the site and get the area cordoned off. Call the Bomb Squad."

I hung up, and the guards had me by both arms, so I told them, "I'm STP positive."

They backed off, and one of them made a call on his radio.

An ambulance pulled into the pickup lane with Kate in the passenger seat, and I opened her door and said to her, "Get out."

"No. I'm going with you."

One of the guards told the ambulance driver, "This guy is STP positive."

Kate said, "John, get in the ambulance. Now! Or I'm going without you."

She meant it, so I moved as quickly as I could toward the rear doors and climbed into the ambulance and knelt between the two front seats.

Kate said to the driver, "Ground Zero. Liberty Street. Lights and sirens."

The driver, a young black woman, hit the bells and whistles and off we went. She asked Kate, "What are we responding to without EMT personnel, and why are we taking a patient to Ground Zero?"

Kate explained, "It's really complicated, Jeena." She added, "And really urgent."

Jeena knew how to weave and bob and blow the lights, and I estimated we'd be at Ground Zero in about five or six minutes.

I asked, "What time is it?"

Kate looked at her watch and said, "Eight twenty-one."

Twenty-five minutes. I said to Kate, "The second plane hit at nine oh-three, and there are more people around at that time. So maybe—"

She said, "Let's go with eight forty-six."

"Right."

Jeena asked, "What are we talking about, folks?"

I answered by saying, "As soon as you drop us on Liberty Street, you turn around and get out of the area."

She thought about that and said, "Sounds like you might need an ambulance down there."

"Yeah, but . . ." I tried to think about how big this bomb could be, and like everyone in this business, I

compared it to the Oklahoma City bombing. That
was a small truck with about five thousand pounds of
explosives that did massive damage. This trailer, if it
was full of the same stuff, would take out fifteen or
twenty city blocks—basically all of Lower Manhattan, from the Hudson to the East River, including the
Financial District right down to Battery Park. And
how many people lived and worked there? Maybe a
quarter of a million, and there was no way to evacuate
them in time . . . Holy shit.

I said to Jeena, "Pull over. I have to drive."

She informed me, "*Nobody* drives my ambulance."

Kate turned back to me and said, "John, maybe we
don't need to be there."

No, we didn't need to be there, but I didn't respond
to that logical statement. I looked out the windshield,
and I could see we were already on Broadway. Twenty-
six Fed and 290 Broadway were right ahead. In fact,
we were already well within the blast zone.

I looked at the time on Kate's cell phone: 8:25.

I called Walsh and asked him, "What's happening?"

He replied, "We got all the construction guys out of
here, and all the crime scene people, and we've cleared
the observation deck and cleared the streets." He added,
"There's no way to evacuate this area so we're trying to
get people underground."

"Where's the Bomb Squad?"

"I see the trucks coming down the ramp."

"You still *there*?"

"Where else am I supposed to be?"

"Tom . . . if that thing goes off, it's going to vaporize—"

"John, I have my hands full at the moment—"

"Did you get the lock cut off?"

"Yes, but the Bomb Squad advised me not to open the doors. Okay, I—"

"We'll be right there," I said.

"What? Where are you?"

"Just speeding past your corner office in an ambulance."

"With Kate?"

He likes Kate. He wants me vaporized. "Two minutes—"

"Get the *hell* out of here. That's an order. Okay, here's the Squad."

The phone went dead, and Kate said, "Eight twenty-six." She asked me, "Where's Tom?"

"Still there."

She nodded.

Jeena had put it all together and informed us, "You got about twenty minutes."

"Thanks."

Kate said to her, "Pull over, get out, and get into a subway station."

Jeena didn't reply and kept going. Up ahead at Murray Street, Broadway was blocked off with police cars. They saw the ambulance coming, and one of the cruisers moved aside and we shot through.

The streets around the site were nearly deserted, except for police cruisers with their roof lights flashing, and warnings blasting out of their bullhorns saying, "Get off the streets! Go down into the subways and leave the area!"

Another cruiser's bullhorn was blaring, "Get away from the windows! Go into your building basement!"

Well, I wasn't an expert on bombs, but I did know that a massive explosion would suck the breathable air out of underground spaces. Not to mention ruptured gas and water lines, falling debris, and collapsing buildings—again.

I hoped to God this day didn't make three thousand dead look small by comparison.

Jeena snapped a hard right on Barclay, a left on West, and within two minutes we were at the open gates to the ramp and Jeena stopped.

It almost didn't matter what time it was anymore; we were so close to the center of the blast that we couldn't get clear unless we turned around now—and we weren't turning around.

Kate threw open her door and said to Jeena, "Get as far as you can as fast as you can."

I was about to open the rear doors, but the ambulance began moving again and we were on the ramp, heading down into the pit. Jeena said, "Too far to walk."

I moved between the front seats again and said to Jeena, "That big tractor-trailer over there." I added, "Thanks."

As we moved quickly down the ramp, I could see one Bomb Squad truck and two guys in blast suits—which weren't going to help them at all—and Tom

Walsh. And that was it. Except for three idiots on the way.

I could also see the yellow crime scene tape that encompassed about an acre around the tractor-trailer, and within the tape was the crane where Vince Paresi had been hanging . . .

The Bomb Squad guys were standing with Walsh at the rear of the trailer, but I could see that the doors were still closed. *Come on, guys.* I said 8:46 A.M.—not P.M.

I had hoped the bomb would be defused by now—and maybe it was. Or better yet, maybe they'd already opened the doors and found masonry supplies inside, and I had some explaining to do.

Kate also noticed that the doors were closed and asked, "Why are they just standing there?"

Coffee break? I said hopefully, "Maybe they're finished."

We were off the ramp now, and the ambulance was fishtailing in the soft earth, but within a minute we were inside the yellow tape and pulling up to the big semi.

Kate and I jumped out, and Kate yelled to Jeena, "Get out of here! Go!"

Jeena made a quick U-turn and gunned the big vehicle back toward the ramp.

Tom was speaking to the Bomb Squad guys, and I could tell they were a little tense—so this was not over.

I looked at the time on Kate's cell phone—8:31—then it changed to 8:32.

I said to Kate, "They don't look happy."

She nodded.

I watched Tom and the two guys speaking quietly, as though a loud noise would set off the bomb.

Bomb Squad people are, by definition, nuts. They volunteer for this. And I knew from past experience that they have a weird sense of humor about getting blown up. But they're highly trained and cool, and these two guys didn't look panicky yet, though Tom was a bit pale. But . . . well, I give him my brass balls award for this.

Finally, Tom turned his attention to us, checked out my pjs, gave me an annoyed look, then said to Kate, "Get in that Bomb Squad truck and get out of here. Now!"

Kate replied, "I'm not leaving unless we all leave."

There wasn't much time left to argue so Tom said, "Okay . . . here's what's happening—we sent the other Bomb Squad team away with the dog, who gave a positive reaction. Also, Dutch"—he indicated the older guy—"and Bobby say they can smell ammonium nitrate, diesel fuel, and whatever. So we have a bomb."

Right. I could smell it, too, and I noticed now that the doors were open just a crack, and Bobby was looking inside with a flashlight.

I suggested, "Maybe they should think about defusing it now."

It was Dutch who replied, "Sometimes these things are rigged with a booby-trap detonator." He added, "If we had time, we'd use the robot, but the robot is slow and you're telling me it could be set for eight forty-six—so Bobby is the robot."

In fact, Bobby was now standing on the rear bumper rail with his flashlight, and he called out, "I still don't see any indication of a booby-trap detonator." He added, "But you never know until you try." He turned and said to Dutch and to Tom, "Your call." He asked, "Open it?"

Tom and Dutch looked at each other, then Dutch looked at his watch and said, "If it *is* set for eight forty-six, we have about ten minutes to defuse it, or ten minutes to get in our truck and get ourselves into a bank vault or something."

Tom Walsh looked at the towering buildings around us, which we all knew were still filled with people, despite the warnings to clear the area.

Dutch informed us, "We're talking about a mile, mile-and-a-half blast radius . . . depending on what they have in that fifty-three-footer."

Tom nodded, but didn't respond.

Dutch also let us know, "If it's a simple detonator— without any tricks—I can defuse it in a few seconds, by cutting some wires or interrupting the power source."

I asked, of course, "And if it's not so simple?"

He replied, "If it looks like it's rigged with a current interruption switch, or maybe a second power source or some other sneaky detonating device . . . then . . ." He shrugged and said, "If I had more time, I could dope it out . . . but we don't have a lot of time, so I just start cutting wires and see what happens."

He went to school for this?

Dutch also let us know, "And maybe it's command

detonated. Like, someone is going to make a cell phone call and that trips the switch."

No one had anything to say about that, and Dutch reminded us, "Meanwhile, we got to decide if we're going to open that door—that's step one. I can't defuse it from here."

Bobby, who I thought had shown a lot of patience, said, "I think our time is almost up to get out of here."

Kate said to Tom, "Open the doors."

Tom glanced at his watch.

To help Tom with his decision—before it was too late to run and too late to defuse the bomb—I said, "I'm guessing that Khalil stashed the PA cops' bodies in there, so the doors have already been opened." Recalling that Boris told me he'd never trained Khalil to work with bombs, I concluded, "I don't think Khalil would risk disarming or rearming a booby trap."

Tom looked at me, then at Dutch, and said, "Open the doors."

Dutch said to his partner, "Bobby—do it."

Bobby grabbed the handle on the left door, and Dutch put his hands over his ears. What the *fuck* is wrong with these people? This is *not* funny.

The big door swung open, and, just as I predicted, nothing happened. Or I was in heaven now. But Walsh was here.

Dutch was already in motion, and he jumped up into the trailer where a stack of cement bags formed a wall almost to the roof. Bobby gave him a boost, and Dutch scrambled up the bags, lay on the top row, and shone his flashlight into the trailer. For a second, I thought he was going to say, "Just cement," but he said, "Mother of God . . ."

Oh, shit.

Bobby called up to him, "What do we have, Dutch?"

Dutch replied, "Well, for starters, five bodies. Two PA cops—male and female—and three males in civilian clothing."

Bobby made the sign of the cross, which these guys probably did a lot.

Dutch said, "Also, about eighty . . . ninety fifty-five-gallon drums . . . with wires running to them."

Bobby asked Dutch, "Do you think it's a bomb?"

I looked at Tom, who was looking at me. And he thought *I* was nuts? These guys just lowered the nut bar to ground level.

Kate took my hand, then surprised me by taking Tom's hand, too. Well, we could sort this out in heaven.

Meanwhile, Dutch had some bad news. "I don't see the power source or the timer or the switch."

They're definitely in there, Dutch. Look hard.

Dutch gave Bobby a hand, and Bobby scrambled up to the top of the cement bags and shone his light into the trailer. He said, "It's gotta be over there. See where the wires are running?"

"Yeah . . . but . . . it's tight in there . . ."

Tom called out helpfully, "Four minutes."

Dutch said to Bobby, "Okay, let's walk on barrels."

They both dropped behind the wall of cement bags and disappeared.

I didn't want to rip my stitches, but in about four minutes that would be the least of my problems, so I hopped up onto the bumper, followed by Kate and Tom. We boosted and pulled one another to the top of the cement bags and poked our heads into the dark trailer.

Tom had a flashlight, and below us was a two-foot space between the wall of bags and the first row of drums, and in that space were five bodies piled on the floor. In fact, I could smell them over the chemical smells. The three civilians looked young and burly, and I could see blood on their faces as though they'd each been shot in the head. I assumed, too, that these guys had something to do with the truck and with Khalil.

Tom was shining his light around, and I looked into the trailer and saw the tightly packed rows of fifty-five-gallon drums, each one covered with a lid. I could now see the wires running into the centers of the lids.

Neither Kate nor Tom said anything for a few seconds, then Kate said, "That bastard."

Dutch and Bobby were walking carefully on the rims of the drums making their way toward the front of the trailer, shining their flashlights between the drums as they walked.

Tom asked them, "Is there anything we can do?"

Neither man replied, and I had the sense that even these two were getting a little tense. I didn't want to look at the clock on Kate's cell phone, but I was estimating about two minutes until eternity.

Dutch said, "Here it is."

Good news.

"Hard to reach."

Bad news.

Dutch flattened himself on top of the drums in the far right corner, and Bobby squatted beside him and kept his light trained into the dark space.

Dutch said, "I see the twelve-volt . . . but I don't see the timer or the switch."

Bobby agreed and added, "They could be anyplace."

I strongly suggested, "Take the fucking cable off the battery."

"Yeah," Dutch replied, "that's what I'm trying to do . . . thanks for the tip . . . tight in here . . . this vise grip was made by the lowest bidder . . . hope there's not a second battery somewhere . . ."

So Kate, Tom, and I lay there on top of the wall of concrete bags, peering into the dark, waiting for some positive statement from Dutch.

Also, I was trying to remember why I thought I needed to be here. On that subject, I said to Kate, "Sorry."

She replied, "It's okay, John."

Right. I already saved her life once—so I was allowed one fatal mistake.

Tom was staring at his cell phone and said, very calmly, I thought, "It is now eight forty-five."

No one had anything to say about that.

It got very quiet in the trailer, and I could actually hear the metallic sound of Dutch's vise grip trying to loosen the nut on the positive cable lead.

Dutch said, "Got it."
Bobby said, "That's the wrong one."
They both laughed.

I shut my eyes, and I could hear the bells of nearby St. Paul's Chapel, which chimed every morning at 8:46.

ACKNOWLEDGMENTS

As in all my novels, I've called on friends, acquaintances, and professionals to assist me with technical details, and all the other bits and pieces of information that a novelist needs but can't find in a book or on the Internet. And, as I always do, I'd like to thank those individuals here:

First and foremost, I want to publicly thank my beautiful wife, Sandy Dillingham DeMille, for the first reading of the manuscript and for her excellent suggestions and also for the patience and good cheer she displayed while I was working long hours on this and other novels. No matter how late I came home from the writing office, Sandy always greeted me with a cocktail, and a smile.

One of those smiles led to James Nelson DeMille, age three, who recently asked me, "Daddy, do you live in the office?" Well, that made me stop and think, so I thank James for the idea that I should do more of my writing at home.

None of my John Corey books would have been possible without the assistance of Detective Kenny Hieb (NYPD, retired), formerly with the Joint Terrorism Task Force. Kenny lived the life of John Corey, and I've been fortunate to have him as my reliable source for technical and procedural details and as my friend.

Another great source of information and advice for this and other novels has been my good friend John Kennedy, Deputy Police Commissioner, Nassau County Police Department (retired), labor arbitrator, and member of the New York State Bar.

When real life and literary license clash, license and drama usually win, so any errors or omissions regarding legal matters or law enforcement are mine alone.

As in many of my past novels, I want to thank U.S. Airways Captain Thomas Block (retired), contributing editor and columnist to many aviation magazines, and co-author with me of *Mayday*, as well as the author of six other novels. Tom and I have known each other since grade school, and we used to be able to finish each other's sentences, but now we can't even finish our own sentences. Nevertheless, when it comes to research and writing, Tom provides the answers to all those pesky technical questions a novelist needs to ask to give the fiction its facts.

Many thanks, too, to Sharon Block, Tom's lovely wife, former flight attendant for Braniff International and U.S. Airways, for her timely and careful reading of the manuscript, and for her excellent suggestions and her enthusiasm and encouragement.

The Russian nightclub scenes in this book would not have been possible without a visit to a real Russian nightclub, with companions to help with this arduous research. I'd like to thank Tom and Joanne Eschmann, and Carol and Mike Sheintul, for joining me and my wife at Tatiana's in Brighton Beach, Brooklyn. Mike's knowledge of the Russian language, the culture, and the food made the evening lots of fun and gave me good food for thought.

The ambulance and hospital scenes in this book would have been impossible to write without the assistance of three people—Dr. Robert Kurrle, former naval flight surgeon; Ashley Atiyeh, EMT with multiple ambulance services; and Bob Whiting, Ex-Captain, EMT, Glenwood Fire Company, NY.

Any errors in trauma care, emergency response, or other medical details in these scenes are a result of my misunderstanding or my decision to omit what was told to me by these three knowledgeable professionals.

One of the most difficult scenes to write in this book was the skydiving scene, and though I've jumped out of an aircraft once, I've managed to suppress any memory of that experience. So, to fill in all the blanks, I went to Bill Jackson, a former twelve-year member of the U.S. Army Golden Knights Parachute Team, and past World Champion in the Classics-event category of skydiving competition. Bill has made over 12,000 jumps—11,999 more than I have—and I thank him for his time and for sharing with me his knowledge of this difficult sport. Again, any errors or omissions in the relevant scenes in this book are mine alone.

It would truly have been impossible for me to write this book without the hard work and dedication of my two assistants, Dianne Francis and Patricia Chichester. Dianne and Patricia have read and commented on the manuscript, chapter by chapter, page by page, and word by word. They've done amazing research and fact checking, and they've freed me from all the distractions that writers are subject to when trying to write. I am truly blessed to have these ladies on my team.

And finally, many thanks to the other individuals in law enforcement and counterterrorism who have helped me in my research, and who wish to remain anonymous.

The following people have made generous contributions to charities in return for having their name used as a character's in this novel:

Andrew Goldberg, who contributed to Joan's Legacy; **Brian Gold, "The Candyman"**—Fanconi Anemia; **Mindy Jacobs**—Crohn's & Colitis Foundation; **Irv Gomprecht, "Gomp"**—Horizons Student Enrichment Program; **Kiera Liantonio**—St. Joseph's Catholic School PTA; **Matt Miller**—Fanconi Anemia; **Ed Regan**—Hospice Care Network; and **A. J. Nastasi**—Crohn's & Colitis Foundation.

I hope they all enjoy their fictitious alter egos and that they continue their good work for worthy causes.